Thank God For The Sinners

A Rick Price Novel

iBooks
Habent Sua Fata Libelli

iBooks
Manhanset House
Shelter Island Hts., NY 11965-0342

bricktower@aol.com • www.ibooksinc.com

The iBooks colophon is a registered trademark of
J. Boylston & Company, Publishers.

Library of Congress Cataloging-in-Publication Data
Magun, Eric.
Thank God For The Sinners—A Rick Price Novel
p. cm.

1. Fiction—Thrillers—Crime.
2. Fiction—Thrillers—Suspense.
3. Fiction—Crime.

Fiction, I. Title.
ISBN: 978-1-59687-394-0, Hardcover 978-1-59687-396-4, Trade Paper

Thank God For The Sinners

A Rick Price Novel

Eric Magun

This book is dedicated to that unnamed teenager,
the one with the shaved head.
The punk who hit me square between the eyes at my first show.
It was the Dead Kennedys at Irving Plaza, and
I was enthralled by the ensuing chaos.
You must have seen the innocence on my face
as I stood outside the pit.
Or maybe it was the fear you recognized as I contemplated
joining the mosh.
You came at me from across the room and flat-out
punched me in the face.
My legs trembled as I hit the floor, barely able to breathe.
I was being trampled as I fought to regain my senses.
A few took pity on me and lifted me back up again.
I looked for you, but never got a good look at where you went.
I wanted to thank you for the beating.
For showing me what being a punk was all about.

My devotion also goes out to my wife and my family,
who through the madness,
never stopped loving, supporting, and believing in me.
I hope this book does not change that!

THANK GOD FOR THE SINNERS *is a work of fiction. Unless otherwise indicated, all the names, characters, businesses, places, events and incidents are either the product of the author's imagination or used in a fictitious manner. Any resemblance to actual persons, living or dead, or actual events is purely coincidental. This book is also not an autobiography; in fact, I have gone through great literary lengths to protect the innocent. I have also taken dramatic license (or fantasies) to create this sensational story. If you think that I am talking about you, I am not. So please do not sue me, my life is already complicated enough.*

CONTENTS

1

Here Comes Sickness, *Dongguan City, China—circa 2003*

The hotel I stayed in was a shitty four-star Chinese type.

Non-smoking rooms were unheard of back then and there was always a struggle at the front desk to speak some English. But it was cheap (about $30 a night) and had the best "recreational" facilities in Southern China. Lit up with lasers and flashing, colorful LED lights, this tacky hotel came alive in the evening, as it was not meant for sleep and relaxation but was a paradise of alcohol and debauchery.

This was China in the early two thousand and those brave enough to venture into those hotels were met with smoky, dirty rooms, inedible food, bug infestations and a fear of being poisoned by the water that came out of the faucets. But these establishments were worth the price of admission as they also doubled as some of best brothels around. The one caveat I can say about Communism back then is that it produced a very unjust balance between the sexes. For Chinese women back then, the only way for them to make money was to serve and entertain the men willing to spend the cash for their company. The more willing the women were to satisfy these men, the more they ultimately made.

In one night, a young lady would make more money than a factory worker could earn in a month! If she was pretty and a "pro," there was always the chance that she would become some wealthy john's boyfriend. And like a fairy tale, the would-be princess, could hope to meet her prince and live happily ever after. That was the dream for these women and the only way out of poverty.

I know this because I've been coming exclusively to China now for about a decade, ever since I took over the family business manufacturing furniture. My Chinese business partner Shu Shu (uncle) knew my weakness was the women and always arranged for me to stay at whatever hotel had the best services. Shu Shu was a titan in this industry, employing almost half the city of Changping to work in one of his many manufacturing facilities. He had that kind of power that most men longed for, and others feared. It's fair to assume that Shu Shu always got his way even if it meant coercion and downright violence. He was educated in Hong Kong; spoke multiple languages and I was glad to be his number one customer as well as his best friend.

China was a man's world and being Shu Shu's wingman, was like having the keys to the castle. If only I didn't have Mei Mei (Younger Sister) monitoring my every move. Mei Mei was my CIA handler and I swear the most beautiful Asian woman I have ever seen. She seemed to fall right out of a wet dream, using her tall figure, high cheek bones, slender but fit body and comic book wide eyes to pierce directions directly into my heart. She was my cupid, and I give the agency kudos for knowing my penchant for the ladies. Except Mei Mie was more than a pretty face, she was downright obsessed with Shu Shu's operation having me record his business activities, especially when they interloped with any government officials including customs brokers and local police.

It was all very stressful for me being recently married as I didn't like spending so much time away from my new beautiful but unaware bride. I married Heather right out of college having fallen in love with her at first sight. She was the epitome of a fit model, and the captain of the university cheerleading squad. I can't say she felt the same about me and the madness that followed me around like a drug resistant plague. It took many years of pushing my own emotional baggage down into a locked place reminiscent of a medieval chastity belt before she felt safe enough to reciprocate my love.

Shu Shu set me up at this hotel appropriately named, "The Hiyatt." Leave it to the Chinese to copy everything with no respect for Intellectual Property. But I was used to this by now and my fondness for all things sinful, overrode my better judgment. I was two hundred pounds of pent-up, *Gweilo* (white devil) man-meat, waiting to be turned loose on the pleasure opportunities of this fine establishment.

The types of entertainment available this evening came in either one of two options:

<u>KTV</u>: *Karaoke.*

<u>Sauna</u>: *Massage with very happy endings.*

Tonight, I decided to skip the KTV and visit the sauna for a massage instead. I was tired after twenty-one-hours of travel from the US. By the time we crossed the Lo Wu border into Shenzhen, my eyes could barely focus on those neon lights as they peppered the now polluted evening sky. The Shifu (driver) took me directly to the front desk and checked me in. He also arranged for my bags to be delivered to my dirty chamber and handed me the plastic room key. There were numbers written on it with what appeared to be a black Sharpie. The numbers were difficult to read as the *ones* looked like *sevens*, the *twos* like *threes*, the *threes* like *eights* and so on.

This was the first time I was staying at this crappy hotel; it was recently erected strategically for visiting *Gweillo* businessmen. The Chinese might not know how to write English numbers well, but they learned quickly about capitalism and how competition worked. Therefore, the newest hotels always tried to outdo the others in the neighborhood by taking men's recreation to a new level. Shu Shu gave me a call to make sure everything was "ok," he told me that, "my room was *1128* and is considered good luck."

The Chinese were highly superstitious when it came to numbers especially the number *four* as it was unlucky and synonymous with death. They also weren't fans of *five, seven* and *thirteen*. I know this as we never stayed in rooms that had those numbers in it. Shu Shu told me to get some rest and highly recommended the top floor sauna for their unusual manipulation skills. He told me that he had already called ahead and made all the arrangements. They were expecting me, so I hung up with him and was suddenly excited to see how their massage services differed from the others in town.

Unabashed, I took the elevator up, holding my breath from the stale cigarette smoke that reeked like an ashtray at an "AA" meeting. The doors opened and I entered the *Emerald Sauna*. The place was brightly lit with large neon Ying Yang symbols and in the center of the room was a large fish tank with what looked like large goldfish with bug eyes and a few carp lying lazily on the bottom. There wasn't aquarium foliage or anything decorative about the tank. Just the fish which I understood was good luck but looked downright depressing to me.

I was greeted immediately by the "Mommy" (an older, postdated massage girl), and was directed to follow her and sit in a small, dimly lit room. Like everywhere else, it reeked of smoke due to bad ventilation eking out of dusty wall AC unit, a small two-seater pleather couch adorned with cigarette burns and a nondescript TV sitting on top of a chipped mahogany dresser. Mommy turned on the TV blaring some bad Chinese Kung Fu soap opera, sat down on the couch and motioned for me to come sit next to her. I did as I was told, taking a seat that was too close for comfort, as our legs touched and was immediately assaulted by her body odor that I can only describe as a mix of sweat, perfume and spoiled milk. Mommy quickly noticed my tattoo sleeves peeking out of my shirt and made a big deal about it, forcefully trying to get a look at the ink that covered my entire torso and back. I didn't give her the satisfaction and knocked her hands away from the endless hours of black, white and grey pain that decorated my well chiseled body.

"Ooh, you bad boy." she managed to say in broken English.

"Bu Hao." (No Good) I said back in Chinese.

She laughed, held out her hand and introduced herself as, "Mommy Bao Bao."

I took her hand which was surprisingly soft and warm.

"Ni Hao, (hello) "I'm Rick" I said pointing to myself.

"Yes Rick." she said and pronounced it like "wick."

"Rick Price," I said not sure why I added my second name. "Hen goaxing renshi ni," (nice to meet you) I continued and then released her hand.

She looked at me and smiled.

"Tsk, tsk," was the sound she made and winked, she followed that by giving me the universal sign for *fucking*, by placing her right pointer finger poking inside the small hole made with left pointer and thumb.

"Wei," (yes) I exclaimed. "Piao Liang!" (beautiful) and "Hen Gao!" (tall).

Sometimes I amazed myself with the Chinese I knew, after all, I spent years working on it but stood up anyway for dramatic effect and used my hands to show her how tall I wanted. Tonight, I was looking for something different than I could find back in the States. I needed eyes to lock into that were not similar to mine. Like a poacher, I was looking for a rare animal for my trophy wall (or my spank bank).

"Okay—aah," Mommy said, and left with a smile.

I am not a complete callous animal and knew this was probably not the best way for a newly married man to spend his evening 8000 miles away from home. But I had rationalized this many years ago as some sort of perverse fringe benefit for the work I was doing. I had to keep up my anonymous front despite the circumstances as I couldn't afford to be exposed for who I really was. There was too much at stake, my family was counting on me to perform, Shu Shu was invested in our business and Mei Mei was up my ass for intel. I felt caught up like I was in some sort of elite *vice squad* and convinced myself that I needed to fit in, and a little relaxation was just part of the role I was playing.

My lizard brain was hoping that this sauna would have a selection of girls from Northern China, which I knew by experience has taller girls. These Northern Chinese women also tended to have pale skin and an attitude that seemed confident of their beauty over their smaller relatives from the South. We were in Guangdong Province which is known as the Chinese powerhouse of the economy. It was also the most Southern province of China sharing a border with Hong Kong. Most of the people still spoke Cantonese over Mandarin and yes, the girls were shorter and darker.

I learned from Shu Shu, that the Southern Chinese girls were often farmers and spent more time in the sun. The climate was also subtropical and therefore, they were darker and not looked upon as beautiful as their taller, paler relatives from the North. Geographic racism in Communist China exists... believe me, it does!

Mommy knocked on the door and six young girls entered the room. They were all dressed relatively the same in tight black miniskirts, with white laced blouses and red "come fuck me" heels. They bowed, introduced themselves in Chinese, and said where they were from. I took my time to look them over and my gaze returned to the second girl. She was shorter than I preferred but had beautiful (almost Korean) comic-book cartoon eyes and a thin, tight body. I think she said she was from Guilin, which made sense as it is known as a city of outstanding natural beauty. I had also learned from Shu Shu that good scenic terrain in China often breeds the more attractive girls. Must be something in the water?

This one was stunning, shy, and afraid to look directly at me.

So, I chose her.

Mommy gave a little *happy clap* and the rest of the girls bowed and then left.

"Wick," Mommy said reaching into her purse.

"Shi," (yes) I said.

Mommy handed me a small bar of soap wrapped in plastic and one toothbrush and toothpaste set.

"Wei Ni!" (For You) she exclaimed

"Xie Xie," I said and put the packages into the front pocket of my jeans.

Mommy Bao Bao began to bark loudly into a walkie talkie that she took off from her belt. I couldn't understand what she was saying from the loud squelching feedback but understood this to be instructions to where we were going next. I took the girl from Guilin's hand as Mommy mentioned for us to follow her. She led us out of the room, put her walkie talkie back on her belt and directed us down a dark corridor. We passed a few shut windowless doors and then an open room filled with working girls. They were sitting around eating noodles and watching TV. Some of them looked at us as we passed, and I quickly recognized the other five girls who were just in the room. I had a shit eating grin on my face as we followed Mommy Boa Boa to the room with the letters "VIP" attached to it. The letters were finished in a brass color and appropriately tarnished almost brown. Mommy opened the doors, turned on the overhead fluorescent lights, grabbed the dirty remote Velcroed to the wall and with a noticeable beep, turned on the small wall AC. With that she said, "Bye-bye," and shut the door behind her leaving me alone with the massage girl from Guilin.

The room was standard size for a hotel of this caliber. Bathroom immediately to the left with a large shower stall and no tub. In front of me was a queen size bed sitting on a small wooden platform. There were two small pillows and only a bottom sheet for comfort. A standard white towel that was too small for my large ass body was draped vertically in the center of the mattress. The floor had beige carpet that was stained with spots reminding me of an accidental Cheetah print. There was a closet to my right and next to that sat a small wooden mahogany desk, no chair, but had the pleasantries of two water bottles that appeared unopened. The massage girl immediately went into the closet and took out an aluminum folding chair with a red plastic cushion on the seat bottom. She opened it up, and I noticed there was an opening cut out of the middle of the cushion, where your ass crack would be if you sat on it. It reminded me of an open wound.

She pointed at the seat and asked me, "OK-aah?"

I nodded my head in agreement, not knowing what I was consenting to. The girl then took the seat into the bathroom and placed it in the center of the shower stall. I followed her, reached into my pocket and placed the soap and toothpaste set on the side of the sink. The girl turned on the shower, handed me another small towel that was folded in the shower door and then started to undress. She quickly took off all her clothes, folded them, placed them on the other side of the sink and was not shy about doing so. I marveled at her cavalier attitude and then focused on her pink nipples now erect like pencil erasers.

Another tidbit I learned is that the Chinese often gauged the age of their women with how light the color of their nipples were. Hence, the lighter the nipple color often correlated with their young age and often the "older" girls would use blush on their nips to mask their age!

She was young, I marveled at her cat-like, thin body and the smooth texture of her skin. She was almost hairless with a small triangle patch protecting her little cooch. I couldn't stop staring at her as she came over to help me out of my clothes.

I must confess at this point, that I am also covered head to toe with a full bodysuit of tattoos. (Another addiction to feed my inner demons).

After twenty something years of ink-filled rage, there is little skin left on me to desecrate. Of course, I obsessively planned my ink to stop 3.5" above both wrists, therefore in a long-sleeve dress shirt (or a business suit), you would never know what was hidden underneath.

My bodysuit depicts a torrent of Asian sea monsters, tiger's, demons and skulls, all crowning in a turbulent sea of waves and wind. I purposefully chose black with grey shading, staying away from color, being *truer* to how I felt about the world. I used to joke that I wear my black heart on my sleeve. However, the large dragon tattooed on my entire back earned me the Chinese name of, "Dalong" (Big Dragon). My skin art, as impressive as it is, was also my armor defending me from having to prove my ability to tolerate pain. Tattoo art was not something you saw back then in China unless you were a "yakuza" gangster. Even though that was symbolic of the Japanese crime syndicate, the Chinese underground mafia, often imitated those tattoos to show off their toughness and solidarity. It was not for the faint of heart and I'm sure was especially scary if you were a massage girl from Guilin!

I helped her by disrobing quickly, shedding off my clothes, excited to be naked with this exotic creature. She jumped back having never seen this many tattoos on a *Gweillo* before, let alone a six-foot, two-hundred-pound, naked American in front of her. This made me laugh, and I found myself completely aroused by her fear. She noticed my excitement, gave a little shriek pointing at my manhood, took the small bar of soap off the sink, opened the shower door and quickly got in. I glanced at myself in the steam filled mirror and imagined that I must have looked look like a monster to this poor young girl.

I tried to convince myself that this was in fact her lucky day! After all, she could have had some smoky, smelly, little, dirty Chinese fuck with long fingernails and hair growing wildly from a mysterious face mole. Instead, she had me, a nice Jewish boy from Long Island, and all my demented glory. I was feeling good about myself and decided to do some stretching to loosen up my hips. Like an athlete going through pregame rituals, I was preparing myself for some heavy exercise. After a couple of half-baked naked sun salutations, I set my intentions and was ready to hit the shower.

The shower stall was big enough to fit four people. The girl had her back to me and was soaping herself up. Her long straight black hair was now carefully tucked into a large transparent shower cap. She looked like she should work in a kitchen instead of this brothel. I knew she did the shower cap thing to keep her hair dry and fake the other *johns* into thinking this was her first trick.

I hated that shower cap, how she looked in it, what it stood for, and ripped it off her head. She shrieked as I flung it over the shower door and out of sight. She protested lightly as I spun her around to face me. I quickly put my arms over hers and held her very tightly. Like a trapped dog, she tried retreating, then quickly gave up resisting and grew relaxed in my grasp. I thumbed her nipples just to make sure there was no makeup, and they were hard reminding me of the candy, *Jolly Ranchers*. I bent my knees, so my erection now rested throbbing between her legs. I felt her body tremor under my tightening embrace.

I lowered my right hand from her nipple and reached between her legs to soap up her private parts. Her body tensed as I brushed her clit with my thumb and forefinger. She exhaled loudly with excitement. I caressed her with my soapy fingers, making sure she was clean. She began to quiver and used all her effort to push me off her.

"děng yi xia," (one minute) she said softly

I released her and she made her way to the red chair with the gash in the bottom and set it up in the center of the shower stall. The aluminum legs forced open and locked into place with an audible 'click.'

"Zuo," (sit) she commanded, pointing at the chair.

I did as I was told and sat down noticing how my ass cheeks now spread open over the open crevice. The girl then got on her knees and like a wet dream, looked me right in the eyes as she proceeded to soap up and work my shaft with her soft hands. She sensed my excitement as she continued to carefully pump me to oblivion. It wasn't long before I felt that familiar sensation of release and relief.

She must have sensed my climatic excitement as she relaxed her grip, now gently scratching and teasing lightly at my attentive crotch. I lifted my head into the shower spray, feeling the hot water dance off my flushed face. I was determined not to blow my wad now, so I lifted her up away from my manhood.

The girl stood up, wiped her soapy hands off, filled her mouth with shower water, spit on the floor, faintly smiled, and excused herself. I followed her naked cat like body out of the shower and sat there for just a heartbeat stroking myself. When she returned, she had the small bottle of toothpaste in her hand. It was red with white lettering, imitating *Colgate* but with Chinese lettering and God knows what ingredients inside. I assumed that might be for my cock, but I thought wrong.

Right before my eyes, she got down on the floor, lying on her back and maneuvered her body so that her head was under the red seat. She put the toothpaste on her right pointer finger, stuck it inside the cushioned seat crack and began to smear it around the rim of my asshole. I tensed up in surprise as her other hand magically began to jerk me off at the same time. Then she lifted her face up to my exposed crack in the chair and her wet, firm tongue began licking the toothpaste out of my ass. The toothpaste burned a bit, but her darting tongue kept my mind from drifting. She skillfully applied more toothpaste as her left hand was again pumping me to near climax. The sensation was overwhelming. It was now or never...

I stood up and quickly doused my ass clean in the shower spray. The girl got up, as well, and I used the shower head to rinse out her mouth. She was now a dirty little girl, and I felt my mind switch from arousal to primal, animal ecstasy. I lifted her small frame onto the red massage chair, spread her legs, and used the shower head to massage her pussy. She was moaning heavily as I increased the shower pressure aiming directly at her engorged clitoris. She started to finger herself under the warm spray and began to tremble uncontrollably, so I soaped back up my fingers and added more pressure.

Suddenly, she let out a long, tremendous moan as her eyes stared off into the distance and then seemed to roll into the back of her head. And just like that, she stopped shuddering, hands dropped to her sides, became stiff a board, then fell backwards off the chair and smashed her head on the floor. I stood there a bit in shock about how suddenly she fell and waited for her to get back up. The water repelled off her naked body as she started shaking violently again. It was then that I noticed the crimson blood flowing from the back of her head, pooling up around the drain. This was no ordinary climax; she was having some sort of seizure, shaking uncontrollably like a fish out of water. A collage of foam, spittle and toothpaste ran down the corners of her mouth like melted vanilla ice cream. I reached down to help her up but suddenly became too afraid to move her. I turned the water off and quickly left the shower to fetch some towels.

When I returned with the towels, she was just lying on the floor, and not moving anymore. I kneeled quickly, gently placing the towels under her head and turned my face to see if her chest was filling with air. I stared at her torso trying hard not to concentrate on the beauty of her small, plump breasts. Her nipples were still erect, but her chest was not moving.

"Hey!" I said rapidly tapping the side of her face.

"Hey, get up!" I exclaimed nervously shaking her body with both hands.

I did this in vain as she continued to lie there in silence, not moving like a wet stuffed animal. Then I felt an emotion that had been tucked away in the recesses of my troubled mind. I felt fear and started to panic, realizing this was China, and I was clearly in some serious shit!

So much for anonymity!

Furiously, I pounded her chest and administered a very poor rendition of CPR. I tried to remember my training, but I was terrified and fumbled for the instructions locked somewhere in my brain. I knew enough to clasp my hands and continually rock back and forth keeping pressure on her chest. I did this for what felt like several minutes and then switched to give her mouth to mouth resuscitation. I wiped the spittle off her lips and placed mine over her open mouth. This time there was no eroticism, as I watched her chest rise up and down while my breath filled her lungs.

I kept switching the chest pounding and the breath work for what seemed like thirty minutes of sweating over this poor, naked girl. I was starting to tire and slapped her a few times in the face in a desperate attempt to wake her up, before deciding to call it quits.

"No, no, no!" I screamed to no one.

I sat down and held her head carefully in my big arms. I closed my eyes wishing this was some sort of bad dream as my brain became overwhelmed with despair. I knew enough about shame to not let her be found naked on the floor of this shower with a mouth full of toothpaste and pre cum. Carefully, I lifted her lifeless body off the floor and held her cautiously in my outstretched arms. I walked slowly out of the shower noticing how much heavier she now felt. I made my way across the discolored carpet and carefully placed her on the center of the bed. Like all mattresses in China, this one was also hard as a rock and did nothing to cushion the girl's lifeless body. I glanced at her nakedness one last time, wishing she would wake up and all this would be some sort of bad dream.

But like the rest of my life, the nightmares followed me like thunderclap to lightning. The storm clouds were ever present, always threatening, and never seemed to pass. I was lost in thought as to what to do next as I gazed at the blood beginning to coagulate underneath her head. I took a few deep breaths and knew I had some serious calls to make to protect myself, my family and my business. With so much to lose, I was also uncharacteristically calm. Death was nothing new to me and has been following me around since birth like a bad omen in some horror movie. A demon always threatening to catch me and drag me down to a fiery hell.

2

Victim in Pain, *Long Island, NY—circa 1969*

Many psychologists have been caught up with the idea that the trauma of childbirth has a definitive impact on one's psychological profile.

They refer to this as "Perinatal Psychology," and have explained to me in no uncertain terms, that the suffering of my delivery into this world was probably responsible for my anti-social and borderline personality disorder. Some have even gone so far as to rationalize it as the reason for my poor life choices, my unstable moods, and my intimacy issues.

I was a pre-teen when my mother (Susan) finally confessed and told me the fantastic tale of the magical doctor who saved my life at birth. It seemed that I had flipped upside down in her birth canal, at the last minute, rendering me a breech baby. This happened in the eleventh hour, just as she was fully dilated and ready to push. The good doctor, attempted to right this sudden detour of our natural course, trying desperately to turn me around forcefully by manipulating my mother's stomach with his hands. My mother said she was in blinding pain as the virtuous doctor tried to work me back around headfirst. After several attempts, he surrendered to my mother's intense pain and suffering.

When I asked my dad (Steven) to confirm this and describe what he had felt, I was told that he was not there during my birth. Instead of being by my mother's side, my father and grandfather (Butch) thought it a better idea to hop into a local bar and drink to this celebration of life. Dad told me with great pride that my grandpa bought the entire bar endless drinks until closing, and that they did not return to the hospital until well after my mom was "done."

As the story goes, there was very little time left to safely deliver me without the need of emergency surgical intervention now commonly referred to a C-section. My mother begged him to keep trying, as she wanted to have a "normal" birth. She told me that cutting her open was just not going to happen. She was determined to push me out, even if it meant more suffering for the both of us. In a last desperate attempt to deliver me "naturally," the skilled obstetrician reached into my mom's cervix with his Piper forceps and ripped me through the birth canal to enter the world... *ass first!*

The force of this trauma, as well as literally being bent in half and forced out with crude pincers, left me wailing from multiple injuries. I was born to pain with a double hernia, undescended testicles, and dual hip dysplasia. These injuries would haunt my young life, as multiple surgeries were needed to fix me. The double hernia operation was performed first and not until six months later. My testicles were also released surgically, but only one descended. It was called cryptorchidism, and the name of this condition is as "cryptic" as the jokes made at my expense. If that wasn't enough, the hip inflammation left me with crippling pain, in and out of crutches throughout most of my childhood. It wasn't until my bones stopped growing during my early teens that the physical pain finally subsided allowing the mental anguish to flourish.

As for my mother, my birth resulted in her suffering as well, in the form of severe postpartum depression. She was left weak with malaise looking after the both of us in our small Long Island apartment. As the melancholy settled over her like a wet blanket, she could not manage herself, let alone be responsible for me. Her mother (Rose) has already checked out emotionally and offered no help or empathy for that matter. My dad in usual fashion, got drunk with my grandpa and then decided that a baby nurse was needed to help care for me. Unfortunately, as black clouds would predict, the nurse they hired was more unstable than my mother.

I was told later in life that the nurse was also an alcoholic that was often caught stealing liquor out my dad's coveted, well stocked bar. Instead of firing her, my dad, who also had a bad temper when it came to his alcohol, put a lock on the bar to keep the nurse out of his stash. As legend goes, the alcoholic nanny brought her own wine with her when she came to the apartment to take care of me. When confronted by my mom, she drunkenly threatened to kidnap me if my mom did not give up all her money, jewelry and the keys to the bar. My mom had enough sense to refuse the abusive babysitter's demands. She told me that the baby nurse then picked me up by my feet in her left hand and grabbed a pillow off the couch in her right, as she threatened to suffocate me! My mom panicked as I started to wail and ran into the kitchen to dial 911. The baby nurse supposedly started yelling at my mom, "to hang up the phone," while, she placed the pillow over my face. My mom said that she started to scream, let go of the receiver, took off her wedding ring and threw it at the drunk woman. The inebriated nurse dropped the pillow and then me on my skull, to grab the diamond ring as it circled towards her feet. My mom shrieked in horror and ran to my aid. The intoxicated nurse then apparently hit her over the head with the wine bottle.

Mom blacked out.

When my dad came home, he found my mom unconscious on the kitchen floor and heard me crying loudly in the bathroom. He panicked and immediately called my grandpa for assistance. Grandpa who I later learned besides being an alcoholic, was also a tough son of a bitch, lived in the apartment just upstairs and came running down. As lore goes, they found me in the bathtub covered in a blanket, tearful but unharmed. My father raged running through our one-bedroom apartment as he realized all their jewelry was stolen. Also missing was the TV, the liquor, and for many years, my mom's ability to smile. Even though my grandfather vowed revenge and told my mom not to worry, that he would find and 'take care" of that woman, it obviously was not enough to erase the trauma. Depression and guilt overcame my mom like a cold, dark shadow.

Growing up, I never gave much thought to how these early traumatic experiences could have shaped my antagonistic personality and messed up my psychological development. Even though the "head shrinkers" tried to convince me differently, I never felt comfortable blaming my emotional instability on my childhood. Truth is, I knew I was fucked up and I had some sort of masochistic desire to own that by myself. No matter how I tried to convince myself that this was somehow all my fault, clearly there were others responsible for my madness.

3

Seeing Red, *Long Island, NY—circa 1971*

My earliest memory was a bloody one.

It was also the day my parents brought my baby brother (Josh) home from the hospital. Dad was celebrating the occasion by making a few vodkas over crushed ice. I can recall the crushing sound of the ice machine as it spit chunks into the glass and watching my father spin the drinks with his left pinky. He danced around our white and brick kitchen telling Mom that, "she deserved a drink" and handed her a frosty glass. Mom placed the baby carrier down, grabbed the cup as the both of them toasted to themselves. I was left standing on my toes trying to get a look at the pink package that Mom placed on the Formica kitchen counter.

Mom caught me trying to catch a glimpse and smiled warmly. Dad knocked back his vodka and extended his left pinky, also smiling in my direction.

I remember the pinky.

"Well Rick, it's time to meet your new baby brother!" exclaimed my mom and dad in unison.

Mom then polished off her drink, lifted baby Josh out of his carrier and gently placed the little miracle on the cold white laminate counter. I remember being mesmerized at how small he appeared to be. The whirl of the ice machine broke the silence as Dad made another round of drinks, his pinky stirring them again. He gave my mom hers, then left to go outside the kitchen door that led to our patio, so that he could have a smoke. My dad loved his *Marlboro Red's*!

"Rick, meet your new best friend, baby Josh," Mom said.

Then she said, to stick out my pointer finger and put it inside my brother's clenched fist. She continued to tell me that, if my brother squeezes my finger, it means he loves me!

Without hesitation, I stuck my finger inside his soft little grip.

He instinctively grabbed my small finger inside his chubby clutch and my mom remarked again how much he loved me. I remember feeling surprised to be inside his tiny grip. It was stronger than I would have thought, and he grabbed it instinctively like he knew who I was.

I was smiling with glee, when my mom bent down to smell his crotch, made a small smirk and remarked that she was going to show me how to change his diaper. She took out the baby powder, a small diaper, baby wipes and some Vaseline from a large bag that had a blue bear on it. The items were placed next to my brother as my mom started to take off his clothes. She seemed frustrated trying to unbutton all the snaps carefully and took another swig of her drink. When he was finally undressed, my brother squirmed under my mother's touch as she removed his soiled diaper, wrinkled her nose, rolled it up in a ball and placed it the garbage pail.

I remember that my brother's skin appeared very pink and wrinkly, like my great grandfathers always appeared to be. I watched my mom clean him up with the wipes and apply the baby powder while attempting to finish her drink at the same time. After that, she rubbed Vaseline on his privates, lifted him gently up by his legs and put on a fresh diaper. She coddled him talking in gibberish like a baby and then asked me to go look in his blue bear bag for the "safety pins." I shuffled around the bag, still standing on my toes until I found a plastic box with silver pins inside.

Mom quickly took the safety pins from me and fished out two large ones from the package that they were in. She put the pins down next to her drink next and opened them up from the clasp, revealing a long sharp point. I can remember being confused at the possible danger and put my finger instinctively back into my brother's tightening grip.

The kitchen phone began to ring, and my mom leaped away from my brother to answer it. My aunt (Sylvia) was on the other line, I could hear her distinctive voice piping in from the earpiece talking about, "planning a party to show off my new brother to the family."

With the phone clutched under her neck, mom continued the conversation walking back over to my baby brother as the white coils on the phone wire unwound from their knotted position. She was talking excitedly as I watched her open the second sharp pin. With the phone still grasped between her neck and shoulder, her free hands hastily held the edges of the diaper together as she aimed the sharp pin through the cloth. She laughed at something my aunt had just said and pushed the pin into the rest of the diaper, carelessly piercing my brother's tender skin in the process.

I remember the scream he let out as, I didn't think something so loud was possible from someone so small!

My mother instantly let the phone drop from her neck as she desperately tried to calm my brother. She quickly pulled the pin out of his skin and then he screamed some more. A trickle of blood ran down the front of his diaper.

I remember the blood, the tears and the wailing.

My father ran in from the backyard with a cigarette hanging from his mouth. He looked at my brother, the blood, then back handed my mother in the mouth. She stood there stunned, blood now trickling from her lip.

My brother continued screaming as my father berated my mother for being, "a careless, drunk bitch!"

I stood helpless and watched as he ripped the bloody diaper off my brother. He balled it up and threw it and the cigarette into the sink. He then looked back at my hysterical brother, gave me a scowl, turned and yelled at my mother to get him another diaper. She stared at him for a moment still in shock, slowly turned, put a dishrag to her bruised mouth and then ran for the stairs up to the safety of her bedroom.

My father looked back at me, bent down so that we were face to face. I remember his cigarette breath as he told me to, "be a man and put a new diaper on my bother." He gave me the bag with the blue bear and then ran upstairs after my mother. Their bedroom door slammed, and the shouting continued. I tried to put my finger back inside my brother's hand to offer him some love, but he was not having it.

I remember him crying uncontrollably like he was in terror.

I shared his fear and did my best to try and calm the both of us down, as I didn't know exactly what to do next. I went back into the blue bear bag to find another diaper and repeat some of what I just saw my mom do. My calves burned as I stretched onto my toes to lift and gently place a new diaper underneath my brother. I put baby powder and Vaseline carefully around the wound in a feeble attempt to heal it. I pulled the diaper folds together, stood higher on my toes, and kissed my brother on the forehead. I remember feeling horrified as I picked out another couple of safety pins. I tried to keep calm, as I squeezed them from the clasp guarding their sharp points. My hands shook with terror as I carefully slid the piercing metal through the gauzy fabric. To this day I am not sure why they called them "safety pins!"

4

Shut the Door, *Dongguan City, China—circa 2003*

The naked dead girl lied still in the bed.

I had since attempted to wrap her in the fitted sheet and used the pillowcase as a homemade tourniquet around her head. She had stopped bleeding, but her eyes remained opened, revealing an unusual light brown color. Her pale skin was now white like porcelain. Even in death, it amazed me how frail and gentle Asian girls looked.

But this was no time to sit and ponder. I had to act immediately and call the only person who could bail me out this mess. It was also the very person I was there to see in the first place. I needed to call my current Chinese business partner, so I picked up my cell phone and dialed him. He, like many other Chinese, felt the need to be introduced as family. Therefore, it was not uncommon that he would introduce himself as my "Shu Shu" (uncle) and that is what I continued to call him.

'Shu Shu, Ni Hao."

"Rick, what is going on?" he asked in perfect English.

He knew me well enough that if I phoned him in the middle of the night, it usually meant trouble!

"Shu Shu, I really fucked up this time!" I exclaimed, trying to keep the panic out of my voice.

"Are you at the hotel?" he asked.

"Yes, I am in the sauna, and... we have a... problem with... the massage girl," I stammered.

"What type of problem?" asked Shu Shu, getting to the point.

"I don't know... what happened," I stammered again. "But she had some sort of... seizure or stroked out... and now she's dead—It was crazy! I mean, this happened as she was cleaning my ass with her tongue!"

"Rick, come on! What do you mean she is dead?" he asked, completely ignoring the part about her tongue doing the *dirty deed*.

"Dead, like not breathing," I replied, starting to unnerve.

"Are you sure?" he asked sounding more perturbed.

"Yes!" I exclaimed, "I applied CPR for like thirty minutes and now I have a corpse in my bed-"

"Rick, I know you better than that, what did you do!" screamed Shu Shu.

"Please, Uncle, I did nothing but enjoy the toothpaste rim job she was giving me!" I exclaimed again, "I swear that didn't do anything to her!"

"Rick, massage girls do not die on their customers by mistake!" he continued.

"Well, this one did!" I screamed. "And I've been thinking about this and maybe it's got something to do with the Chinese toothpaste!"

"What toothpaste?" he asked seeming not to hear about my exploits.

"The toothpaste that mommy gave me," I continued, "The toothpaste she put on her finger, stuck up my ass and then ate it out—"

"Mommy gave you the toothpaste?" he asked quickly cutting me off.

Ignoring his question I continued to explain, "yes... I mean we all know not to use the toothpaste in China! You've even warned me that there's no telling what's inside."

"Are you saying there was something wrong with the toothpaste?" he asked but felt like he was mocking me.

"Yeah, like maybe poison?"

"So, If I'm following, are you suggesting Mommy gave you the *poison toothpaste*?"

"I don't know for sure at this point what the fuck happened, except I have a dead girl now in my bed! If there was something wrong with the toothpaste, well now I am feeling very alarmed as it was in my asshole!" I exclaimed in fear.

I heard Shu Shu hobble out of bed and mute the phone with his hand as he muffled directions to someone else in the background. It took a few more beats before Shu Shu came back on the phone.

"Okay, Rick, listen to me well, as I will not repeat myself. You need to stay where you are and remain calm while I figure out what to do. Do not leave the room or answer the door. I am going to call the Mommy and let her know that you have decided to take the girl for an overnight. This will buy us some time to get rid of the body."

"Get rid of the body!" I exclaimed as this thought started to sink in.

"Would you prefer to go to a Chinese jail instead!" he screamed.

"Shu Shu, I swear I had nothing to do with this!" I exclaimed.

"Rick, we now have a lot to be concerned with. I told you that you needed to lay low and stay out of trouble."

"Listen, Uncle, I am innocent this time... I promise"

"Just stay where you are and for God sakes clean your ass and don't brush your teeth!"

He hung up the phone, leaving me alone with the silence.

I put the phone down on the on the side table next to the no smoking sign, which was situated behind an ashtray. I was never super religious but decided it was probably a good time to pray. I put my hands together and summoned a prayer to Buddha, to Christ, to God, to my wife, and to anyone else who would listen.

I thought about how badly I just wanted to feel "normal." I always long to be *normal* with *normal* thoughts and a *normal* life. I began to quietly obsess on my existence, especially my compulsion for the darkness. I knew that I had hurt others and thought that this was maybe some type of karma consequence. After all, it was just a matter of time before life hurt me back. This contemplation just made me angrier, and that anger turned into rage. I preferred the fury over feeling vulnerable. I couldn't stand weakness, and that is why I never had capacity for empathy.

I kept my eyes closed and let my mind drift to Shu Shu, and how the hell he was going to get me out of this mess. I knew he was connected to the local authorities, and they were adamant in helping us ship containers to the US. Considering the sudden increase in business we were doing together; I became confident that Uncle and his "friends" would do the right thing to save face... to save me.

I also knew that I needed to alert Mei Mei about this. She would be furious for sure, never underestimating the trouble that I could make for our operation. No matter how much time she spent preparing me for this intel job, she knew I was a risk. This *death* was not part of the plan and would threaten my cover and her ability to protect me. I thought about this a bit more, my mind still going to the possibility of poisoning. Mommy gave me that toothpaste. Maybe it was meant for me?

I let this sink in for a bit longer and remembered that Shu Shu recommended me the Sauna. I decided then not to let Mei Mei know for now as I needed to get closer to Shu Shu and understand if something nefarious was in the works.

5

Think Again, *Dongguan City, China—circa 1999*

The first time that I met Shu Shu, I was relatively new to the China scene.

The family company I worked for was involved in domestic manufacturing, and I was hoping to expand our efforts into what seemed at that time, an untapped China. I was currently the product development director of our New York facility, had just finished college, and was spending a lot of time overseas already.

The plan was to find a Chinese partner with good manufacturing capabilities that would also act as our agent, broker, and production warehouse. My previous experience with China had been a rough start, fraught with inconsistent vendors, horrific travel experiences and the looming danger that always seemed to follow me. No matter how bad I wanted to make this work, we were still mainly buying component parts that we would import and assemble in our US facilities. My grandfather (Butch) along with Mei Mei helped arrange the relationship with Shu Shu, just as they have always done whenever we needed help finding partners in China. Shu Shu was one of our more reliable Hong Kong vendors. He had opened a tremendous plant in Changping, China and was keen on winning our business. He was ten years my senior, shared the same birthday, enjoyed a similar lust for pleasure and quickly became my good friend.

Shu Shu wasted no time getting me familiar with his expansive factory and sharing his corrupt knowledge of China. Technically, he was from Hong Kong and considered himself a "Honky," not necessarily Chinese. At least not in a Mainland Communist China sort of way. The *Honkies* back in those days did not assimilate as Chinese, even though they might have looked it and sounded like it to the untrained ear. It was their knowledge of China's forbidden language, Cantonese, and their American values of capitalism, including English, that set them far apart from their rural Mainland cousins.

The Chinese at that time had no Western manners. They just never learned about what we considered "normal" behavior or hygiene. They would smoke in elevators, continually spit on the floor, drink to absolute wreckage (often during the day) and wear ridiculous polyester pants with gold belt buckles and pointy shoes. Their teeth were a *yellow, black* combination, breath always stunk, and they had random hairs growing out of their cheeks or chins. Their fingernails were kept long like talons and were used to clean snot from their nose or dirt from their putrid orifices. They ate everything that moved (except cars), and it was not unusual to find them munching on a plate of steamed cockroaches or drinking rice wine laced with Cobra blood. They were flat-out the grossest people to do business with back in those days. And Shu Shu, their Democratic brother from another mother, appeared to want no part of these peasant pieces of trash!

Hell, we even had to travel with our own toilet paper (or napkins), as toilet paper was considered a luxury—so there would never be any in the bathrooms, or it would be stolen. And forget about hand soap or even a proper toilet bowl to sit on! No need for these western luxuries, either.

I would say the only thing that these Chinese had in common, was their absolute belief that women were second-class citizens, whose sole purpose was to pleasure men... any man and so us *Gweilos* (white devils) quickly learned to overlook their missing modern pleasantries. Turning a blind eye in favor of sexual pleasantries, we fell right in line doing business in Communist China.

I was a fast study and quickly learned as much as I could from Shu Shu—*warts and all.* He set me up with a tutor to study *Putonghua* (Mandarin of the people) and often bought me along to social functions with the various government and police types. I was being trusted to learn how to assimilate with the people and I was determined to win their hearts and minds. Even if they grossed me out, I wanted to make Shu Shu proud and befriend these little tyrannical fuckers. Especially because it was good for business!

Shu Shu was a *Honky God* in those days and had a small army of 1,500 people working for him in his factories. He was generally respected by all his workers, and in return he built them dorms to live in, a canteen to eat at, and even provided a doctor (Doctor Dave) with an infirmary, to boot. They had no reason to leave him if the work was steady. I was committed to help build the business by creating products produced at ridiculously low prices to resell them at tremendous markups as "bespoke" or "hand done." In return, retailers would buy these (at what they thought was a fair price) and mark them up another four times, before selling to the consumer for what the final customer thought was a fair deal. With the help of the local town officials, we kept three shifts of exploited labor busy twenty-four-seven to fill our pockets. With all the steady work and profits, I did not feel anything except contentment and entitlement! I was blind with ambition and not able to see the warning signs of something reprehensible that was going on in the background.

Instead, I was impressed with the productivity of workers making cheap shit and the overwhelming size of the facilities in which these products were made. Even more remarkable was the amount of heavy machinery and equipment Shu Shu owned. There were machines to accomplish anything from casting metal, grinding, spinning, polishing, stamping, welding, plating, finishing, and painting. They appeared to be able to make anything in those plants and I often questioned Shu Shu about the thousands of brass casings being produced along with my decorative furniture items. The casings shining with fresh brass polish, were in various sizes but all shaped to hold what I could only imagine was a projectile of gunpowder and bullets. Shu Shu just didn't like to be questioned about anything non furniture related and quickly yelled at the closest factory manager who had a red arm band with the words

"QC" sewn into it. The *quality control* (QC) man quickly threw a tarp over the casings as we climbed the cement stairs away from the metal shop that we were now in.

The noise, pace, and pollution of factory life was overwhelming and exhausting. After eight hours straight in the heat and dirt, I was ready to relax, and Shu Shu knew exactly where we needed to go. He offered to take me for a foot massage and explained it to me as "China's last great kept secret!"

Shu Shu mentioned to me, "that the Chinese (in the know), considered these foot massages as routine health visits, like going to the doctor or pharmacy."

The foot massage center was situated above a nondescript restaurant in the busy part of the downtown. It was nothing luxurious and certainly did not resemble any sort of modern-day Western spa. We were greeted by a line of overly made-up women in stained robes who shouted at us in Chinese and then directed us to a private room down the end of a dirty hall. The room had two tattered recliners and a small TV blasting Chinese news. Air was thick with stale smoke, and the small wall air conditioner hardly worked at all. Shu Shu was unfazed by the conditions and yawned in anticipation. I cautiously sat in the dirty chair and tried to make myself comfortable. There was a small pillow for my head that I was apprehensive about using but was too tired to protest.

The massage girls were very young, homely looking, right off the farm, but quick to the chase. They assisted us with taking off our shoes, socks, and rolling our pants above our knees. Hidden under each of our ottomans was a porcelain tub that they began to fill with scalding hot water. When the water was filled, they poured special herbs into the foot tub reminding me of loose tea leaves. I sat up in my chair, following exactly what Shu Shu was doing, and quickly stuck my feet into the burning water.

Shu Shu noticed my discomfort and quickly told me, "Not to move my feet or the burning would be worse!"

I did what I was told and sat still in the scalding water as sweat began to pour down my face. The girls made a big deal about this and played uselessly with the air con unit, trying to get more cold air to blow on me. This effort was in vain, but in a matter of minutes the fiery temperature subsided and immediately my feet did not burn anymore. The girls, sensing my enjoyment, began to give me an intensive back and shoulder rub. They had strong hands that pulled and pressed, releasing the pain that was lodged in my neck and traps. They even did this little move where they squeezed my forearms above my wrists to cut the circulation from the fingers and then slowly released the pressure until the blood flowed back into my fingertips. They blew on my fingers, and it felt like butterflies were sitting in my hands.

After my head, arms, back, and hands were turned to marshmallow, the girls removed our feet from the tea-like mixture, drained the tubs in a sink in the corner of the room and wrapped our legs in fluffy towels. They then reached into the side of the chair and released the back rest so that I was now lying flat. My girl placed another towel across my midsection to replicate a blanket. A huge smile spread across my face as the girl took off the leg towels, applying thick lotion to my toes, feet, and calves. Then she rubbed my pressure points on my feet with her fingers, causing me to scream in both pain and delight. The girl continued to work up my legs, paying particular attention to my calves and shins. At times, the pain was unbearable, and at others, it couldn't feel better. I was enjoying every moment of this, and tried to relax as the girl wiped off the lotion and wrapped my feet in hot towels.

That was when Shu Shu dropped the bomb on me.

"Rick," he said. "I hope that you are enjoying yourself now because tonight we have some very special dinner plans that I need you to be prepared for."

"No problem," I said with a yawn, "This massage is starting to get me hungry."

"Good because tonight will be a different dinner than you are used to, and I was hoping that this foot massage would put you in the relaxed mood."

"You mean no cockroaches will be served?" I laughed.

Shu Shu looked at his phone and had a concerned look on his face.

"No worries, Shu Shu, I'm relaxed and could use some food."

"Okay, Rick, then please enjoy this little foot vacation because tonight we eat dinner with the local government officials."

"Government officials, that sounds cool, I guess?"

"Not just *the Government*," he continued, "but also *local police, border control, security advisors*, and anyone they invite," he answered.

"Sounds like we're having a party?"

"Kind of, but this party is not something I usually enjoy."

"C'mon, you love a good party."

"Rick," he interjected, "these parties are obligatory and happen about once a month. They call all the shots, and I must comply with anything they ask. For business reasons, I have no choice but to be at their mercy."

"Have no fear, I'm here to help," I quickly replied.

"I know, and you will do what I say and make things easier for me."

"Easier in what way?" I asked.

"Well, this will be the first time that they will have the privilege to eat with you, an American businessman." He let a sly smile escape. "And you can bet they will all have a lot of fun trying to show you face!"

I took a second to let this sink in and thought about all the drunken nights of debauchery that were blamed on saving face. I closed my eyes and tried to shake off the feeling of being, "Shanghaied."

"Rick, no matter what happens tonight, you cannot lose your cool! Think of this as a test. They will all be judging you and by proxy also me. I need your absolute trust tonight. We are partners now and these men are also part of our business."

I thought about the business reference and knew this was an important event. The closer I got to these people, the more I had to report back to Mei Mei. I took a deep breath and willed myself to unwind. I concentrated once again on the massage and tried to let myself drift off into oblivion. I was searching for deep relaxation, but that elusive muse was nowhere to be found. I was caught up with tonight's festivities and my mind simply would not cooperate.

6

In My Head, *Long Island, NY—circa 1979*

Ever since I was a young boy, I have had the same reoccurring nightmare.

The night terrors always began by watching myself in bed, sleeping in my bedroom. Everything about the room was always the same, retro wallpaper, twin bed, knit blanket, and a two-draw beige nightstand with a pierced porcelain lamp. Even though I knew I was asleep, it felt like I was awake. Like an apparition of myself floating above my body, I could see myself unconscious, in my platform bed and sound asleep.

The feeling I always associated with these episodes was that of losing control. I would watch myself and drift away further away into a deep sleep, from which there was no waking up. It was then that I began to panic, afraid that if I did nothing, I would surely slip unconsciously into sudden death. Concentrating hard, I tried to gain all my strength and will myself to wake up by forcing my body to move. When that didn't work, I would try to scream like I was in a silent horror movie. In an act of final desperation, I would count to three and thrust my energy into waking up—because every moment I remained unconscious was another moment I feared I was slipping closer to death.

The gratification of waking (and not dying) was quickly shattered when I saw that zombies had entered my room and made their way towards my sleeping body. I watched this happen while I was subconsciously willing myself to move, to scream and to wake up. I saw the dead fiends hover over my body, and I felt the intense pain as they ripped chunks of flesh from my limbs. I could not escape the pain and horror as I was being torn apart limb by limb.

I tried to scream again, desperate to wake up and escape the agony of being eaten alive. But every attempt I made to awaken only made the monsters fervor into a more intense feeding frenzy. I could see it and I could feel it as they tore into my soft flesh. I would verbally protest but my teeth, unlike the undead, always seemed to crumble and fall out of my mouth. I could feel them crunching into pieces as I bit down in pain.

On the brink of feeling inevitable death, I would awake screaming and clawing at the air. I sat up quickly, breathing heavily, switched on the lamp and checked my limbs while I scanned the room for the undead. There were none and thankfully, I was whole again. My body was intact, my tongue skimmed my mouth for missing teeth. They were all there and now I was up, hyper conscious, and sweating profusely. Surprisingly, my prepubescent pecker was engorged and standing at attention. I tugged on it feeling more confused by my youthful arousal. I tried to catch my breath as I realized there was no going back to sleep.

It would take many years and many more near death dream experiences before I learned that this disorder had a name. It was explained to me by my shrink (Dr Hurtz), that this was called sleep paralysis, also known as "the demon in my bedroom." Apparently, it is associated with panic or anxiety disorders and no matter how much I learned about it; the nightmares would not subside. Beside the fear, I was also embarrassed and did not tell Dr. Hurtz that all those night terrors excited me somehow.

The older I got, the worse they became. The flesh-eating zombies turned into frenzied sharks, and the sharks eventually turned into gun-toting madmen. My nightmares were all destroyers of flesh and bone—they were terrorizing, and I felt unbelievable physical pain throughout my entire body. My teeth continued to crumble in distraught as I spit them on the ground. I was rarely clothed in these nightmares and my naked vulnerability fueled my anxiety and that all manifested itself in my inability to sleep.

I was horrified of the evenings and learned how to masturbate at a young age hoping that this would help me sleep soundly. Unfortunately, jacking off in the evenings did put me to sleep but did nothing to stop the night terrors. In hindsight, I should have expected this. God knows I had sinned, and I certainly deserved the nightmares. I believe that saying about payback being a bitch... or is it, Karma? Or maybe it was some psychobabble I learned in college about Erik Erikson's theory regarding childhood trauma and its correlation to a negative outcome of personality development.

Whatever it was, either awake or asleep, I was certainly doomed from the very beginning.

7

I Hate Children, *Long Island, NY—circa 1974*

I can remember being forced to attend summer day camp at the ripe age of six.

This was not my choice; it was the "right thing" for a boy my age to do during the summer. After all, it was what the Long Island *Jones's* did with their kids! All I wanted during the summer was to stay home and have my mom's full attention. But I quickly learned a big lesson that would repeat itself over and over again.

My parents had no intention of spending more time with me than necessary.

The summer was, in fact, their vacation from the kids! We children simply did not fit into their seasonal escape plan. Children were not to be heard in my house, and I was going to camp whether I liked it or not. I might not have had a voice, but I had a personal choice, and I was determined to make my parents miserable for their decision to abandon us.

At day camp, I made no attempt to interact with the other boys, refused to play sports, hated the heat, the counselors, the bugs, bad lunch, and orange *Creamsicles*. Having no interest in playing along like the other kids, I was picked last for all sports (including kickball). But what I hated the absolute most about the day was swimming. I couldn't stand changing into my bathing suit and then being forced to jump into the freezing water. I tried anything to escape this misery and often hid in my favorite spot, the proverbial sandbox. There was something so peaceful about burying myself in the cool dirt and pretending to disappear. I was self-soothed by escaping the world that I wanted no part of.

You can only imagine my disappointment when the counselors repeatedly had to dig me out of the sand. Some say, "Insanity is doing the same thing over and over and expecting a different outcome." If so, I must have crossed that line every day imagining that finally, they would just leave me alone as I pretended to be dead and buried.

When I was no longer allowed in the sandbox, I hid in my tall plywood clothes cubby. Hiding in the cubby didn't go over well with the other boys, who expressed their concern for my obscurity by repeatedly spitting on me.

Shamefully, I crouched in the cubby, covered with spittle as the boys took turns throwing insults my way. The adults as always just turned a blind eye as I held back my tears and waited for the boys to disappear. I just wanted to be left alone to wallow in my despair. There was only one solution I could think of that would help my problem, one final way to be left alone...

I shit in my pants!

Yeah, you hear me right, it felt gross, but hey, it worked!

At last, I was finally left alone by the kids and the counselors. Just me and my crap-stained drawers. I couldn't even stand the putrid smell of myself, but finally alone, things were better this way. And I learned a great life lesson: Anytime I did not want to not participate in life, to be left alone, all I had to do was shit myself... such simplicity. Boy it was just great to be six!

Unfortunately, my mother (now fed up with cleaning my clothes) got in touch with the camp to come up with the brilliant plan of matching me with an older camper who would act as my "big brother." His name was Joey, and, like all older brothers, he enjoyed tormenting me more than protecting me.

Every time I shit my pants, he would hit me in the side of the head and taunt me without mercy. He taught the other kids to "hock loogies" from a distance, and would laugh out loud, joining them in the ridicule.

Joey liked to abuse me, even when I wasn't shitting myself. The counselors turned a blind eye *again*, and I realized for the first time that I was feeling truly helpless.

It was then that I learned another important life lesson as shitting my pants wasn't an option anymore. That night, I had trouble sleeping and certainly didn't want to invite the monsters into my room. Instead, my mind tried to think of a plan to avenge the wrongdoings of Joey and the rest of the boys. I obsessed on revenge, thinking of every scenario until a possible solution popped into my head. I had the formation of a plan and replayed it over and over in my young mind until it became crystal clear. I was excited for the first time in a long time! I finally knew what I needed to do, and I was convinced that the result would allow me to be left alone! I ran the scenario in my head all night long, feeling strangely satisfied and consumed. In the morning, I had the plan worked out, it was clear what needed to be done.

The next day during swim, I quickly changed into my tight bathing suit. Joey was the first to notice my change of clothes (and attitude) and quick to warn me, "Don't shit in the pool!" I said nothing and made my way to the water's edge. The pool was long with the deep end at the opposite side of where I now stood. I dipped my toes in first and recoiled as it was as cold as I always remembered. I was determined to seek retribution, mustered up the courage and jumped in *feet first*.

Joey and the other boys jumped in soon after. The swim instructor was busy yelling out drills for us to do with the kickboards. I took my board and kicked quickly to the center of the pool approaching where the bottom began to slope into the deep end. I was out of breath but excited as I noticed Joey kicking towards me. I slid off my board holding it by my face and just hung there silently, like an animal stalking its prey. The water was just below my eye level and did not feel cold anymore.

Joey made his way to the center of the pool coming right for me. I watched him get closer, pointing and laughing at me. As he approached, I let go of my board and I slid silently under the water. I kept my eyes open and when he was almost on top of me, I sprung off the bottom of the pool and landed on his back.

I had played this scenario in my mind obsessively about a hundred times the night before. I quickly grabbed the back of his head with both of my hands and threw him off the board and into the water. I knew I had the element of surprise and used all my pent-up anger to hold him close to my chest while my legs forcefully strangled over his like a python. I tried to position myself on top of him letting my body weight sink and slowly drag him to the bottom of the pool.

Joey began to flail his arms and legs as my grip tightened around his head. I imagined being one of those giant snakes squeezing the crocodile and tried to imitate the same response. I would not let go, no matter how hard he protested. I looked up to see the sunshine over the water and felt suddenly at ease. I did not panic and felt no need to breathe as he struggled in my embrace. It was empowering to hear him scream under that water. I felt stronger than ever and the more he protested, the tighter my grip became. I repositioned my legs over his to stop him from kicking and willed myself to continue sinking to the bottom of the pool. I heard strange noises, like muffled screams, but held my breath and tried not to pay much attention to them. The lifeguard blew his whistle, but all I could hear was my heart beating.

In my eyes, the sun turned to red as Joey began to spasm and puke inside the pool. Some of the other kids began to scream and suddenly counselors appeared in the water like sharks, prying me off my catch. I succumbed and let go of Joey as the puke continued to fill the pool. The counselors quickly manhandled me to the shallow end. I was breathing hard and my eyes teared with happiness for the first time in a long time, as the realization of what I had done sank in. I tried to catch my breath, slowly turned to look at the other kids and then at Joey as he now sat in shame on the pools edge. I noticed that no one was returning my stare, the counselors quickly hustled the other kids to the opposite side of the pool. All attention was now on Joey, the puke and others who were try-ing to contain the situation.

At last, I was alone in the puke-filled water with no one around to bother me. I felt omnipotent in my close call with death. It was a powerful feeling that finally I had done something about my misery. I could make them stop hurting me if I hurt them harder. If I made them afraid of me, they would leave me alone. I was careful to make a mental note of this. This is one of many life lessons that I would cherish forever.

8

Family Tree, *Long Island, NY—circa 1976*

My grandfather (Butch) had two charms around his necklace that summarized it all:

So Bad (written like the Superman logo)

And a *Scorpion* (for his Horoscope sign).

The first was a reference to how he ended every sentence when talking to you:

"Blah blah blah... you're so bad!"

But really, we all knew it was given to him because of his nature. He was not liked by many and, more importantly, he did not like most. Either he was "so bad" to everyone or everyone else was "so bad" to him. It was an elusive saying that he proudly wore. He was a good-looking man to say the least, full head of silver hair, broad shoulders, large retro aviator glasses and held himself to high standards, especially when it came to drinking.

My grandfather was also the town's kosher butcher for a period when he was a lot younger. He supposedly had an uncanny knack of remembering everyone's name and I was told that he spent most of his time in that meat market of a store, where he would chop and grind animal flesh with his bare hands. As family legend goes, he was something of a savant with that meat clever and very popular with the married women of Long Island.

He quickly adopted the name "Butch" and when he wasn't knuckle deep in dead pulp, he was either drinking at the local bar or caught up in some sort of shady business that the family was not keen to talk about. He did keep the family flush with cash, and they pretended to like him, especially when it came to Thanksgiving, where he would dissect the bird with the skill of a surgeon.

He had the temperament of a man that could not be bothered with small talk, was known as a mean man to many and for this reason adored his Scorpio nature. He was proud to be one. He identified with his Scorpio charm, wore it proudly and always told us kids the fable of the *Scorpion and the Frog.*

Grandpa would recite his version:
A scorpion asks a frog to carry it across a river.
The frog hesitates, afraid of being stung by the scorpion,
but the scorpion argues that if it, did that, they would both drown.
The frog considers this argument sensible and agrees to transport the scorpion.
The scorpion climbs on the frog's back and the frog begins to swim.
But midway across the river, the scorpion stings the frog,
dooming them both to die.
The dying frog asks the scorpion why it stung him,
to which the scorpion replies, "
I couldn't help it. It's in my nature!"

The moral of that fable and my grandfather's mantra is the very nature of the scorpion, vicious people cannot help hurting others even when it is against their best interests. That was often his excuse for the rage and anger he let fly at those caught in his crossfire. For my mom, she describes his moods as absolute terror. She goes on to explain how he literally would pull her hair and kick her down the street.

"Down the street?" you ask. "Out in public?" It's amazing how times have changed...

Luckily for me, I was not one of those left in his carnage. Grandpa liked me and my peculiar behavior. Either that or he felt some sort of innate kinship to protect and look over me. I didn't care why but felt lucky for the first time in my life. Lucky to be recognized and in Grandpa's good graces.

Sadly, I cannot say the same for the rest of my family, whom he kept in line with a sharp tongue and an iron fist. Grandpa was old-fashioned macho, large "Popeye like" forearms, big, scarred fists and a "farmer's tan" even in winter. Although he did not grow up poor, he carried himself like a man who been through the shitter and now expected to be revered. I can remember High Holiday dinners in which we were not permitted to talk. Those dinners went on for hours and even though we fasted (and were starving), you just could not interrupt Grandpa's Seder. No laughing, no talking—hell, no coughing. If you were caught making noise, Grandpa would stop the Seder and stare with pure ice in his veins. If that didn't work, he would leave and go outside to have one of his long cigarettes and if he was mad enough sometimes, he had more than one.

Grandpa was also a world-class smoker and did so with effortless gallantry. He was one of those who looked cool smoking. A natural Marlboro man. His ashes would stay intact throughout the entire smoking session, never to fall on the ground or go unlit. I am not sure how he did this, but at the end, all that was left in the ashtray was a smoky snake that looked like it was giving birth to the paper filter. The ash was the same size as the unlit cigarette. We all thought it was some sort of miracle or divine intervention for Grandpa to have such a skill. Especially with his shaky hands and overgrown yellow fingernails. How could this old man make smoking look so enjoyable? How does one possess such talent?

Practice.

At least that is what he would tell me when driving his large Crown Vic deftly after a few vodkas, while smoking cigarettes that would not ash on their own.

"Son," he would say, "you have nothing to fear. I am a professional."

And then he would finally flick the cigarette with its long ashy carcass out the driver's window. Like clockwork, it would fly back in the open window behind him and land in the back seat where I was sitting. I learned the hard way to watch for this burning ash as it would often land on my unsuspecting lap. There were many holes not only burned in my clothes but in the back seat. It was littered with soot pock marks and finished butts. Grandpa never used the ashtray, and it always amazed me that the car just didn't go up in flames. But this was Grandpa, and he was "so bad!"

But let's stop here for a moment and talk about my great-grandparents. Specifically, my great-grandfather (Joseph). All that I knew of him was that he was born in Poland. During the war, he was sent to America with nothing, only to find his cousin (my great grandmother, Sarah), marry her, have a family, and start a plumbing business on Long Island. As the story goes, his father (my great-great-grandfather) was an engineer back in Poland, who befriended the Polish President to help retain passage to freedom for my great-grandfather. The rest of his family, like all my historical relatives, all perished from the Nazis.

Alas, my family in America was started on incest, which I believe was not so unpopular back then. It was different times and people were desperate. I can only imagine coming to America as a teenager with nothing except a raging hard-on for freedom and the need to start a family! Like so many of the *great* generation, great grandpa Joe continued in his father's footsteps using his engineering background to start a small home plumbing business. That business flourished, and a second entity was created to cater to all the plumbing needs of Long Island. These plumbing companies quickly blossomed into Air Conditioning and Heating conglomerates to service both Nassau and Suffolk Counties.

My great-grandfather was also a child molester. I shit you not! At one point, he was actually sent back to Poland (by the authorities) after being caught multiple times "hanging out" at the local elementary school. My family is unclear exactly how long he stayed overseas, but when he returned, he apparently went back to his same old tricks.

He worked feverishly on expanding his business until he had all Long Island locked up for their home plumbing needs. This was way before Home Depot and there was a lot of money to be made. With money comes the power to have others turn a blind eye and with that dominance, he became more of a tyrant. He would choose which grandchild to have over for the weekend, claiming that they all belonged to him.

His grandchildren lived in horror of being the "lucky one" selected for the weekend slumber parties. My mother and the rest of my aunts would only refer to him as "that monster!"

I never had any reason to not believe them, and now understood why my grandfather Butch might have viewed the world as "so bad." What I remember of my great-grandfather Joe was that he appeared to be a man of infinite strength. He never used a cane or assistance in his old age. No, he was broad-shouldered and mean looking. He never talked much and when he did it was with a thick Polish accent. This only added to his toughness, and I quickly learned that the strongest guy in the room was usually the one who never talked. Or bragged. As a matter of fact, I remember a distinct time around my Bar Mitzvah when, as a present, I received my first weight set and bench press. Great-Grandpa Joseph just happened to be over the house and came down in the basement where I was "working out."

He said gruffly, "Son, put all the weight on that bar."

I looked at all the heavy weights scattered around the bench and began to protest.

"Great-Grandpa, I don't think this is such a good idea."

"Do it!" he cut me off with a hint of violence in his tone.

I placed all the weights on the bar and leaned over to give him a spot. He slowly made his way onto the small bench and lied down into position. I had a quick moment of panic that I was not going to be strong enough to help him if he couldn't push up the weight. I was fearful that I would fail, and the iron would come crashing down on his chest. I mean, what if he had a heart attack. What if I killed him?

Before I could reach a full state of panic or call anyone else to help, he placed both hands on the bar and lifted the weight off the hooks. He gave it a beat and then my great grandfather cleanly benched all the weight I had. He cleared it effortlessly! He put the bar back on the hooks, sat up, walked out of the basement and up the stairs. He did not say a word to me, but I understood it all, loud and clear. Hence my fear of the silent "tough guy," especially if that tough guy was also a child molester.

My Grandfather Butch spent some time in the Navy to escape his old man. He told me he was in "special operations," and I had no reason not to believe him. When he was back from serving his country, he started his kosher butcher business. From what I have been told, the family had no idea how he learned this business and was in awe that he seemed so comfortable in his bloody smock. Butch enjoyed the carnage of his work and kept that shop open all hours of the day (and night). My grandmother who never was one for words, did not discuss those days and would never refer to him as Butch. When my great grandfather became ill with heart failure, my grandfather shuttered the butcher shop and joined his molesting father—*not in molesting*, but in the plumbing business. Quickly surpassing his illiterate father, Grandpa appeared to make serious money expanding his father's empire and taking no prisoners.

Now, if I already told you that Grandpa was also a highly functioning alcoholic and his poison was Russian vodka, *Stolichnaya*. "Stoli and soda," to be precise. He would tell me that the Russians knew their vodka better then they knew their own history. Butch would often brag about the "commies" he met overseas and their religious penchant for alcohol.

"Never to be mixed with tonic," he would tell me. "Tonic is just quinine and used in the military to cure malaria."

He continued, "Vodka should never be mixed with fruit, and this includes lemons and limes!"

"And orange juice?" I would add, knowing the answer.

"Especially juice!" he would say with a grin. "Juice and fruit have sugar and so does vodka. If you drink too much sugar, you will become diabetic!"

Which he was (a diabetic) after a lifetime of drinking Stolichnaya vodka. He knew the rules firsthand and made me repeat them in unison. Stolichnaya held a special place in his heart, as it did with the rest of my family.

"Son," he would explain, "the Russians know misery; they know hard times and they know how to make vodka!"

"You seem to know a lot about the Russians," I would add.

He ignored that comment and continued, "Only repressed countries know how to drink. They drink to forget about their shitty lives, while we drink to celebrate ours!"

Then he would toast to me, always in a tall glass. And *never* with a straw! These were simple drinking lessons from the master. And like a good apprentice, I took it all in and practiced every chance I could.

For some reason grandpa was always looking after me. Which is one of the reasons I knew he loved me. Even if that included my escalating drinking habit. Nobody ever cared about me like that. More importantly, though, Grandpa was always there for me. To rescue me and take care of me. Whenever I was in trouble, whether at camp, or school, in college, mental hospitals... He never gave up on me, and for that I've always loved him.

Even when we were smuggling Stolichnaya and cigarettes on his private plane, I knew this was just his affection for me. See, Grandpa became rich enough from the plumbing business to invest his money in things he cared about, like buying prized cattle, professional sports teams, and purchasing other plumbing and AC companies. He even retained a few butcher shops spread throughout Long Island. Butch was not flashy with his money and never seemed to mind when he lost it on any of his passions. I guess when you have enough of it, you need to lose a little in the process. And when Grandpa had a good year, he would donate half his earnings to the poor and needy. At least that is what he told me, and I had no reason not to believe him.

I would like to believe that his biggest regret was that he didn't own his own liquor company; he was proud, however, of keeping Stolichnaya (and the Russians) well infused with cash.

Between his habits, my family's habits, and my parent's friends' habits, the smuggling business was a good way to wash his hard-earned money. When you had money, I learned that life became easier for you and everyone who surrounded you. Again, lesson learned.

Like clockwork, every Christmas he paid for the entire family to vacation at St. John, where he leased us, apartments overlooking the sparkling blue Caribbean. We all looked forward to this vacation and, like clockwork, we were magically transported out of the snow and into paradise. Having a break from the brutal cold of the fierce New York winters, was idyllic fun for me and my cousins. For my folks and my "Scorpio" Grandpa, it was just another excuse to get tan and drunk. I mean, it was in his nature...

It seems the tanner they got, the drunker they became (maybe it was vice versa?). I am not sure if there is a correlation, but I could bet that if you polled people who drank, say, Corona, you would quickly see that sun, fun, and alcohol were, "all in the family." And we were the poster children in the generation of the Coppertone Tan. Nothing screams carcinoma more than a family of well-to-do white folks, sunning themselves in the Caribbean with reckless abandon. When we got beat red and real burnt like lobsters, we were thrown in cold showers to scream in agony. The pain would eventually go away and, if not, there was the ceremonial lubing of aloe vera and *After Tan* sun lotion. We appeared to be that perfect 1970s family, soon to be plagued with skin tags, sunspots, and the removal of skin cancer.

When the vacations came to an end, my family boarded propeller water taxis and the continued home in jumbo commercial jets back to the frigid Northeast. Only Grandpa and I remained behind. See, Grandpa knew that adults were only allowed a certain amount of duty-free vodka back in the States. Accordingly, he loaded everyone up with the correct number of bottles of Stoli to take on their commercial flights and then hired himself a private plane. The private plane allowed him to enter the US with as many duty-free cases of Russian vodka (and cigarettes) that we could fit onboard. They apparently did not seem to have customs check on international private flights back then and certainly Grandpa was going to take advantage of that loophole.

I can remember the excitement of settling into the leather seats of the sleek jet. The cabin was adorned with polished wood reminding me of the inside of a yacht. There was fresh carpet on the floor and window drapes which I opened to get a glimpse of my grandfather. He was on the tarmac smoking with a bunch of gruff looking native men in blue jumpsuits. They were hovering around a luggage cart with filled cases of vodka and canvas bags. I could not make out what they were saying but my grandpa looked serious. In the end, he gave them a thick envelope, shook their hands and extinguished his cigarette. He made his way to where the captain was outside checking on the engines and then boarded the plane with a big smile on his face.

"Son," he'd say. "Those men outside are *So Bad*, just like you."

"You and me both," I would say back and that always made him laugh.

I watched in back as the men filled the small plane with cases of vodka. They put them everywhere—underneath in the storage hold, and in all the empty seats and other spaces in the cabin. Any other remaining openings were quickly stuffed with the canvas duffle bags that my grandfather said were filled with *cigarettes*. I remember a few times when the captain complained that we were too heavy to clear the mountains just off the Island's runway. Grandpa would give him hell in return for being afraid and scaring me! In no way would he ever compromise and agree to lose some of the cargo. Instead, he would always tell the captain and co-pilot, "to take out some gas and land somewhere in South Florida to refuel."

Also, to compensate for the heaviness of the contraband, we were instructed to either sit at the very back or front, depending on what weight we needed to displace to clear the mountain tops. Often, I was instructed to sit in the cockpit's jump seat. This was by far my favorite way to fly. I was absolutely blown away to be in there and watched the crew with silent intensity as they worked all the buttons, turning the engines alive with the fury of a dragon's breath. It was always an exciting ride as we flew down the short runway and lifted upwards quickly exposing a close encounter with the mountain tops. We left the island behind as we flew the bird up to the sky like Icarus's journey to the sun. And just like myth, it felt like a short time before our ambitious trip needed to land back on earth.

No matter the weight, it seemed that we always had to stop in Miami (or close by) to refill the gas that the strained aircraft had used. In my grandfather's defense, the stop gave us a chance to stretch our legs, find him a Vodka and some candy to pacify me. We would sit in the private lounge while he ordered, "the usual" for himself and then we munched on mini-Hershey's chocolate bars, while they refilled the plane and removed the canvas bags. My grandfather always seemed to know everyone in the lounge, calling them "so bad" and always introduced me as, "his partner in crime." After a few trips, I also recognized some of their heavily tanned faces, Hawaiian shirts and aviator sunglasses that were tucked in their shirt pockets. They called him "Butch," referred to me as "little Ricky" and were always pleased to see us. I always looked forward to those trips and felt blessed to be asked to join as his partner—especially when I got a chance to sit in the cockpit!

For a brief period, I considered myself the luckiest grandchild alive! I went to school upon our return, full of fantastic memories and a sunburn that slowly faded in winter's gloom. These early excursions flying with Grandpa seemed to be my only salvation in what would become a *life of agony*.

9

Unsung, *Hong Kong, China—circa 1997*

The first time I met the old man (Buddy), was synonymous with the first time I went to China by myself.

The opportunity mixed with the unforeseen violence was the perfect foreshadowing to what would come. You see, back then, I was anxious to find a new supplier in Asia that would promise to deliver completely assembled goods at very competitive prices. Grandpa knew Buddy back when he was in the Navy, who happened to now live in China and owned a factory. He introduced me to Buddy over a long-distance call, that seemed like we were talking to someone who was literally at the other end of the world. The conversation was full of lags in time where we only heard silence, then clicks like someone was listening in to our call. What I learned was that Buddy seemed to have his own furniture factory in a small town, about five hours away by boat from any hotel in Hong Kong. This factory was not your "usual" Chinese vendor, conveniently situated an hour's drive into neighboring Shenzhen. Instead, Buddy was in a remote city in Guangdong province called Zhaoqing and far away from the safety of Hong Kong.

This factory was in a completely remote part of China and would require a slow boat up the Pearl River to a part of Guangdong where few

Americans ever traveled. Buddy mentioned, "that unfortunately there was no hotel for us," and the old man confided, "that an old army barrack would have to suffice."

"It's small rooms but very clean," he said with a slight Brooklyn accent. "I tell you what, let my office fax you over some of the products that we are working on, and you can decide for yourself if the trip is worth it"

"Thanks Buddy, great to hear from you again," my grandfather said and hung up the phone.

"Army barracks—are you kidding me?" was my dad's response. "There's no way I will ever visit this factory!"

My Dad was something of a narcissist and did not venture anywhere his pampered needs were not met. He was used to "the good life" being a creature of habit and did not like new experiences, especially those that did not cradle or stroke his self-esteem. If he could not enjoy a comfy night's sleep in one of Hong Kong's five-star hotels with a well-stocked bar, then the trip was off for him.

I tried to persuade him that this trip was worth exploring for the chance to set up a "pick and ship" operation. One where we could buy already assembled goods at a better price than we were currently getting. Even better, the goods once delivered, would be packaged and ready to ship directly to our U.S. customers. We would save on labor costs in the U.S., and it was our opportunity to get out of the manufacturing business to become a leaner, more profitable operation. Dad completely agreed with that initiative and then doubled down on his refusal to join.

"I am not going—this is a job for you, my son!" He slurred. "After all, that is why I have *you* in my business."

"I got this dad. You can count on me." I said somehow feeling vindicated for the years of his negligence.

My grandfather shot back his vodka and gave me a wink. He seemed to know this was going to be my dad's reaction and reassured me that, "I had nothing to worry about." He confided, that the old man, Buddy, was a 'special friend' who owed him a 'few favors.'

"Rick, you will meet another friend of mine named Mei Mei," he added. "Mei Mei practically runs the operation. I'll make sure she'll meet you in Hong Kong to ensure all goes smoothly."

"Understood," I nodded, barely able to hide my excitement, knowing that my grandfather would take care of everything, as he usually did.

Over the next few days, Buddy's office faxed us pictures of elaborately painted furniture items and vases already turned into lamps complete with wiring and shades. He proclaimed to have started the porcelain factory in that town because this is where the mud was the best in all of China. Judging from the pictures and his notes, these lamps looked better than what we were used to receiving. Intrigued to find out more, we sent him packages of fabric swatches to paint onto the porcelain blanks (or shapes). Within a few weeks, we received back incredible faxed images of completed lamps and (of course) at very competitive prices. The decision was solidified for me to check this vendor out and teach them how to make assembled furniture along with complementary lighting products.

We arranged another phone call with Buddy to confirm that I was committed to making this happen and he extended the invitation again to visit him with great enthusiasm. At last, it was finally decided that I was to go on my first sourcing trip alone overseas and I was psyched.

My grandfather gladly took on the responsibility of booking my tickets with his travel agent. In those days, you could not get a direct flight from New York and had to stop either in Vancouver or Guam, or even Tokyo. Hell, like I cared. I was young, naive, and looking forward to this adventure. More importantly, I could not wait to take this trip without my greedy father and all his emotional and physical baggage!

The plane was a TWA Boeing 747, and I was fortunate enough to be booked in business class on the upper deck. I must admit that it was a privilege to walk up those winding stairs, away from economy, to be sat in a wide, reclining seat that grandpa arranged directly across from the bar! Even though we stopped to refuel in Vancouver, the service and comfort made the long trip bearable and somewhat enjoyable.

However, landing in Hong Kong back then was a harrowing experience onto itself. The airport, destined to become the hub into Mainland China, was disproportionately situated in what seemed like the center of the city. After an excruciatingly long flight, the plane touched down between huge buildings to what seemed like an impossibly small runway. Not only was the runway short, but if overshot, it would leave you right in the South China Sea. And on the way down, I swear you were close enough to see inside the apartments that surrounded the airport. It was not a landing for the timid as we touched down quickly and came to what felt like a sudden stop, deftly reminding me that these pilots must have practiced this to perfection.

Once landed, I debarked off the giant plane and queued up with the other passengers as we slowly waited to be let through Hong Kong immigration. With my passport now stamped, I made my way downstairs to the luggage carousel to retrieve my baggage. Bags in tow, I left through the green exit under the "nothing to declare" sign. Outside immigration, I was overwhelmed by the number of Chinese people waiting to meet up with the now landed travelers. I scanned up over the sea of people to look for my name on a placard and was amazed to see my name in the hands of one of the most beautiful Asian women I have ever seen. She was a tall woman, slender build and a face that looked like it was carved from the softest soap stone, with alluring eyes and a pearl white smile. We locked eyes as I waved in her direction. I quickly ran my hands through my short spiky hair and walked over to meet her.

"Hi Rick," she said seemed to purr and outstretched her long fingers. "I'm Mei Mei."

I shook her hand noticing the strength in her grip.

"Hi Mei Mei" was all I could muster up to say.

"You can call me your 'younger sister' if that's easier?" she smiled showing off perfectly white teeth.

I held her hand and her gaze for an uncomfortably long time, while my brain tried to come to its senses.

"Ah ok, younger... I mean Mei Mei," I said. "I like that better."

"Good," she said releasing my hand. "Shall we go? I have my car waiting just outside."

She took my bags from me without protest. I followed her from behind and got a good look at a body that has been carefully sculpted by hard work and genetics. She walked confidently past the crowds, out the automatic doors, to the outside and got into the back of a blacked-out, four door Mercedes Benz S500. The driver was waiting outside dressed in a black suit with dark sunglasses that seemed too small for his well chiseled face. He opened the door for her and then nodded in my direction. He quickly opened the other door for me, took my bags and put them in the trunk.

Once inside, Mei Mei took out her Motorola StarTAC flip phone started talking in Chinese. The car quickly left the curb as the driver fought his way out of the airport and to the highway. I admit that I could not stop staring at her as she talked into the phone. Mei Mei caught my gaze and smiled back. She hung up the phone, and then mentioned to me, "get a good night's sleep, we have to catch an early ferry in the morning." She took out a Montblanc M164 pen out of her black Prada purse and wrote her number on a piece of paper.

"Rick, take this number, save it in your phone and call me if you need anything at all."

I let this sink in for a moment, staring at the number as Mei Mei jumped back on her phone talking in English this time. I heard the Old Man's voice in the receiver. She told him, that I landed without incident and that she would get me on that Ferry at 7am. I was surprised at her English; she talked with the accent of someone schooled in London. She hung up and returned my smile once again

"Rick, please enter my number into your phone," she added pointing to the paper in my hands.

"Sure," I said taking out my blue Nokia 5110 and adding it into the contacts.

I put the number in my back pocket as the car made a few quick moves avoiding any traffic and pulled up to the Marco Polo Hong Kong Hotel. Once at the hotel, she shook my hand goodbye, as the driver opened the door and handed me my suitcase and green Jansport backpack.

"Your room is all taken care of." She said, "You only need to show them your passport."

The car drove away as the porter took my bags and led me into the hotel. I checked in quickly and asked where I could get some dinner, I was starving from the long flight. The concierge took out a map and directed me to an American style deli around the corner from the hotel. He offered to hold onto my bags while I ventured out to eat and relax. It was getting late, so I didn't object, I left my bags with the concierge and took off.

That night's dinner was exactly what the doctor ordered. I had feasted at the New York themed deli, craving a good turkey sandwich, sweet potato French fries, a side salad and of course, a couple pints of draft beer in a frosty mug! I knew I was headed "deep in the jungle" tomorrow and wanted to carb up with something familiar while I still had the chance!

After dinner, I walked down Nathan Road to ride the Star Ferry across the picturesque Victoria harbor. I was on my way to Lan Kwai Fong (LKF), the "party street" of Hong Kong. But first, I would enjoy the short but sentimental ride on this well-worn passenger ferry painted and weathered in green and white. The Star Ferry founded in 1888, carried over 70,000 passengers a day, was the cheapest (and most scenic) way to cross travel from Hong Kong Island to Kowloon. It was like stepping back into time and on that boat, you literally felt like you were on the other end of the world.

It was a short boat ride from Tsim Sha Tsui (TST) ferry pier to the Central pier on the other side of the harbor. I disembarked the wooden ferry boat climbing the steep streets of Central district until I arrived at my destination in Long Kwai Fong (LKF). LKF was a horseshoe street, intersecting with D'Aguilar Street, where there were no cars so that throngs of patrons could frequent the copious number of bars (and restaurants) without fear of being run over. I always made sure to visit this area every time in Hong Kong, since it was not only fun but filled with expats.

I had learned a while back that expats (short for expatriates) are businessmen and women who live and work outside their native country. Hong Kong being a British province, meant the bars were filled mainly with Aussies and the English. They were loud, brash, and always spilled onto the street like drunken sailors. It was right up my alley (literally).

I was still young (and new) at this as I barreled my way through the crowded streets to the Mexican-themed Tequila bar, ordered a margarita, light on the syrup with no salt. I marveled at the way they squeezed fresh limes into the icy goodness. I was about to pound the first one when I was approached by a rather striking Asian female. She was tall, thin, had a purple silk scarf around her neck adorned with gold dragons. Her face was unusually defined with sharp, angled features that reminded me more of a Native American Indian than Asian. Her skin was darker than I had seen before, and she had fierce accentuated eyes that also sparkled with intrigue as she smiled and climbed into the empty chair next to me.

I was immediately captivated as she leaned into me, our legs now lightly touching.

"Buy me a drink?" she questioned but sounded more like a command.

"Sure," was all I could offer.

"I'm Saran," she said in perfect English, "but please call me Moon."

"Ok, Moon—I'm Rick," I stammered and then reached out my hand.

Instead of shaking it, she held on to it, interlacing her long fingers with mine like we were a couple. Then she flagged down the bartender and asked for the "house special" speaking with an English accent just like Mei Mei.

"You alone Rick?" she asked flirtatiously.

"Yep!" I said a bit to proudly.

"First time?" she asked softly.

"Shit, how did you know?" I answered, a bit stunned. But later realized that I must have been an easy mark.

The bartender returned with her drink. She thanked him and called him by name. This seemed too familiar and rubbed me the wrong way.

"You look lonely," she added.

"How could you tell?" I said, looking at the crowd at the bar. They all seemed to be remarkably female. "Usually, I come to Hong Kong with my dad, but not this time."

"So, your first time at this bar?" she asked.

"Um, yeah, I think so. I mean, I passed it many times."

I quickly downed more of my drink with false bravado.

"I like the way they make margaritas!" I exclaimed.

"What about Mongolian girls?" she asked coquettishly, as she slowly removed her neck scarf revealing strong trapezoid muscles that seemed to lift and define her bare collarbones. She proceeded with wrapping the scarf around my neck.

She smiled leaned into me, grabbed my thigh, and whispered into my ear, "700."

"Seven hundred?" I asked and took a nervous gulp of the remaining tart green liquid.

She shot back her "house drink," and ordered another round for the both of us.

"Okay, six hundred, but only for a short time," she continued. "And because your Daddy is not here."

I let this resonate as I felt her body quickly occupy whatever empty space was left between us. Then it hit me harder than I thought it would. My mind shifted to overdrive as I began to laugh to myself. This is a "working girl" who just propositioned me to have sex with her for, like, what... seventy-five bucks? I smiled broadly and thought, *Hong Kong is a great city!*

She smiled and looked lovingly into my eyes as the bartender returned with both our drinks. I quickly pounded mine. I called the bartender over, asked for the check, and paid for both our drinks on my company credit card. I smiled back at her as she got even closer in my personal space, pulling us closer together with her scarf around my neck. I let the flirtation continue and then raised my left ring finger to let my wedding ring do a little dance between her eyes. She kept smiling and gave me that sexy vixen look, like, "yeah, so fucken what?"

She was resolute and confident. I wanted to seal the deal right there, but truth was that even with all my sexual proclivity, prostitutes scared me the shit out of me back then. I had only been with one and it was when I was a lot younger. The experience was not the sexual conquest that I expected and traumatic to say the least. When we first got our drivers licenses, my friends and I had a big plan to drive into the city from Long Island and cruise 42nd Street looking to get blow jobs. We thought that was what men did when they were old enough. Like some sort of pornographic rite of passage.

We drove around in my friends' Cadillac Deville until we found a group of prostitutes and pulled into an adjacent alley. The group quickly followed us, and I insisted on going first. I sat in the back seat with the questionable girl while my friends got out of the car, huddled together, smoking cigarettes and making small talk with the other whores. I was the "brave" one in the bunch and quickly "dropped trou." What I remembered most about sitting pant less in the large back seat of the 4-door coupe, was that *she/it* had the worst body odor, smelling like an unwashed jock strap. I had trouble concentrating while she slobbered over my pubescent cock. She worked me quick and insisted that I, "tell her when I was about to cum." I closed my eyes, letting my mind wander to something sexier and soon enough that special feeling started to take

Eric Magun

over my body. She must have sensed this and increased her sucking and slobbering. I tried to keep silent, ignoring the stench, wanting to just finish in her mouth.

"I'm going to cum," I ended up confessing like a guilty boy.

And just as I was about to empty, she released me from her mouth and let her hands do the pumping. As I exploded, she started to scream, and bang on the roof, "He's coming! He's coming! It's time! It's time!"

Before I knew what was happening, there was turmoil outside of the car where my friends were gathered. Two Hispanic men approached quickly, flashing switchblades at their faces. The she-devil I was with took out her own blade from her purse and told me to, "get out of the car and join my friends."

I quickly pulled up my jeans and underpants, put my hands nervously over my head and exited the vehicle. I joined my friends, hands held high as we were all frozen in fear. Especially me, who just came all over my shirt, and was looking at a sharp end of the double-sided blade now pointed at my throat. The girls were yelling at us, "to keep still or we would be stabbed."

No one dared move as the dangerous men with blades told us to quickly give them our wallets. We carefully reached into our pockets and handed over our billfolds as the girls ripped off our gold chains. These necklaces held our Jewish stars that were given to us at our Bar Mitzvahs. We all stood in shock, and I was beyond humiliated. It happened so fast that it almost seemed as if we were frozen in time. The men broke the surrealism with a threat that we needed to "leave fast and not call the cops!" They reminded us that, they had our IDs and would "kill our families if we told anyone about this!"

That was an experience my friends and I swore to never to repeat to anyone. We were in shock, embarrassed and needed to get our stories straight about our missing chains and wallets. We rode home in silence, too humiliated to speak, let alone stop at Wo Hop's 24-hour restaurant on Mott Street in China Town. It would be a long time before we went back to the city and was also the last time any of us went to 42nd Street looking for sex.

So naturally I was too traumatized back then and wanted nothing to do with this current sex worker, even if she was Mongolian and had a great British accent. I wrestled with my conscience a bit more as I was

56

alone, sans Jewish star, but it just didn't feel right to spend the night with a sex worker, even if I was far away from home. I didn't want anything to fuck up this opportunity to finally do something good. It was a tough decision, but I gave the scarf back to Moon, excused myself, went to the bathroom and then took off out the back door. Cowardly, I ran down D'Aguilar Street, hailed a cab, made my way to the Cross Harbor Tunnel and back to the safety of my hotel.

The next morning, I met Mei Mei in the hotel lobby. She was immaculately outfitted in a tight fitted (Double G) Gucci dress, Prada shoes and carrying a small Hermes bag. A big contrast to my baggy grey washed Levi's, faded black T-shirt and Converse Chuck Taylor high-tops. I followed her out to the same car as yesterday and was assaulted by the hot, humid weather that hit me like a warm water balloon. The sun glassed driver opened both doors for us, took my bags and loaded them back in the large trunk. The car was frigid and felt good as we drove through the busy Canton Road to the China Ferry Terminal.

"Rick, I hope you had a good night sleep?" Mei Mei asked peering into my eyes.

"Not really," I replied. "Guess I have a bit of jetlag."

She continued to stare into my eyes and started to smile. I felt the urge to look away, but I was too mesmerized by her beauty. She grabbed my hand lightly as a sly smile appeared on her wide face.

"Too bad, you couldn't find anything to help you sleep."

"Excuse me," I stammered.

"Well, did you at least see the beautiful *Moon* out last night?"

She let my hand go but continued to lock eyes.

"Maybe another Margarita would have done the trick?" she said and gave me a wink.

I wasn't sure where she was going with this conversation, but I started to feel very uncomfortable. Just then her phone rang which she flipped open like second nature.

"Morning," she said. "We got him and will make sure he makes the boat."

She listened intently for a few more minutes as the car made its way to the Ferry Terminal and pulled up to the ticket counter.

"Yes, he'll have the package." She said and hung up.

Mei Mei told me to "wait for her," she got out of the car and headed inside the building toward the ticket counter. The driver also got out and pulled my suitcase along with two army green duffel bags out of the trunk. He followed Mei Mei inside and handed the bags to a porter who promptly left with them.

Mei Mei and the driver returned as I got out of the car to meet them. Mei Mei had the ticket in her hand and gave it to me along with a sealed manilla envelope carrying what felt like two USB jump drives. She told me to "give the envelope to Buddy," and then apologized for having to go back to the office instead of escorting me to the factory. "Sorry Rick, something urgent came up and I need to leave," she said.

"Yeah sure, no problem," was all I could muster.

I was unfazed by this. If anything, I felt confused by this Mei Mei and wasn't sure what I would do on this five-hour boat ride alone with such a beautiful and mysterious woman. Besides, I wasn't much of a conversation starter and right now would rather listen to my punk rock CD's and watch the scenery. I waved "goodbye" to her, placed the envelope in my backpack, put on my Sony Discman headphones and made way through the immigration counter and onto the rickety wooden ferry boat.

My ticket allowed me to sit in the back of the one-story boat that had a small but private section. There were cushions on the seats and although they were ripped in places, still offered me a bit of comfort for what would be the next five grueling hours in the immense heat. The boat carried 25–30 passengers upriver and was in no hurry to reach its destination. I took notice of the landscape as it quickly changed from urban jungle to, well, the jungle.

After countless near water buffalo encounters and dozens of men in wooden skiffs throwing nets into the air, we finally pulled up in between two patches of rock and rubble. I chalked this down to what must have been the jetty and the entrance to the ferry dock. Alas, I had arrived to where the old man was making the "best porcelain in the world." I sat on my proverbial "wooden horse," thinking that finally I would make my family proud. It would take a sojourn across the world, flirting with Malaria ridden mosquitoes, on a slow boat to literally to China, while visiting someone I've never met before, to gain the attention I have always craved of my parents. Man was I fucked up.

10

Last Caress, *Dongguan City, China—circa 2003*

I stared at the dead girl in the bed, looking at the starchy fabric as it made a perfect outline of her naked body underneath.

I gazed at her delicate frame, hoping to see some movement as I wished once again for her to wake up and for this to be just another one of my bad dreams. I even gave her a little shake, then a tug, and lifted the sheet to quickly fondle her breasts, anything, hoping the shock of my touch would somehow startle her alive. Instead of life, I received death's stare as the sheets remained still and the blood continued to stain the makeshift torniquet around her head. I couldn't look at her open eyes anymore, no matter how pretty they were, so I used my shaky fingers to gently close them.

I took some deep breaths to try and gain some composure. I needed to think quickly about my next moves and try to find something to calm me down. Unfortunately, there were no drugs or alcohol in the room to numb my brain. I would have finished a mini bar to its bare bones, but this was not that kind of hotel room.

"Fuck!" I exclaimed and proceeded to hit my head several times with an open fist. A dead girl is not exactly the type of attention that I desired. I felt panicked, alone, and needed to hear a familiar voice.

Someone to shatter this nightmare and bring me some reality. It felt perverse but I decided to call my wife to redeem some sort of normalcy. It might have been 5 A.M. in New York, but it was the only thing I could think to do now.

I got off the bed, reached in my wallet to fish out my international calling card, picked up the hotel phone, dialed the long list of numbers to get an outside line, and finally a long-distance connection to the U.S.

I sat on the floor next to the bed and after several rings, the phone was picked up.

"Rick if this is you, I'm caressing your wife right now," said Robin teasingly.

Robin was my wife's yoga teacher. She stood 5 foot 7 inches of lean muscle, blond hair and piercing blue eyes that could stop a moving car with her stare. This was not the *grounding* voice I needed to hear.

"Robin, I need to speak to Heather... it's urgent!"

"Jesus, Rick," she whispered in a tired voice. "She is passed out; can't this wait until a little later?"

"No!" I said firmly. "I need you to wake up my wife now!"

I heard some rustling and Robin talking quietly behind a muffled hand. Recently, Robin had made it a point to stay over at the house whenever I was away to "keep my wife company." They met in Robin's hot yoga class, became fast friends, sharing similar passions for salads, veganism, working out, and "Namaste."

Now they were sharing my bed—not sure when this escalated from keeping my wife company to spending the evening, especially on a school night. Normally, I would be fine with the thought of these two hot broads in the same bed, but not without me! I felt a wave of jealously rise over me, reminding me how lonely I really was. Finally, my wife got on the phone.

"Rick, honey, is everything alright?" Heather said in a tired voice

I ignored that question with my own.

"Why is Robin over now?" I answered abruptly.

"C'mon, sweetheart, let's not start that again."

"Right, I'm not allowed to ask my wife why she is sleeping with her yoga teacher?" I said defensively.

"C'mon Rick, we went through this before and you were okay with me having some company when you were gone," she interrupted. "You even encouraged Robin to be here for me."

"Okay, but maybe we can try this sleepover thing when I am home?"

"Rick, there is nothing going on here, why are you calling so early?"

"As it turns out, I am having a shitty night!" I exclaimed. "And I would do anything right now to be in that bed with you... or the both of you!"

"Rick, are you dunk or something?"

"C'mon hon, let's not start that now."

"Well then what is it? She asked. "Was everything ok with your flight over there?

"Flight was the same ole."

"Then why is your night so bad?" she asked and yawned loudly.

I turned to face the dead girl in the bed.

"Nothing I can explain right now," I said slowly, feeling rejected as depression started to rear its ugly head. "I guess I just miss you already."

"You are definitely drunk!" she exclaimed with exasperation.

"No, I'm not!" I answered short. "I just wish I wasn't *here* right now; I would much rather be home with you and the kids!"

"Don't worry, I'm taking good care of your family!" exclaimed Robin loudly into the receiver.

I heard the rustle of the phone as my wife regained control.

"That's sweet, Rick; I miss you, too, babe. Just think, we will see each other in a few more weeks."

This was the best I could get from Heather.

A few more weeks, I thought. Shit, this could blow my cover. I could be in jail by then. Or even dead! I turned and stared at death under the sheets of the bed. I swallowed hard, knowing I needed to do something about this, and I was running out of time.

"You're right, honey, just a few more weeks," I said glumly.

"Love you, baby," she said. "Try to relax, sober up and get some sleep."

"I don't think I'm going to get much sleep tonight."

"Why don't you go downstairs and get one of those massages you talk about so fondly?" she asked.

"Yeah, sounds like a good plan," I said, and swallowed hard at the idea.

"I love you, Rick. I need to go back to sleep now, I have to get up soon and help the kids get ready for school."

"Love you, too, Rick," said Robin from a distance, and Heather hung up the phone.

"Love you, too," I said to the empty receiver.

I placed the phone back on the base, walked across the room and turned on the TV. There was nothing in English, just some Chinese kung fu soap opera. It's strange but the same TV series seems to be on no matter what time of day (or night) it is. At least I think it's the same show, but who can really tell? Every TV show looks and sounds the same in China. They are always a blend of melodramatic bad acting, cheap stunts, uneven sound, and very cute girls.

I needed to relax and figure out what to do next. I needed a break. Some time to clear my head. I laid back down on the bed, careful not to touch the cadaver under the sheet next to me. I closed my eyes, praying that some decent thought would overcome me and give me divine direction as to what to do next. Instead of any solutions, all I could think about was my wife's naked body next to Robin's. I let that thought resonate and felt a familiar stirring in my crotch. As habit would have it, I began to rub myself quickly in anxiety and desperation. It didn't last long as eroticism was quickly replaced with intense fear. That brought on my *fight-or-flight* instinct, and, in this instance, I wanted purely to escape.

I thought of my only two options to help me and had already called on one of them. Shu Shu would come over with Dr. Dave and I was confident they would help. I also knew that I needed to call Mei Mei but was too concerned now to let her in on my dirty secret. Although she knew almost everything about me, there are still some things that I wanted to keep sacred or pretend that they were mine alone. Even if what I was doing for her, was in some ways helpful for the greater good, I still couldn't help feeling guilty for my betrayal to Shu Shu, even if he was up to something wicked. We were still business partners, making decent money and have been through so much together. Mei Mei would have to wait for now, but my better sense knew that she would soon find out and I would have no choice but to make that call.

Man, I needed a drink or a smoke! I could murder a bottle of vodka right now and kill for a joint!

11

Suburban Home, *Long Island, NY—circa 1977*

My parents wanted to grow strawberries.

I was delighted by the idea and eager to learn more. It was not every day that my folks decided to call a family meeting to share such exciting news! To think we would be farming on the small plot of land that consisted of my backyard, right here on suburban Long Island. We didn't have much property and often joked that, "we could reach out of our windows and pick up our neighbor's phone." The homes were all two stories, uniformly built close together to maximize property value. Besides a common exterior with suburban curb appeal, the property lines did allow for backyards large enough for a swing set and often separated for privacy by 8-foot wooden fences outlined with tall pine trees. I couldn't imagine where we would be planting this fruit farm but was intrigued to find out more.

I mean, my dad was far from "handy." I don't think he even owned a hammer, let alone any tools, especially those needed to farm with. My mom was also not the type to sweat or get her well-manicured hands dirty. That left us kids, namely my brother Josh and me to handle the dirty work. So, it was not a surprise when my parents mentioned to us at the family meeting that any of our friends would also be invited to help cultivate our majestic strawberry farm.

The plans explained to us were rather simple to grasp. As a matter of fact, we were already prepping and didn't even know it. My dad explained it in great detail, "that first step was to separate the seeds from the grass." I smiled in delight, as I had been doing this for years and did not even know these were strawberry seeds! "Easy peazy"—the grass gets put into a big strainer, then we work the grass with our small hands, separating the stems, pushing the grass through, and leaving just the brownish seeds. Then we dump the seeds and whatever remaining grass was not strained onto big pieces of cardboard paper. My dad handled the cardboard carefully, standing it up forty-five degrees. That was the tricky part, so Dad would be generous enough to pitch in and help at that point. He showed us how to carefully take a butter knife in one hand while holding the paper up with the other hand. We slowly scooped the seeded grass up the paper, and let gravity do its work. Eventually, the seeds would roll down the paper, leaving just the grassy residue.

We would gather the all the small seeds that fell down the paper and put them with the remaining seeds from the strainer into small white plastic buckets. The buckets would be filled half with water, allowing the seeds to float on top of the water like sprinkles on ice cream. The strained grass and the grass residue left on the paper was removed and put into plastic Ziplock bags that Dad and his friends would smoke later.

My father was kind enough to also teach us how to miraculously turn this strawberry grass into cigarettes. I watched intently as my dad opened the *Ziplock's* and placed a handful of the strained grass back onto the cardboard. He took out a small package of incredible thin paper and proceeded to show us how this *Zigzag* rolling paper had a sticky side on one end. He pulled out two sheets, one for him and one for me. They were wafer thin with a crease already set in the middle. He had me copy him as he licked his right fingertips and felt for the sticky side. I did the same and, after a few tries, found the paper to stick to my fingers with ease.

Then I watched in amazement as he pinched a large amount of grass, placing it onto center of the paper very carefully to not spill any. With both thumbs, he did the incredible feat of effortlessly rolling the bumpy grass into an even tube-like shape. In a blink, he put it to his mouth, ran his tongue along the sticky length of the cigarette and with his thumbs still working, sealed the strawberry grass into a perfect cigarette.

I sat there stunned and amazed. I never saw my dad do anything so perfectly before. He smiled in satisfaction and continued to roll the rest of the strawberry grass. He even generously gave me some papers and grass so I could practice, too! It was much harder than my dad made it look. My hands were just too small. I was clumsy and made a mess. Dad didn't seem to mind and even let me lick a few that he rolled closed. We were really bonding for the first time. I enjoyed the strawberry business as the whole process made a lot of sense to me. It was also my first practical lesson in the usefulness of mother nature. To think that some fruit I loved could be grown in our backyard and smoked! I could only imagine the lovely strawberry taste of those hand-rolled cigarettes.

The hand rolled cigarettes were put back into the *Ziploc* plastic bags that my dad put into the center draw under our kitchen counter. We carefully bought the buckets of strawberry seeds down in the basement and placed them under the small window that looked out over our future farm. Next to the window was a life-size poster of a man named "Alice Cooper." He was wearing makeup and had a very large snake around his neck. He was frightening and the fact that he had a girl's name terrified me even more. There was nothing else remarkable about the basement except for my great grandma's, stained yellow floral couch and an old Zenith TV set in a wooden sideboard that was not plugged in and just sat there as secondhand junk.

The poster scared me, as did the barren basement, but the seeds were more important than my young, frightened nerves. Dad told me: "check on them every day and soon you will see them sprout." When this happened, it would be the day to call all our friends so we could begin to plant them in the farm!

In a few short weeks, to my amazement, the seeds began to sprout. Short white and green tentacles began to sprout out of the seeds. A few days after reporting this to Dad, a small team of Spanish speaking landscapers began clearing a small patch of grass in the bottom-right portion of our well-manicured backyard. The grass was ripped up and replaced with fresh dirt and bordered with a low but tightly wound plastic fence.

When I asked Dad about the fence, he told me, "It was there to keep out the bunnies." I didn't remember seeing any bunnies, but it seemed to make sense to my young brain.

The following week, I had my small clan of friends over for the farming experience. They were all as excited as I was to grow our own strawberries. No one I knew grew fruit in my town, let alone their backyard. We all fantasized about what we would make with the strawberries we would grow. Some talked about ice cream sundae's, others mentioned strawberry cake with whipped cream. We all loved *Reddi-Wip* and imagined filling our mouths with the berries and then directly shooting in the sweet, cold sugary cream!

With ear-to-ear smiles, we walked onto the small patch of dirt and waited for Dad. He emerged with my mom. He was carrying the seed buckets, and my mom had a handful of plastic shovels that we used for the beach. Dad set the bucket down and walked around the side of the house to retrieve the hose. My mom divided us in half, giving shovels to those on her right. She explained that "The diggers on the right would dig small holes, evenly spaced in the dirt. Those on her left, without shovels, would be responsible for putting a small pinch of seeds in the holes. When that was done, we would take turns replacing the dirt and covering the holes." First my dad and then my mom demonstrated. We watched with determined faces.

The farming went exactly as planned. Mom and Dad supervised to make sure the holes were evenly spaced; the correct size and depth was dug, and finally the right number of seeds was placed inside. Within an hour we were done. It wasn't a lot of work, and we were anxious to play with the hose. Dad turned it on and set the nozzle to a widespread arc. We all took turns watering our crops and then spraying down our sweaty bodies. It felt good to be alive and even better to be a farmer in America! Even if this backyard was the suburban epitome of entitled middle class white folks.

In the weeks that followed, we frequently checked on our *field of dreams*. Sometimes I checked it twice a day, once before school and once afterwards. Then on a sunny Sunday, my brother and I woke to find small green stalks fighting their way out of the dirt. We jumped up and down, hugged and ran back inside to wake up Mom and Dad. Later that night, they had friends over to show off what we'd done. They were all smoking that strawberry grass and congratulating us on a job well done. They must have been really happy, as they could not stop laughing!

The strawberry field grew fast, and, by the end of summer, it was almost as tall as the 3 foot fence protecting them from the bunnies. My friends and I checked every day for signs of the red fruit only to be disappointed to find nothing but green leaves. It seemed that we would never see *the fruits of our labor*. My father seemed concerned as well, came out to grab some of the weeds, pulling them out, smelling them and then placed them gingerly into another plastic bag. He didn't look overjoyed, and I had to ask him, "when will we see our first strawberry?"

That night, both Mom and Dad sat me and my brother down to tell us, "That they might have made a mistake with the strawberries. We needed to prepare ourselves that the fruit might never come!" We were shocked and in disbelief. Dad continued to explain, "That we might have unfortunately planted only male seeds by mistake." He continued to explain to us that, "Without female seeds there would be no fruit." I was heartbroken and told the news to my friends who were also disappointed.

We stopped checking on the plants, and by the time October rolled around, Dad had the landscapers cut it all down. He told us later, "That he was thinking of building a hot tub in place of our strawberry field." That way everyone could still enjoy the outdoors. While we loved the idea of having a hot tub, we were still crushed that the fruit didn't work.

Dad felt sympathetic and told us, "We might have more luck if we tried to grow them indoors." Thus, to our delight we replanted a new crop of strawberry seeds into small pots. Dad moved our portable farm downstairs into the basement. He set up a bunch of lights on clips and a few box fans. He told us, "That we were going to recreate nature, and all we had to do was make sure the lights were turned on in the morning and off at night."

He and Mom said they would make sure it was watered, and that we were welcome to have our friends over to help at any time. He also explained that "This time we will have strawberries, and they will taste better grown inside than any we had tried before!" He pointed at the poster of the man with the snake around his neck and mentioned, "that makeup man will help keep our strawberries safe."

I didn't believe that a poster of a scary man with a snake offered us any safety, but I was optimistic that we would have our berries and that they would be delicious. Sadly, the berries never came but the grass was bountiful. As it turned out my old man had something of a *green thumb* after all. My parents proceeded to build that hot tub and used it all hours of the evening, in any weather conditions. Their friends would come over, smoke the strawberry grass, get naked and take turns bathing with each other.

It would take years before I eventually learned what that grass really was. I spent many an evening watching them get stoned, party naked in the hot tub that was in the strawberry field, directly under my bedroom window. My folks did a nice job of robbing me of my young innocence and destroying any trust I had left in my parents or in any adult for that matter.

12

Furniture, *Zhaoxing, China—circa 1997*

We came to a sudden halt as the passenger boat drifted onto the sand bank by the river's edge.

An incomprehensible message in Chinese was muffled through a single loudspeaker. I saw the others gather their things and lifted my suitcase from the top of the impromptu roof rack. Embarrassingly, it came crashing down on the deck unexpectedly heavier than I remembered it to be. I was tired and cramped up from sitting in the same position for hours. My body felt as stiff as the wooden board I was seated on.

I grabbed my backpack and followed the Chinese people off the boat onto a waiting dock. I looked over the crowd to see a western old man in the back smoking what appeared to be a cigarette. He was a bit out of shape, wore faded cargo shorts with a short sleeve polo shirt and had a fantastically long ponytail of silver hair. He was also rocking a pair of black Ray-Ban Wayfarers. We caught each other's eyes at about the same time and followed that with a cordial wave A few Chinese men, also in sunglasses, stood austere next to him. The silver-haired old man said something to one of the Chinese men and pointed to me. The Chinese man, dressed in Levi's with an unrecognizable T-shirt, quickly came my way and outstretched his hand in a warm welcome.

"Hi, Rick, I'm Sunny. So glad you can make it," he said in perfect English.

I wasn't prepared for that but quickly shook his hand as he grabbed my suitcase and backpack. I didn't resist his chivalry and followed him as he made his way to the old man.

"Rick, great to finally meet you," the old man said as he extended his hand and exhaled smoke.

"Hey Buddy," I replied quickly grabbing his hand. He had a firm handshake and a broad smile of astonishingly straight but yellowing teeth. I let go of his hand and quickly recognized that he was either smoking a hand-rolled cigarette or a very skinny joint. He saw me looking and quickly offered it to me.

"Where are my manners?" he said passing me the hand rolled cigarette.

I took it from him and hit it hard. I'm not sure exactly what it was, but it made me cough wildly. The old man started to laugh and then patted my back. I regained my composure and out of the corner of my eye, saw the other two men who were with Buddy, walk over to the boat and retrieve the two army green duffel bags that were loaded on by Mei Mei's driver.

"Rick, I'm so happy you made the trip," he said interrupting my inquisitive stare.

I took another deep inhale, coughed some more, and gave it back. He gave me another big smile before taking a tremendous inhale and finished the joint like a pro.

"Rick, we're Familia now, and I have so much to show ya!"

Again, I detected that Brooklyn accent.

"Let's skedaddle," he said and entered the car. Sunny put my bags in the trunk, made a motion for me to get in and then sat next to me, putting me in the middle seat between him and the old man. The old man took another joint out of his shirt pocket, gave it to me and leaned into my ear.

"One of the advantages of having your own factory is that you can do or grow what you want," he said with that big grin.

I quickly pocketed the joint as the other two men took the duffels, put them in the trunk and got into the front seat of our large black car. It was not a brand name car that I recognized. Something Chinese that looked American. Like a fake Ford.

"Rick how was your journey?" asked Sunny.

"Long," I said sheepishly.

"Cut the shit, Sunny," said the old man, laughing. "He's been traveling for 24 hours and just rode that flea bag boat to see us. He must be tired, confused, and hopefully a bit stoned."

"I'm cool."

"See, Sunny, he's cool. Not like the rest of you girls!"

"Now, now," said Sunny, "no need to show off your big balls in front of our guest." Then he repeated something in Chinese and the others began to laugh. The old man ignored them and turned to look in my direction.

"Rick, Sunny here is the best English-speaking Chinese person in the country." He let that sit for a moment. "Too bad about his small balls, though!" He laughed loudly and coughed vigorously at the same time. I admit to laughing with him.

"But seriously Rick, Sunny is an English teacher at the Rural Farm College nearby."

"True," said Sunny quickly. "The first day I found out about the factory being built, I showed up and asked for a job."

"And now Sunny runs the place," the old man answered while Sunny blushed.

"Mainly you will be dealing with him. I can't speak a word of Chinese and really don't care to learn. Besides, Sunny knows everything, can get you whatever you want and is basically here to do whatever he can for you!"

Buddy winked at me, and Sunny smiled in appreciation.

"Except for pricing, the old man continued, "when we get into pricing, well, that's all me."

"Got it" I replied.

"I knew you would," he said. "Now before I forget, I believe Mei Mei gave you an envelope for me."

"Oh yeah right," I said embarrassed that I forgot and reached into my backpack exposing the envelope.

"I'll take that," said Sunny quickly.

I gave him the package

The large car labored through unpaved streets, flooded roadways, and long stretches of third-world poverty. In between the destitution, in the distance, produced crag-like structures towering their rocky cliffs over dark blue lakes. Zhaoqing's natural beauty mixed with the poverty confused my young Western mind. They were like polar opposites colliding into a scene best left to my Canon Powershot digital camera. So, that is exactly what I did, fished out the small camera from my backpack, and opened the windows to take pictures of the breathtaking natural hyperbole.

We drove through slowly with the windows still open, when children appeared out of nowhere to approach and wave to us in the car. We drove even slower so that the kids could catch up and very carefully the old man leaned out the window to shake the kid's hands and wave, "hello." He seemed something of a celebrity or an oddity and the kids just kept on coming. I took a few snaps of the kids and then put my camera down.

Buddy told Sunny to stop the car, reached into his briefcase and handed me a package of common party balloons in various colors. He kept another bag for himself.

"Hey Rick, take these and let's go have some fun."

He opened the car door and exited. The kids began to swarm around him as he reached into the balloon bag and begin blowing up several balloons. I quickly opened my door and joined the old man as he labored over filling them with air. The kids squealed in excitement as I began blowing up balloons like a mad clown. I heard a few, "hellos" from the kids as I passed out the blown-up balloons. I took out my camera and started to take pictures of all the kids and their plastic balloons. They were all smiling, a few with missing teeth but happy, nonetheless. After a few minutes of pure excitement, the old man threw the balloon bag in the air letting the deflated colored rubber pieces fall to the floor. The kids started to scream in joy as they quickly retrieved the fallen inflatables. I stared in awe at the innocence of these children and the joy they had in something so simple. Sunny broke the spell as he yelled out the window.

"Buddy, we need to get a move on!"

I imitated the old man and threw my empty balloons into the air and away from the car. The kids continued to scream in delight as we entered the car and slowly drove away. We continued to what appeared to be the center of a very sleepy town. Most of the buildings consisted of a ground floor workshop, where the family did their craft and lived on the top.

Sometimes it was metal work, sometimes painting, cleaning or repairing shit. Others just sold stuff like clothes, shoes, miscellaneous household goods and food... yep, food. However, it looked more like a zoo than a market. What I saw shook me to the core of disgust and it took me a moment to recognize what I was witnessing. I was eyeing straw cages packed with chickens, and metal cages with what appeared to be too many mongrel dogs or feral cats, or something in between. There were pigs, snakes, and fish laid out on mats with no ice. Like a horror movie, the old women had dirty bibs and held bloody cleavers. The men sat around (or squatted) and smoked cigarettes. I've always been amazed at their ability to squat so close to the ground. Squatting in China is an untold cultural event. It's hard to describe if you've never seen it. The men squat down real low, where their butts rest on the back of their calves, hovering inches above the ground. They are seated upright, as if unfazed by gravity, with incredible flexibility, posture and balance. It is their "normal" sitting position and looks uncomfortably obscene by any Western standards.

We made our way slowly through the zoo of a town, and pulled up to what I could only imagine was an old temple or a museum of some kind. It was a very large wooden and cement building, ornately decorated with classical Chinese sculptures, angled, tiled roofs with dragons in the corners and a pair of very large ceramic Foo Dogs at the entrance. The car stopped in front of a guard booth. The guard dressed in a polyester green uniform, gave us a toothless (and shoeless) salute, and opened the gates so that the car could enter. Once inside, the old man turned in my direction again.

"Rick, mi casa es su casa." He laughed and got out of the car and lit a cigarette this time. Both Sunny and I got out as well.

The old man continued with outstretched arms, "Welcome to my home and as you can see it was an old temple that I was able to buy only with Sunny's help."

Sunny said, "Since there is no hotel in this town, we always keep a few rooms open for anyone visiting."

The old man gave me a wink and took another deep drag of his cigarette. I stood there in awe looking at the temple, letting its beauty and physical prowess overwhelm me.

"This house is part of the deal we have with the locals," the old man added. "They let us buy this temple, refurbish it to live in and in return we rent out some of the rooms to anyone willing to visit our humble town."

"And when we're done with it, we will return it back to the city, where they will convert it into a museum," Sunny added.

"What about the Army barracks?" I asked puzzled.

The old man and Sunny just laughed.

"Had you going, didn't I?" the old man said, still laughing. "Butch told me that your dad would never come if he thought we only had the barracks and quite frankly I wanted to meet you alone."

The old man proceeded to give me a side hug with surprising strength in his embrace.

"Rick, you are the future," he added. "I also owe it to your grandfather to take good care of you!"

"Thanks, he sends you his regards as well." I added

"Well let's get you inside," he pointed to the entrance and continued, "I'm sure you're exhausted and could probably use a cold beer by now."

The guard used both hands to pry open the large wooden doors that were intricately carved with Chinese lettering. Both Buddy and Sunny made their way in as I stood there dumbfounded by the sheer size of the place. The two men in the front of the car got out, opened the trunk and took out my bag along with the two large duffel bags that they took from the boat. I took one more look around, slung my backpack on and then followed them inside.

I stood in the entrance for the few moments that it took for my eyes to adjust to the dim light. What I saw (and felt) was an odd, cold place reminding me more of a mausoleum than a museum. The vaulted ceilings were extremely high, and the walls were a mixture of clay, tile, and exposed wood. There was very little light except for the small bit of natural daylight that fought through the building's small windows that were strategically placed on the second floor. To my right I noticed another large door with the old man's company logo on it. The door was ajar, so I took a glance and saw a grand porcelain blue and white lamp with dragons expertly hand painted on it. The lamp was very large, switched on and sitting on top of an intricately carved mahogany table. I took a few cautious steps toward the entrance but did not dare cross the threshold uninvited. However, I was now able to make out many ornate antique furniture pieces, tall decorative vases on rosewood stands and a gold gilded display case with a large picture of Buddy shaking hands with someone in a Chinese military uniform. Quite honestly it looked more like a history museum then an office. Buddy came in and stood quietly next to me. He startled me when he put his arm around me again and told me, "I have some other people I'd like you to meet."

I followed him through the cavernous catacombs until we reached a grand open room with towering ceilings, large stained glass windows and approached three Chinese women sitting on an old antique opium bed. The bed was exquisitely adorned with carved deities in weathered red paint and with what looked like fourteen karat gold paint that highlighted the embossed parts of the carved antique.

As we approached the women, they stood up and smiled in our direction. The oldest woman was small-boned, frail but stood without any help from the others. She had very long hair braided down to the bottom of her back. The other two standing were young, much taller than the older woman and looked like sisters. All three of them had the same broad smiles, long hair and pronounced cheek bones. The oldest of the sisters was just an inch taller than the youngest. They were thin, well dressed in traditional silk outfits and appeared overjoyed to have a visitor. The old man approached and kissed all three of them on the cheeks. He held the hand of the eldest woman and turned towards me.

"Rick, meet my family," he said. "Ladies, this is Rick Price from the United States."

Sunny interpreted as they all smiled and waved, "hello" to me.

"And this beautiful woman is my Ma Ma." Buddy said proudly as he dropped her hand and replaced it with an overly zealous hug. She yelled something in Chinese as she hit him lovingly.

The old man then turned and took the hand of the taller sister. They looked lovingly at each other and then back at me.

"Rick, please meet my wife, Ai." Buddy said with a big smile.

He pronounced it as "eye" and then let me know that "her name means love."

She reached out to shake my hand and I stepped up to reciprocate.

"Nice to meet you, eye," I mustered.

"You too-ah," she said in broken English, and then turned to introduce her sister.

The younger of the sisters didn't need an introduction and proceeded to shake my hand.

"Hi Rick, from USA, please call me Xiao Mei," said the young girl.

I quickly noticed that she seemed more confident both in her English and her eye contact. I shook her hand without hesitation.

"Ni Hao Xiao Mei" I said inquisitively, holding her hand a bit longer. "Your name is almost the same as Mei Mei's?"

"Yes, she explained. "Mei Mei is Younger Sister, and I am Little Sister!"

"We're all family here," said the old man, catching me give Xiao Mei the faintest of smiles. "Let's leave Ma Ma and the girls to prepare dinner while we give Rick a quick tour of the factory."

The girls waved goodbye and then left through another large wooden door to what I imagined to be a big kitchen. Sunny returned with two cold Tsingtao beers in green, and gold cans with red lettering. He gave one to Buddy and another to me.

"None for you Sunny?" I asked.

"No." he said

"Sunny don't drink," chimed the old man. "Against his religion."

He laughed, then pulled off the tab as the can let out the familiar sound of air escaping the cold chamber. He chugged it instantly while I went through the machinations of trying my best to clean the top with my now soiled and sweaty T-shirt. After a few deliberate wipes, I opened mine and drained it quickly. Amazing I thought to myself how satisfying a cold beer can be, even a Tsingtao! Both Buddy and I belched in unison as the old man crushed his can and placed it on the small marble table next to the opium bed. I followed suit as Sunny left to call for the car.

I followed Buddy out of the museum, careful to pick up my backpack and then made my way over to the car. The two men and Sunny were already inside. We entered as they rolled up the windows and cranked up whatever AC the foreign car could muster. The guard opened the gate and saluted as we acerated away. I felt compelled to salute back.

After a short drive down the main street, past the outdoor fish market, we climbed up another steep hill and made a right on what looked like the only completely paved road in the town. The cemented road led us to the factory grounds that were surrounded by an intimidating high white metal fence. On top of the railing were sharp posts and jagged pieces of glass glued haphazardly to ward off any potential interlopers. This crude form of extra security caught me a bit off guard for a furniture factory. But I guess having the best porcelain needed protection this far away from "normal" civilization. The structures inside the fence were very large and reminded me of crude airplane hangars. Outside these buildings, workers appeared to be very busy painting, hammering, drilling, and carrying cartons inside an empty container box.

I didn't see much of the porcelain product the old man bragged about. Instead, the factory was more like an antique wood furniture workshop. The grounds appeared to be littered with ornately painted cabinets, bed frames, altar tables, mahogany chairs, rosewood stools and abstract patterned wardrobes. Some were in pristine condition and others were barely recognizable. I started to feel a bit unsettled as none of this was something I was familiar with.

We drove to the front gates and were immediately surrounded by a small crowd of people loitering around the entrance. They started to look menacingly into the car windows, and some were banging on the hood in anger. There was a guard in the crowd, wearing cheap flip flops and a green uniform that had seen better days. He was armed with only a small baton and appeared to be arguing with the mob. When he saw us approach, he yelled loudly at the men, stepped up on a high block and saluted us. Sunny and the old man saluted him back. Then Sunny and the other two men got out of the car to address the crowd, when more shouting erupted from the crew. The old man turned to me and put a reassuring hand on my shoulder. He looked a bit uncomfortable but still had that stoned grin on his face.

"Don't mind all the shouting," Buddy said dismissively, "The people here are very emotional, and strangers, well, let's just say, some of them never saw another American before."

With that, Sunny jumped back in the car, said something to the driver and then the two men and the guard opened the big white gates just enough so we could pass through. The men and the guard closed the gates quickly and ran over to help us out of the car. The crowd outside the gates continued their shouting as Sunny and the guard shouted back at them. The driver and the other two men escorted all of us into a very large building, shut the doors quickly and left. Sunny immediately locked it from the inside.

When my eyes adjusted to the darkness, I saw rows of what appeared to be more antique furniture, clay vases, porcelain statues, paintings with Chinese characters and other historical items I couldn't identify through the thick layer of dust. Sunny quickly turned on the overhead lights as they buzzed to life, leaving me with a clear view of what I can only assume was a treasure trove of ancient objects. The building was larger than it looked from the outside, about the length of a football field and stacked floor to ceiling with wooden furniture, chests, drums, fishing nets, bamboo poles, troughs, tables, cribs... I mean, everything was very old and Chinese. Some of it was dusty and broken, while others appeared to be in pristine condition. I sat slack-jawed, clueless about what this all was, but impressed, nonetheless.

"Welcome to my factory!" said the old man proudly. He seemed unfazed by the commotion at the entrance, slowly walking down the aisles, perusing the items like a pirate opening a treasure chest of gold for the first time. I watched him put his hands behind his back as he blew dust away from the spoils of another era lost in history. He picked up a large piece of carved jade, wiped it clean on his cargo shorts and placed it back gently from where it sat.

Sunny interrupted quickly. "Rick, why don't we go upstairs to see your samples. You must be anxious to finally examine them. Plus, there is air conditioning up there."

I didn't need to be told twice, as it was very hot and dusty in the building. But the old man had other plans and mentioned for me to follow him instead. He slowly walked towards the center of the building as I noticed for the first time that he had a swagger, like an athlete who had a knee injury early in his career. He would stop frequently and run his fingers lovingly over the dusty furniture. Then he stopped suddenly and turned to face me.

"Rick, in case you're wondering what you are looking at, this collection comes from dynasties that do not exist anymore." He explained and then opened his arms wide. "All this furniture, and all these belongings, have been collected by my team of 'experts.' This team is led by Sunny and is very well respected throughout the province." He continued and then turned to Sunny. "My boy Sunny has gotten us into even the furthest of small towns, all the way to Mongolia and beyond!" he beamed with pride.

"I can honestly say that I never saw anything like this before." I continued. "It's like stepping back in time."

The old man liked that response as he continued to beam.

"Sunny and his team are the best at scavenging the country looking for the rarest of pieces. As you can see, we don't care what shape they are in, as we can repair almost all to their full glory. And well, now they belong to me and Sunny."

Sunny smiled shyly and said, "that is until we sell them."

"Rick," the old man continued, "we have buyers all over the world paying fortunes for these items and what's inside of them. You must imagine that most of these pieces go back tens of thousands of years. What you are witnessing are some of rarest reminders of China's history and only certain museums can come close to owning what we now have."

"Yes, this is true," Sunny chimed in. "But Rick, you are not here to see this, so please, let's go upstairs to our business at hand."

He turned anxiously away and made a gesture to follow him as he walked towards the cement staircase at the end of the cavernous room. I followed right behind him as the old man stayed downstairs with his fortune. We climbed a few flights, passing even more floors packed of furniture. Some of it was being meticulously worked on and others were being carefully packed into wooden crates. Everyone was silent and appeared to be working at a fast clip.

We approached the top floor and entered another room. Sunny hit the lights, and alas I saw my samples on a gigantic wooden table. He then went to the corner of the room and pushed a few buttons on what I assumed was a large free-standing A/C unit. It hummed as it slowly pumped out cool air. I was sweating through my clothes and made a bee-line to the air vent for some comfort. Unfortunately, it was not pumping cold like I was used to, but it was at least a relief from the stagnant air downstairs. I stood in front of the vent and closed my eyes. I felt out of place and a bit overwhelmed. I shook off these feelings as weakness and then chalked this up to being jet-lagged.

Sunny brought me a bottle of water with the logo of a frosty mountain top. Unfortunately, it was room temperature, warm, but I drank it anyway and followed him to the table to examine our samples. The vases were painted with precision and matched perfectly to the counter swatches we'd sent over. There were two sets of each, one that was unassembled and the other that had an electrical assembly attached. We went through the machinations of comparing the lamp bases to the finish swatches. I took out my notebook from my backpack, took copious notes and then shot the samples with my digital Canon camera. This took longer than I would have imagined, and my eyes were beginning to close with exhaustion.

Finally, Sunny suggested that we "find the old man, go back for dinner, and continue this work tomorrow." I told him, "That is an excellent idea" and followed him down the stairs. Above the first level, next to the men working, were a series of small offices. Sunny led me to the old man's headquarters. He was sitting on a mahogany chair behind an outrageously large wooden desk. It had similar intricate carvings as the other items, but with more gold gilded paint, the wood color was much darker, appearing almost orange and blackish red. There was a large glass top covering the antique monstrosity that had a large porcelain bowl on it, being used as an ashtray. The old man was smoking and looking out the window as we approached. I glanced outside to see that the crowd we encountered was still there and looked larger than when we first entered. Sunny also took notice of this as I detected a look of concern spread over his face.

"How did we do, kid?" the old man said, breaking the silence in the room.

"Awesome. I mean, everything looks great!" I exclaimed.

He smiled and said, "I told you this trip would be worth it."

I wasn't sure if this was directed at me or Sunny.

"Tomorrow, we should finish the shade selections and then move onto the furniture items. And if time allows, we'll show you more of the factory," Sunny said. "Right now, we need to get you back for dinner!"

There was a knock on the door as the two men from the car entered with another security guard. This guard appeared more together than the one at the gate. At least he had on tall boots, a green helmet with a red Chinese star and a wooden baton strapped his waist. He looked like he was in charge and had a few tense words with Sunny. Sunny then handed him the envelope that Mei Mei gave me, and this seemed to calm him down. He quickly pocketed the envelope, saluted me and left.

Sunny turned to me and asked, "you wouldn't mind following the two men to the car and wait for me and Buddy?" I nodded, gathered my knapsack, and followed the men downstairs, past the graveyard of antiques and out the large building.

Once outside, I noticed the crowd was definitely larger than before. Thankfully, the car was pulled up just outside the door. I quickly jumped in as the crowd turned to face me and the car. Both guards and the two men who now I can only assume were more security, started shouting at the crowd. The booted guard pulled out his Billy club and held it above his head in a threatening manner. There was a lot of yelling as things got very tense. I was on full alert, scanning the crowd and then the way out should I need to bolt quickly away. Suddenly, Sunny appeared from the building and jumped in the back seat with me. He left the door open as he turned to face me.

"Rick, we must stay here for a bit and talk with these people outside. They are our employees and as you can see, there are some matters that we must clear up. Nothing for you to worry about, but we probably will not make it to dinner with you. I will call the girls and let them know. They will take good care of you tonight, and tomorrow we will get an early start... say eight a.m.?"

"Sure," I stammered a bit confused, "See you tomorrow."

"Thank you, Rick," he said. "You must be exhausted. I hope you have a good night's rest." He said something to the driver, and then quickly left the car, slamming the door shut and ran back inside the building. The driver hit the automatic door locks.

The guards pulled open the gates as the crowds threatened to overtake the car. I saw clearly that this crowd was made up of men, they were angry and persistent. We took off quickly disregarding anyone in our way. The driver kept his foot on the gas and his hand on the horn, as we sped away drowning out the muttered shouts from the crowd. I looked back through the rear window as the guards and security men worked the gates closed after our departure. I was glad to get out of there but wondered what Sunny and Buddy where up to. I felt exhausted, confused, and looked back at the crowd, the fenced in buildings, and the shattered pieces of glass as they reflected a now-menacing setting sun.

13

Born To Lose, *Dongguan City, China—circa 2003*

I paced the bedroom floor waiting for Shu Shu to arrive and help take care of this problem.

It was taking longer than expected and I was tired of looking back at the dead girl in the bed. I was filled with anxiety but brought up enough nerve to make that call to Mei Mei. I knew it was the right thing to do, but also that she would be more than pissed off as she instructed me (more than once) to keep a very low profile and not attract any attention to myself. I admit that this is a very tall order for me to comply with. Keeping attention away from myself was just not in my nature—kind of like the scorpion...

I pulled out my small Nokia cell phone and dialed the numbers that have burned into the back of my mind. Numbers that I deleted from my contacts, as I would never forget them and never repeat out loud to anyone. She picked up immediately.

"Mei Mei" I said.

"What's wrong Rick?"

"Shit, why is something always wrong?"

"You don't call unless something is wrong," she quickly replied.

I looked back at the girl and exclaimed, "Well there's a dead girl in my room!"

"Rick shut up! Stop talking!" she commanded.

"But she's dead." Is all I could think of saying.

"I told you to shut up and not say another word!"

"I swear it was not my fault!" I continued.

"Enough!" she shouted for the first time.

"I think maybe someone was trying to poison me." I tried to explain.

"What are you saying?"

"Something in the toothpaste."-

Did you call Shu Shu?" she asked ignoring me.

"Of course," I replied.

"Does anyone else know about this?" she asked.

"No!" I exclaimed a little too loudly.

"Rick, we've run through this drill before, no talking to anyone else."

"I understand" I said meekly.

"No Rick, you don't understand, you cannot possibly understand!" she said sternly.

I let that sit for a moment and felt angry at her accusatory tone.

"Listen carefully, here's what we are going to do. When you hang up, I want you to take photos of the girl, the entire hotel room, the room number and the hotel address," she said.

"I can do that"-

"Then you will text me all the photos from your phone. When you are done sending, you are to permanently delete them from your phone."

"Ok, I'll shoot it all and send it to you."

"Then you must take the SIM card out and destroy it as well."

"How do I call without a SIM card?" I asked.

"I will have Shu Shu get you a new one." She replied and hung up.

I made a mental note of all the instructions and made my way over to the dead girl again as I delicately pulled the covers off her. I stared at her naked body one more time, feeling guilty about my entire life, took out my phone and started to take the requested photos. I shot her from every angle I could think of, including turning her over to shoot from behind. I took close ups of almost every inch of her body, including untying the pillowcase, revealing the gash on the back of her head.

I didn't enjoy this photography shoot at all but was at least comforted that the bleeding seemed to have coagulated and stopped from its flow.

I then took pictures of the entire room, the key with the number and hotel address. I took more photos of the shower, the red chair and the toothpaste. When satisfied, I sent all the photos to Mei Mie, took out my SIM card and crushed it under my foot. My mind was still in disbelief and my stomach started to turn sour. I ran to the bathroom and wretched whatever acid was left in my abdomen. I took some deep inhalations caught my breath, took the pieces of the sim card and flushed it down the toilet with the bile. I was all nerves now, needed to settle my mind and again wished to be anywhere but here.

14

Lust for Life, *Zhaoqing, China—circa 1997*

When we got to the old stately home, I took my backpack and followed the driver inside.

He went directly to the security guard. The guard gave me a small key and made a signal for me to follow him. I looked around for the girls but did not see anyone, so I followed the guard up a flight of narrow wooden stairs and towards the back of a cavernous hall.

At the end of the hallway was another very large wooden door. This one, like the others, appeared to be very old and had Chinese letters expertly painted across the top. The guard motioned for the key, slipped it in the lock and gave it a turn. The door belched a loud creaking noise as it opened slowly. I instantly felt the noxious heat escape, assaulting my lungs with a combination of dust and stale air. I made quick tracks to the closest windows, and opened the shutters as wide as they would permit. Sunlight spilled into the room, illuminating a dusty replica of what I saw in the factory.

The room was decorated with another antique opium bed and on it sat two small pillows on top of an ornate patchwork blanket. There were several framed paintings on the wall of Chinese calligraphy, a large carved wooden chair reminiscent of an open dragon's mouth, and an oversized rosewood desk, painted with ornate scenes of water and wind. The pattern reminded me of that famous Japanese painting, *The Great Wave*, it looked like my tattoos, and I felt immediately at ease. Above the desk was a light switch that I promptly turned on. It lit up a small hand-painted porcelain desk lamp with an old shade made from rattan. The lamp gave off a muted glow. The guard pointed to my luggage in the corner and turned to leave. Before he left, he flipped another wall switch, and a ceiling fan began to slowly hum, circulating the stale air as it mixed with whatever warm wind was coming from the open windows.

I took stock of my surroundings, sat on the opium bed, took off my shoes, sweaty socks and let it all sink in. The room reminded me of something straight out of an *Ang Lee* movie set. In the very far corner was a doorless entry to a small bathroom. I got up to take a look as a cold shower was exactly what I needed. What I saw was a handheld shower head hanging next to a small sink, and a drain in the corner of the mildly sloped floor There was no shower curtain, and a small towel was folded on the small sink next to a small piece of soap. I turned on the shower faucet and fought with the shower head as it strained to stay in place. I ended up taking off the holder and dropped it to the floor as it sprayed in the direction of the floor drain.

I went back into the room, opened my bags to take out my personal belongings and a new set of clothes. I started to undress and noticed there was also no mirror in the room. A smile stretched across my face as I thought that perhaps this room could be haunted with its unique history. I walked nude to the open windows to look outside to see if there was any way for someone to notice me. All I saw was a slow-moving stream fighting its way through large rocks and clumps of wild bamboo that towered over the roof of this historical home. I smiled to myself, chalking this up to some sublime moment and knew that I would probably have some crazy dreams tonight.

I entered back into the mirrorless bathroom, gathered up the shower head as it spurted water aimlessly and waited a few more minutes until if finally got lukewarm. It was impossible to gauge how long the tepid water would last, so I quickly started to wash myself with the small bar of hotel soap left on the sink. There was no shampoo, so I used the soap for my short hair as well. I turned the water off and promptly wrapped myself in the small towel. It barely fit around my waist. I did my best to dry myself with what was more of a washcloth, than towel and put on a new pair of shorts and a Minor Threat T-shirt. The room was still warm, but the breeze from the fan was welcoming. I felt dizzy with exhaustion, took the quilted blanket off the bed and threw it in the corner of the room. I shut out some of the light from the open windows, turned off the desk lamp, and climbed on top of the carved bed. Thankfully there was a thin foam pad that acted as a mattress. I huddled the pillows together and closed my eyes, imagining those who slept here before me. I quickly nodded off.

The knocking on the door startled me awake. It was not very loud but continuous, and it did the job. I opened my eyes, looked around, got my bearings, and got out of bed.

"One minute," I said rather loudly.

I opened the door and saw Xiao Mei with the guard from outside. He was carrying a tray of food, nodded in my direction, came in and placed it on the desk. He took off the cover, revealing a steaming plate of something that looked like soup or stew, some green grassy-looking veggies and white rice. Xiao Mei looked uncomfortable and very shy. I tried to make eye contact with her as the guard left us alone the room.

"Hi, Rick," she said, pronouncing it like Wick. "Sorry to disturb you, but we thought you would like some dinner."

She then outstretched her hands and presented me with another Tsingtao.

"Xie xie," I said taking the beer and placing it on the desk. "And where is everyone else?"

"Oh, no one else. We eat already" She stopped and looked nervous.

"What about the old man and Sunny?" I asked.

"Still at factory," she said and looked at me in the eyes for the first time. She still had that timid look on her face. She was very pretty with flawless skin and wide eyes that looked like they had permanent eyeliner accentuating her features.

"Your English is very good," I said, trying to change the subject.

She blushed. "No good," she replied with a nervous smile.

"Hey, why don't you come in and keep me company while I eat?" I asked. "We can at least talk some more."

She seemed to consider this for a moment, but again that timidness returned. Then she walked in, over to the desk and opened the first row of drawers. Inside was a Panasonic VHS player, a small portable RCA TV, cables, and a few Western movies.

"Thank you," I said, examining the contraband and movie titles. I took them out, placed them on the desk and tried one more time to get her to stay.

"Why don't you keep me company while I eat, and then we can watch a movie together?"

She looked at the movies and then back into my eyes as if contemplating this gesture.

"You should eat and get some rest. Maybe we watch movies tomorrow," she said.

I tried to change the subject to keep her with me just a bit longer.

"Xiao Mei, you look like a younger Mei Mei. Are you guys related or something?"

"I know Mei Mei," she said quickly, "but we are not related. You already met my sister Ai and my Ma Ma. That is *my* family"

"And Buddy," I said.

She nodded in silence.

"So, how old are you?" I asked. "Eighteen?"

"I am sixteen." She answered and smiled.

"Wow, you look older," I said with complete ignorance.

"Good night, Rick," she said and left the room, closing the door behind her.

The heavy door shut with an audible 'click' as I stood there for a moment, letting all this weirdness sink in. I needed a cold drink and went right for the Tsingtao. It was not as cold as I wished but downed it anyway, wishing that there was a mini bar in the room. I made my way curiously to the food, examined the contents in the steamy soup, thought better of it, and went straight for the white rice.

I must have passed out soon after.

When the knocking on the door woke me up again, sunlight was burning through the wooden shutters on the window. This time I was slow to awake and had no idea where I was. I tried to shake the cobwebs out of my brain when the knocking started again. I saw the uneaten food, the CD player, and it all came flooding back.

"Hold on," was all I could muster. I got out of the large bed and made my way to the sink. My bones cracked as I did a quick stretch and ran some cold water in my mouth. I was about to swallow it when I came to my senses. No way was I digesting this water. I promptly spit it out and then brushed my teeth waterless. I spit out the toothpaste, put my hands under the sink and ran my wet fingers through my hair. I washed my face and made my way to the door.

I opened it, expecting to see Xiao Mei. Instead, it was Sunny and the driver. They entered quickly and shut the door. Sunny didn't look so "sunny" today. I noticed he was still in the same clothes as yesterday and looked like he'd been up all night. Under closer examination, his red eyes confirmed that he has been crying.

"Good morning, Rick," he said. "Listen, I do not have a lot of time to explain but something bad has happened last night and I need to get you out of here now. You must get your things together so that you can catch the next ferry back to Hong Kong."

"What?" was all I could manage to say.

"Rick, we need to go now!" Sunny said sternly.

The driver was taking whatever I had around the room and throwing it into my suitcase.

"Where's Buddy?" I asked.

"Please get dressed, make sure you have your passport, and I will explain in the car."

I threw back on my Minor Threat T-shirt, my Converse, sprayed some deodorant in my pits, dumped my toiletries into its bag, and zipped up my suitcase. The driver took my bags and left with Sunny. I grabbed my backpack, checked for my passport, and followed suit.

We passed the women who were all gathered around a table, holding on to each other and crying loudly. I tried to catch their attention but only Xia Mei looked up in my direction as tears streamed down her pretty face. I stopped for a moment about to ask what was happening, but quickly felt the strong hands of the guard grabbing at my backpack. I held on to it tightly and took this as a cue to leave swiftly.

I followed him outside to the car, slung my backpack in the backseat and jumped in. The car quickly exited as the guard shut the gates behind us. I looked out the window at the crumbling village and the unpaved roads as we quickly made our way to the Ferry terminal. A few mopeds were following us, and I recognized the fatigues, as the same as the guards from the factory. Sunny was sobbing into the phone as he listened to whomever was on the other side. He hung up, blew his nose into a handkerchief as we continued to drive fast and in silence.

"Where's the old man?" I said breaking the silence.

Sunny turned around to face me. He was swollen red as he appeared to be holding back a sob. He struggled for the right words to say and what he said next shook me to the core.

"Rick, Buddy is in hospital."

"What, are you kidding me?" I said incredulously.

The look he gave me was as serious as a hand grenade.

"He was admitted last night."

"What, what happened, I stammered, "Did he have a heart attack or something?" I asked.

"No, nothing like that," he said glumly. "He got hurt."

"Hurt?" I questioned, "How?"

"I am afraid he was stabbed." He said holding back a sob.

"Stabbed!" I exclaimed, turning furiously to look at him.

"Yes, he was attacked at the factory," he said, and then turned away from me. I heard him quietly weeping to himself.

I was stunned and confused. I thought about the scene at the factory, and it all came crashing down.

What was I doing here?

What kind of place is this?

Now what?

Confusion turned to sadness as I ran through my brief encounter with the old man. I thought of the antiques, the samples I worked on, and my need for this sourcing trip to work out. But that was just a fleeting emotion. I was quickly consoled by familiar feelings of fury and rage. Either way, I rapidly sank comfortably into the darkness of my soul and thought about the framework of my life. Especially the violence that has followed me like an angry shadow. I wanted revenge and I had the anger (and skills) to do some serious damage.

"Please Sunny, take me to him!" I pleaded.

"I cannot do that!" Sunny said too quickly.

"You must!" I exclaimed. "I am sure I can help"-

"Rick, Buddy is dead!" he sobbed suddenly.

"What!" I exclaimed in disbelief.

"Listen, you need to get out of here right away," he continued. "Mei Mei will meet you in Hong Kong and she will get you on the next flight back to the US."

With that Sunny handed me another envelope that seemed filled with papers.

"Please give this to her when you see her," he said sternly as he wiped his nose on the sleeve of his shirt.

"What is it?" I asked with frustration. "Why all these envelopes?"

"Please don't concern yourself." He said with tears gathering back in the corners of his eyes.

I took the envelope and put it reluctantly in my knapsack. The car was gunning it to the Ferry Station, but I did not want to leave so quickly. I had the familiar urge to stay and fight for the old man, as he reminded me of my grandfather in so many ways. I wanted to avenge his death, find the scumbags that did this and pay them back tremendously. I wanted vengeance for Buddy. I needed the violence and longed for the danger. I was on high alert and knew this was going to be a long torturous ride back to the civilization of Hong Kong.

I was confused, at a loss for words and didn't know what to do next. I needed to calm down, reached into my backpack pocket for that joint and lit it up in Buddy's honor.

15

High Hopes, *Long Island, NY—circa 1975*

It was the Jewish High Holidays, and, like our traditional nomad ancestry, this meant a trip was necessary.

Our trips consisted of taking a two-hour car ride to visit our relatives in rural Connecticut. My father was the son of the town's pharmacist, and all of his side of the family still lived there. Incidentally, my Poppa's name was Paul, and my dad spent his adolescence working behind the register of their family drug store. My dad would often wax poetic about "how much he hated the work, the long hours and the old people who were constantly asking for drug advice or to find something amongst the stocked shelves." He did, however, confide in me (later on in life) that there were "perks" to the job as he had access to pocket some valium, quaaludes, cigarettes and of course condoms for any of his friends. Even though he hated the work, he became some kind of a celebrity drug dealer amongst his small group of friends.

I once asked my Poppa Paul before he passed, if he knew dad was stealing drugs from the store. He would smile, wink say, that he was glad that dad "didn't steal the cash instead." I guess he had a point, although I wouldn't put it past my old man to pocket some twenties if the situation presented itself. I remember my Poppa Paul as a jolly man, good hearted with an infectious laugh. He was also a modest man with limited means compared to my Grandpa Butch. But he made up for that with always bringing us presents as kids, filling the trunk of his Plymouth Valiant with candy and toys that he obviously had taken from his drug store. Poppa Paul left this earth at a young age from severe cardiac arrest, leaving his widow, my Granny Jeanette the store and whatever possessions they owned. Granny sold the store and rapidly declined in health, dying of a broken heart and joined her husband soon afterwards. I remember my Granny to be full of love, always cooking for us and her large family. I have fond memories of both my Connecticut grandparents and never understood my dad's reluctance to visit with them and the rest of the Price clan.

Still, even with the "convenient" job, Connecticut was not Dad's favorite place and he left as soon as he could to continue partying at the University of South Florida, where he apparently majored in suntanning and drinking. My Mom told me, "That when she met my dad on campus, he was jumping off the roof of his car and projectile vomiting at the same time." They apparently dated for another year, until my dad graduated with a bachelors in the "Art of Partying." He was also the Jewish fraternity Social Chairman and planned all their bashes and mixers. It must have made an impression on my mom as she said "yes" to marrying him and then they moved to NY to settle down so that my dad could join my other grandfather Butch's business.

My parents didn't try to hide their disdain for these sojourns back to Connecticut and tried to make the drive as fun as they could. That meant killing three hours of driving by smoking that strawberry weed, listening to rock music, and ignoring us children. We had a black Cadillac Seville with shiny spoked hubcaps, grey tufted leather seats and a burlwood dashboard. This was the seventies and although having seat belts was the law, they were seldom used. The same went for any other form of safety like infant car seats or rear seat belts. It's amazing that we made it out of those "reckless" years alive!

I remember my younger brother and I making the most of this drive by building a fort in the back seat. We did this by carefully placing our blankets across the top of the back seat, hiding underneath from the reality of the long drive. But there was no escaping my parents, as they included us in showing off their new ceramic smoking device. My father stopped off at *Te-Amo* on the corner of Sunrise Highway to buy this special tool for this holiday drive. He had showed us all how perfectly it held his strawberry joints in place, explaining that when the joint got smaller, this smoking tool would make sure he would not burn his hands. My brother and I were kind of pot apprentices by now, learning the ins and outs of this weed culture. It is fair to say that in my family, weed was a bonding experience.

The drive always turned special when Dad put on Pink Floyd. He rifled through a pile of eight tracks until he found *The Dark Side of the Moon*. Once the music began, he cranked it, lit up the strawberry joint and instructed my mother how to "hit it." It was a small ceramic orb, that looked like a smooth rock with a hole on each side. Dad put the perfectly rolled joint in one side and pushed it through to the other side, keeping the orb in the middle. He held the ceramic holder between his fingers, lit the exposed end and inhaled through the other side. He exhaled strongly filling the car with smoke and rolled down the windows. He passed the joint holder to my mom, and she copied his actions. They seemed content, coughing out smoke and concentrating on what they were doing, as they passed the smoking tool back and forth. It was no wonder my dad often took his eyes off the road for what appeared to be a long period of time. But it was nice to hear them laughing, coughing, and singing. It was a familiar and comfortable scene to my brother and me. Hence, we retreated under the safety of our blankets, completely unaware as we swerved across the opposite highway lane and clipped another car at sixty miles per hour.

The sound of the impact was sickening. This was multiplied by screeching brakes as Dad tried to gain control of the car. And as he did this, the vehicle behind hit us with tremendous force sending my small body airborne, flying into the front seat. I heard my brother hit the back of one of the front seats and bounce off. My mother started screaming at the top of her lungs. My brother and I both started crying in horror as the car finally came to an abrupt stop.

For what seemed like a long time, my parents didn't say anything. When I opened my eyes, I remember seeing them hugging, checking each other out, and then turning around to attend to my screaming brother. My mom gently picked him up from the back seat, cradled him, and using her shirt began wiping blood off the small gash over his eye. I lied motionless on the floor in the front. I was in shock and afraid to move. My father looked down and asked me, "if I was okay." I nodded my head yes, as he reached down to pick me up, but then quickly let me drop back on the floor.

"Jesus Christ!" he exclaimed. "You smell that?"

My mother turned around to take a whiff and scrunched her nose in disgust.

"The boy shit in his pants!" Dad exclaimed.

"Oh, God," she said, and shook her head in disbelief as if this was the biggest tragedy of the day.

That is when people started to make their way over to the accident to make sure we were all okay. I sat up slowly, still woozy, with a cut like my brothers over my right eye. I was now conscious of the shit squishing in my pants and did not want to be bothered anymore. I shut my eyes, lied back down, and pretended to be dead.

My father had carefully helped my mom and bother out of the car and to safety on the side of the road. He came back, opened the door for me, reaching in to grab the ceramic pipe, which he quickly pocketed. He didn't pay me much attention as I slowly sat up again and looked out of the fractured windshield. All those shards of uneven glass seemed to be speaking to me.

"Hi, kid" said a strange woman (not the glass). This rocked me back to reality. "My name is Jane, and I am a nurse; do you mind if I take a look at your eye?"

"Okay," I said looking now at her. She was older than my mom, had short hair but a bright smile that made me feel calm.

"What's your name?" she asked as she gave my eye a closer examination.

"Rick," I said.

"Well, Rick, you're a lucky boy. That cut looks superficial."

"Lucky?" I asked meekly.

"Yes, you are going to be okay," she said reassuring.

She then opened her purse took out a clean bandage placed it carefully over my eye. She had a very calm voice, a gentle touch, and asked me, "to hold the bandage there until the ambulance came."

I sat in the driver's seat with shit in my drawers, clutching the bandage tightly and watched as Jane walked over to attend to the rest of my family. I glanced at the back of the car and saw that the trunk had smashed in reminding me of an accordion. There was also a similar dent to the front of the car as smoke and fluid seemed to be mixing in unison under the crumpled hood, making hissing noise.

Jane was a tall, thin woman, who reminded me of someone on the TV news. When she was done bandaging my brother's head, she quickly went over to help the people in the car my father had hit first. When she was through, I saw her walk to the car that hit us from behind. She got in it, and then walked around it, surveying the damage. It appeared to be her car and I remember feeling thankful she was not hurt in the accident.

Within a short period of time, the ambulances, fire department, police, and tow trucks came. They took statements from the adults, looked us all over again, and huddled my family in the back of the ambulance. My mom still had my bother crying in her arms. My dad simply stared out the window as I lied on the gurney, sickened by the smell of my own mess. Jane peeked in before the doors closed and told us, "She would meet us at the hospital."

The hospital thankfully was a short ride away. Once there, my dad told me he was going to find a pay phone and call my uncle to come get us. The doctor came over and gave us another checkup. He was very thorough with my brother and me, removing Janes bandages, cleaned the wounds and then taped large Band-Aids over the cut on our heads. Then I saw Jane enter the room. She said a few things to the other nurses. They shook their head in understanding, and then she called my name.

"Rick, do you mind coming with me to another room?" Jane asked.

I looked at my mom, who nodded her head in agreement. I took Jane's outstretched hand and left my family. Jane led me to a different room where another nurse was dropping off some cleaning wipes and a pair of hospital pajamas. Jane helped me out of my soiled clothes and never left eye contact with me as she cleaned me off and fit me into the pajamas. When finished, she smiled warmly and winked at me. She never made mention of my accident and didn't seem bothered by the task at hand.

When done, she brought me back to my family, spoke to the doctor, and then winked at me again.

The doctor checked out my parents quickly, filled out some papers and declared that we were all okay to leave once my uncle arrived. Jane gave my brother a big smile and his boo-boo a little kiss. Even though there were tears in his eyes, he managed a laugh at her warm affection. Then she came over to me, picked me up, and gave me a big hug.

"Happy New Year," was all I could think to say. She looked confused by this but smiled, said goodbye to my folks, and left. I believe that was the first time I realized that not everyone was Jewish. More importantly, I learned that you didn't need to be a Jew to be a kind, good person.

At that night's Rosh Hashanah dinner, Dad and Mom got very drunk with all my uncles and aunts. I remember with shame and embarrassment how funny they all thought the accident was. There was no remorse about getting stoned and almost killing us. In fact, they were all hysterical that I had shit my pants. It became a running joke among my family. My aunts, uncles, cousins, and distant relatives laughed while shaming me by holding their noses in mock disgust. I felt like that crash had somehow become my fault and nobody made mention that my father was a drug addict who almost killed his family.

The joke was on me and often retold in jest for the next few years. It became the real "High Holiday" story. Forget about the blowing the Shofar or eating Challah with white horseradish that burned your nose and made your eyes tear. It was the crap in my pants story that everyone loved and that became another chapter of my shitty existence. I never looked forward to Jewish New Year's again, and that accident changed me as a person and shaped my view of traveling forever.

16

Betray, *Hong Kong—circa 1997*

The slow ride back to Hong Kong felt especially long, uncomfortable and downright depressing.

I sat most of that ferry ride in a *stoned* trance-like silence, without moving much, listening to punk rock CDs to keep my sanity. It was five hours of sweaty misery as I thought about the Old Man, Sunny, the antiques, his family and the shock of what I just witnessed. Let alone how this will affect the questionable future of my family business. I was torn is so many directions and didn't have a sound solution for how to deal with all of this. For the first time, I actually felt that this was something bigger than myself and that thought made me more uncomfortable than my usual forlorn disposition.

Alas, the boat finally made its approach into the China Ferry terminal in Tsim Sha Tsui (TST), Hong Kong. I waited to be the last off the boat as I was in no rush to see Mei Mei and what could possibly come next for me. I grabbed my bags, exited the boat and took the rickety ramp into the entrance hall. It was unusually quiet inside as if every passenger was in mourning. I cleared customs quickly and made my way through the double doors to where Mei Mei was already positioned to greet me. She approached me immediately, dressed to the nines, while her sun glassed driver took my bags.

"Hi Rick," she said with a hint of sadness.

She surprised me with a big hug, which I reciprocated more as reflex then concern. She felt warm, smelled good and I held her for a few uncomfortable minutes before letting her go.

"How was your trip back." She continued while looking directly into my eyes. I held her gaze and felt like she was looking into my soul.

"Thankfully quiet," was all I could muster, then looked away from her stare.

"I know you must have a lot of questions, so let's get some lunch and I will try to provide you with some answers."

"Yeah, but I think I need to contact my dad and Grandpa first."

"They have been notified," she said surprisingly fast.

"You called them already?" I asked

"Come, lets grab some food before your flight back."

"Lead the way," I said still feeling defeated and confused.

I followed Mei Mei and her sun glassed driver outside the Ferry Terminal to the parking lot where her black Mercedes S500 was waiting. The driver opened the door for her and then placed my bags in the trunk. I let myself in the back as the driver got in, turned on the car and blasted much needed AC. We took a right out of the parking lot and slowly fought our way through lunch time traffic on Canton Road. The driver took a left on Peking Road and stopped on the corner of Ashley Road in front of *Hing Fat* restaurant. The restaurant looked like every other restaurant on this busy road with a window full of hanging roasted meats and aquarium tanks of seafood.

The driver opened Mei Mei's door to let her out and then came over to do the same for me. Mei Mei told me to grab my backpack as I followed her inside the crowded restaurant. The driver stayed outside with the car and my luggage. Once inside Mei Mei flagged down the apparent owner who appeared to be waiting for us. He waved in our direction, led us through the que of patrons, to the back of the restaurant and opened a door into a small private room.

The room had a round table that could fit six people comfortably, in the center was a carved wooden lazy Susan, that was already full of tea pots, Char Sui (BBQ pork), Siu Yuk (Roasted pork), assorted dim sum (Sui Mai), Bai fan (white rice) and Bok choy (green cabbage). Thankfully, there was a small wall AC, as well as, a standing fan that helped with the brutal heat coming from the belly of the restaurant. A waitress followed us in and put both of them on full blast.

The food looked good, as my stomach growled in anticipation. It was a long boat ride without much to eat but a few granola bars. I loaded up some BBQ pork on top of a small bowl of white rice. I was a vegetarian in China, but this was Hong Kong and that was good enough for me. Mei Mei poured some tea for me and then herself. I gave her the obligatory sign of respect by tapping my pointer finger and middle finger twice on the table in quick succession.

As the story goes, sometime back in Qing Dynasty (1644), the emperor hid his identity in order to eat with the common folk. The servants had to help with the ruse and instead of bowing, which was customary, they tapped both fingers simultaneously on the table to represent gratitude. One finger representing the bowed head and the other fingers representing the outstretched arms. This gesture is still common today when someone fills up your cup with tea, as a high level of respect and a way of saying, "thank you!"

I shoveled in two mouthfuls of glazed pork goodness before Mei Mei spoke.

"Rick, can I have that envelope that Sunny gave you please."

I put my chopsticks down on their porcelain holder as I reached into my green Jansport backpack to take out the stuffed envelope. Mei Mei took it from me, turned the lazy Susan so that the vegetables were not now in front of me. I reloaded my rice bowl again as she opened the envelope to examine the papers inside. I noticed that she did not have any food on her plate.

"Not hungry?" I said with a mouth full of rice.

"No, not particularly," she added solemnly.

"So, what's with all these secret messages?" I asked shoveling some greens inside the bowl. "You want to tell me what the fuck is going on?"

Mei Mei got up opened the door, screamed something to the waitress and then shut the door again. She poured me some more tea. I gave her the two taps.

"Rick, what I am about to tell you cannot be repeated to anyone else."
I stopped eating for a moment and gave her my earnest stare.

"First, I am really sorry about Buddy, he was a good man, but he was tragically flawed." She said with a hint of sadness.

"Enough to be killed?" I added hastily.

"That was not supposed to happen!" she said quickly, hitting the table with obvious anger. The porcelain teacups rattled under her strike. She turned her attention to the papers that I gave her.

"Rick, in this envelope are the shipping manifests of four containers that have set sail for, Rome, Amsterdam, Abu Dhabi and New York."

"What's that got to do with me or his death?" I asked impatiently.

"Buddy was peddling antique furniture on the black market. Some pieces were the real deal, fetching a lot of money, and others, well they are duplicates being sold as the authenticate."

"And how do you know this?" I asked and took a sip of hot tea.

"Rick, I work with other people who are very concerned about this situation." She said and got my attention.

"What kind of people would be involved in this mess?" I asked. "And who really cares?" I said with sarcasm.

"The Chinese government cares intensively," she added quietly as she physically got closer to me. "These antiques, for all intents and purposes have been stolen and the Chinese Communist Party (CCP) believe they have sovereign right of ownership over all of them."

I let this sink in for a moment thinking of the number of antiques he seemed to have amassed.

"So, let me guess, they want them back," I said indifferently. "Is this why Buddy had to die?"

"I'm afraid it's a little more complicated than just that," she continued, "There are reasons why so many people in that factory were angry at the old man and Sunny. Many of the workers knew what they were doing and either wanted their fair share of the cost or they just plain wanted their ancestors' "possessions" returned."

"So, why am I and my family now involved with this?" I asked with confusion and anger.

"Rick, we also believe Buddy was involved in money laundering."

"What the fuck!" I exclaimed and stopped eating.

"We have people on the inside that claim he was also hiding cash in the inner framework of these antiques." She continued. "Once those pieces cleared customs, well the declared price of the goods and the undeclared cash got the attention of many of us. We just can't look the other way."

"Now I am really confused and who is this *we* shit?"

"The *we* are a larger network of professionals that need to ensure U.S. and China relations are always paramount." She continued in a hushed voice. "Your grandfather is a bit of a lynchpin in this arrangement, as he always made sure that his interests benefited the country that served him so well."

"Are you saying my grandpa has something to do with this?" I exclaimed and stood ready to defend his honor.

"Please sit, calm down and eat." She said coolly.

"Not sure I'm hungry anymore," I added. "Maybe best to just take me to the airport now."

"Your grandfather always talked so highly of you, and your determination to get the job done at all costs." She replied getting my attention.

I let this sink in and then sat back down with a head full of questions.

"How do you know of my grandfather?" I asked.

"You can say that we work with each other, she continued, "Your grandfather has helped a lot of people. He is immensely regarded and in return, many owe him favors."

I let this thought stand for a minute as I quickly remembered all that he has done for me and my family by proxy.

"I assume Buddy owed him favors as well?" I asked.

"Butch was critical for Buddy's business to survive as he always managed to help him expedite and clear those containers." She continued. "They started bringing in contraband together during the war and well that was just the beginning of one of the many businesses your grandfather has involved our organization with."

"So, what are you, some sort of spy?" I asked feeling a bit reticent.

"You can look at it like that or you can say I am a problem solver for interested governments" she said in a hushed voice.

"So, my grandfather is involved and now I am?" I asked not wanting to be in this secret society. "Why me, what's my role in all of this?" I asked.

"Rick, your grandfather has been looking after you for your entire life. You are the product of his love, guidance and support. We needed someone to trust on the inside to get close to Buddy's business to confirm all this was fact."

"You used me to get close to a criminal?" I asked incredulously.

"It's not necessarily all that," she said, "Buddy was supposed to be a solid vendor for your family's furniture company. Your grandfather paid for that furniture company to help all of you, and us. None of this was supposed to happen now and certainly without your prior awareness."

"The old man was killed!" I exclaimed feeling used.

"Yes, that's most unfortunate, but it's not the end for you?" she said and took a sip of tea.

"What if I say it is?" I added in a sudden burst of rage. "Maybe I don't want any of this spying *bullshit*! I have a family of my own but I'm sure you know that already!" I exclaimed knowing I was being gaslighted.

"Rick, from what I read in your dossier, you are very prepared for this *shit*," she spoke. Then opened her Gucci bag and produced a folder with my name on it and the words "Confidential" stamped in red across the top. She put in on the lazy Susan and then spun it for my review.

I apprehensively took the folder from the wooden circle and opened it with disbelief. I couldn't believe my eyes as my entire life seemed to be within those A4 papers. I quickly scanned the documents reading about *my childbirth, my school reports, England, Boaz, my medical reports, Heather, my parents, my kids and Dr. Hutz's assessment of my mental proclivity to depression and my propension for violence.* I began to feel sick as old photos in various stages of my life leaped from the pages and spilled on the table. I admit for the first time in my life that I did not know what to do. Anger was the only solution that I immediately went to for solace. Mei Mei must have sensed this as she reached across and grabbed my hand inside of hers. I tried to pull away, but she held tightly, and I acquiesced.

"Rick, I know all of this is a shock and a lot to unload on you now. But believe me, we have been waiting for the right time to divulge certain information and privileges to you," she said.

I dropped the dossier on the table feeling completely embarrassed and taken advantage of. I spun its' contents in Mei Mei's direction.

"I'm not your man!" I exclaimed not wanting to be here anymore and pulled my hand away from hers. She moved even closer directly in my personal space.

"Rick, you have been training your whole life to be *that man*!" she continued, as I sat in silence. "There is also a checking account opened for you here with *Hang Seng Bank*."

She opened the dossier to the very last page and handed me a bank slip that had my name on it with too many zeros in the balance.

"Your grandfather opened up an LLC in your name, he will give you further instruction upon your return. This account will be yours to do with what you want for yourself and your family."

Then she opened her purse and gave me a green bank card. It also had my name on it.

"And what do I do next, I mean, what the fuck do I tell my dad and the family about this trip?" I asked in disbelief about all of this.

She showed me the manifests in her hands again.

"These shipping documents are crucial for us as we will use *our influence* to intercept the deliveries and return them to their rightful owners," she continued. "All you need to do now, is tell your dad that Buddy had a container load of samples he is putting together for you. It is important that you tell him and your grandfather that you are skeptical about the quality and the pricing. You need to downplay this trip and the container of samples."

"And what about the container?" I asked. "Dad will certainly question this."

"That container will never make it to you." She replied

"So, you want me to lie about the container and what about the old man?" I asked.

"In a few days, your grandfather will let you and your dad know that Buddy had a heart attack and died."

"Well, that's convenient" I added.

"You will need to reach into your inner dramatic self and react shocked," she continued. "Then you must corroborate this by reflecting that Buddy did not look well when you met, explaining that he smoked heavily, was out of shape and had deep phlegmy cough."

"Right, Buddy was sick," I continued in disbelief.

"Your grandfather will also vouch for his health." she confessed.

"And what happens now?" I added and filled her glass of tea.

"When we finish our meal, I'll drop you off at the airport," she continued. "You'll get back home for some rest, spend time with your family and then meet with your grandfather as he is anxious to speak with you." she answered with a wink and that winning smile.

"I can't help to feel used and wish you would have given me more of a *heads up* before I visited with Buddy!" I said still angry.

"How about I tell you what happens next?" she added. "No more secrets."

"Ok, let's try that for a start." I added.

Mei Mei turned the lazy Susan grabbing back my dossier, placed it into her leather bag and pulled out a picture of a thin Chinese man, around my height, sitting with a much larger man in the front gates of a very large factory. In the picture both men are smiling and have lit cigarettes in their hands. Mei Mei pointed to the slight man around my size.

"I will introduce you to this *operative* we have working in South China. He is also in the furniture industry, but not in antiques, more your style of *home fashion*. His name is Richard, goes by *Shu Shu* (Uncle) to his friends and runs one of the largest manufacturing plants in Guangdong Province. Richard is originally from Hong Kong, made his fortune in China and works with his enforcer, *Dr. Dave*." With that she pointed at the much larger man with huge forearms.

I took a moment looking over the photo.

"Together they make a formidable pair," she added. "You will find Shu Shu to be an absolute ally in creating a fortuitous business together. I have known him for some time and believe you two will hit it off smashingly." She said in that English accent.

"What about this Dr. Dave character?" I asked pointing at the picture of the man.

"Dr. Dave is not to be trusted. He is only there to look after Shu Shu's empire and is known to have a bad temper with violence running through his veins." She said.

"I sympathize with that" I added sarcastically. "So, what's the catch here?"

Me Mei leaned in closer again and spoke, "We believe Richard may be making weapons for the People's Republic of China (PRC)."

"No shit!" I added, "You want me to befriend a potential weapons dealer?" I asked with an incredulous smile.

"He may be more than a dealer and as a manufacturer, we are not sure just where his loyalty lies." She added "You will find Richard, *your Shu Shu*, to be an opportunist and I do believe his first priority is still his furniture business."

"That's comforting" I added again.

"Shu Shu has a *spirited* nature and I believe you will enjoy each other's company," she continued, "I am positive he will pull you into his inner circle."

"And what do I need to do?" I asked.

"You just need to keep him close and your eyes open for anything that may be considered *nefarious*."

"Nefarious" I asked almost choking on my tea.

"Shu Shu is highly connected, with a lot of people on the payroll and not just those in his factory. We will need you to take some pictures and report in from time to time.

"Report in?" I asked.

"Yes, you have my number. She continued, "I will arrange all with your grandfather."

"So now I am what—some sort of spy?"

"As I said, you have been training for this your whole life."

"And my next mission is to meet with this Shu Shu weapons guy?" I asked sarcastically.

"Please think of this as an opportunity to finally find a vendor that can help your family business achieve all of its financial goals." She added quickly. "You are doing the right thing for your family and your country."

With that she picked up the photos, put them away, opened the door and called for the check. She paid the bill in cash, as we picked up our belongings, made our way to the car outside and headed for the airport.

17

Human Fly, *China—circa 1998*

China never seemed ready for the experience of mass flying.

It came quickly and was embraced by the common people as just another convenient form of mass transportation. It never had the glory days of flight that we experienced in the states. In fact, there was nothing celebrated or spectacular about any domestic flight within China. On the contrary, it was feared and avoided by all of us Gweilos. But sometimes, we unfortunately had no choice as it was a necessary part of the job.

Chinese airports were the exact opposite of what I was used to in the U.S. They were filthy, unorganized, and incredibly unsafe on every level. Instead of efficiency, there were endless lines of confusion, queued around all corners of the airport. Common decency was pushed aside as the Chinese people fought each other for more advantageous spots in long lines. "Normal" suitcases like what we had in the U.S. were not used back then in China. Instead, they were replaced by cheap plastic bags, held together with packing tape, or often just a tattered brown carton that was being checked underneath the plane.

There weren't clear directions (at least not in English) as to what counter was for what plane or airline. The Chinese had what seemed like unlimited amounts of domestic airlines, all with related names, going to the same or similar destinations. It was total chaos to figure out which were the right ones. Forget about trying to find a customer service agent, as those were few and far between. And, of course, if found, they had the longest lines, all with non-stop shouting in Chinese.

It was a major clusterfuck just to check in. You had to have nerves of steel or be completely *out of your mind* to handle the onslaught of what was seen as "normal" airport travel. To make matters worse, flights were often delayed for hours or just cancelled. There were never explanations or apologies, and certainly there was no one available to re-book you on another flight. This was Mainland China and communism meant shit happened and no one ever asked why. It was, "what it was" and you just had to bend over and take it!

In those early days, if we needed to go far, we chose long arduous car rides instead of flying. Even taking dirty buses filled with scurrying cockroaches was better than dealing with the airport. But sometimes it was unavoidable, and when Northern China began to show some promise, I was quick to make sure I would be the first one in. Eventually, the destinations were too far for automobiles and there was no choice but to travel through the dreaded mainland airports.

To make matters worse, the lack of security or surveillance created a haven for confusion and uncertainty. While the rest of the world had common sense protocols of what was (and was not) permitted on airplanes, China was, once again, way behind. This thought crippled me with fear and apprehension. It seemed that anything outside of carrying an obvious weapon was permitted through security. There were no restrictions of liquids, lighters, sharp objects, etc. The process was actually quite simple and terrifying. It was every man and woman for themselves, and it went like this:

Fight your way to the security counter (literally).

Show your ID and ticket to the man in the outlandish polyester costume.

If you were not from China, your passport needed to be checked by several *clowns*, who never knew exactly what they were looking at, as if they had never seen a U.S. passport before.

After several minutes of confusion, your ticket was stamped with red ink (that came off on your hands and clothes), and your ticket and passport were handed back to you.

Then you had to put your carry-on luggage on an incredibly short table and push it through the "luggage security detector."

Next, step through the body scanner—it goes off automatically (no matter what).

Step on a block while someone pats you down with an incredibly large and outdated handheld metal detector that also always goes off (no matter what).

Of course, you have on a belt and in your pockets are metal coins, pens, lighters, whatever... as you were never instructed to remove these items. No problem, just toss them on the floor with everyone else's contraband, and there were no garbage pails.

Get another quick pat down.

Grab your carry-on and get the fuck out of there.

Then you frantically search for your gate and queue up behind whatever resembles some sort of ridiculous line. Since there was no boarding by class or row, again it was survival of the fittest. Announcements were made in Chinese through tiny, inaudible speakers or bullhorns, squelching muffled directions that sounded like a noisy feedback loop.

If you were at all like me, by this point, you were agitated beyond belief and would be quick to take someone down. I must admit that all those years *moshing in the pits* helped my airport boarding skills. I let my elbows fly out as I pushed through the crowds. I aimed my luggage at knees and other weak points, anything to get me in the front. Usually, it was the elderly that were the most combative as they fought their way to enter the plane. I took absolutely no mercy on them as well and felt no shame to hurt those around me as I boarded.

Once on the jetway, the frenetic pushing continued as people fought their way onto the plane. This also meant queuing up several more times to have your ticket validated, torn, and stamped again with the same red ink that you just wiped off your hands earlier.

Exhausted yet?

Wait there's still more—

Once aboard, the pandemonium continued as people struggled to find their seats. You see, most of the Chinese were illiterate and reading the plane seating chart (although obvious to those from the U.S.) was a foreign language to them. It still dumbfounds me how confused the Chinese were (and still are) about understanding their row number and seat letter. As a result, many just ignored this and sat wherever they wanted... first come first serve. *Ha! Take that Southwest Airlines, guess your seating directions weren't so groundbreaking after all!*

There was one flight in particular that will always remain locked in my psyche.

It was raining particularly hard that afternoon and I had no choice but to fly to Shanghai to attend a trade show. As mentioned, flying in China had become a necessary evil and, on that day, the rain just made matters worse. I thought about the pilots and their training (or lack thereof). It was common knowledge back then that their pilots were all ex-military fliers and lacked the sophistication of commercial aviation. Because of this, most flights took off on time (or early) but without warning or having concern for the several hundred people on board. Flights went up quickly and then came down to a sudden, crippling stop when they reached the destination. It was not uncommon to hear the sudden shrieks of those on board as we hit the ground hard, and the luggage racks opened from the impact.

Back to this particular flight. When everyone finally boarded, I noticed that this plane, like so many others, was extremely beat up and past its time. There were still ashtrays in the seat arms, and I couldn't help thinking about the number of miles on this bird. Even worse was the appearance of condensation dripping from the ceiling. Was it possible that the rain was leaking inside the plane? Was there a hole in the fuselage? Were there safety checks being ignored? Why would I trust this airplane and its pilots to safely reach our destination?

I mean, why would the Chinese care if a few planes went down? There was already no regard for human life in China and way too many people. Who cared if a few hundred Chinese were suddenly gone? Who would sue the communist government? Who would miss them/us? All this brooding became common sense, as I was convinced, we were all going to die!

The Chinese passengers settled into their seats, oblivious that some were taped off with plastic covering as the water continued to drip. To make matters worse, the flight attendants handed out Chinese newspapers to everyone for the ride. Listen, I need to make this very clear: Chinese newspapers were extremely popular on airplane flights. They were a necessary evil, dirty, badly printed, and the ink came off everywhere. They had a hazardous smell to them, and I was sure the ink itself was poison. Now wet, they had become even more toxic!

You may be thinking, Rick, why are there newspapers handed out if the Chinese can't read? Well, that might be a gross exaggeration, as "Putonghua" (common Mandarin) is mainly pictographs so that the common people can understand. However, on airplanes (and other mass transit), newspapers also doubled as crumpled, makeshift pillows for comfort. Yes, the plane was now filled with human stench and the incessant rolling of toxic newspapers into balls as foundations for their heads (and faces) to lie on. It was too much for me to take.

Again, it gets worse as the common Chinese, in what have must have been a cultural custom to get comfortable, took off their ratty shoes and sandals. This meant an even more noxious odor was now permeating through the cabin. Lucky me! That is why I always traveled with a light scarf, which I constantly sprayed with cologne. I kept this scarf locked in a *Ziplock* bag, specifically for these glorious occasions. I wrapped it around my mouth and nose like a burka. I always practiced this ritual, when I was in mass public transit situations such as this.

So now I was sitting in my seat in absolute horror, thinking that the plane was definitely going down. I was wrapped like a Muslim, staring at the dripping water, and noticing the flight attendants as they helped everyone into their seats. They were teaching passengers how to use their seat belts. Apparently, understanding the function of a seat belt was also challenging...

Finally, everyone seemed to have been settled in, so I slipped on my headphones and cranked up some good old-fashioned New York hardcore to settle my nerves. That is when I noticed the man next to me. He had a small child on his lap. The child was squirming and began to cry loudly. The plane started to taxi without warning. The man unbuckled his seat belt and stood up with the child in his arms. The stewardess (yes, I can still use this) promptly came over to put the man back in his seat. There was a loud commotion, but now the plane was in perpetual motion. The stewardess was very stern with the man whose child began screaming, and the man ultimately sat back down.

That is when the unthinkable happened. I watched as the man as he reached in the seatback in front of him and pulled out a vomit bag. *Oh no*, I thought.

No fucking way!

But no, he did not vomit.

Instead, he instructed the crying boy to stand up. He then proceeded to pull the boy's pants down and placed the now opened vomit bag under the boy's small penis. He said something that stopped the boy from screaming. The plane began to ascend just as the boy began to urinate into the vomit bag. The old man did his best to fight gravity and capture the urine as it splashed over his clothes and seat. Thankfully, the boy was easy to manipulate, and the man gained control over the stream as it filled the bag. When the mission was complete, the man folded the urine/vomit bag closed and placed it back into the seatback. He then dressed the boy and they both lied back into a ball of newspaper.

Due to the weather, we hit a lot of turbulence on the way up. The plane rattled and bounced as the water dripped sideways from the ceiling. My heart felt like it was literally in my throat. I began to pray as we hit more bumps. I noticed out of my peripheral vision the urine beginning to leak out of the bag onto the floor. The cabin smell was compromised again by the onslaught of olfactory offensives. I began to think about my death and questioned (once again) what I was doing here?

When the plane seemed to level off, I stared intently at the seat belt sign, waiting for it to turn green. It did not, but I was determined to get out of my seat, anyway. I stood up, opened the overhead compartment, and removed my notebook and pen from my backpack. The flight attendant made a motion for me to sit down, but I ignored her and made a beeline for the bathroom in the back of the plane. I passed the plastic seats, the water, the pee, the rolled-up newspapers, the feet, and opened the small lavatory door.

Inside, the small bathroom was dirty and smelled like feces. The ashtrays were still intact from days long gone by. There was no soap near the sink, but that was okay since I was not there to wash up. Instead, I put the down the seat and checked for turd remnants. There were none, just permanent dirt from years of use and abuse. I sat down on the small throne. My pants were on as I did not need to use the facilities in that way. Instead, I thought of my family and began to write them a letter. It was my goodbye letter. I let the emotions flood over me as I professed my love for each of them—line by line, page by page.

Surprising, I welled up with tears that have refused to fall for almost a quarter century. I was a bit embarrassed by this moment of weakness as I stayed in the bathroom for a very long time. I tried to write the note despite the constant turbulence. My handwriting was terrible to begin with but now it was illegible. I knew this letter was useless as there was no way anyone would be able to read it. But I was determined to finish and gathered myself as the plane continued its roller coaster ride. I noticed the ashtray again and wish I had something to smoke!

I was convinced that I would die on this flight; however, I was somewhat comforted that if I went out now, at least it would be on the crapper. Shit followed me my whole life and I imagined to myself that when they found me, there would be crap in my pants once again. This was my fate. I closed my eyes, waiting for the plane to crash and burn.

18

Bloodstains, *Dongguan City, China—circa 2003*

The loud knock at the door snapped me back into reality.

I jumped up, looked through the peephole, and was relieved to see Shu Shu with Dr. Dave standing there. I opened the door and Dr. Dave rushed in. He brushed past me and went straight for the bed. Shu Shu entered carefully, not making eye contact with me but staring directly at the lifeless girl on the bed. Dr. Dave threw back the sheet, took out a penlight from his shirt pocket, and gave her a quick examination.

It was fair to say at this point that Dr. Dave was not a real doctor, at least not in any Western way. His medical skills were learned by treating battle injuries for the Chinese Communist Army. I was told that he spent years working as a "specialist" in Inner Mongolia, interrogating prisoners, and this experience had given him a cold, ruthless demeanor. Not to mention his resemblance to a "Chinese Popeye," with bulging forearms and unusually large hands. Dr. Dave was not a tall man but made up for this with brute force and sheer intimidation.

Dr. Dave flipped the girl over, shined his light on her, and examined her small private parts very carefully. He then took out his phone and shot a few pictures, getting closeups of her face and her genitals. I'm not sure why he was doing that, but I too was consumed with looking at her naked body, ashamed, I tried not to stare. Then he looked over her blood-stained forehead, felt her nose between his thick fingers and then checked the inside of her mouth like a dentist would. He took several more pictures of the corpse and as with other Asians, it was easy to notice the *red anger* on his face. He talked quickly with Shu Shu and walked over to me in a fury. I am not usually scared of confrontation, but Dr. Dave always made me feel very uneasy. I knew he could read my fear as he stared at me with absolute disgust.

He said something loudly to Shu Shu but kept his eyes on me.

Shu Shu sighed in response and looked directly at me. I saw the sadness in his eyes.

"Rick, you really fucked up this time," he said shaking his head.

"It not my fault," I added.

"Mei Mei even had to give me a call," he said ignoring my innocence. "I need you to carefully walk me through this again."

I did my best abbreviated version to recount of all the events including the toothpaste. I looked at both of them for some sort of support and understanding. I again proclaimed my blamelessness and theory of some sort of poisoning resulting in the sudden death of this young girl. I couldn't explain her demise to anything else except the fact that she had some sort of deadly seizure. Shu Shu remained steadfast in his disbelief. I guess he's seen enough of my demons to know I am often *out of control.*

"Rick, we have been through a lot together and I know you very well. This is just too hard for me to believe!" he exclaimed and then nodded to Dr. Dave.

Before I had a chance to react, Dr. Dave quickly outstretched his hands, cupping them and then violently boxed both my ears at the same time. The pain was intense as my ears rang in revolt. I became dizzy and disorientated and before I could catch my breath, Dr. Dave hit my ears again with even more intensity. My knees buckled as I hit the floor.

I could not hear and struggled as I tried to inhale.

Instinctively, I managed to curl myself into a defensive ball on the floor. I managed to take a few gulps of stale air and looked up at Shu Shu but saw no kindness in his eyes. I couldn't find the words either and in a pathetic gesture of friendship, I grabbed for the jade Buddha charm around my neck. I held it out to him, hoping this would remind him of our alliance. After all, it was a gift from Shu Shu after the night I saved his life in the Philippines.

Shu Shu saw my peace offering, walked over and ripped it off my neck. He put the necklace with the jade charm in his pocket and then flipped what appeared to be a SIM card in my direction.

"This is from Mei Mei." He said, "She instructed me to give it you!"

I caught the sim card and cradled it to my chest as Dr. Dave walked over and forcefully placed his foot on my neck. I let go of the SIM card as I reached out to try and stop his overpowering pressure on my neck. I struggled to breathe, and frantically punched wildly at his leg as I began to lose consciousness. Dr. Dave reacted to my fury by increasing his pressure as I lost my breath and after a short time, started to float into darkness. My last conscious thought was whether Shu Shu would take mercy on me, especially since we had done so much business together. I could only have hoped that Shu Shu would remember how I saved his ass in Cebu and in return, would save mine.

19

Sailin' On, *Cebu, Philippines—circa 2000*

Shu Shu and I had a master plan to steal manufacturing techniques and precious raw materials out of Cebu.

We would use my U.S. company to buy the containers of Filipino products, which we would ship to my freight forwarder in China. Once in China, the consolidator, with the help of Shu Shu's connections would send the goods directly to his factory. It was there that we would attempt to reproduce these Filipino items at a fraction of the price.

The Filipino's besides speaking English were masters at their craft. They had perfected the use of natural materials, wood carvings and anything that required skilled hand labor. They did this with precision and with an amazing eye for decoration. The plan included hiring the Filipino technicians to work in China and teach the Chinese how to perfect these Filipino techniques. Therefore, it would be possible to mass-produce the rich Filipino natural look in China without having to pay the high price for handmade Philippine craftsmanship. The practice of stealing intellectual property from others was a rampant epidemic in China and one we were eager to capitalize on.

The timing was perfect as we heard from our Cebu sources that the untimely devaluation of the Filipino peso made buying anything on this island nation extremely affordable. This included semi-precious stones such as rare, marbleized limestone which we were eager to use in our product offerings. We knew that this also meant the opportunity to stay in five star lush tropical resorts and enjoy the rampant red light districts that made the Philippines so attractive to tourists. *Did we need to be told twice?*

I gave a quick call to Mei Mei to let her know of our upcoming trip including our plan to steal local marble and smuggle it into Shu Shu's factory. She listened carefully and then gave me the name and number of a local "connected contact" who would act as our agent and look after our shipments. She said, "to call him 'Señor Gabriel' and that he would know how to best advise us."

I hung up from her and immediately called Señor Gabriel to discuss the trip and our plan to visit most of the local factories. I briefly introduced myself and what we were looking to produce and what materials we needed to find.

"Rick, thanks for calling as Mei Mei has told me a bit about you already." He said with a Spanish accent.

I thought that was strange as she never mentioned him to me before.

"I hope she didn't leave out the good parts?" I answered smirking.

"She mentioned you guys like to work hard and party harder!"

"Well since you mentioned that party part"-

"No need to discuss further," he cut me off. "However, unfortunately, I will not be able to accompany you this time as I have the Canadian Ambassador in town. So, I've arranged for you to be picked up at the airport by a mutual friend (and local cop) whose name is Manny."

"Ok, Gabriel"-

"That's Señor Gabriel to you Rick," he continued. "You will be in good hands with Manny. He is one of my best men and he also knows all the clubs in town. You will find him to be a great entourage for you and Shu Shu. He will show you around and more importantly, he will keep you safe."

I let that sink in for a second, how did he know Shu Shu and safe from what?

"Have a nice trip Rick and if you need me, you now have my number."

With that Señor Gabriel hung up. I called Shu Shu to tell him about Manny and confirm the trip once again. Shu Shu appeared to be very enthusiastic about our upcoming journey.

On the short Cathay Pacific flight over from Hong Kong, I did some light reading to learn more about what we could expect to find in tropical Cebu. What I learned is what many "sexpats" have known for years: that after a long American occupation by the U.S. Armed Forces, the Filipino people were schooled about our love of sex, drugs, and rock'n'roll. They perfected learning the English language, became gifted musicians and nightlife entertainers. Thanks to the American military, the smart Filipino women became nurses, and the beautiful became sex industry experts. The weather was hot, the local beer was cold (and cheap), and we both knew this trip was going to be a great change from the mundane pace of Communist China!

I must admit that the overseas police make me uncomfortable, so I was uneasy about being picked up from the airport by a cop. However, I was quickly reminded in the book I was reading about the random kidnappings, extortion, and violence that often went hand in hand in this country of political corruption and sin. I also trusted that Mei Mei would make sure we were all sorted.

Shu Shu and I were in good spirits as the plane touched down on the small island nation. We were excited for this adventure and the spoils that would result from this trip. That good natured feeling was quickly soured, as we faced an immigration line that rivaled nothing that I have experienced before. It's not for lack of immigration counters or incoming passengers, rather it was the lack of immigration officers and any semblance of direction as we queued in what seemed like an impossibly long line. The heat and humidity hit me like Miami in the summertime. After an agonizing hour, we made it through the sweat fest and out the doors.

Manny was waiting for us with a large sign that had our name written on it. Flanked on his sides were two beautiful Filipino girls. He introduced himself, the girls and told us they were "sisters." Manny had a strong handshake and spoke with a heavy accent. He continued to explain that the sisters were a welcome present from the *Safe House*, which was a local club we would visit later that night.

We followed Manny and the girls outside to a palm tree laden parking lot. We walked up to a dirty Jeep with no doors. Manny threw our carryon bags into the back and then the girls climbed in. We followed quickly, with me in the back with the girls, while Shu Shu rode shotgun. Manny got in the driver's seat, belted up and started the car. He then turned to the girls and spoke to them in their native tongues. The girls smiled at him, looked around coyly, lifted their braless shirts, and showed us their young perky breasts. I quickly noticed that their skin was dark like a deep tan, different from the milk-white skin of the Chinese women we were used to.

"Sir Rick, do you like what you see?" asked Manny.

"Hell yeah!" I said a bit too proudly.

"Welcome to the Philippines, Sir Rick," the girls said, giggling in unison.

I must admit that I liked the "Sir" respect thing.

Manny and Shu Shu laughed as the girls let us know that there was no shortage of beautiful women at the Safe House. Again, we didn't need to be told twice!

"First," said Manny, "let's check you into your hotel so you can get washed up, and then the fun begins."

"We can help you wash up, Sir Rick," the sisters said, and giggled some more.

"Wait, what kind of sisters are you?" I joked.

"These sisters are very close," said Manny with a wink.

With that, he reached into his pocket, pulled out a skinny joint, and lit it. Manny exhaled the fragrant smoke and passed it to Shu Shu, who gladly took his turn and coughed up a strong hit.

"Sir Rick," said Manny. "You should know that Marijuana is highly illegal here in the Philippines; you can get in serious trouble for smoking it!"

"I thought everything was legal here." I replied.

"Only if you are with me," said Manny with a big smile.

With that, he took the joint back from Shu Shu and inhaled once more before reaching back and giving it to me. I took a long drag and exhaled as the car made its way over the Marcelo Fernan bridge to our resort on Mactan Island.

The sun was warm, the sky blue, and the palms swayed with gentle indifference. I took another drag, smiled at the sisters, and closed my eyes as I turned my face to the sun. I let myself relax for the first time in days, drifting off into a light stoned slumber.

It was a nice break from the normal chaos in my life.

20

I Don't Wanna Hear It, *Hong Kong—circa 1995*

The phone rang, startling me out of a deep Ambien-induced sleep. I fumbled to make sense of what was happening:

Strange room ✓
Hotel ✓
Clock ✓
2 a.m. ✓
Phone ringing ✓

I fumbled for the receiver.

"Hello?" I said, a bit unsure.

"Hi, Mr. Price," came the soft Chinese female voice on the other end. "I am so sorry to wake you at this early hour, but we have a situation with your father."

"My dad?" I asked, now fully awake.

"Yes, sir, Mr. Steven is your father?"

"Yes, he is." I sat up, getting ready brace myself. "What kind of situation do you have with my dad, what is going on?" I asked nervous to hear the answer.

"Well, sir," she said, and cleared her throat, "it seems that your dad has locked himself out of his room."

I sighed.

"Not again!" I said a little too loudly.

"And sir..." she continued in that soft soothing voice.

"Yes," I grumbled.

"I am afraid he is naked," she said quietly.

"Jesus Christ!" I exclaimed. "I am so sorry."

"Well, sir, I must also let you know that he is also bleeding from his head."

"Whoa! What? Bleeding?" I started to get out of bed and threw on my nylon adidas gym shorts.

"Yes, sir, we have called a doctor to attend to him, but I am afraid that we will need you to come down, as he appears... well, to be a bit confused."

"You mean he's drunk!" I exclaimed.

"Sir, we appreciate if you would come down to help."

"I'll be right there!" I hung up the phone, finished getting dressed, and checked myself in the mirror. I gave myself a few cold splashes on my face to wake up and raked my fingers through my short hair. I looked like shit after spending two weeks of nonstop traveling. I was tired and thought for a moment about just leaving him downstairs. God knows, I'd had enough of this "rescue dad" bullshit. But hey, he was naked and that gave me a sly chuckle.

We were staying in Hong Kong at the five star Renaissance Harbour View Hotel on the way home from a tough, ten-day trip in China. It was end of summer, brutally hot and I knew he was looking forward to getting out of here and going home. The factories we visited were "sweat fest" with little to no AC and even though we stayed at the newly opened Dongguan DongCheng International hotel, I knew my father had a tough time on this trip. He was a "creature of comfort," and mainland China was void of any Western pleasantries back then. If you were easily grossed out and privileged (like my dad), this was not a trip you looked forward to taking.

For this reason, we (like all who did business in China back then) enjoyed the end of our journey, especially crossing the border back into Hong Kong. It was freedom, the promise of a decent meal, the comfort of a great hotel and, of course, going home. I can remember literally kissing the ground in Hong Kong on several occasions!

We'd gone out for a nice "victory" dinner at the hotel's Mirage Restaurant and Bar to reward ourselves and decompress before the long flight back home. It was our usual go-to with stunning views of the Hong Kong harbor. In case you forgot, Dad was a drinker, and he was honored to pass that torch onto me. I couldn't really only blame him, as the vice of alcohol runs rampant in my family tree. Therefore, like good partners, we tossed back a few vodkas, ate well, and went back to our rooms for sleep.

Except this time, (like others before), I needed to save his ass again!

I entered the elevator and rode it down to the lobby, as my mind raced to the scene that would quickly unfold. I swiftly walked to the front desk and was immediately greeted by the woman on the phone.

"Hi, Mr. Price?" asked the woman.

"What happened? Where is he?" I answered.

"Your dad is in the back office with the doctor."

"How bad is he?"

"His head was bleeding when he arrived here fifteen minutes ago."

"Arrived?" I asked.

"Yes, sir, he took the elevator down and stumbled up to the counter asking for his room key. We immediately sat him down, grabbed a towel for his head, and another one to cover himself with." She said shyly.

"Shit, I am so sorry." I said embarrassed to have just cursed.

"No need to apologize," she said in that same pleasant tone. "If anything, we are sorry that it took so long to contact you."

"Because he was naked?"

"Well yes," she said embarrassingly. "And he because he was confused and didn't know who he was. But he kept insisting for us to call his son, Rick."

"He never even gave you, his name?" I asked now a bit concerned.

"No, your father was adamant about calling you. Hence, we checked the register, and you were the only Rick on file."

"Can I see him?" I interrupted.

"Sure, he is with the hotel doctor."

"This hotel has a doctor?" I asked.

"Thankfully the doctor does not live far away and is always on call for us."

I followed the clerk behind the large marble hotel counter and into an office that was hidden behind the back wall by a door that swung inward. When I entered, I saw a small Chinese man standing over my father, wrapping a white gauze bandage around his head. There were two other men in the room kneeling beside my father. They were dressed in suits, and I took them to be hotel security.

"Dad!" I exclaimed.

"Look who decided to show up?" he slurred and burped at the same time.

I walked over to examine the work being done. There was a thick bandage over the right side of his forehead. It was coated with congealed blood. I could see a nice golf-ball-size lump beginning to form. The doctor nodded to me and continued to wrap my father's head in gauze.

"Nice one, Pop," I said. "Not only naked this time, but naked and bleeding!"

"Like I need your shit now... again?" he stumbled for words.

It was always a toss-up with my dad. You never knew how things were going to end, just that they would finish badly. It reminded me of the time when he "tripped" on the curb during one of our trade shows in Dallas, Texas. After an evening of heavy drinking with our sales reps and best customers, he went outside *Javier's* restaurant, lost his balance, and face-planted into the curb. Just like that, he was unconscious, concussed, with two missing front teeth and bleeding profusely from his nose. The most embarrassing part was that this happened right in front of our executive team and our major customers in town for the show. It would take twenty-four stitches, a new mouth bridge, and an operation to repair his broken nose. Still, nothing would shatter his tremendous narcissistic ego—once a drunk, always a drunk.

Even buying a new sports car would not stop my dad's incessant drinking. You would think that after acquiring his first Porsche 911 Carrera, my dad would have a bit of humility. Somewhere in his self-absorbed brain, his bravado should have been fully appeased, especially considering the staggering 270 horsepower underneath the hood. But no, he turned the occasion of being able to go 0 to 60 MPH in under 5 seconds into a bizarre spectacle that would haunt me for the rest of my life.

All the neighbors came over to witness the fire-breathing beast of German engineering. My father unveiled his black beauty for all to see and opened several bottles of champagne as if he'd won some sort of Formula 1 race. His friends marveled at the engine, the leather wrapped upholstery, and the aggressive racing lines. I was too young to appreciate such a fine automobile, however, I was required to sit in the passenger seat with my brother while my dad revved the engine to the delight of the neighbors.

It was loud, and I remember my brother being upset by the noise. I held him close as Dad slowly backed out of the driveway. He waved to the audience and then punched it into first gear. Later, I would learn that Dad had revved the engine high enough to shift seamlessly into third—forgetting second gear altogether. The car lurched unexpectedly with blinding speed and, as Dad rounded the corner out of control, the tires lost purchase and we smacked face-first into a thick Red Maple tree. The neighbors came running over as the fire trucks and ambulances were called. My dad climbed out of the car and looked at the damage he had done.

I remember him swearing up and down over the smashed-in front of the race car. He exclaimed to all who gathered round that, "the tree must have jumped into the curb and hit him!" The crowd of his male friends joked along with him as me and my brother cried in shock. The women grabbed for us and tried to coddle us as they searched for my mom. Thankfully, dad was coherent enough to strap the seatbelt over both of us, as if he predicted that something bad might happen. We were miraculously not injured in that wreck but unfortunately that would not be the last time that he had an intoxicated accident with me and my brother in the car.

Presently, I shook off this memory and quickly returned my gaze to the sorry excuse of a semi-naked man that I called my father.

"I need you to call your mother," he slurred.

"No way!" I said. "You need to get upstairs and sleep this off."

"Actually," the doctor chimed in with that English accent, "he will need to be observed every hour to make sure he did not suffer a concussion."

I let that sink in for a moment. "Are you saying I need to stay with him?"

"That is correct, or we can admit him to the hospital for observation, but I am afraid if we do that you will miss your flight home tomorrow."

"I'm not going to no damn 'Honky' hospital," he protested.

He tried to stand up but ended falling back on his ass as the towel fell off his waist and on to the floor.

"Take it easy dad," I said, and turned to the doctor. "I will stay with him."

With that, the hotel clerk covered my dad's embarrassing nudity with the towel and asked me, "to go to his room and retrieve some of his clothes."

"Good idea," I said, thankful to get the hell out of there and gather my thoughts.

"You will also need to get him to a doctor in New York when you land to follow up," the doctor added. "I'll write down an incident report for you to have for them."

I grabbed Dad's key from the nice woman, nodded my head in agreement, and made my way to the elevator to the Club floor. On the way up, I thought of the chaos that would await me. There was always a mess from him for me to clean up. I am not sure why this burden always falls on my shoulders and why I offered to even help anymore. I thought about the choice I made to work with him and reminded myself that it was to help the family business and all the relatives that we employed.

I ruminated on this a bit more as I walked slowly down the well-lit hallway to his room.

I took a moment to steady myself, took out the room key and opened his door.

What I saw stopped me cold in my tracks. The room was trashed. I mean, first-rate-rock-star-status trashed!

"Fuck me!" I said loudly looking at the carnage.

The minibar was toppled over; glass was shattered in several spots. The desk lamp was on the floor next to several open pill boxes. Empty airplane-size alcohol bottles and his clothing were strewn all over the bathroom. In the corner by the tub, he had defecated on the floor. There was blood on the rim of the tub.

I saw it all instantly like a scene in a crime movie:
- perp drains the mini bar
- gets drunk
- pops pills
- becomes delirious
- chaos sets in as he smashes things
- takes off clothes in bathroom
- falls
- hits head on tub
- shits on floor
- passes out
- wakes up confused
- bleeding
- leaves the room naked
- locks himself out
- rides elevator downstairs to get another key
- hotel staff are horrified.
- He can't remember who he is
- son is called to help
- the boy must deal with his dad
- roles are reversed
- son becomes the parent and is left to clean up the mess—that is his life!

21

Cause for Alarm, *Honesdale, PA—circa 1980*

Adults always seemed to let me down, especially when I needed them the most.

At the tender young age of twelve, my parents decided to send me away for the summer to sleepaway camp. Summer was their holiday time, and it seemed that the best vacation for them was to get rid of us kids. Summer was their chance to enjoy time together with their friends or make new ones. It was a time for them to imagine life without any kids to interrupt or bother them. They wanted to party. A chance to swing with each other, drink excessively, and smoke weed out of large pipes. This was not an all-ages show!

Because we were children never given a choice, I (of course) protested this decision as a form of abandonment. But like the rest of my life's grievances, they often fell on deaf ears. There was no getting out of this one as my parents and their friends had summer plans that did not involve their pestering children. They already put in ten months of hard parenting and now it was their well-deserved break.

My younger brother and I were sent packing, in the form of filling large green duffel bags with our summer clothes. The bags and our clothes had our names written on them with permanent markers. We all met up at the Nassau Coliseum parking lot and were put on several yellow school buses for a three-hour journey to the great outdoors of Pennsylvania. The buses were filled to capacity with other bratty Jewish kids from "The Island." It was surreal to see all of us Jews being bussed away from our families. I remember sticking my head out the window, screaming for them to rescue me. But all the tears and protests had no effect on my parents who promptly proceeded to their car. They were dead set on having themselves a memorable summer without us. And just like that, busloads of Jewish children were taken from their parents and brought to a camp. *Kind of ironic if you ask me.*

The long bus ride through unfamiliar terrain made me anxious about not knowing where we were going or what was waiting for us. Even though the camp had arranged a home visit to show us a video tape of surreal settings filled with smiling children, the camp video haunted me more than The Who's *Tommy* movie. At least Tommy was a rock opera and had music in it that I had grown to know from the endless hours that my father played it in the evenings. Right now, sitting next to my brother with his head on my lap, I felt the furthest away from, "I'm Free" than ever before. It was more of a, "see me/hear me" moment and I was ready to "smash the mirror!"

When the school bus finally arrived through the camp gates, we were quickly led off by counselors who looked like several of my older teenage cousins. They had whistles around their neck and clipboards in their hands. They asked us our names and then sent us to our designated bunks. The bunks were more like army barracks, small, primitive wooden houses where twenty children and two counselors lived. The counselors were college kids looking to earn some extra scratch by babysitting us. We all lived in close quarters, sleeping in cots, showering, and shitting together. It was all very militaristic as we unpacked in small cubbies and marched like good soldiers to the sacred flagpole.

It was here that we started every morning with reveille being piped through the camps PA system at full blast. The bugle signaled the beginning of each day, where traditionally we would stand in single file lines while the American flag was hoisted up the pole to declare the glory of another camp day. This revered flagpole was also where we were given our daily announcements and mandatory schedule of activities. Events of the day involved playing sports in the dead summer heat, often against our will. The camp did a good job of trying to make sure we were always busy and therefore we were kept orderly. I detested every moment of it and like my Jewish ancestors before me, I was determined to flee from this camp of cruelty. After all, where was our freedom to do whatever, we wanted for the summer and why was their no goddamned air-conditioning? Imagine the barbarism!

According to *my nature*, I rebelled by refusing to partake in any camp activities. I would sit on the sidelines during games, trying to ignore the insults thrown at me by other campers (and even counselors). But worse than the activities we were forced to play, was the food (if you want to call it that!). It was more like chow thrown together by teenagers pretending to be cooks. I was already a picky eater, somewhat neurotic about proper hygiene and would protest by not eating anything at all. My hunger strike did not sit well with the counselors. They were nervous about my rejection to eat and tried to find something to satisfy me. What was offered as enticement was a "substitution," which consisted of peanut butter and jelly sandwiches. I detested PB&J and continued starving myself like I was on a hunger strike protesting some sort of political activism. In a way, I guess I was feeling like a prisoner and the only control I had was over what I ate... or chose not to eat.

After several days of protest, the camp decided this was a battle best taken to my folks. As a result, they moved me to the infirmary to try and coax me into eating some ice cream while they placed a phone call to my parents. My folks, of course, could not be reached, as they were off enjoying themselves at some naked grown-up hedonistic Club Med. Accordingly, the camp tracked down my aunt, as she was on the emergency contact list. My aunt listened to me cry but offered no help, as she was also about to leave on her childless summer vacation to Europe.

When self-induced starvation failed to get me home, I resorted to some sort of insanity or my first mental break. My thoughts began to race as I obsessed on how I would get free from this "concentration camp." After days of ruminating on this, a plan had started to take shape, backed by a constant hunger in my belly, I put my obsessive thoughts into immediate action. Just as I planned in my head, when everyone was at the flagpole, I retreated to the bunk pretending to need to use the toilet. When I got back to my bunk, I shut the door and quickly packed up all my clothes into my green duffel bag. I exited in sheer determination as I dragged my heavy bag to the side of the country road where the entrance to the camp gates were. It was there that I decided to sit on my duffel and wait for someone (anyone) to pick me up. I convinced myself into a false reality, in which my parents somehow heard my cries and were on their way to save me. If not them, then maybe some "townie" would take pity and rescue me.

I obsessively did the same routine every day, sitting on my bag, just off the camps grounds on the other side of the country road, waiting inevitably for my parents to come and take me home. It was there that the camp would now leave me alone with my thoughts of salvation... well, sometimes. Mostly, by the afternoon, I would hear my name announced repeatedly on the campus PA loudspeaker. Off in the distance, I would hear, "Attention, Rick Price. Please return to your bunk. I repeat, Rick Price back to your bunk. No one is coming for you today!"

This was always painful to listen to. But it paled in comparison to the feeling of neglect and the constant taunting I endured from the other campers. The counselors hired to protect me, were of no help, as they just turned a blind eye, hoping I would one day soon be miraculously picked up. I was a pain in their ass, and I knew that they were looking forward to the time that they would finally be rid of me.

In solace, I finally gave up waiting to be saved and had another idea that had been spiraling through my pre-teen brain in an endless loop. I was stuck at this camp with my younger brother and the only salvation I found that I remotely enjoyed was spending time on the archery field. There was something so satisfying about the range and shooting deadly projectiles at a target. I learned to enjoy the strain of my muscles and the sound of the arrow as it solidly hit its mark. I felt peaceful for the first time in camp, as I placed on the protected arm guards like some medieval warrior and pulled back the taught bowstring. Not only was I satisfied by the projected violence, but my hunger returned, as archery released my inner energy and nervousness. I still ate very little but realized that I needed some fuel to make the arrows fly farther and hit harder, so I began to eat only sugary cereals. The camp was delighted that I stopped waiting to be picked up. They were so thrilled by my change in behavior that they made special arrangements for me to be at the archery field all day, every day. It appeared much easier for them to bend a few rules than fight incessantly with a hell-bent child.

I was amazed to see that archery was not very popular with the other campers. I couldn't imagine that they would rather spend time in the cold lake or sweating it out on the basketball court! I didn't relate to what planet they were on but was relieved to be left alone with an active imagination and a deadly weapon.

My archery counselor's name was James, and he was on an exchange program from England. I loved his accent and enthusiasm as he taught me how to tape photos from magazines to the archery target's bull-seye as we practiced shooting them. He also appeared to reciprocate my company, and together we plotted to shoot arrows in imaginative ways, often pretending we were Indians or Gladiators. James was a great counselor, and I admired his archery skills and the "fags" he would sneak to smoke in the woods. After a short period of time, I would convince him to allow me to try and smoke one of his cigarettes. I loved the idea of smoking as I felt cool and mature by doing so. I had seen my parents and family do this so many times that it never looked strange. Even the head rush, although making me extremely nauseous was exciting to me. And the cough, well that was something I tried not to do and after some practice that seemed to dissipate along with the nicotine induced dizziness.

But nothing gave me more satisfaction than ripping arrows through photos of some megastar's skull. I enjoyed shooting the magazine and newspaper photos imagining that I was actually executing them. My counselor also liked doing this, and we formed a special bond as we called out their names and "sentenced them to death!" James was different from the others, and I liked him. He also seemed to have a dark side, at least in music. He was responsible for my first taste of metal music and turned me on to English bands like *Led Zeppelin, Deep Purple and,* of course, *Black Sabbath.*

Camp was beginning to grow on me as my archery skills continued to improve. Under the guidance of my new British mate, we tore through photos of celebrities, politicians, and pop musicians. It gave me such a thrill to imagine sending an arrow through these people's skulls. It actually improved my aim, my forearm strength, and my grip. I was getting good and was often left alone while James sneaked away to smoke as he tried to hook up with the American female counselors. Thankfully, the archery field was remote from the rest of the barbarians. No one knew what we were up to and that was solace gave me the courage to face another day.

And so it went, I was always on my best behavior on the archery range and because of that, James trusted me alone with a bountiful quiver full of arrows. I would practice every day and when the targets got shredded and the magazines gone, I was on the lookout for something new to shoot at.

Often, I would sneak around random bunks while all the "good" kids were doing their mandatory sports and steal family photos from them. Once alone, I would tack up the photos and shoot arrows through their moms, dads, siblings, and family pets. I imagined the screams as the arrows pierced the targets. Once finished, I carefully took all the shredded photos down and hid them in an old nylon bag used to hold the archery gear. The bag was nestled on top of the shed, full of cobwebs and never used. I would deftly hide the torn stolen family photographs in that blue nylon bag and use a wooden crate to hide it in the shed's attic. My compulsion to steal personal effects and destroy them might have helped with the hunger but it did not quell my anger. If anything, I needed more and started to take photos and letters from my bunkmates—especially from my counselors.

There was definitely something in the air going around camp, and it was not my paranoia. At our mandatory flagpole meeting one night, the General Manager of the camp gave an impassioned plea for all of us to respect each other's property. I was looking at the ground but could imagine his eyes burning a hole through the top of my skull. And on the way back from the meeting, my counselors both grabbed me and roughly threw me to the ground. One of them sank their knees deep into my chest, pressing the wind out of me, while the other one stood guard. They were angry and told me that they knew I was "stealing their personal photos." Even though they could not prove it, there was apparently no one else "creepier" on campus who would do such a thing. I bit my tongue and once again took my beating.

Unfortunately, the hazing did not stop, and the next evening they got to my younger brother in the mess hall. I heard the commotion and saw out of the corner of my eye as my kid brother was held down. A group of older kids, protected by the counselors, proceeded to pour a pitcher of red fruit juice over his head that they commonly referred to as "bug juice." My brother started to cry as everyone laughed. I was in fight mode, so I grabbed the closest fork and ran over to avenge my brother. Two counselors, who were particularly egging this on, anticipated my action and tackled me to the floor. I quickly turned to my left and with my newfound strength, planted that fork into the top of the hand of one of the counselors who held me down. He screamed in agony as he continued to try to restrain me. I knew that they were afraid of seriously hurting me, so I used this to my advantage as I kicked, clawed, and bit my way out of their grasp. They released me as more counselors appeared. Frantically, I ran over to my soiled brother and held him in my arms. He was crying hysterically, and, at that moment, I swore revenge on everyone at that camp.

A whistle went off as the rest of the boys were quickly escorted out of the dining room. The counselor I forked was screaming at the Boys Head Counselor, who told him to calm down, and then escorted him out to the camp doctor. The Head Counselor returned with a clean towel and took my brother from my arms. I ran out of the dining room as fast as my feet could fly. I knew where I was going and ran into the safety of the woods. I was heading for the archery range, as I knew where the key to the weapons was hidden.

Once inside the archery shack, I found a few cigarette butts and a lighter. I lit them with shaky hands as I tried to calm my nerves. After a few lightheaded puffs, I put out the butt with my foot, careful to make sure the flame was extinguished. I found my favorite bow and placed twelve arrows in a quiver. I looked above in the attic for my bag of damaged photos but could not find it. I panicked for a moment but thought that perhaps I just misplaced it. Either that or James had found them and either got rid of the evidence or ratted on me. Regardless, I was now armed to the teeth and needed to think of a plan to get my brother and myself out of this Nazi camp.

It was then that I heard my name reverberate over the PA's loud-speaker. Apparently, there was an urgent phone call for me, and I was wanted at the boy's head shack. This is where the General Manager presided. I smelled a rat, but they had my brother, and what if there really was a call for me? What if it was finally my parents and they were calling to come rescue us?

I quickly took the bow and arrows and re-locked the shed. I stashed the weapons deep in the woods in case I needed them for later and made my way down to the office. Once inside, I was greeted by a large group of counselors. They stood around in a circle and had venom in their eyes. I looked for my archery counselor James but could not find him in the group. In the corner was my brother, who shot out of his seat and into my arms. I held his quivering body tight and whispered that I had a plan to get us both out of here.

The boys GM (General Manager) entered the room and made his way to where the counselors were standing. They parted as he entered, and I could now see that he had my nylon bag of desecrated photos. With a lot of unnecessary drama, he opened the bag and scattered the photos to the ground in a large circle with me in the middle. The counselors began to scream as they saw their personal photos shot to shreds. Some even made attempts to grab and shove me and my brother against the floor. I screamed back and told them, "I'll kill you all!"

The GM told me to calm down and explained to us and the others that my brother and I were leaving tomorrow morning. He said he'd just hung up with my grandfather Butch and that someone was finally coming to pick us up. With that, the other counselors pried my brother out of my arms and took him away from me. He was screaming and so was I. The GM made a gesture to grab me as he was mentioning something about, "pressing charges for destroying property, etc." I anticipated his advances, ducked between his legs, and once again fled the scene. I ran as fast as I could into the wild, dark forest. Barbed branches attacked my small frame as I ducked and weaved to the clearing where I'd hid my bow and arrows. I might not have had a flashlight but thankfully the moon was full and bright. Blood began to trickle from my forehead and mixed with my salty tears.

Something inside of me snapped as I once again felt numb and hollow inside. I knew those feelings well and they were welcomed with a comfortable rage. I felt in control of my angry emotions and knew that those feelings would not go away without action. I needed to do something drastic, and my mind raced, searching for an answer. I scanned my brain looking for a tape of what to do next. When none was found, I made my own playlist. I thought about the events to come and then thought some more. Letting them play out until I felt the plan turn into reality.

I ran out of the woods armed to the teeth and took a direct path for my bunk. By this time at night, all lights were off inside. Besides those I imagined were looking for me, all was relatively quiet. Knowing exactly where my counselor slept, I aligned myself outside the wall of the bunk and took aim with my first arrow. I pulled back the bow with all my might and released the arrow. I didn't think the arrow could miraculously pass through the wood planks, but by good God, I was going to try. The first arrow hit hard, rocketing the night with a hollow *thud*. Instinctively, I drew another arrow, held the bowstring until it felt as if my shoulder was going to break, and released the arrow a bit higher.

The projectile flew with a loud crash into the bunk's window. It did not go through, but glass crashed and sounded like a small explosion. The lights came on in an instant. I had automatically reloaded one more arrow. This time, I quickly aimed at the other window above where my other counselor slept. This arrow soared through the glass shattering it to pieces inside the bunk. Campers started to scream as the front door flew open.

I quickly grabbed another arrow and aimed it high at the now open door. I heard it pierce deep into the wood. I didn't look to see if I hit anyone and took off running instead. I was heading quickly in the direction of the boy's headquarters where the GM slept.

I rounded the corner of the HQ shack and was immediately stopped in my tracks. A smile spread across my face, as instantly it was clear what my next target would be. Sitting out front was the GM's big diesel Mercedes Benz 300D. He loved that car and would often use washing it as a punishment to kids who did not follow his rules. I have washed it many times and now it was time to destroy the beast.

I quickly skidded to my knees, ignoring the road rash and took aim at the back-left tire. An explosion of air was expelled in an instant as the arrow pierced the rubber with Olympic precision. I kept methodically slinging arrows into the remaining tires, the doors, and then the back windshield. I was in an all-out rage, an out-of-body experience that I was having for the first time. I was consumed with the impact of the arrows and did not hear the others when they quickly approached from behind and tackled me to the ground. Then someone hit me with something that made all the lights go out in my head.

When I awoke, I was lightly restrained in a white hospital bed. My eyes opened and tried to focus on my brother sitting in the chair next to me. He appeared to be silently watching TV and had his "blankie" with him. I thought this was strange because I remember the day he threw it in the garbage. We had a family party to commemorate the occasion as my folks toasted my six-year-old brother's braveness. They gave us both a celebratory sip of what they were drinking, and I believe that was my first taste of alcohol. I remember it was hard to swallow as I choked on it and immediately felt woozy, like I had been drinking all day. I tried to shake this memory by moving, but my insides hurt and so did my head.

Through the hospital curtain, I swore I heard my grandfather's voice screaming at what I believe was the camp's General Manager. I heard the words, "lawsuit!"; "broken ribs" and "concussion!" and knew my grandfather Butch was taking care of business. My father once told me that my grandfather was the most ruthless man he had ever met. He had even once fired his own son from the family company and then my father was the next to be terminated!

I knew my grandpa Butch was always good to me and I felt safe knowing that he was here to protect me. My head was ringing as kept listening to grandpa rage on about the camp, the hospital or anyone that appeared in his way. I took one more look at my brother and encouraged him to come sit with me on my hospital bed. He quickly climbed in and found his way into the safety of my arms. My grandfather peeked in to see us together and then turned to me with a wink.

"Son," he said, "you're so bad!

22

The Eliminator, *Cebu, Philippines—circa 2000*

Manny met us in the tropical lounge of the Mactan Shangri-La hotel.

We polished off our ice cold beers and left in his police cruiser. We traveled for fifty minutes over the scenic Marcelo Fernan Bridge and to our destination on General Maxilom Avenue. We were going to visit the sisters at the Safe House, and we were all jacked about the evening to come. We parked illegally outside the club, and at the entrance I noticed two burly doormen armed with menacing sawed-off shotguns. They did nothing to conceal their weapons. I asked Manny about this, and he said it was for our own protection due to the recent rise in crime targeting foreign tourists. I let this sink in and looked around more closely. I was scanning for marks and exits as I did not feel as safe as I usually did when we were in China. Manny saw me tense up and smiled, reminding us again that, "he was a policeman, and the only bad thing we could catch tonight was a case of crabs." We laughed at his joke, took his advice, relaxed, and passed armed burly doormen. We entered the club, and we were immediately met by the two sisters with the small brown breasts.

"Paradise!" is how Shu Shu described it when we walked in the club. Inside were numerous dance floors with half naked Filipino women working the crowd. The music was loud, progressive, the air was thick

with smoke, sweat, and sexual tension. When the girls finished dancing, they exited the stage to sit with the male patrons, drinking, eating
pizza, and having a good time. The crowd consisted of horny white
sexpats from around the globe. They were taking advantage of the free
Internet, making this the best virtual office to work from, drinking
cold San Miguel Beer and having a blast. Manny was quick to tell us
that in the Philippines, and anywhere there were Filipino girls, it was
proper etiquette to order a *San Miguel* beer or "Send-Me-A-Girl" as one
would have it!

Manny and the sisters led us to a private table close to one of the
stages. The stage was lit up with neon lights, flashing LED's and a several
dancing poles. The conversation took a turn south once the sisters found
out we were visiting from both China and the U.S. The girls became
adamant that, "Filipina hygiene was far superior over what we were used
to," and were not shy about showing us their freshly shaved bushes. I
must admit that their personal grooming was a nice change to what I
have witnessed in China, but I was still not convinced that they were
superior. So, to prove it, the very friendly and confident Filipina girls
quickly got the rest of the working women together to start a contest on
who had the best looking pussy.

The rules were simple: The girls would line up one at time, Shu Shu
would pull back their bikini bottoms to take a look and I, of course,
volunteered to be the judge. I know this sounds perverted, but Cebu is
not for the faint of heart and we were there to enjoy ourselves! Soon the
entire club was a buzz participating in our little game of show and tell.
The competition began to heat up when Shu Shu put up a cash prize of a
$100 U.S.D. bill. An announcement was made over the club's PA and all
the girls screamed with delight. We were at the center of a "pussy riot,"
with girls lining up to exhibit their genitalia, allowing us to enjoy the
"fruits" of their labor.

As the night progressed, we all got completely trashed. The contest
quickly turned south from "best smelling" to some girls claiming to have
"best tasting!" That's when Manny reminded us that even Cebu had
rules and perhaps this was a good time to leave? Being the consummate
host, he told us we should check out some other clubs on the island,
and offered to take us to an after-hours bar where the girls went when

they got off work. We didn't need to be told... *you guessed it*. We paid the bounty to one of the sister's, said our goodbyes and left the club, laughing as we passed the bouncers with their sawed off shotgun's.

Once back in the cruiser, Manny opened all the windows and blasted progressive American rock from his elaborate car stereo as he set course for the next destination. We were all smiles and laughing loudly as we recounted the competition in play-by-play fashion. When we stopped at the next red light, I happened to notice an inconspicuous pickup truck pull up alongside us. Inside the truck, three dark skinned Filipino men pointed at us, in what my instincts felt was a menacing and threatening manner. Manny and Shu Shu seemed not to notice as they listened to music and continued to laugh about the "pussy contest."

The pickup truck followed us closely for a few more blocks. When we stopped at the next traffic light, the truck quickly pulled up beside us. Before the light turned green, one of the men suddenly jumped out of the truck with a baseball bat. Then all hell broke loose.

In what seemed to be slow motion, I watched the man with the bat make his way directly to Shu Shu. Manny noticed this as well as he suddenly turned the music off. I counted backwards as the figure approached and let my years of martial arts command the warrior in my soul. I felt oddly at ease with the impending violence I knew was about to go down.

"Hey, dude!" I screamed distractingly through the open car window.

The guy turned, smiled a rotten grin, and then quickly walked in my direction. Like a cobra, I shot out of the back window with a tight fist and struck the guy on the side of his face. Before he had a chance to react, I kicked open the door, striking him in the knees and sending him flying onto the pavement.

I swiftly got out of the car, lifted him by his hair, released my right hand, and struck him hard in the center of the face. His nose flattened with a small crunch under my knuckles and blood instantly flew out of his mouth as he started to choke. I quickly grabbed the bat as it fell out of his hands, and proceeded to deliver three quick, devastating blows to his right knee cap. His body crumpled into a bloody mess as he howled in pain.

Instinctively, I focused my attention back to Shu Shu and Manny. They were still in the car, intently watching the driver of the truck, who was now in the street pointing a shotgun at them. I looked at Manny and saw him reach slowly under the seat for his police revolver. I dropped the bat, shot my hands out to the sky in defeat, and began screaming incessantly at the guy with the gun, "to calm down." He looked in my direction and leveled the shotgun towards my approaching body. I never had a shotgun pointed at me before, but this did not stop my advance.

My commotion distracted him enough for Manny to produce his loaded revolver and point it at the guy. I continued to scream in English, and Manny started screaming in Filipino. During the commotion, my hands waived in in the air while my footsteps quickly closed the gap between me and the armed man. The standoff was quickly filled with confusion, as we all continued to loudly shout in unison.

This was the perfect storm of alcohol, violence, and rage. My endorphins were firing on all cylinders, and I was prepared for what I needed to do next. Without fear or hesitation, I immediately sprung towards the gun, grabbing the barrel forcefully away from my head with my left hand. Instinctively, I turned my body counterclockwise so that my right elbow smashed into his jaw and sent a few more elbows straight into his face as I kept the gun pointed high over my head.

I continued the attack with my right fist pummeling into his face and neck with quick, incessant blows. Each punch landed repetitively on strategic sensitive spots that I had been trained to identify. It felt as if I was punching my way through the guy's neck. His knees began to buckle as he lost all control of his breathing and his body. I twisted the gun free from his hands and pointed it at his face as he hit the ground. He did not look up at me or make a move, so I spun around and ran to the third guy, who sat nervously in the passenger seat of the car.

I threw open the door, grabbed him by his shirt, and shoved him to the ground. My adrenaline was pumping as I hit him straight in the face with the butt of the shotgun, cracking his face and jaw. Manny joined me, placing his hand on my shoulder, letting me know that he was there to help. He pointed his revolver at the man with the bloody face as I turned away to examine the violent scene. I was crazed with bloodlust and alcohol. I saw the first assailant slowly making his way up off the ground as he began to limp over to me. He was about to say something when met I him halfway and pointed the shotgun to his face. I used the gun forcefully to push him towards the truck's hood and his damaged body followed as I pinned him down with my fury. I screamed at him, "to open his mouth wide" and then shoved the shotgun inside his face.

His eyes widened in shock as he began to choke on the cold steel. I heard some muffled voices screaming my name, but I was more focused on the tactile feel of the trigger on my finger. I racked the shotgun and increased the pressure.

Then I did the unimaginable and pulled the trigger.

It happened fast... the trigger succumbed, and then was followed by the click of the empty chamber.

"What the fuck!?" I said loudly and pumped the shotgun again.

"Rick stop!" I thought I heard Manny scream.

I pulled the trigger and, again—nothing but an empty payload.

My heartbeat pounded in my head. I heard nothing else as I removed the shotgun from his mouth, grabbed it by the barrel and began to smash the butt repeatedly into his face with rage.

The man fell fast as I continued my assault, pummeling his head like a ripe melon. It took both Manny and Shu Shu to tackle me and rip the gun from my clenched fists. Manny was screaming in my face with his gun now tucked in his pants.

"Get the fuck in the car!" he shouted.

I was somewhere else and did not respond as I tried to catch my breath.

"Get the fuck in the car!" he repeated two more times.

I looked around, dazed at the carnage of the three bloody men lying in the street.

Shu Shu threw the shotgun into the police car as Manny wrapped his arms around my now silent body and manhandled me roughly into the back seat of his car.

Shu Shu jumped into the other back seat and looked at me incredulously. Manny was now yelling into his cop radio as he stepped on the gas and sped away from the crime. I gathered myself, still shaking, but looked at Shu Shu and saw him smiling. This put me at ease until Manny turned around and started yelling at me.

"Amigo, not a word of this to anyone!" he yelled like I was far away from him.

Maybe I was mentally not there but nodded in understanding.

"You are a fucking lucky man that that gun was not loaded!" Manny exclaimed and then turned on his flashing cruiser lights.

I recounted the scene, step by step and let the fact resonate that I almost blew someone brains out. There was a stretch of silence as we were all lost in thought, and maybe in shock. Manny broke the silence:

"Where the hell did you learn to fight like that?" he asked.

I thought of Boaz's classes but didn't answer his question.

"You just saved our fucken lives!" Manny continued as he shook his head in disbelief.

"Did you see all that blood?" Shu Shu kept repeating to himself as he stared off in thought.

"Shu Shu, are you okay?" I asked in a surprisingly calm voice.

He didn't answer so I put my arm around him and gave him a supportive side hug. This seemed to snap him out of his thoughts.

"Yeah, man, you were amazing," Shu Shu added, cracking a smile.

"I always got your back brother," I replied.

"Thank you," he said solemnly.

"Yo, Manny, do we still get to go to that after-hours club?" I managed to ask with a devilish grin.

"You are fucking crazy!" Manny screamed. "No more parties for you!"

"Then where are we going?" I asked.

"I need to get you off the island tonight!" he replied quickly.

"But Manny-"

"You listen carefully to me Rick," he continued. "There is no telling how connected those guys are or who they might be working for. If they were targeting tourists, then there is a good chance they will have people looking for you. And that means in every bar and hotel on the island."

"Isn't that a bit far-fetched?" I asked.

"You, my heavily tattooed American friend, are not an easy mark to miss and I fear you will not be safe here!" he exclaimed and stepped harder on the gas.

I let this sink in as the cruisers lights reflected hypnotically over the now empty street. I took stock of myself, glancing at my bloodied knuckles and soiled shirt. I made a few painful fists and tried—but failed—to wipe some of the blood off my hands and face.

"Look, I'm arranging a police escort to the Mactan Air base where you will catch a helicopter to Manila." Manny said breaking the silence again. "Once there, the police will ask for a brief statement. You will tell them that you were targeted for being an American and Shu Shu for being Chinese."

"We were definitely targeted," I commiserated.

"Rick, it is important that they know that I was the cop that stopped those men." He continued. "You can mention that this was all in self-defense and that all you want to do now is go home and forget about this!"

I started to laugh at this pathetic story but realized that Manny was in charge and probably right. This incident needed an explanation, even if it was a stretch of the truth. I wasn't concerned about the cops, but someone needed to let Mei Mei and Señor Gabriel know what happened. There was no hiding the truth from Mei Mei and that thought alarmed me more than the men that attacked us.

"In the meantime, I will go back to the hotel and gather your things," said Manny.

"Manny, c'mon, you're overreacting! I mean, we were attacked for God sakes!" I exclaimed defensively.

Manny hit the brakes hard as I instinctively used my bruised hands to cushion the blow. The pain shot through me like an ice storm and pulled me back to reality. Shu Shu let out a soft moan. Manny defiantly looked me dead in the eyes.

"As an island nation, we depend on tourism and cannot afford any more bad press about attacks occurring to foreigners. You are not to breathe a word of this to anyone! No one can know *the truth* about what happened here tonight." He added.

Again, I began to protest in earnest.

"But, dude, you already said that it was all in self-defense!"

"Yes, it was, but you almost killed a man, and we do not take kindly to this kind of violence on the island. So do not think of coming back to Cebu in the near future. If I were you, I would not consider the Philippines in any of your upcoming travel plans!"

I looked at Shu Shu knowing that the Philippines was a big part of our company goals.

"But Manny, we need this for our business," I pleaded.

"Your business is not worth your life!" he exclaimed. "Now, both of you hand over your room keys and your passports."

We handed Manny our keys and passports as his words resonated in my head. I mentally began to play back the tapes of what happened tonight. I know Shu Shu must have been upset that we didn't get to that marble limestone or complete our mission. But he didn't show any remorse, if anything occasional laughter erupted from where he sat. He appeared to be pumped by the action of the evening and, of course, happy to be alive.

Manny made a quick call to Señor Gabriel, who refused to talk with us. I thought about making a call to Mei Mei but couldn't find my cell phone anywhere on my body. Manny hung up, then picked up the police radio and did a lot of explaining as he shouted into the receiver. After his fiery rebuke, Manny shoved the earpiece back in its cradle. He turned around to look at the two sorry foreigners in his back seat. He shook his head in disbelief, and then started to laugh. This put me at ease as he cranked up the music, lit another joint, handed it to me and sped us to the Air Base.

I opened the window, took a long hit of the joint, stuck my head out like a dog and breathed in the hot, humid night's air. I smiled a shit eating grin and for the first time felt "happy" to be alive.

23

Teen Age Riot, *Long Island, NY—circa 1981*

I am convinced there are several distinct times and places when innocence crumbles, slapping you into a new reality.

The first, of course, is childbirth. The second usually comes around puberty, and that collides with Bar Mitzvah time when you become an adult in the eyes of God.

As children we were trained for this moment for years, being sent to Hebrew School, where we learned to read (and sing) from the Torah and then celebrated like we were the Mashiach. Sure, learning to read from the Torah and then singing it in front of everyone you knew took nerve. I also get the historical significance of a life event signifying your transformation into a man (or woman). But really, we were not even close to being adults. We were just awkward, pubescent teens, trying to understand what was happening with our bodies, our voices and confused with new emotions and emerging sexuality.

Our parents were the "real" adults in the room and this "rite of passage," became just another excuse to throw a big party. The only difference this time was that our parents felt at ease to celebrate with their kids. Not that we were doing the same type of partying, but we were doing it completely visible to one another. For many, it was the first time seeing their parents for what they were; out of control adult children.

I am not complaining about the party, our folks tried their best to make it about us. It's just that maybe a full-blown vodka bar, complete with ice sculptures, wasn't necessarily something thirteen-year-olds needed to be around. Unless, of course, we were free to sample the goods. After all, most of us had been around vodka our entire lives. And my family certainly held the torch for the Russian liquor.

We were young teens copying our parental role models by learning to take liberties at the vodka bar. I would like to believe that my friends and I became quite the esteemed drinkers as these vodka bars became standard fare at many of our Bar Mitzvah's. Sometimes we were enticed even further to develop our taste for the "finer life," when the vodka over ice was paired and served with cocktail shrimp platters. I would like to take this opportunity to thank my parents for such lovely tutelage, as we became astute students of this vodka and shrimp cocktail grouping.

As the weekend festivities intensified, we quickly learned to steal the full shot glasses from the sculpture bar, hide them in our oversized suits, and then sneak into the men's room where we'd shoot them down our throats with intensity. It didn't take much for us to feel the burn, cough, and get woozy. Learning how to drink at these parties was a bonding experience amongst my friends. And while drinking in the bathroom had its advantages regarding our inexperienced livers, it wasn't necessarily the best hiding spot.

We quickly noticed that our parents also liked to congregate in the bathrooms. It seemed they spent a lot of time in those stalls, snorting, coughing and blowing their noses. We tried to keep it quiet, hiding our vice from the adults in what appeared to be their secret sanctuary as well. We might have felt guilty, but they never paid us much attention, they were quick to snort, wipe their noses, and leave without saying a word. It was as if they were afraid of being busted by us as well.

We didn't want to be around them either, so we quickly learned to take our drinking outdoors to the parking lot. This usually happened around dinner time when all the adults appeared to be eating. The live band on stage was on "lounge mode," and everyone seemed to be content with their meals. This is when we left the ballroom, took our shot glasses, cigarette butts, lighters, bravado, and marched outside for some much needed fresh air.

We were usually trashed by then, but that was nothing in comparison to the adults. As it turned out, they were also quick to use this down time to move outdoors where we would find them huddled around smoking joints and coughing some more. It felt like we could not escape them and maybe they felt the same since they always scattered like mice when we approached. Thankfully, they never seemed to care what we were doing outside. Instead, they were quick to take a few more tokes, extinguish their smokes, and move inside to celebrate some more. Occasionally, we were lucky enough to find half-extinguished joints smoldering in the parking lot. We took them and added them to our treasure trove. This is when things got interesting!

Our newly adult sexual urges were on eleven and that meant no female was off limits. We were just beginning to explore our sexuality, the drugs and the alcohol only added gasoline to our proverbial fire. It was not uncommon back then to break out into full-blown make out sessions with any of the girls who joined in our debauchery. Sometimes they were willing accomplices and other times it took a lot of coercing. We all learned that the drugs and liquor certainly helped ease the tension. Either way, we all were on a sexual binge and easily became *orgasm addicts*. It was not uncommon for many of us to hit on any of the girls who were partying with us. Whether drunk or stoned, everyone seemed to end up on the grass, kissing and groping each other.

Those times of sexual exploration were nothing compared to what we all encountered on the "Bar Mitzvah bus." Those bus rides (to and from) the party were something special and a big part of our precocious puberty conquests. I'd like to think this phenomenon was regional just to New York. *God, I hope so*. Our parents often rented school busses as a convenient way to *safely* get us kids to the party. Considering our parents partying behavior, quite frankly, they could have used busses themselves. But we were protected from them with a hired driver in a bus full of sex-crazed, often drunk and stoned-out minors. In reality, we needed to be protected from ourselves, as it was here that many of us learned how to french kiss, copped our first feels, and felt confusion between sexual exploration and aggression.

The bus was not safe for those that were timid to our gang-like mentality. But there was really nothing you could do about it, as we were bussed almost every weekend of our entire thirteenth year of life. We were without adult chaperones and the more we practiced our sexual behavior, the more we looked forward to these bus rides. We were at an impressionable age and thought we were being like the drug addict adults we admired. Therefore, we carried on like a pack of substance induced wild animals in heat.

It took one night, for reality to slap us back into the children we so desperately didn't want to be. We were partying at a Bar Mitzvah in New York City. This was generally more exclusive than the celebration we usually had on Long Island. That meant a fancier affair with more chances to secretly score drinks, drugs, and more time with the ladies. It was a large party at some supper club on the Upper East Side. The parents were wealthy, connected, and really wanted this celebration to show off in front of their friends, family, and business partners. There was a large band playing classic disco and *Le Clique* hired to entertain us kids. *Le Clique* was an entertainment ensemble the wealthy hired to dance at Bar/Bat Mitzvahs. They were outlandishly dressed in costumes, used props, and basically got the party going in an outlandish frenzy.

The party ended late into the evening, and as always, we were trashed. The Bar Mitzvah bus this time was a rented motorcoach, outlandishly luxurious and parked around the corner from the affair. We were instructed by the adults to walk double file to the neon lit charter bus, as this was Manhattan and not as "safe" as our suburban neighborhoods.

We proceeded our march around the corner and as we approached the bus, we heard a woman across the street as she started to scream, "for help!" We all stopped and turned to look at the scene as it unfolded. The screaming woman was dressed in a fur, high heels, tight mini skirt and had just been punched in the face by a very large man. We all stood in shock as this was something we had never seen before. The beating continued as the man pushed, screamed and continued to slap the woman around. It was frightening, but at the same time, I felt suddenly exhilarated by the violence. Instinctively, I started running in her direction, away from the bus line. I am not sure what overcame me, but I don't think it was out of bravery. Rather, I genuinely thought this man would stop beating her if he saw us kids running over.

I screamed for my friends, "to follow me" and then started yelling at the guy to, "stop hitting her!"

He paid me no attention and by the time I crossed the street, he had the woman pinned against an iron fence, continuing to slap her bloody face. I imagined that my friends were closing in behind me, when I decided to jump on his back.

He didn't expect this inconvenience, moved quickly, grabbing me off him and tossing me to the ground. I sat there for a moment, feeling pain in my shoulder. I looked desperately at my friends for help, but they remained across the street frozen with fear.

Then the man lifted me clear off the ground with one hand. The woman started screaming at him as blood ran out of her mouth. I noticed one of her eyes was swollen shut. This is when he delivered an open handed palm strike me to the center of my face. I was then thrown against the iron fence and crumbled to the ground as my legs offered me no balance.

I saw stars for the first time in my life as I gasped for air. The world started to spin out of control and I threw up all over myself. I was struggling to breath as the puke and blood now soiled my Bar Mitzvah suit. The man quickly grabbed the woman and they both bolted around the corner and out of sight.

The girls across the street started screaming for "help!" as my boys finally made it over to offer me assistance. In a wave of extreme dizziness, I felt my eyes closing and the world went dark.

When the ambulance arrived, they revived me with smelling salts, placed a butterfly bandage and a pack of ice over my nose. The police were talking to the parents who threw the party. I heard the words "pimp" and "john" and struggled to understand what they were talking about. The police also questioned the parents as to the obvious intoxication of us minors. They seemed to be more concerned with that than the woman I was trying to help, and the beating I took.

It turned out that my nose was not broken, just bloody. After a brief medical check inside the ambulance, I was escorted back to the plush Bar Mitzvah bus with a taped-up nose and a mouthful of Tylenol. I had the beginnings of a black eye and a monster headache. After some more conversations among the police and the adults, my parents were notified of what happened because the cops thought I might be concussed.

I sat alone in the front seat of that decked out bus with an ice pack and a sore face. My friends and those around me were all unusually quiet. Instead of our usual celebration of pubescent proclivity, we were all sullen and confused. I must have been in a bit of shock, as I just couldn't understand how an adult could hit a kid like that. It just didn't seem possible in my once-sheltered world. Even worse, I felt like my boys all seemed to have let me down. They didn't have my back when I needed them. I felt extremely alone and confused by the violence. It was the first time I was physically assaulted by an adult and unfortunately, not the last.

24

Give Me the Cure, *Dongguan City, China—circa 2003*

My ears finally stopped ringing as my eyes opened and began to refocus again.

I lifted my head and saw Shu Shu carefully dressing the dead girl back into her clothes. I still had the SIM card in my hand and after a few minutes fumbling with my phone, I inserted the chip and re-booted it. Dr. Dave seemed to be missing, but then crashed through the front door, carrying an army-green wool blanket and two large rolls of shrink-wrap. I recognized the blanket from the dorm rooms at the factory. Sometimes, I crashed at the worker's dorm when we all got too drunk for anyone to drive me back to the hotel.

Dr. Dave spread the woven blanket beside the girl. He had become a very instrumental cog in our wheel of business success as Shu Shu's protector or enforcer, depending on the circumstances. In a corrupt China, with factories filled with raw materials (and cash), you needed all the muscle you could afford. The factory workers knew all about Dr. Dave's reputation. Hell, it seemed everyone in this city knew about him, and that underlying fear kept things working as they should.

Dr. Dave once told me, "He knew how to break every bone in the human body." He also said, "He was a healer and could then mend those broken bones with his bare hands." This skill set came in handy in a devious sort of way as Dr. Dave literally ruled with an iron fist. I envied him for this, admitting that I always wanted to see him do that—break bones and then heal them with the threat of re-breaking them again... vicious.

But there were other strange powers Dr. Dave claimed to have, and with the help of a lot of Baijiu (rice wine), he was quick to share them with me. One night, I remember him telling us that he could "tell how horny a girl was by feeling her nose." In addition, he claimed, "their noses would also reveal whether they had recently had sex, if they liked sex, and how good they were at it." I wasn't sure about this claim but did not refute it. Clearly, Dr. Dave did a lot of nose checking back in those days.

Perhaps the greatest lesson Dr. Dave ever taught me was to judge a woman's grooming habits by how she treats her eyebrows. The theory went that the well-manicured eyebrow usually meant the same for her underarms and, even more importantly, her bush (or lack thereof). The logic made perfect sense—that a correlation between a thin eyebrow and personal grooming habits existed. This was a country where the carpet matched the drapes! Even though. China was years behind in first world "body scaping," I often caught myself staring first at the eyebrows of any Chinese woman that I met. This included factory workers or any female on the street, anywhere—it was enough to drive any man nuts. Especially one (like myself) with full blown OCD.

It was also Dr. Dave who reinforced the finer points of admiring the different types of Chinese women. He told me, "That northern woman tended to be taller, with pale complexions, and were revered among Chinese men for their soft skin. While their relatives from the southern Canton region were known to be smaller, darker, and would eat anything that moved (except cars). He was most fond of the Western Sichuan girls, where he claimed that, they were the "spiciest, most adventurous, and had fiery tempers to match their appetites."

Regardless of where their families were from, all Chinese working girls shared one thing in common—they enjoyed drinking and mastered in getting you drunk. They also loved to sing karaoke songs, usually had beautiful voices, and even though the sappy songs they chose could make any Western male want to shoot himself, Dr. Dave (being the master he was) could outdrink and out sing any one of them!

This very "esteemed" doctor was now wrapping the dead corpse tightly in the green blanket. He saw me watching him and threw me the shrink-wrap. I caught it, stood up, and made my way over to the bed. I knew exactly what he wanted me to do, so I began to wrap the plastic shrink over the blanketed body. I lifted the body up as I wrapped her in plastic, starting head to toe, then back up to the head again. I was amazed at how heavy this lifeless little girl was as I wrapped her tighter and tighter. She wouldn't be able to move, even if she were alive.

I took one last look before cutting the shrink-wrap with my teeth and lying her head carefully back on the pillow. Her pale face was deformed under the plastic and reminded me of that horrific painting, *The Scream*. I stared at death, clenched my fists, and felt oddly sickened. This was someone's daughter, or sister or best friend. I thought of my own family and the guilt washed over me like a storm darkening my already foul mood. I was mortified and ashamed by my fear as I saw fatality staring back at me. My life has certainly been filled with trauma and I wanted to scream back at the *horror of it all*!

25

Back Against the Wall, *Long Island, NY—circa 1982*

With our Bar Mitzvahs now completed, we were congratulated for being adults, and then bussed to Middle School across the proverbial "railroad tracks" to the northern part of our suburban town.

The north was the non-Jewish section and, just like our ancestors, we had no choice but to ride together into antisemitic hell like those described in history books. We were the proud graduates of various Long Island Hebrew Schools where we learned about hate and were taught to "never forget" the Holocaust. We were told that Jewish persecution should have ended with the defeat of the Germans in WWII. Only they forgot to inform us that, Jews were always hated, and this hate would never stop. It didn't matter where you lived as there was always a Jew hater in the crowd, and the shocking news is that they were closer than you thought. In our case (like a bad cliché), they congregated just north of the town's railroad station. There in that enclave lived a special breed of Jew haters. They were often the blue-collar workers our parents called to fix the toilets or paint their houses. We kept them busy, flush with work that our fathers did not know how to do or didn't have time to be bothered with. Accordingly, *the haters* came south to our big houses to find work, and what they found was comfortable wealth and an air of elitism. And for this, they resented us!

When middle school started, the antisemitism took us all by surprise. We grew up a sheltered bunch, thinking everyone knew the difference between right and wrong. We were wide-eyed optimists and looked forward to middle school. I remember the excitement as we marched off those school buses with our new haircuts, stone washed Edwin blue jeans, and white Reebok sneakers. I remember smiling at what looked like an angry mob of older kids in white tank tops with ripped jeans and dirty sneakers. I assumed they were older because they were physically larger than us and sported facial hair. These were our northern counterparts, and they were not happy to see us "*Southern Hebes.*" Our silly grins were quickly extinguished as they leered at us and started spitting venom our way. We were greeted with insults as they spat the word "*Jew*"in our direction. Nothing can prepare you for the first time you are called that "*J*"word! Your first reaction is to look around at who they could be directing this hatred towards. Only to realize that it was no one in particular; instead, it was all of us! No one taught us how to deal with such hatred. How to react to it? And finally, what to do once you realized there was also no one to protect you from this antisemitic hate.

There was no safety in this middle school, as we were terrorized daily. Suddenly benign places of congregation such as hallways, the cafeteria, and locker rooms became spaces for physical and mental abuse. Even more shocking was that this level of hatred was not hidden from the adults, our teachers, the guidance counselors, and our parents. The beatings were celebrated by our northern brothers and done at almost any time and any*where*. My friends and I were bullied into submission, while the faculty and our own families turned a blind eye. I remember feeling that those in charge perpetuated this, like we were all getting what we deserved. After all, we were the spoiled "bagel benders" from the south who never had anything to worry about! Until now...

We came home from those first weeks of school with visible bruises on our bodies and invisible scars to our egos. It was the first time for many of us to be abused like this. We panicked, cried in shame, and tried to tell our parents about this horror show. They did nothing to help us. They either didn't believe this could happen in a public school or they were too busy with their own lives to be bothered by their whining children. Either way we found ourselves alone with our misery and our bond together became that of survival.

The adults failed to protect us and once again let us down when we needed them the most. Even when we showed them our bruises and told of our brushes with terror, they belittled our experiences and looked the other way. We were flat-out fucked for the first time in our young lives. Without a plan to save ourselves, we thought it would be important to try and at least win over the admiration of these Jew haters. To do this, we would have no choice but to join them at their own game. And that game was football.

For this reason, the bravest (or dumbest) of us tried out for the regaled team. It appeared that football *up north* was celebrated as strictly being played (and enjoyed) only by the gentiles. Jews, while having every right to try out for the team, were certainly not welcomed. However, we wanted to win over this violent club, and were determined to win the respect of these modern-day Nazi's, boy, were we delusional!

During tryouts where we were singled out, used as blocking or tackling dummies, we were targeted, beat on, and exercised to physical exhaustion. At the end of a vicious hell week of being yelled at and humiliated, only my friend Drew and I made the cut joining the Varsity team. I might have been the physically stronger Jewish boy having owned my own weightlifting set, but Drew was a natural competitor. He was fast, smart, and blessed with great athleticism. In *the south* Drew was something of a phenome, probably the best sportsperson we had, especially on the basketball court. But this was no B-ball court; it was a field of brutality where we had to constantly prove our manhood. Drew had speed, coordination, but most of all, he could also throw the ball in a perfect tight spiral. He would hit receivers with a perfectly thrown ball, while I could take a hit and if permitted, would be quick to give one back. This got us noticed and instead of building kinship, we ended up infuriating the others. They could not deal with our physical prowess and in return, they would try desperately to get us to quit.

Our athleticism also caught the attention of the coach, who called us into his office before practice one blustery Fall afternoon. The coach was a crusty ex-marine with crude tattoos on his forearms and a

close-cropped crew cut. He made no bones about letting us know that even though we made the team, we were "not welcomed on the team!" And, unless we liked punishment, we should "probably quit while we still had our health." Of course, Drew and I, having gone this far, feigned bravado and refused to give up.

"Well, boys, you are a stubborn bunch," the coach said, implying our collective Judaism. "If you are to remain on this team, then it is important to remember, there is only one person in charge here and that is me!"

With that, he pointed at a sign affixed on the wall next to a large crucifix and asked us to read it aloud. It said:

Rule #1: The coach is always right.

Rule #2: When in doubt, refer to Rule #1.

Posted next to those rules were framed pictures of what appeared to be the coach in his high school football days, as well as some military photos of him dressed like a soldier. Coach promptly excused our presence by telling us, "*Boys* to go back and join the other *men* in the locker room to suit up for practice." We were so excited by making the team that we did not notice the gang of manly boys standing intimidatingly outside the coach's office. They stared at us with absolute hatred as we cruised past them and into the locker room.

It should have come as no surprise that the first day of practice would go down in history as our last. The practice was designed to separate the *men* from the *boys* and, since we were the only *boys* on the field, most of the punishment was directed at us. The sadistic coach seemed to have fun putting me and Drew in tackling scenarios, where the others could practice inflicting maximum damage on our unsuspecting bodies. We practiced getting hit; we ran more than most; we were chased, tackled and ran some more. In the end, we were winded and hurt but not broken by the unusual punishment directed to single us out. Finally, when the whistle blew to end practice, we limped to the locker room to undress, change, and rest our sore bodies.

That is when we discovered just how cruel the world could be. The coach entered, slamming the door shut and demanding silence from the team. He yelled with such violence that spittle flew from his pit bull mouth. Most of this venom was directed at us the *boys from the south* that his *men* on the team could not break. He was furious at them and embarrassed for their families. He made no bones about being disgusted about having to let us join his prestigious team. With that, he rubbed salt in their wounds by reminding them of Drew's blazing speed, his accurate arm and then my recapped my physical endurance. He painted a picture of us taking their starting positions, embarrassing their friends and families by opening the door for more *southern boys* to take over their team. With that, he spit tobacco on the floor and left us alone in the locker room.

Drew and I stared at each other in silence as we knew that we were in big trouble. It took less than a minute before the entire team pounced on us, kicking and striking us madly. We had no time and no strength left to defend ourselves. Instinctively, I curled into a ball to protect my face and midsection. As quick as it started, my beating suddenly stopped as I heard Drew wail in fear. The others still held me pinned down as Drew was lifted from the pile and thrown against the lockers. They held his arms and legs in place while the others took turns wildly throwing a football against his defenseless body.

"Take that, you faggot quarterback!" they screamed as the ball bashed his midsection repeatedly. He was screaming for them to "stop," but this just incited the pack more. It wasn't until he stopped screaming and started sobbing that they finally stopped the attack. They released him as his bruised body (and ego) fell mercilessly to the floor. I tried to find the strength to escape their grip and fight back, but quickly felt a cold blade of steel against my throat.

I immediately stopped, wild-eyed, and afraid for my life while voices called for the "Jew pig to be still or be gutted!"

What I saw next cannot be explained without absolute horror and disbelief.

Drew, now curled up in his own ball on the floor, was forcefully being undressed by the others. They pulled, grabbed, and ripped his football pants off. By the time they got his underpants down, the room was in raucous laughter, making fun of his small, circumcised "Jew dick."

I frantically tried to resist the blade. I wanted to help but I was scared, as the knife pierced through my skin and blood began trickling down my neck. I remained absolutely still fearing for my life as poor Drew got flipped onto his belly. The savages continued retraining his arms and legs as he bellowed in pain and fear. I thought we would be rescued any moment by the coach. After all, he was an adult...

No one came to our rescue and the scene only got more incomprehensible as the terror raged on. In an instant, one of our *teammates* grabbed an orange practice cone and, with the shaft down, began to assault Drew's ass with it. Drew screamed something horrible as blood now stained the rubber orange cone. It was too much to watch and I couldn't bear to hear him scream like that. I tried to close my eyes and wish it all away, but they would not stop. He screamed and sobbed as I witnessed the mob taking their turns sodomizing Drew with that practice cone.

I needed to do something to get them to stop and gave one last scream for the coach's help but was quickly punched in the face by the assailant with the knife. I felt woozy with pain and then absolute terror as my body was lifted off the floor and shoved into the nearest full-size locker. The door immediately shut out all light and I was left in the dark, feeling completely helpless. I heard the mob yelling at Drew to remain still. Then they directed their rage at me kicking at the locker I was trapped in. I heard voices instructing me to, "never tell anyone what happened here, or you will be killed!"

Then that same knife that held me by the throat was forcefully pushed through the metal locker, just missing the top of my head. My feet gave way as I crashed to the bottom of the locker, sobbing in fear. The knife made a few more attempts to get at me but the blade was not long enough. So, the kicking continued rattling the metal cage with forceful blows.

I closed my eyes wondering what we did to deserve this abuse. After a period of time the kicking stopped, and their loud talking became whispers mixed with laughing. Soon, the mockery stopped and I hoped that meant that they finally left the locker room.

I sat on the bottom of that cold, smelly locker for what felt like hours. By now, I could clearly assume that they had left us since the only thing I could hear was Drew sobbing quietly in the near distance. I summoned whatever courage I had left to open the door and help my friend. What I saw next, I would never be able to unsee.

When my eyes adjusted to the blinding light, I saw Drew naked, crumpled on the floor and sobbing in shock. I made my way cautiously to my friend, bent down to hold and comfort him. He pushed me away at first, but I held him tighter, and eventually he held me back. We both lied there in each other's embrace and sobbed like the victims we now were.

I knew that this day would haunt and change me forever. I swore at that moment to never be the victim again, and promised Drew I would never repeat what happened to him. Not to anyone. His secret was safe with me. I also promised him vengeance. But Drew never came back to school the next day and, shortly afterwards, his family moved far away from this town. I never got a chance to say goodbye, apologize for what happened to him, or even avenge his abuse. Drew might have moved out of my life, but he was never forgotten.

As for me, I kept my mouth shut, quit the team and allowed that rage to turn inward into bottled violence. I was angry at everyone, and I was ready to pop off at any moment. I needed to find somewhere to channel this wrath. I wanted revenge and, more importantly, to find someone to teach me to fight. I didn't want any self-defense *karate* bullshit. I was looking for pure offense. I wanted to learn how to kill with my bare hands. I was looking for ferocity, and I was determined to find a martial arts teacher who would show me how to become a vicious opponent.

I was looking for an assassin.

26

Hard Times, *Long Island—circa 1984*

Boaz learned how to fight, first as a necessity and later as sport.

He was born just inside the West Bank security wall that separated Israel from Palestine. His father was a commander in the Israeli Defense Forces (IDF). Boaz spent his childhood around elite soldiers and lot of time with his dad. He learned at a very young age how to defend himself, as the area where he lived in Israel was under constant attack.

Boaz was a good student and took his Torah studies very seriously. He was big for his age, and his height gave him a physical advantage over the other boys. Although socially shy, it was competing against his peers that he enjoyed the most. And at an early age, he studied marksmanship with his father who was also a sniper. Boaz learned from him how to control his breath, steady his nerves, and shoot the *Galil rifle* like a pro. He also mastered the calculated art of stripping down and cleaning the internal components of various guns and assault rifles. It was not uncommon for the men in his father's regime to leave their weapons with Boaz for a super tune-up and field strip cleaning. He would earn some shekels doing this and saved every last cent.

As part of the compulsory service to Israel, all children learned the art of Krav Maga's style of *hand-to-hand combat* when entering the military. It was Krav Maga that allowed Boaz's talents to really flourish. It did not take long for his father (and others) to see that Boaz had a natural talent for this brutal form of self-preservation. At sixteen, he was sent to learn Krav Maga from infamous commando trainers in the esteemed Israel Border Police.

There he learned the essential skills of disarming, maiming, and killing a man with his bare hands, or using a blade along with various firearms. This style of self-preservation was quick, brutal, without rules, and suited Boaz just fine. He loved the history of its humble beginnings, from founder Imi Lichtenfeld to its current incarnations, being perfected through many years of actual use. It was by far the most effective means of self-defense and violence prevention. Krav Maga provided Jews the self-defense tools needed to deal with ruthless enemies hell-bent on killing its people and destroying Israel as a country.

It did not take long for Boaz to win multiple Krav Maga competitions and be recognized by Israel's elite soldiers, *The Sayeret Matkal*. It was in the Sayeret that Boaz excelled at completing top-secret commando and recognizance missions deep behind enemy lines. In homage to the British SAS and the US Delta Force, the unit's motto is, "Who Dares, Wins!" (מי שמעז - מנצח)

Boaz was always practicing and would often challenge other foreigners to hand-to-hand combat contests. He was on a quest to learn what skills others had as he tried to perfect his deadly art. He particularly enjoyed studying various Asian martial art styles including Aikido, Judo, Karate and the philosophy behind them. Boaz also became a leader in tactical knife fighting and with all this experience he turned his attention to becoming a teacher.

He considered it his rightful duty to train other Jewish children how to protect themselves. After many years of teaching Traditional Krav Maga (TKM), he set his sights on opening a school in America. He understood the importance of Jewish preservation and knew there would be plenty of Jewish students in New York who needed his expertise.

As a fully decorated soldier and a master of combat, Boaz set his sights on Long Island. He learned that the U.S. was not so different from Israel with respect to the deep-seated pockets of hatred and anti-Semitism—especially from those living beside large concentrations of affluent

Jewish families. Where there were Jews, there was animosity among their neighbors. This would never change, and the large Jewish population in Long Island seemed like the perfect place to teach the deadly Israeli martial art. Boaz firmly believed that Jewish survival depended on being able to protect oneself. He was determined to teach the Long Island Jews to, *"never forget!"* (לעולם אל תשכח) that they were targets of hate and *always* would be.

When Boaz opened the first Krav Maga School in Long Island, My Grandfather Butch drove me over to meet the Israeli self-defense master. Apparently, they must have talked about me before hand, because upon my arrival, I was greeted with a stern, "Shalom," and handed an outfit consisting of camouflage fatigues and black combat boots. I immediately looked at my grandfather who gave me a wink and a nod of his head. He then took Boaz aside for a private conversation, shook his hand and went outside for a smoke.

The first class took me by surprise as I was uncomfortable training in the stiff fatigues and new boots. Boaz was also not the kind of teacher who supported his students with flowery praise or pats on the back. He was ruthless, tough, and had a very thick Israeli accent. In broken English, he made no bones about the violence that must be learned, and he vowed to teach it to us until it became *second nature.*

He explained Krav Maga to us as, *"emphasized aggression designed to be flexible to real life threatening scenarios."* He continued to defend that, *"we would learn the primal reaction to ending an attack, more fierce than other practiced forms of martial arts or katas."*

Therefore, we often trained outside in the cold or inside with the heat blasting. Sometimes we were blindfolded and other times we trained in full protective gear to simulate what it was like be hit with bats, pipes, and knives. Sometimes we even changed into civilian clothes to train as he screamed mostly in Hebrew, teaching us how to blind, break, and kill opponents. The most perfect memories of my post-teenage years were spent in that dojo. The violence for me was like a drug, similar to punk rock, I was addicted to the frenzy, the adrenaline and the ferocity.

When it was time to graduate to the next level, Boaz felt confident enough to award us with our own Israeli commando knives. These were not fixed-blade knives but folded smoothly with ambidextrous clips to hold in either front pocket of our pants.

We were trained with both hands to redirect, control, attach and disarm with our knife fighting. Boaz congratulated us and told us it was now our duty to carry these knives and protect our Jewish brethren. Both in the real world and of course, in his class.

"Who dares, wins!" (המעז מנצח) he would have us repeat with blades open.

He was convinced that this knife was necessary not only to save our lives but also to disarm and dismantle a threat in any situation. We trained incessantly with those blades, learning with precision and speed to attack the opposition's weaknesses. This meant targeting critical soft-flesh spots, such as arteries, ligaments, neck tissue and, of course, the human heart. We learned to inflict pain so great (and so fast) that it would stop an attacker in his tracks.

With the knife fighting under my belt, Boaz decided it was time to teach his advanced students in handgun training. This not only included disarm techniques that we had practiced until second nature, especially under realistic high stress situations. The training also taught us the necessary skills of redirecting the line of fire, control of the weapon, counterattacks and target shooting. Boaz also found it necessary to instruct the very best of us in more advanced tactical firearms training. This incorporated not only respect for the weapon, how to dismantle for safety but also included the fundamentals of firearm proficiency and marksmanship. When we advanced from dryfire to live ammunition, would often go to the private gun range in Hempstead, where the local police practiced and honed their skills. Boaz was highly respected among our *brothers and sisters in blue* and was often invited to instruct them on the fundamentals of tactical Krav Maga. They all respected Boaz and by proxy took interest in his students, especially me, who turned out to be quite the marksman. I would often accompany him as his assistant when he trained local law enforcement and government agents.

With this new confidence and skill, I was no longer afraid of my classmates from the north. Instead of fear, I was busy working on my body, my killing skills, and my aggression. I became infatuated with punk rock and found its violence a perfect companion. I shaved my head and adorned a pair of 1460, eight-eye, cherry-red Doc Martens boots that I kept spit shined like I was in the military. I walked with a well-deserved swagger and a scowl. My confidence must have been apparent because I was never bothered again. Word got around that I was training to be an Israeli assassin. There was even rumor (started by me) of my wanting to go to Israel to join the army. This was true, and life seemed to finally be getting easier for me. Especially since I was no longer afraid of it!

27

Minor Threat, *Long Island, NY—circa 1985*

The first time I used my new skills in hand-to-hand combat shocked me as much as my parents.

We were driving home from our Sunday night ritual of Chinese food (it's a NY *Jew* thing) when a red and white Ford F-150 pickup truck ran a stop sign and plowed into the side of our white BMW 325e Sedan. Time seemed to stop while we all processed what just happened. I quickly scanned my family to make sure everyone was okay. My brother started to cry as my mom checked him over for injuries. I quickly looked out the window and saw a bearded man jump out of his truck as he checked out the damage to his front bumper and hood. After a swift examination of his truck, he came threateningly toward our car, screaming all sorts of obscenities at us.

My dad's instincts were to quickly lock the doors but mine were faster. I immediately jumped out of the car and quickly approached the sizeable man. Amazingly, I had no hesitation and, in my head, knew exactly what to do. I was also confident how this was going to end. I was on autopilot now as my hands shot up in the air in a posture that resembled defeat.

"Kid, get in the fucking car," the guy said. "I want to speak with your father!"

I kept apologizing to the man and confusing him with my non-confrontational body language. He reached out to grab me—after all, I was just some teenage kid. I instinctively twisted my left foot counterclockwise, coiled my hips and unloaded a right roundhouse kick to the man's right knee. It was a thunderous blow that struck his knee with an audible *crack*. He never expected the blow. How could he?

The man yelped falling on his other knee as I cupped my hands and struck both his ears with intense strength. Before he could react, I grabbed the back of the man's head, forcefully directing his face to hit the top of my head. This ferocious head butt instantly broke his nose, spraying blood in my hair. With one hand still holding the back of his head, I sent my other elbow into the crux of his neck. This devastating blow was used to stop the oxygen from going to his head, and momentarily short-circuited his brain.

The man was in shock by my forceful, deliberate blows. He was delirious with confusion and pain. I never let up and rejoined my other hand behind his head, holding him tight to my shoulders. He wanted to go down; he wanted this to end... but I was not done with him yet.

Holding him upright took the strength out of me as I sent continuous knees into both sides of the soft flesh around his ribs. I amassed whatever training I had left and pulled him around in the opposite direction, while I continued to deliver overwhelming blows with my knees. This kept him off balance and in a constant state of surprise. He was getting heavier to hold to my shoulder and exhaustedly I grabbed his beard with my left hand. I sent my right elbow up to hit him with an upper cut under his chin and then let him collapse to the floor. His face took most of that fall and he was moaning loudly.

Convinced this was now over, I looked back at my family. There were safely locked inside the car, motionless, with shock on their faces. My dad had his Motorola 8000x mobile phone in his hand and I could tell they were trying to process what they had just seen. It was evident they did not recognize their son anymore. Instead, I had transformed into some sort of demon, covered in blood and smiling. I waved to them and then heard the man trying to get up. He was moaning and spat blood in my direction.

"Fuck you, kid," is all I heard.

I gave my folks the "one minute" sign, turned to the prone man, and forcefully stomped on the back of his right ankle. Again, I hit pay dirt as the bearded man began to howl in pain, clutching his right foot.

I calmly walked back to my parent's car, took off my shirt to wipe off the blood and knocked for them to unlock the door. This startled them some more. Once the door was opened, I casually got inside and slid next to my brother and took his hand. My mom asked, "if I was okay, and if I needed any help?" I did not say anything and just looked out the window at the man in the street. I felt justified and proud. My father must have felt emasculated since he didn't say anything to me. He jumped out of the car (now that it was safe), examined the damage, got back in, looked at me in surprise, shook his head and then peeled away from the scene.

The next few days were awkward at the house, we never discussed this incident again. As for me, I tasted violence, knew I was capable of it, and couldn't wait to share this story with Boaz. I also couldn't wait to tell my grandpa. I finally felt empowered for the first time in my life and this time the *price was right*!

28

I Love Livin' in the City, *New York City, NY—circa 1983*

I was fifteen the first time I saw someone die.

Ironically, it was at a punk rock show. Where else can a teenager die doing what they loved without anyone seeming to give a shit? *The Sex Pistols, Bad Brains, Dead Kennedys, Black Flag,* etc., were played on my Sony Hifi stereo every time I came home from school. I always made sure at 4:30 p.m. that my radio was tuned to 89.1FM, WNYU's (NY's college radio station) "The New Afternoon Show." I taped each episode on cassettes with religious fervor. On that station, I heard college music or *underground music* from all over the country. At this time, the only place to hear hardcore and new music was on that college radio station. Sure, we had Long Island's now infamous and defunct WLIR, but that was mostly weak *new wave* disco to me. I needed aggression and found it right in my backyard with New York's own infamous hardcore bands like *Murphy's Law, Cro-Mags, Sick of it All,* and the great *Agnostic Front.* Thankfully, WNYU also played evening hardcore programs like, "Crucial Chaos" and "Hellhole" to satisfy my musicophile angry self.

I even went so far as to buy a special external FM antenna from *Radio Shack* and installed it on my roof to make sure I picked up the college station's signal. Listening to punk music became my entire identity. I cut my hair into a mohawk, spiked it with Gelatin, hung suspenders from my ripped jeans and finally found an outlet for my intense teenage angst. I even pierced my own ears with safety pins and made my own clothes by destroying the ones my folks bought me. I was a walking advertisement for the *Salvation Army* and proudly marched through high school with my 10 eyelet oxblood Doc Marten boots.

The first punk concert I attended was *The Dead Kennedys* at Irving Plaza. I had all their albums, knew every song, and yet was completely unprepared for what I witnessed at that show. There were punks, skinheads, long hairs, and mods everywhere. When Jello Biafra, (the lead singer), finally arrived on stage, he greeted the crowd by spitting on the skinheads. The skinheads retaliated by storming the stage to attack the brazen singer. It was then that the music started, and pandemonium erupted on the dance floor turning it into a mosh pit. The skinheads began to slam dance, beating the long hairs out of the chaos they'd started. I never saw such brutal hostility as fists, elbows, feet, knees were flying everywhere. For me it was a beautiful sight, and I was instantly hooked...

Totally immersed in the viciousness, I bravely ran directly into the mosh pit, flailing my arms around like a madman. The loud music, heightened pace, muted screams, sweat, and violence were addicting, like a drug. I was pummeled, punched, then pulled from the pit, bloody and half-crazed. I just smiled, ignoring my injuries, and knew that I had finally found a home for my rage.

This experience quickly escalated into weekly trips from Long Island into the city for Sunday's, at CBGB's *all ages* "Hardcore Matinee." It was the one (and only) thing I looked forward to. By the time Friday came, I was jonesing for some mosh pit violence. The adrenaline rush from the brutal sounds, the oppressive crowds, the heat, and the physical viciousness was my drug of choice. By Sunday afternoon, I was a powder keg ready to blow, and on Monday after the chaos, I returned to school badly bruised but relaxed as a baby with a pacifier.

Every weekend, punk rock bands and punks alike would converge into Manhattan's "Alphabet City" for the Sunday matinee show. Some were local NYC bands, others were from DC, Boston, and the West Coast. Often, we would fight each other, proclaiming our allegiance to New York Hardcore. Even though punk hailed from the UK, we all felt a kinship to make it known that our local hardcore scene was also the best. This did not go over well with the LA hardcore bands, who brought an intensified violence and rage to the NY shows, that was fiercer than what we were used to. Even though we had our different scenes, secretly, I loved just about any punk music I could find, and this included a new crop of music hailing from the Midwest and the South.

One of those bands, whose show changed my life forever, was *The Meatmen*. On the day of the Meatmen show, I adorned my favorite ripped camouflage pants, white T-shirt, and plaid suspenders. I laced up my cherry red Doc Martens and headed to the Long Island Railroad train station for the big *"rotten"* apple. At this odd hour in the early afternoon, every punk who entered the train was headed to the same destination. We all sat holding back our nervous energy by drinking beer from paper bags and not paying attention to each other as the train slithered its way into the city like a venomous snake.

By the time The Meatmen hit the stage, the crowd was going wild with anticipation. A mosh pit immediately began to form as the band sang their single "Crippled Children Suck." I loved this song and immediately jumped in, swinging my arms and pumping my knees. The skinheads were spinning themselves around, slamming their bodies into anyone in their way and knocking to the floor those that dared to *"pogo dance!"*

Out of the corner of my eye, I saw a punk climbing up the wall of stacked Marshall amps. The crowd caught on and started to scream for the boy to jump. I braced myself, knowing I was in the middle of this slam dance and would most likely be one to help catch him. He climbed higher and with the crowd behind him, chose to then dive off the stack of speakers. Unfortunately, he was not the only thing to fall into the crowd. As he jumped, he accidentally knocked loose one of the large amps off the pile. The boy and the amp went crashing into the crowd below.

I remember the amp seemed to fall in slow motion as it crashed into to the dense crowd of people. The boy fell first into the mass of people and then the large amp followed, crushing his now limp body. Blood escaped from the corners of the amp as the boy's head seemed to absorb most of the impact. The dance floor became an instant scene of pandemonium as no one seemed to know what to do next. The loud music was still going and everyone around the boy was slipping in the gore. The band finally stopped, and the punks started screaming, "help" as they tripped over each other on the slick bloody floor.

The house lights came up and that is when the full extent of the panic set in. The boy's crushed carnage was smeared all over the dance floor. Dazed punks seemed to be staring at the bloody kid, whose feet stuck out of the amp, like the wicked witch's feet from the house at the end of *The Wizard of Oz*. Some of the punks were playing with the blood, while others panicked, falling over each other as they tried to flee the dance floor. I sat there stunned, starring at the bloodshed and the boy who was no longer moving. I turned to notice that I was not the only one gawking. It was surreal to see so much blood coming from under that amp knowing there was a crushed teenager's head somewhere in that mess.

I remember feeling thankful that it was not my brains splayed all over the floor. I took a deep breath, inhaling the noxious fumes of blood, sweat, and fear. I stared at it for a while until the bouncers forcefully pushed me and the crowd of punks toward the exit. I didn't know it then, but this would be the first of many times I would have a close call with death.

29

World Peace, *Dongguan City, China—circa 2001*

China's face to the world appeared to be disciplined and moral, but saving face was its true *nature*...

As previously mentioned, once a month, Shu Shu was obligated to entertain top government officials (and their friends) in the bustling town of Changping where his factory was situated. In return for an all-expenses-paid evening, he was allowed to work undisturbed and was sometimes aided by those officials, who would normally bribe him for apparently more than that one night would cost him. After all, that was the *price* of doing business as a "Honky" in Mainland China. I recall thinking it was like the *wild west* back then; you needed to watch your back as rules did not apply in this communist country where lawlessness was rampant. Some people needed *enticement* to look the other way, while others required a flat-out bribe to facilitate the heavy business we were pumping out of that town. There was a *price* to pay to receive the "special ROI" from those monthly dinner expenditures.

Shu Shu was quick to let me know that even though these dinners were important, he "despised them and the corrupt Chinese politicians who attended." These were the ones who abused their power, insisting on getting drunk (and crazy) on his dime. He would explain further that "these men were often illiterate and not worthy of their titles." Entitlements that they wore as a *badge of honor* were often bought, inherited, or taken. And unlike their educated (and free) Cantonese cousins, these communist officials were just a necessary nuisance to Shu Shu and our operation. He knew that we needed them and thus we had no choice but to oblige them in these monthly mandatory dinners.

I learned from Shu Shu that this event had the same "MO" every time. The corrupt bureaucrats would take advantage of him by inviting everyone they knew to a free night out, which involved drinking themselves to unconscious oblivion. The main purpose of these machinations was first to beat their *Hong Kong brother* down with incessant toasts and random games meant to induce alcohol poisoning upon him.

As I was about to find out, China was very much about this macho masculine mentality, which meant never turning down a toast or you risked the dreaded "losing face," which is the same as losing your self-respect. The plan for the evening was as simple as the men involved. The dinner was aimed at targeting the host to drink to excess, every time, until they gave up by becoming unconscious from being *overserved*. Saying, "No" to the crowd was not an option and that also meant you were responsible for paying the *price*... and the tab!

I quickly learned that toasting in China is referred to in Mandarin as, "ganbei" and is equivalent to our "cheers!" However, do not underestimate this as a pleasantry as this is more of a challenge because the more you "ganbei'd," the more respect you'd show. Therefore, it is impossible to turn down a drink, no matter how drunk you were, especially when the room is screaming at you to "ganbei!"

Luckily for Shu Shu, I was his wingman that night and he knew they would all be gunning for my submission. It was made clear that this would be my introduction to international relations with China, and they would stop at nothing to prove that I (and the USA) was weaker than them. Shu Shu explained that "most of these men never met an American before," so drinking with me would be "quite the experience for them" ... and me!

That evening we arrived at the crowded restaurant, which specialized in Peking duck, and were led to a large private room. When we entered, I was assaulted by the amount of thick cigarette smoke that wafted around me like a toxic cloud. The Chinese loved to smoke and eat at the same time. This disgusting habit, along with their random spitting on the floor, was something I never got used to. Hence, we coughed our way into the room, where I was introduced to two dozen uniformed military and policemen. They all stood up to greet me with shots of Chivas and chasers of warm Tsingtao beer.

I was warned and responded with my best, "ganbei, motherfuckers!"

At dinner, I sat around choking on Chinese cigarette smoke and toasting incessantly with the most powerful men in that corrupt industrial town. Like most meals those days in China, the food was inedible, indescribable, and certainly not like what we are used to in the states. But to *save face*, I tried to eat as much as I could handle, disgusting parts and all! I was also not one to back down from a challenge; it isn't in *my nature*, so confidently; I obliged them all by swallowing whatever was put in front of me. We might have struggled through a language barrier, but there was no denying they wanted me drunk and sick. They wanted to show *the American* a hard initiation into Chinese hospitality.

So, there we sat around a large circular table with a glass lazy Susan in the center and spun it with great intent to get me to eat whatever was being spun around. In between the unrecognizable *food* that was served were ashtrays full of cigarette butts, glasses of alcohol, and soy sauce in small dishes piled with steamed chicken feet. Underneath the spinning glass was a cigarette burned, dirty tablecloth, ceramic chopsticks, and packages of tissues that served as napkins.

I was an easy target, and this night, while things were quickly getting out of hand, I had still managed to stand my ground. I felt a strange sense of pride that this was not only about me, but also about Shu Shu and for the good of my country. While these little men of power smiled through their yellow-stained teeth, I gave them the pearly white smile of a healthy, competitive nation they were so quick to try and fuck with. I felt proud about my drinking abilities, as I had a lifetime of practice. At last, my familial alcoholism was being put to worthy use as it was good for business!

When the Chinese finally succumbed to my intensive competitive drinking habits, they decided to turn the evening up a notch and go after my other weakness—the ladies. It was decided by the spitting men, that the party would continue across the street to the closest (KTV) karaoke club.

Shu Shu paid the bill with cash in the form of a mound of dirty renminbi (RMB). Let me explain that the *dirty* part was only stating the obvious, the money was filthy, often creating a layer of dirt on your hands when you touched it. Drunkenly, the mess that was our party, held up traffic as everyone walked across the busy street to the KTV club. Once inside, the girls quickly lined up in their evening dresses, bowed and wished us, "Wangshang hao!" (Good evening). Shu Shu spoke to the head mommy in charge, since he was obligated to arrange for the largest VIP room that the KTV had to offer. The mommy was an older plump woman, who winked at me and then began to shout into her walkie talkie.

We were led up a gilded staircase to a huge, decadently furnished room with plush couches, low tables, mirrors, disco lights, and a dancing pole. It also held the largest flat screen TV and karaoke computer system that I have ever seen. The room even had its own bathrooms (no toilet paper) and a private balcony with more pockmarked stained couches and tinted windows.

There was absolutely no way a visitor to China could guess what these gaudy places looked like on the inside. All that was evident from the outside world was a giant cement building, like a windowless amphitheater that had fluttering neon "KTV" lights above the stadium-like parking lot. Since the night sky was full of these neon lights, you would have to be a local to know where the best ones were. And since I was with the most powerful men in town, you can bet that this party was in the best facility that the town had to offer. Yes, you guessed it, *shit* was about to begin.

First the mommy re-entered the room to say, "Ni Hao," (hello) to all the men and take their requests for the type of girls they were looking for. Then the warm beer arrived by the case and, of course, more bottles of brandy. Boys dressed in black uniforms placed fruit platters, nuts and ashtrays on the tables. They turned on the karaoke system and immediately, the smoking and singing began as sappy Chinese love songs were played at full volume. After a round of toasts, the mommy came back, yelling again in her walkie-talkie to bring in the girls.

The girls paraded in by the dozens until there was no room left for anyone to stand. They quickly introduced themselves (in Chinese) and mentioned what province they were from. The government men wasted no time in yielding their power to force the girls into a compulsory personal body inspection. The girls were harassed, teased, and required to show their nipples. Some were stripped of their sheer dresses and fondled against their will. Others started to protest and were commanded to leave the room, never to return. I began to feel even more uncomfortable than the girls as my anger quickly turned into rage. I saw Shu Shu looking at me with concern as I tried to *save face*, despite my repulsion for these men.

I felt pity for these young girls and disgusted by these low-life officials that I felt compelled to entertain. I have never witnessed such sexist barbarism as it dawned on me just how far away from home I really was. China was its own cruel fire breathing beast, and their customs made me feel more like a guilty *Gweillo* than ever before. I know I was a visitor in this strange land, where men forced women to follow their rules, but I was quickly losing my patience with this *saving face* bullshit. I could also tell that Shu Shu was feeling uncomfortable and embarrassed by the behavior of the men. To his credit (and experience) he acted quickly and chose four girls to sit with us in the corner table and play a harmless game of *dice*.

Playing *dice* in China is a skill everyone learns at a very young age. It is a lot like playing poker, with the loser having to drink excessive amounts of alcohol. There is no money involved, and the strategy is to guess what your neighbor has hidden and hope that your roll is higher than theirs. The girls sitting with us were very experienced dice players, they kept a *poker face* as we continued to lose. Our punishment was always to drink more as the girls continued their experienced onslaught of trickery and skill. They were *professionals* in every sense of the word, and the more we lost (and drank), the more commission (from the beer) they were earning from the club. In a way we were chivalrous, being happy to lose, even if that meant to extreme inebriation.

Across from us, the uniformed men were having a party of their own, wielding their power to further humiliate and embarrass the girls. The drunker they got, the worse the abuse became. I was losing my tolerance as their smiling rotten teeth, incessant smoking, and bad singing voices began to boil under my skin. I never had high respect for authority figures, and these men hiding behind their communist uniforms were no exception. As a result, I lost my cool... or *my face*... whatever.

I got up from our benign game of dice and approached the policeman sitting closest to me. He got my attention by holding down a young girl against her will to fondle her breasts. He was also threatening to burn her with his cigarette as she continued to scream in protest. The rest of his party was laughing and cheering him on. That's all it took for me to snap.

I knocked the beer out of his hands. It crashed to the ground, and I screamed a loud "FUCK YOU!" pointing my finger directly in his face. He must have understood this bit of English as he smiled at me and immediately walked across the room to where Shu Shu sat. He grabbed one of the girls I was sitting with off the couch and tore her blouse right off her body. The girl started to scream, hiding her nudity with her hands, while the rest of the room continued to laugh and encourage more of this rude behavior. Shu Shu stood up in protest, trying to diffuse the situation by quickly putting himself between me and the belligerent policeman. I thought I heard him say my name as he placed his hand on my shoulder, but I was already at the point of no return.

I lunged past Shu Shu towards the cop, who now held the naked girl up by her long black hair, exposing her nakedness. Without warning, I pounded my right fist into the soft part of his neck that held his ugly face. Before he could react, I followed with a left elbow uppercut that caught him under the jaw and sent him flying backwards against the wall. Suddenly, the singing stopped.

I turned my crazy *Gweillo* round eyes to meet the rest of the crowd. My fists were loaded for attack, as I placed my weight on my bent left leg, keeping my right foot light and ready to use. The first one to move was the oldest uniformed man in the crowd. He stood up rather swiftly for his age, knocked the glasses off the table, reached into his pocket and pointed a small .38 caliber revolver toward my face. He was not smiling a dirty teeth smile anymore. I checked the cylinder to see 5 brass slugs resting in the chamber.

Shu Shu stood in front of the gun and me and started talking fast in Chinese. The girls (and the mommy) began to scream as they left the room in a hurry. I opened my fists and raised my hands in a universal sign of defeat. That was when someone blindsided me with what I can only imagine was a wooden nightstick. I remember feeling my knees go weak as I hit the floor.

There was a lot of commotion, and many hands were grabbing at me. I heard Shu Shu continue to protest as the men shoved me to my feet and forcefully pushed me out the door, through the hall and down the stairwell. I felt blood coming from my right eye, was woozy, beyond drunk, and couldn't manage to stop them from manhandling me. I tried unsuccessfully to regain my composure by planting my feet, but the men kept lifting me up and slapping the back of my head with force. They managed to drag me to the back of the club, opened a side door, and tossed me out like a sack of trash into the parking lot.

I lied there curled in a fetal position by myself, trying to gather my breath and without warning, began to puke. That is when I heard the side door open again and looked towards it hoping to find Shu Shu. Instead, I saw the initial cop I'd hit exit with more of his police friends. I tried to scramble to my feet but couldn't get them to respond. The men were on top of me in no time, kicking my ribs and head. I went into an immediate defensive posture on the ground, hiding my face between my forearms and knotting into a tight ball. I sat there for a few moments, absorbing the blows, and praying they weren't going to kill me. I was not scared to die; I just didn't want to go out in this dirty, shitbag, communist country.

I tried to plead with them in English, "to stop," and after a few more hard kicks to my ribs, the men started to yell back at me. I couldn't understand most of what they were saying but heard *two words* that resonated the bad dream that I was in.

"You lucky," said the main policeman in broken English.

Funny but I didn't feel *lucky* as I saw him point that revolver back at my prone body. I froze as he gave me that big toothless grin, spat on the ground next to my head and then re-holstered his weapon.

"Lucky American" he said again as the other cop that I previously assaulted, got right in my face to spit bloody phlegm in my mug. They

laughed at that, opened the side door and then stormed off inside the KTV.

I sat there alone for a few moments as the spittle threatened to creep into my open mouth as I gasped for air. Afraid to move, I listened for the side door to open once again and feared that the beating would resume. When it appeared that they had left for good, I gently unfurled from my knotted position, took stock of my injuries and then tried to lie straight out on the ground. I opened my eyes to focus and thought I saw stars twinkling in the distant sky. After a few moments, the stars disappeared and were replaced by China's ever-present smog and pollution. I tried to take a few deep breaths of this noxious air, but my ribs hurt too much. I decided to stay still until my pocket began to vibrate. It took me a moment to realize it was my cell phone.

Slowly, I fished the cell phone out of my pants and with shaky hands, read the caller ID. It was Mei Mei. It was not who I was expecting, and I don't know why but I felt like laughing as a shit eating grin spread across my face. In fact, it was the first time I had smiled in days, as I recognized that it was a miracle I did not lose any of my pearly white teeth.

"Wei, Ni Hao?" (Yes, you good?) I answered in my best Chinese as I coughed up more blood and mucus. Mei Mei ignored my Chinese and began the inquisition.

"Rick, I just got an alarming call from Shu Shu!" she exclaimed

"Yeah, I got in a fight," I barely got the words out.

"I told you before that it's imperative that you keep a low profile," she continued.

I ignored her and thought only of the violence that had just occurred.

"By the way, I'm feeling just peachy, thanks for the concern," I said sarcastically.

"Rick did anyone take your picture?" She continued in rapid fire, "Did you get the names of any of the commanding officers, is Shu Shu with you?"

I let the phone drop from the cradle in my ear, promptly turned my head, and spit more blood onto the cement. I heard her still talking in the receiver and wondered if I was the right man for the job? After all, I wasn't the easiest person to handle. I let that thought settle as the neon lights overhead seemed to dim and then turned into darkness in my head.

30

Orgasm Addict, *Long Island, NY—circa 1984*

My menacing demeanor and lack of impulse control made it *acceptable* for me to hang with the older kids.

I was never comfortable in my own skin, certainly not with the kids who were my age and lived in my neighborhood. The teens I went to school with always seemed to act younger than me and had what I considered juvenile interests. I was often lonely and confused that I wasn't like the others. After all we went to the same schools, same temples, and played together as children. I take some responsibility; I was not the friendliest guy and really had no "gift for gab" like the others. I wasn't one for small talk or gossip and really didn't give a shit about sports, pop music, or whatever else they were into.

So, while the other youth's my age stayed at home in their *safe zone,* I was making friends with the older kids. We lived in a *"jappy town"* (slang for Jewish) with *McMansions* overlooking the harbor and had a town dock that I would sneak out to in the evenings. All the older kids from high school would be there, getting stoned and hanging out. Like a ninja, I quietly learned to climb out my window on the second floor and weave a path down the roof until I was grounded, where I would ride my bike to meet up with the crew on the dock. It was these special evenings where I learned to party with peers much older than me.

I handled the alcohol pretty well for my age as I already had a lot of practice with this vice. But perhaps my greatest talent was smoking weed and rolling joints—*thank you, Dad!* It was because of him and his friends that I always had weed on me. It was easy enough to steal since it was everywhere in my house and in copious amounts. This helped me tremendously to form friendships with the older group. Hell, I even went so far as to sell it to them.

But definitely the greatest drug I became infatuated with was sex. Or what I imagined sex to be. And the older kids appeared to be having some sort of sexual exploration anytime I was around them. There was definitely something erotic about those evening on the dock, overlooking the moonlit water. The alcohol, the drugs, and the flirtatious older girls only added to the intoxicating scene. These girls were practically women now, fully developed and dressed in sexy outfits to show off their newly developed bodies. My head (and boner) couldn't take their sexual prowess, and my mind compulsively thought of only lustful feelings—twenty-four seven. I was like a walking hard-on and besides music, sex was all I thought about, I would masturbate obsessively trying mentally to fulfill my insatiable urges.

The only drawback was my age. I was still physically young looking, especially with my hairless face. I tried to make up for this by building up a muscular physique, but I still lacked the self-confidence needed to get laid. I watched in envy at my older friends getting it on with the girls I so desired to be with. I would smell their fingers as they waxed poetic about their conquests and then laugh and tease me about my innocence. The girls were equally as cruel and would mock my inexperience at the same time as they sent their sexual energy towards me. They sauntered and teased me, knowing this was driving me bat shit crazy.

But I was a keen observer and like to think that I learned a lot about sex during those days. Especially, when we began to mix angel dust with the weed, the girls went wild losing their inhibitions. There was so much raw sex and madness that my older peers would have intercourse in their cars and let me watch from the outside. I used this enticement to hide in the bushes, pull down my pants, and masturbate outside in the bushes that surrounded the dock. The embarrassment I felt was fleeting, I was out of control and the sex—or lack thereof—was driving me to become a self-professed *orgasm addict*.

I quickly became obsessed with sexual thoughts and that fixation followed me to school where I was stuck with girls my own age. There, I would spend so much time analyzing their young budding bodies, imagining which ones would blossom into insatiable women and those who would want me to be their first lover.

I would tell sex stories to the kids my age that would blow them away and they always wanted to hear more. I told, "little white lies," about touching boobs, what that felt like, how the girls reacted and how that led to my imaginary sexual conquests. I became a self-professed gender expert presenting as a sex-crazed teenager with a penchant for drugs and imaginary finger banging. I thought I was the shit, and that the girls my age deserved me and my newfound skills.

I fantasized about having *Iggy Pop's* sexual energy as he squirmed shirtless through a sea of manic fans.

Unfortunately, the girls my age were not convinced I was Iggy Pop or anyone else famous, to them I was still a punk rock weirdo. I called them, "prudes" and pressured them to "let me work my magic on them." When this didn't convince them, I tried to offer them drugs or alcohol. Instead of making them horny, it just made them laugh at me or get terribly sick. None of my tricks or tales seemed to work as not one of them let me have my way with them. These young girls were still innocent and much different than my older friends. I couldn't find the keys to their crotch, and my fantasies started to become creepy obsessions.

I'd tried to drown out these compulsive thoughts with loud music. But listening to punk rock only made me angrier and more desperate. I would masturbate in every corner of my house, or with anything I could find to put my penis in. This included melons, the vacuum, or every pillow I could dry hump into oblivion. I was insatiable and dangerous enough to try and convince a younger female relative to get naked for me. I even offered her drugs, alcohol and would have even given her some angel dust if I had some.

My day consisted of obsessive thoughts about sucking tits, finger banging, vaginas, and having sex. I was losing my mind and confided in one of my older friends about my condition. He laughed and then cruelly explained (again) about how it is to eat pussy like a man. He even used a peach to show me how to lick off the juices and then drew with a magic marker on the fruit, how to find the clit. He teased me relentlessly, was a real asshole, but had a *PhD* in vagina, and this made him my hero. One night, he even showed up at my house with a carton full of pornography. The box was held together with strips of peeling tape and inside were well-worn magazines, old black-and-white photos and even a few VHS tapes. *Jizz Galore!*

But it was my older male cousin who taught me how to illegally tap into the Playboy Channel on our cable box system. It had something to do with pushing down a series of channels together and then toggling the clarity wheel. Of course, this would have been a lot easier if my parents just paid for the Playboy Channel... but no, I had to get it illegally and it didn't always work. But when it did, it led me into a fanatic fervor of beating off until I was raw, slapping on some more hand lotion and doing it again! I was a sex-crazed adolescent monster with one hand on the cable box and the other on the tissue box.

I collected porn from older friends, cousins, and even stole it from other parents. I had quickly built up quite a collection and would often find myself in the bathroom beating myself raw and limp. I was masturbating at an alarming rate, cumming in the shower, on the toilet, during school, after meals, outside, before bed... you get the picture. I was an obsessed young man with only one thing on my mind. I needed to lose my virginity!

My older friends also noticed my obsession and one drunken evening, promised to take me to a house party where they swore, I would get laid. We drove to a neighboring town on Long Islands' exclusive North Shore, where the houses were much larger than ours and the girls were noted to be much, "looser." My friends would explain that "something about having wealth made these girls appear to be sexier, mature and even hornier." My heart almost stopped when we pulled into the driveway of what appeared to be a real mansion. I never saw a house that size in person as the driveway (and lawn) were littered with European cars. There were groups of older kids all over the grounds, drinking, smoking and making out. The air was thick, reeked of marijuana mixed with perfume, pheromones and smelled like lust to my imaginative mind.

We entered the house as one large group and stuck to each other's sides until we made it out back to the pool. The pool was kidney shaped, lit with blue lights, filled with inflatable floats and bikini-clad girls. Around the pool sat chaise lounges jam-packed with teenagers funneling beers from the many kegs that strewn the lawn. It seemed that these rich kids had no trouble buying alcohol. People were screaming drunk with laughter, dancing, kissing and splashing half naked in the large pool. If it wasn't for that shitty old-school disco being blasted out of the speakers, I would have sworn I had died and gone to heaven!

We stood by the kegs, getting shit-faced and making small talk with any of the girls who would listen. We were a rebellious gang of stoners, interloping bravely from the South Shore to mix it up with our Northern brethren. We were a different breed than what they were used to, and to their credit would politely laugh at our jokes as they sauntered past us with an air of superiority. I was quickly becoming punch drunk with lust, completely *chubbed up* by the bathing beauties and the mix of alcohol. Soon I felt that familiar pressure in my groin, I needed to release and made a beeline to find a bathroom.

I went inside the cavernous house, passed the crowds of people and made my way around, searching for relief. I was exiting the large kitchen, now strewn with empty liquor bottles, bongs, half eaten bags of chips, when I heard some chick on the second floor yelling for, "help!" I didn't need to be asked twice and ran up the steep flight of stairs two at a time. She saw me coming, gave me a quick, "hello" and then proceeded to tell me, "That her friend had passed out in the bathroom, banging her head, and seemed to be knocked out." I told her, "I knew a thing or two about head injuries having had a few myself and would see what I could do." She kissed me sloppily on the mouth and then led me into the bathroom.

When I entered the restroom, I did my best to quickly assess the situation, and what I saw amazed me. There was an *angel* passed out with her head on the side of the toilet. She had puked on herself and had some running out of the sides of her luscious lip sticked mouth. Overlooking the vomit, she was absolutely beautiful, appeared to be tall like me, had dark olive skin, and jet-black hair. She was wearing a leopard print bathing bikini top and skintight Sassoon designer blue jeans. The bathing top was askew releasing one of her dark nipples that I noticed appeared to be standing at attention. I couldn't stop staring at that nipple and knew her perky breasts just wanted to free themselves. This gave me a great idea.

I began to fill the double-ended bathtub with water and told her friend, "That we needed to get her into that cold bath." I made up some story about potential *alcohol poisoning* and needing to wake her up before she went into shock. The friend was either as drunk as me or completely dim as she bought the story. Before I could say another word, she was working the soiled clothes off her unconscious friend. She laughed as she took off the girl's bikini top, and voila, two of the perkiest breasts I ever saw were staring right at me... or me at them. I stood in shock as my enraged boner pressed against my jeans. Her friend must have caught me staring, hesitated for a moment, looking me up and down for the first time.

"Quickly!" I yelled interrupting her thoughts, "We need to get her in this bath!"

That seemed to get her back on track as we both peeled off her jeans, revealing a matching leopard bikini bottom, and pulled her over the porcelain ledge and into the tub. The shock of the cold water must have done something to the girl, as she opened her eyes for the briefest moment before retching whatever was left in her, directly into the bathtub.

"Yuck, gross! What a bitch!" her friend exclaimed, quickly removing her hands from the polluted water. "I am not dealing with this 'ho' anymore! She's your problem now!" and stormed out of the bathroom, without looking back, leaving me alone with the almost naked mermaid.

I quickly ran to shut the bathroom door, turned the handle latch and locked us in. When I returned to the girl, I took a few moments to stare at her in disbelief. She was amazing looking, and she was all mine! But I must admit that the puke was ruining it for even a "horndog" like myself. Hence, I decided to do her (and me) a favor and clean her up. I rinsed out her luscious mouth with my pointer finger and ran warm water from the shower head over her body. I scooped her halfway up, making sure to cup the bottom of her ass with my left hand as I rinsed the puke out of the tub with my right hand. She was heavier in her naked dead weight than I initially thought and almost dropped her back into the tub.

I then drained the tub empty and refilled it with warmer water. I gently laid her back into the bath, staring at her leopard panties, which were sopping wet and gathering up her cheeks like a string bikini. I thought about removing them completely but settled for just a quick peek.

I got down low and gently raised her waistband to take a look. It was like looking at *Venus Rising* the first time and was more beautiful than anything I saw in those magazines. My heart felt as if it would explode in my chest as I lifted her bathing suit bottom down towards her hips to take a better gaze.

There it was, the holy grail, her mons veneris, her pussy! My personal Mount Everest! I kept staring at it, imagining what it must feel like. The outside, the inside. I bent down low from a bird's eye view to a more microscopic exam. I was trying to find the clit but couldn't see past the thin hair on her outer lips. I knew enough that this was becoming *rapey* and thought enough to pull her bottoms back up and show some restraint. I wanted my first time to be reciprocal and even though this was a dream come true, it could have also turned quickly into a nightmare.

The tension in my groin was becoming painful, snapping me back to reality as I was staring so hard that I forgot to breathe. In the corner of the tub, I saw a bar of soap, washcloth, took a deep breath and quickly went to work. I bent down on my knees on the side of the tub, soaped up the washcloth in the warm bath water and gently stroked her breasts with it. Under the suds, her nipples became rock hard again. She began to make a low moaning noise but still couldn't manage to keep her eyes open.

I couldn't believe my luck as I soaped her breasts some more, and then reached the cloth down between her legs over her suit bottom. Even with the soapy cloth, and the bathing suit fabric, it felt soft and smaller than I imagined it to be. I took another deep breath, restrained myself for going further and then rubbed my rock-hard erection as it threatened to *bust a nut*.

Instinctively, I stood over the tub, rubbing my manhood over my jeans and began to fantasize that she was awake and able to fulfill my every desire. I thought *hard* about what her small vagina would feel like and imagined entering her for my first time. I couldn't control my teenage virility, began stroking myself and thought to release my manhood and continue to masturbate to this fantasy. It took an iron will not to make this a reality and I felt a shameful embarrassment at how weak I was to my sexual urges.

I quickly grabbed the nearest towel off the rack, turned back at my bathing beauty, and after a couple more minutes of staring in disbelief, I decided to pull the drain and release the foamy water. I continued to watch the water disappear, leaving her half- naked body exposed and helpless. In a random act of *kindness*, I took the bath towel and gently covered my naked angel's exposed breasts.

I leaned down, gave her a gentle kiss on the lips, and quickly bolted out of the bathroom. However, in a state of sexual confusion, I must have used a different door than the one I entered as I now appeared to be standing in a very large master bedroom. I shut the door behind me, was happy to be alone as jumped on the large bed. I lied on my back, arms and legs spread like a snow angel. The comforter was amazingly soft as the different size pillows, stacked four high were plush and cradled my confused head. I closed my eyes, drowning out the sounds of the party downstairs, stayed still for a few moments, savoring the excitement of what just transpired. I replayed the erotic scene over a few times and couldn't believe my luck.

I slowly began to come back down to earth and realized that I should get the fuck out of there before someone came looking for her... or me. Besides, I couldn't wait to get back to my friends and tell them of my good fortune. I got up to leave when something shiny caught my eye in the vanity mirror. On the Brass gilded dresser was a gold Cartier woman's watch, in a glass dish with some more gold rings and hoop earrings. I quickly stashed them in my front pockets and thought they would make a nice gift for my next girlfriend, whomever that lucky girl would be. Then I did a quick search of the other drawers, hoping maybe there was some porn in there. Instead, inside the underpants draw, what I found was a large roll of hundred-dollar bills and some more loose jewelry. Jackpot! This would buy me some bragging rights and maybe even some sexual favors at the town dock! Quickly, I pocketed it all and ran out of the room, down the stairs, through the kitchen, ignoring the party and to the pool to find my friends. I was riding on an emotional high and for a fleeting moment, felt like a real man. The only thing I needed at that moment was to lose my virginity!

31

Pay to Cum, *Macau—circa 2002*

Shu Shu told me that he had a very special surprise for me.

We were going to take a trip to Macau before I left for home. We were having a particularly good year together, the economy was strong, our business was at an all-time high, as I pimped my furniture goods to every major big box retailer. Mei Mei also seemed to be complacent over this year, seldom bothering me as long as I continued to send her the messages and photos that she required. Everything felt to be a bit "normal" for me and I was sure to take advantage of this invitation before that all changed.

Shu Shu had it all planned in advance and told me, "That we would head to Macau for a bit of well-deserved relaxation." At this point, I had never been to Macau and only knew that it was a high speed ferry ride away from Hong Kong. Also, I had read that it was a Portuguese colony back in the day, had great food and was the only place for legal gambling in China—or Asia, for that matter.

Shu Shu had told me a lot of stories over the years about Macau. Mostly about the cuisine, but also about the infamous Thai massage parlors the island nation was famous for. He didn't give me many details but insisted, "it was an experience we needed to have together." Shu Shu never steered me wrong about massages and after a particularly long trip abroad, I was anxious for some relaxation before the long flight home.

We took the *TurboJet* ferry from Shekou Port in Shenzhen, China. It was a high speed passenger ferry that traveled the sixty miles to Macau in about an hour. The boat was *hydrofoil* with jet engines and appeared to float above the water while it was in motion. It was modern, European built, conveniently holding 150 passengers and we sat in the VIP premiere cabin. Even though I was feeling physically beat up, the ride was fast and the boat intoxicating. I was already hooked on this trip, and we had yet to even step foot on the Portuguese island.

Once we arrived, we took the short walk to the only five-star hotel back then in Macau, the now infamous *Shangri-La Hotel*. This was way before Las Vegas took the island over striving to duplicate the Vegas Strip for the Chinese and cater to their incessant need to gamble. In those days, the casinos were run by the Chinese Mafia and were mostly smoky, miserable establishments. I learned from Shu Shu on the way over that the Chinese came to Macau to gamble, eat, and spend time with the "white" Russian whores who dominated the casino scene. He made it appear that Macau was somewhat lawless, where anything can happen and hence the competition of Thai massage parlors made them the best outside of Thailand.

Once inside the extravagant palatial hotel, we left our bags with the concierge and took a short walk over to the three story strip mall that housed the *Heavenly Thai Massage Parlor*. We were greeted outside by a friendly man with a beautiful girl, who stood at a wooden podium. Shu Shu talked to him briefly in Cantonese. They smiled, laughed, and the friendly man pushed the elevator button behind him.

Once inside, we rode the small claustrophobic elevator up three floors and when the doors opened, we spilled out into what can best be described as the outside of a large fishbowl. It was dark inside but when our eyes adjusted, we saw half-naked girls loitering inside a small round stage of glass. We stood there gawking as we were greeted by another Cantonese man. He was quick to give us binoculars and then motioned for us to follow him as he led us to sit in stadium-like seats.

The girls were all in motion, ignoring us, putting on makeup, changing clothes, talking, laughing, eating... it was all too much. I quickly realized they were on display, and we could see them, but they could not see us. However, they (of course) knew they were being watched and put on a sly but overexaggerated show to get our attention. They had on bikinis, sheer dresses, high heels, make-up and numbers attached to their hips. The numbers were boldly printed in circles of different colors. Shu Shu had a small conversation with the man who gave us the binoculars, laughed, and then turned towards me to explain.

He told me, "That these girls were from all over Asia, and that the colors represented the countries they were from." Shu Shu went on to explain that "Green was Thailand; Yellow Vietnam; Orange Taiwan; Red was China."—you get the picture. Also, he said, "the numbers were on either the left or right hip. On the left meant she was up for anything. On the right meant it was her time of the month, and therefore she was only good for massage."

Shu Shu went on to explain that we should examine them carefully with binoculars and choose the number of the one that we wanted to come out of the *fish tank* and onto the main stage. From there, we would have a further chance to look them over, up close and personal and pick out the one we wanted for our massage.

Soon a few more men entered where we were standing, received their binoculars, and directions. A message in Chinese was then pumped over the loudspeaker. Suddenly, all the girls stood at attention as music started to play and they seemed to smile in our direction. Some danced in place, while others spun around and bent in provocative poses. I gripped those binoculars and made my way through the sea of female bodies. I felt like a perverted Magellan searching for new land. After a bit of teasing, Shu Shu asked which numbers I wanted to see more closely. I took a moment and tallied up a few girls—most from Thailand but a few from Vietnam and one from China. Shu Shu only picked Russian girls, and tall ones at that.

The loudspeaker went off again as the numbers were called. The girls chosen gave a little cheer, exited the tank, and took their place on the stage directly in front of us. When the other men in the room had their pick, the music started to play again. All our choices were now dancing directly in front of us. I saw some of the men get out of their seats and carefully examine their selections. I followed suit, letting my binoculars get up close and personal. It was a bit bazaar to have binoculars as we were less than a few feet away. But hey, this was the most surreal scene I had ever encountered, and the girls seemed to enjoy putting on the show.

After a few minutes, I knew who my massage girl would be. She was Thai, tall, young, and very thin. My binoculars did not detect any physical flaws. I gave Shu Shu her number and he told the man who both of our choices were. The man spoke into a walkie-talkie and then had us follow him out of the room to the cashier. I heard Shu Shu laughing with him, a lot of nodding, and then repeating of my favorite three letters, *VIP*.

Shu Shu gave them his credit card and then turned to let me know what the deal was.

"Rick, you can do whatever you want with the girl; however, the manager suggests that you hold out until the end and ask for a massage first." He added, "All the girls are very skilled in relaxation, so let them do their jobs."

I smiled in anticipation as the girls came to meet us. They grabbed our hands; some pleasantries were exchanged and then I was led away from Shu Shu and up a small flight of stairs. We walked down a tight but brightly lit hallway, passed a lot of closed doors and old women who had mops, cleaning supplies, sheets, towels, etc. They all smiled and said, "Haalow." I smiled back.

The girl led me through an open door and turned on the lights. The room was smaller than I imagined. There was a small single bed with red sheets, no pillows but had mirrors on the walls and ceiling. There was also a small TV built into the wall over the bed that had porno playing loudly on it. *(Nice touch)*. However, the most impressive part of the room was the two-person hot tub in the corner. Next to it on a small bamboo table sat a big bottle of soap, a large sponge and a few small towels. I was happy to see that, as my body instinctively began to relax. It had been a sweaty few weeks, and I was definitely in need of a good washing. As if reading my mind, the Thai girl started the bath and pumped the soap directly into the running faucet. She turned to me and asked my name.

"Rick Price." I said, not understanding why I mentioned my last name. She told me to call her, "Waan."

I laughed and said something stupid like, "I waan what you got."

She smiled, then pointed to the bed. I sat down and she started to take off my clothes. I felt chivalrous and helped her expedite this process. Once naked, she looked me over, smiled some more, and gently traced the tattoos that surrounded my body.

"You like?" I said.

She nodded and said, "Wow."

Then Waan removed her clothes, which consisted of a tight sheer dress and a pair of dental floss panties. Her skin was like milk chocolate, tight and smooth. Her tits were plump, full, her nipples were dark, long and sat inside small circular areola's. Her pussy looked small and was groomed into a little triangle bush. I started to become very excited but remembered Shu Shu's advice about the massage first. Therefore, I relented, lied back on the bed, and flipped over on my stomach. She sauntered over, removed her high heels and covered me with a towel. Then she checked the temperature of the bath, came back, and straddled my ass.

She kneaded with skill my tight neck, broad shoulders, lower back, and made her way down my legs, calves, and finally my feet. My eyes were closed as I felt my muscles untangle and give in to her strong hands. My head began to float, and the pressure was perfect.

Then she popped off me, went back to work the bath, checked it, and turned the water off. I watched her in disbelief as if examining an exotic animal for the first time. She caught me staring, smiled back, and seductively lowered herself into the immense bubbles forming from the tub. She took her hand out and pointed at me to join. Steam was coming off her fingers. It was magical.

I entered the tub and submersed myself in the steamy water. Waan floated her way over to me, gently held onto my shoulders, and let her body hover on top of mine. She slowly slid her warm physique up and down mine. I tried to grab her, but she put her fingers to my lips and said, "Shhh." Then she grabbed the porous sponge, soaped it up, and began to scrub my body. She concentrated on cleaning every part of me from head to toe, front to back. I closed my eyes and took it all in, completely aware of her touch and her nakedness. I tried again to sneak a touch, but she held my hands and directed me to sit on the edge of the tub.

Waan stood up and soaped her breasts with the sponge and then pumped some more soap on her hands. She worked this into a ball-like lather and then spread the foamy bubbles between her legs. She worked her bush until it resembled a soapy luffa. And then she provocatively began to rub her *vag-luffa* up and down my thighs, turned around, and sat herself between my rock-hard cock and my stomach. She gyrated and cleaned me inch by inch. I thought I was going to lose it. I cupped her breasts and thrust under her in anticipation.

She turned her head, gave me a quick kiss, and then stood to drain the bath. She got out, grabbed a towel, and began to dry herself with quick determination. I slid back off the ledge and sank down beneath the bubbles, watching her intently. When dry, she made her way over to the bed, placed her towel in the corner, and removed a small box from a hidden draw. She opened it and removed its contents. Tissues, baby oil, more lube, condoms, and mouthwash. She opened the mouthwash, took a swig, and spit it out right there on the floor. It was so hot.

Waan then grabbed another towel and made her way over to me. I carefully made my way out of the tub, grabbed the towel and watched myself in the mirror as steam escaped off my body. I looked like a monster coming out of a smoky cauldron. My head felt light, and I needed to sit down. I slowly walked with Waan's help over to the small bed, and willfully face planted on the thin mattress. Waan jumped right on top of me and let her full weight rest on my back. She then sat up while still on me, reached for the baby oil and rubbed the lubricant all over my back, legs, buttocks. She then continued to oil herself, as well, paying attention to greasing her most private of parts. She worked her hands and her body in a rhythmic well-practiced motion. She kneaded, pulled, rubbed, stroked, and slid her body over mine. I closed my eyes, exhaled, and let myself drift away into oblivion.

32

Am I Demon, *Long Island, NY—circa 1985*

They called it *"The Leadership Committee,"* but nothing could be further from the truth.

This noble idea was the brainchild of our High School principal, Mr. Cohen. It was designed to give us disenfranchised youth an open forum to discuss all that we hated and all that we wished to change. We were the complete opposite of anything resembling Leadership. What we excelled in was a common disrespect for authority and a complete disdain for the rest of the students, let alone the faculty. They called us "at risk" students. We were the rebels, the dirt bags, the bullies, the poseurs, and I was the school's token punk rocker. I also led this cherished committee for the past two years. My entry to this esteemed club was solidified after I wrote my own eulogy for the school's newspaper, *The Magnum Opus.*

The story went something like this:

Eulogy of Rick Price

Rick Price underneath it all was a good kid who loved to skate and punk rock. He shaved his head, made his own clothes, and wore combat boots (even to gym). Rick didn't like authority and didn't trust his teachers. He never felt comfortable among his peers. Couldn't fit in, didn't like popular music or expensive cars. Rick felt happy being alone. He owned an Iguana named Sid and tried to take Sid to school in order to keep him company. The school wouldn't allow this and suspended Rick each time he brought Sid. Rick didn't mind being suspended as he was safe at home with his punk music and his dreams of being a DJ on the radio.

At school, Rick was at the mercy of his teachers and the other students. Especially the older kids and the jocks. They were the ones who felt threatened by Rick's individuality and these classmates tried to destroy Rick's spirit by taking away his voice and freedom of expression. But most of all they were angry at Rick for reasons that he (and they) could not understand. Even though Rick tried to disappear, there was no denying his outlandish behavior.

Rick simply didn't back down to a beating. Nor did he follow the same rules as the other kids. Rick did as he thought he should, and this did not go unnoticed. The teachers were quick to punish him and the others, well, the others wanted him to suffer. Rick was subject to daily abuse both verbal and physical. He was berated, threatened, and finally beaten on a regular basis.

The adults were indifferent and soon Rick didn't care either. He accepted his fate and took his beatings as if they were his new normal. The others relished in his spiritual defeat, and this flaw incensed the group even more. Like a pack of wild animals that attacked what they considered weak, Rick became their prey. It didn't take long for them to demolish his skateboard, destroy his soul, and finally kill his iguana, Sid. Rick felt as if he didn't belong to this world and soon decided to leave it by overdosing on sleeping pills and alcohol.

So today, we are all gathered here to say our final goodbye to Rick Price. Rick was a good kid and even though you did not understand him, may we all take a moment and give our condolences to his family. It is tragic to have someone you've given birth to go. He paid the price and made the ultimate sacrifice, taking his own life. Hopefully, you will all learn something from this Eulogy and treat others who are different than

you with empathy and compassion. If not for yourselves then do it for Rick. He was
a good kid. He was better than you.

That eulogy story, when printed in the school paper, went *viral* in what was a non-viral world. Meaning we had no social media back then. But there was the telephone, and I believe every adult called my folks to see if I was "*okay.*" My mother responded by having another *convenient* nervous breakdown. She became inconsolable, crying hysterically as if I actually killed myself.

My story even caught the attention of the local paper, as mandatory suicide awareness programs were formed at high schools throughout The Island. I was even asked to do a local interview for Long Island's newspaper, *Newsday*. Shit, the last thing I wanted was this kind of attention and turned them and everyone down. I also became despondent, isolating further from everyone, staying in my room and listening to albums.

My folks felt the pressure to do something and decided to increase visits with my psychiatrist, Dr. Hurtz. The esteemed doctor was referred to us from my grandpa Butch, who seemed to know everyone and always came through when needed. Like everyone else he introduced us to, Dr. Hurtz was also someone he served with in the military and was a valued member of his *PSYOPS (psychological operations)* team. I've been seeing Dr. Hurtz every other week since I was 14 and he has become a trusted advisor in making sure I was well medicated with the best the *shrink industry* had to offer. Dr. Hurtz had assured my folks that this story was a therapeutic outlet for my creativity and should be used to entice me to write more and worry less. The good doctor then switched up my meds from *Monoamine-oxidase inhibitor's (MAO's)* to more experimental class of medicines called, *selective serotonin reuptake inhibitors (SSRI's)* in the form of fluoxetine, or what we now refer to as, *Prozac*.

But it was my principal who capitalized the most on the situation, forming the "Leadership Committee" to show the community he was aware and sensitive to us, the "alienated student body." The committee was held every Friday after school and not open to the general student body. As a matter of fact, it was by invitation-only. We had just one rule, and that was whatever was discussed was to be held confidential. Not that we discussed anything relevant, after all we didn't trust adults, let alone each other. But the confidential part that we kept private was that we were allowed to sit in the faculty lounge and smoke cigarettes. Sometimes the teachers, including principal Cohen, smoked with us and sat in to hear us complain about whatever was on our mind. Important things were discussed, like the amount of homework, the cafeteria food, the need for mandatory hall passes, and why the need to learn *home economics*? I would sit in one of the well-worn recliners and start the meetings by snapping my fingers. Soon, the rest of the merry band of misfits would also start snapping, followed by the adults. When we were done getting everyone's attention, I took a short roll call, and then we moved the seats into a therapeutic circle. I must admit that I enjoyed this small slice of time bullshitting like an adult and it became the only positive thing about going to school on a Friday.

Normally, I would have never talked with the other members of our committee. We were not from the same social circles, nor were any of us very friendly in general. I guess that this was the idea and when we began to talk, our differences became normalized. We were all hand-picked to attend by the faculty and for many of us, it was the first time we were ever asked to be involved in anything, let alone something that seemed worthwhile.

When the committee ended, we all walked outside, shared some last cigarettes and said "goodbye." It would be the last time any of us would *enjoy* each other's company until the following week. When we saw each other in school, none of us would even bat an eye at each other. We were a leadership of loners, tough kids, and losers. We weren't social by nature and had some big reputations to live up to. For many of us, it was only those Friday afternoons that we had to look forward to. After that meeting, it was back to our dysfunctional homes and abusive lives.

It was me (and my story) that started this empathetic revolution, and it was me that ended it for everyone. Of course, yours truly, punk rock extraordinaire couldn't just have my cake and eat it too. No, I had to destroy anything positive for myself and only left carnage in my wake.

Although I never meant to shut this down for the others, it was my usual arrogance that fucked it all up again. This time, it was my own innate disregard for authority that put the Leadership Committee out of business.

We were all hanging in the parking lot before school, as we often did daily. We would meet up a half hour before that bell rang, smoking and loitering. Often, I made it a habit of premixing Bloody Mary's and serving them out of my trunk to whomever was brave enough to approach me. I had an *original* method of dumping half the *Campbells* tomato juice mix out of the bottle and then filled the rest with Russian vodka. I would mix it with some black pepper, maybe garlic powder if it was in the kitchen spice drawer and then give it a vigorous shake blending all the simple ingredients together. It was a crude, warm concoction, but it did the job to start the day off with some much needed Vitamin C. Usually, it was just a bunch of girls and few of my childhood friends who congregated to the back of my Electric Blue Datsun 208ZX. We kicked it early, sitting in my hatchback, drinking from big red plastic cups, smoking cigarettes mixed with weed. It was Spring and we were all in the spirit to get loaded.

We must have seemed like a lively bunch, at least to a very large stray dog who nervously approached us from across the parking lot. He was a Rottweiler mix, looked too skinny for his frame but muscular, nonetheless. One of the girls nervously pointed him out in the distance. We lived in *suburbia* and stray dogs were not a usual occurrence. He was definitely a strange sight, large and menacing like a demonic apparition. I was enthralled by this *devil dog*, feeling a kinship and made no hesitation about calling him over.

"Danzig!" I shouted, and then whistled.

"You know this dog?" one of my friends questioned.

I ignored him, continued to whistle and then reached for a bag of Doritos that I had stashed in the trunk for later. I opened them up and ran cautiously over to the beast.

"Danzig, here Danzig. How about some food?" I coaxed.

The dog saw me coming and retreated to a safe distance.

"C'mon boy, I ain't gonna hurt you. Here, I'll leave these for you."

I placed the bag of chips on the ground and ran back to the bunch.

We all watched as the large dog made his way cautiously to the open bag of chips. He sniffed around and then went right for them. We drank and cheered, as we watched him devour the chips. When he finished munching, he lifted his powerful head and panicked as it was still stuck in the bag. He yelped and ran around in large circles. We laughed out loud as the bag flew off his head and into the street. The dog then ran away to safety, hiding under the bleachers that surrounded our football field. I tried to call him over again and entice him to come. But I was shit out of luck. He was scared.

I continued to keep my eye on him as the parking lot filled up with sport cars and the students prepared for another day of school. I closed down *Rick's Bar*, collected the used cups, drained the rest of the vodka mix and made the quick decision that I wasn't going to leave Danzig alone. No telling what would happen to him, especially if someone called our overzealous suburban police force. The dog would be put down for sure as he was strong, dangerous, and nervous. Afraid of humans... I completely sympathized.

When the bell rang to signal the beginning of school, I stayed in the parking lot. It was now devoid of other students. It was just me and Danzig off in the distance. I extinguished my cigarette on the sole of my DMs and slowly approached the scared dog. I got close and knelt down in an unthreatening manner. I clicked, whistled, and tried to be as friendly as possible.

"Hey, Danzig. Here, boy," I pleaded.

The dog seemed to be looking my way as I reached into my pocket and pulled out a half-eaten Slim Jim. I opened it, showed it to the dog, he sniffed the air and to my amazement, carefully approached me. I kept my cool and reached the jerky stick out. It must have smelled like food to him, and he reached his massive head out and snapped it out of my hands. Instead of running away, he lied down at my feet and began to eat all of it with tremendous speed.

I gathered my nerve and began to pet the top of his head. It was bony, huge and felt like *raw power*. I liked the way he his strength was on display 24-7 and knew instantly that this was my dog! I also decided that my parents would have to deal with this animal as well, but first, being my dog meant I would not take a chance to lose him. I decided that the only way to keep him was for the *hell hound* to come to school with me. And after school, I would take him home with me. As I mulled this over, I continued to slowly pet the rest of him. He seemed to enjoy the affection. After some time, I decided it was now or never.

"Danzig, follow me. We're going to school," I said.

I turned and started walking away. I kept whistling, clicking and calling his name. To my amazement, the dog began to follow me. He stayed just behind me in caution but the both of us slowly made our way to the front doors leading into the school. I opened the doors, took a peek around and then called for him to follow me in. The dog stood there for a moment, looked up at me, as I gently grabbed the fur on top of his neck and led him inside. In an instant, what I can only chalk up to a rare moment of *trust*, the large canine and I were walking the halls of my high school. I felt empowered, like I just won something special. It was as if I found a new best friend. I couldn't believe my luck and thought there was no way this was happening to me. But it was real, and Danzig followed me through the empty hallways, his nose twitching, smelling what I could only imagine was food coming from our school's cafeteria. He looked hungry, so I decided to lead him to the lunchroom where they prepared meals that always tasted like *dog food* to me.

It only took a few minutes before I saw Principal Cohen round the corner of the hallway. Before I had a chance to react, I saw him look at the monster dog and then back at me. Principal Cohen raised his voice as it boomed and echoed through the silence.

"Rick, what the hell are you doing with that dog!" he exclaimed loudly.

I threw up my hands in a submissive posture.

"Sorry, he kinda followed me in," was all I could muster.

"Rick, get that dog out of my school!" he continued his rant.

I didn't react as Mr. Cohen made a quick threatening move towards Danzig and that is all it took for the massive dog to attack!

Danzig unleashed a series of loud barks, and then started to growl menacingly in an attempt to warn all of us that he was on the defensive. I knew that feeling well and tried to grab again at the dog's neck scruff. Unfortunately, Mr. Cohen continued to move quickly to the dog in what must have looked like an offensive measure. He was in mid yell and reaching out when Danzig made his move. It happened in a flash as the large 100 pound dog leaped on the principal's chest, knocking the stunned man to the floor, where he started to tear at Mr. Cohen's ankle. The principal put his hands up in a defensive posture, protecting his face, and started to scream. I know they say dogs are 2-3 times stronger than man and I can now attest to the brute force of the attack. I stood there frozen in disbelief as the animal tried to drag the adult principal to the corner of the hall. I was stuck somewhere between fear and happiness as a sly smile spread across my face.

"Help me, God help me!" Principal Cohen continued to scream as his cry's permeated through the hallways.

Suddenly classroom doors flew open as other teachers and students arrived to witness the carnage. The screaming morphed into pandemonium as the others yelled and tried to get the dog off the helpless adult. I yelled for Danzig as well, using my feet to try and dislodge the animal with some well-placed kicks. I wasn't trying to hurt the dog but had enough of a conscious to know that this was completely my fault and I needed to try and stop this.

Just then the janitor ran through the chaos armed with a mop and bucket. He proceeded to continually hit Danzig over his bulky head with the wooden mop. The dog stopped attacking our principal and turned his threatening attention to the janitor blaring his growl and baring his teeth. The janitor in a move of genius, pick up the bucket and threw the dirty water at the dog. This move stunned the dog (and the rest of us) as Danzig seemed to shriek in shock and rapidly bolted away from the chaotic scene. I chased after him as he backtracked to the entrance, looking to escape and I quickly opened the door for him.

The dog ran like lighting, disappeared across the parking lot and out of sight.

The Nassau County police came shortly after, along with an ambulance and the county dog catcher. They took statements, removed Principal Cohen to the hospital for his rabies shots and stitches. I gave them whatever information I could, took my verbal beatings, and swallowed my pride as I was then suspended for next few weeks. This incident became a permanent stain on my record and the Leadership Committee failed to ever meet again. Mr. Cohen finally made it back, but our relationship had appeared to be over. Again, I had a good record of fucking up anything positive for myself and others.

So be it. Once a Misfit... always a Misfit!

33

Anarchy in the UK, *Cambridge University, England—circa 1986*

After the demise of the short-lived "Leadership Committee," I must admit I was a bit fucked about what to do next.

My folks didn't know what to do with me as they tried to make sense of my latest school antics and the suspension I received. Dr Hurtz increased my *Trazadone* hoping its sedative properties would help keep me in check. Thankfully, my grandfather stepped in for me once again and offered that I go live with him and my grandma (Rose). My grandpa never seemed fazed by my troubles or my general emotional malaise. On the contrary, I think he was happy just to have my company, and I temporarily moved in with them during my junior year of High School. My grandma always made the best chocolate chip brownies and had a freezer full of them for my arrival. My grandparents lived in a three floor condo in central Long Island. The condo had its own boat slip for Grandpa's prized *22' Grady-White Seafarer*, that he appropriately named *"So Bad."* Yet despite the boat and the brownies, the condo also had a guest room that became mine during my short stay. The room like the rest of the house was decorated with vintage furniture that they must have had with them for the past 30 years. There was an old six drawer hand painted chest, that was emptied for my things. My room had a

208

brown plaid pull out couch, but best of all, Grandpa was proud to show me that the room also had *Cablevision* and he made sure to order the *Playboy Channel* for me. Thanks again, Grandpa!

While the school was busy trying to figure out what to do with me, I continued my punk rock crusade of malevolence and anti-authority posturing. My parents were desperate to find a direction for me that I would succeed in. As a result, they spent some dough and hired a private career/guidance counselor. She was an older lady and obviously out of touch with what I was all about. I went back home so she could give me some school-like vocational tests designed to point out my strengths and ultimately to give my folks, her perspective on what I would be good at when I finally grew up.

I remember being adamant that the only thing I wanted to do when I was older, was to be on the radio as a DJ personality. That was my dream job, to find and expose new punk groups who needed the airtime, and to play the music that I liked! I often thought how amazing this would be, especially if I had the chance to interview and discover these new bands... it would be heaven. I was already doing this with passion in my spare time and thought it would be a great job for me.

Unfortunately, the paid career counselor didn't agree with my vocational decision. In fact, she was horrified by this idea! I recall her gathering my parents around our kitchen table to explain that being a DJ was a *dead-end* career. She explained to my folks that DJs made no money, and I would end up in constant poverty. This was not what my parents wanted to hear and looked to her for some guidance. She was obviously paid to give my parents what they considered the suburban antidote to successful living. So, she strongly recommended that I abandon this disc jockey dream and think about applying to either a premed school to save lives or become a lawyer and fight for social justice. This was exactly what my parents wanted to hear, and they both nodded in agreement with her assessment.

I was beside myself with sudden rage. I screamed at her and my parents for being so predictable and fucking stupid! I defended myself by explaining that *Howard Stern* was my personal hero and even though he started on AM radio, he was now responsible for the largest syndicated radio show in the world, and you cannot tell me that he was living in squalor. Besides, Howard was doing what he wanted and wouldn't take no for an answer. He was brave, defiant, and totally punk rock. I explained loudly that I wanted to do the same, and music had always been my happy place. It had been this way since I was an adolescent, listening to WNYU, collecting more punk albums than my local record store and seeing more live music than anyone I knew. I couldn't imagine that anyone would think I was suited for any other profession. Hell, even being an MTV "*VJ*" was better than what she was proposing!

I was angry again about not being heard or recognized. I couldn't stand being told what to do by adults who didn't bother to try and understand me. I felt invisible, unsung, so I stood up and threw my desk chair across the room. This got everyone's attention as I flipped them the bird and then made my way to the safety of my Datsun and back over to Grandpa's house.

I never saw or spoke of that old lady again. However, she left some literature on the table as a parting gift. To my folk's credit, they put it in my bedroom on my beige Formica desk. The next time I came home, I went directly to my room to play the new album *EVOL* by *Sonic Youth* and saw something on my desk regarding Cambridge University and England. Now, *that* piqued my attention. Anything *England* symbolized the roots of punk rock to me. I read the brochure a few times amazed that it was advertising a summer program at Cambridge University in the UK. They were apparently giving scholarship opportunities to students wishing to explore the creative arts in writing. I reread it again and was now stuck on the aspect of living a summer in England. Yes! Now, *that* spoke to me. The only caveat was in the fine print... that being; I had to be recommended by my school, submit letters from the English Department and, of course, from my principal.

I was determined to live in London, at all costs and returned to school on my best behavior. I approached my principal for the first time since the mauling, asking to meet with him and did my best to reflect sadness for my past indiscretions, making a promise of solemn change. There was a quid pro quo agreement made to outline my behavior for the rest of the year, as my atonement for all those I had hurt (either directly or indirectly) and this of course included the recently attacked Principal

Cohen. I tried my best to act solemn in my apologies and kept my eye on the prize... *Anarchy in the UK!* I was *"all in"* asking for forgiveness. After all, God saved the Queen and maybe I could be saved, as well!

After an Oscar-winning performance, I convinced those whom I offended that self-change was imminent. The required forms for the summer program were completed and sent out along with my Eulogy short story, the press it obtained and a letter of recommendation from my English teacher. I got news a few weeks later in form of an acceptance letter that I was admitted to the college for the summer. I couldn't believe my good fortune as I wasn't accepted into anything before, and now I had the chance to go to where the birth of punk originated. Nothing was going to stop me. I worked hard with Dr. Hurtz to make good on my promises, kept my head down, stayed out of trouble and the school year ended without incident.

They day of my departure to the UK, I put all my punk regalia into a large surplus army duffle, got into our *Beamer* and made the laborious journey down the Belt Parkway to JFK's International airport. There at the Pan Am counter, I met the other summer students as we checked in and said our goodbyes to our folks. We were a small group of about a dozen. We were being chaperoned by an older distinguished man with a cane and an amazing English accent. He introduced himself as the chancellor for this summer session and said that we would be meeting the others when we arrived at Cambridge. My first glance at the bunch was a bore fest. That was until Kat arrived. She was very tall, like as tall as me, with black Doc Martens and a closely shaved head. She wasn't very pretty but she was definitely punk. I was intrigued enough to give her my best Sid Vicious snarl. She laughed at me and then approached and told me her name.

"Katherine, but please call me Kat," she said and the stuck out her hand and gave me a strong-arm shake.

"Hey, I'm Rick" I said.

"You from New York?" Kat asked.

"Yeah—Strong Island." I answered.

"Figures," she said, and then let me know she was from Massachusetts.

We shared some small talk about her drive down to New York and a general conversation on the merits of straight edge punk, versus the new metal fusion that punk had evolved into, especially in big cities like Boston.

We boarded the large 747 together but sat separately as the chancellor did not to allow the boys to sit next to the girls. The flight was uneventful. I sat next to a kid named Jay who looked like Elvis Costello. We talked a bit about music and then I drowned him out with my Sony D-55T Discman and a collection of punk rock Discs that rivaled *Virgin Records*.

By the time we reached Cambridge, I was completely distraught by how far it seemed to be from central London. I sat on the bus with Jay for about three hours, looking out the window, trying to find something punk rock in what seemed an endless valley of sleepy villages and farms. Cambridge looked just as unimpressive to my untraveled, child-like mind. Everything was old, set in stone; it felt cold and boring. The only cool things I saw was an outstanding gothic graveyard and some massive castle-like buildings. The entire campus was what I imagined Dungeons & Dragons to be. It was a far cry from NYC, and I wasn't really prepared to be in a Hobbit novel.

We met the other students outside the austere stone residence towers and were given a tour around the part of campus we would be attending. Our dorms were small, and the classrooms looked very old. Actually, everything was old, almost ancient. I couldn't comprehend what I was looking at but felt anxiety about being here. Thankfully Dr Hurtz gave me a pocket full of Xanax should I ever need it. I must have not been the only one uncomfortable because Kat quickly came over to join me.

"Rick, we need to check out that insane graveyard later and then we need to find out how to take the tube to London," she said.

"The tube?" I asked.

"Yeah, the subway. We need to find out where it is and how to get out of here." She answered.

"That sounds like a definite plan," I said reaching into my ripped jeans for a Xanax.

I pulled out my small bottle and then offered her one. She gladly took two from me. It took us at least a week to find out how to get to London. We had our classes during the day, suffered through shitty food in the cafeteria, and technically only had Sundays off. Saturdays were considered a "rec day," where we could choose some recreational activity to do, like water skiing or canoeing. Water sports were not in our cards, so Kat and I skipped this in lieu of finding out where London was.

The Tube, as it turned out, was not that convenient to where we lived. Instead, we had to walk a few miles to take the train one and half hours from Cambridge Station to Kings Cross. Once there, we switched over to the Tube finally arriving at Oxford Circus, it was there on *Carnaby Street* that we hugged for the first time proclaiming in our best punk rock sneers, "God Save the Queen!"

Kat had an unusual talent for begging strangers for change. She even had this amazing English accent that I swear was Oscar worthy. Thus, we targeted Americans, pretending to be English punks; we offered to take pictures with them in return for money. We walked hand in hand, exploring Carnaby Street, begging, and trying to fit in with the Euro punks who littered the streets like a homeless gang. Later that night, Kat had convinced some older punks to buy us some warm Carling beer. She handed over our change and soon we were all loitering, drinking and singing the dirty streets. I was in my punk rock heaven.

It didn't take long for Kat to convince me to die my mohawk black. We did this on one of our weekend forays into London. And on the way back, we panhandled enough money to buy black hair dye, gelatin, and some more beer. It was getting late, so we dumpster dove, found something to eat, and made our way to the Tube. When we returned to our dorms, it was way after midnight. No one was around so Kat told me to meet her downstairs in the women's locker room. I was the submissive in this relationship and became accustomed to follow whatever Kat instructed me to do. It was the first time in my life that I let someone else tell me what to do.

Kat had me take off my Ramones T-shirt and bend over the sink as she dyed my hair jet black. When this was done, she mixed up the gelatin with warm water and began to blow dry my hair into stiff spikes. It was amazing to see the transformation as my hair stood straight up and pointy. The spikes were at least ten inches long. I looked like a combination of *Danzig* and *The Exploited*! It was all too much, and I could not hide my excitement. I was aroused with pent up eagerness and, apparently, so was Kat. She looked me over, felt my cock harden in my ripped jeans, screamed in delight, then got on her knees and began to blow me.

I sat back against the soiled sink, letting my jeans and underpants drop around my ankles. I was able to look at my reflection in the mirrors across the bathroom, while joyfully watching her shaved head bobbing and slobbering over my crotch. I closed my eyes and silently exploded in Kat's hardcore mouth.

The next morning, Kat and I were called into the chancellor's office. He told us not to sit. He was abrupt.

"Rick and Kat, your behavior is not acceptable on this campus. I have had numerous complaints about you skipping rec days, appearing drunk, and now I have a women's locker room fouled with black dye and God knows what else."

He looked at me when he said that. I did not meet his stare and looked at my combat boots instead. Kat was quick to reply in her best English accent.

"So sorry, sir, we were wrong. What can we do to be back in your good graces?"

He thought about this for a second as I tried hard not to laugh.

"You two need to clean up that awful mess! And there will be no more missing classes or taking trips to London."

"Of course," Kat said solemnly.

"And absolutely no more drinking! One more mishap and you both get sent home!" he said resolutely.

He looked at me again, I did not return his gaze as he stood and then dismissed us.

Kat and I went back down to the women's locker room. There was a mop and some cleaning supplies waiting for us. The sink we used was stained with black dye and hardened gelatin. The mess wasn't just contained to that one sink. It was splattered over the entire bathroom reminding me of a crime scene. Kat grabbed my hand reassuringly and then handed me the mop.

We spent most of that morning laughing at ourselves and trying our best to clean up a mess that, well, didn't want to be cleaned. It was either permanently stained or we just didn't have the right supplies. Either way, we decided this program sucked anyway, and we should take advantage of being in Europe. Kat said she always wanted to go to France and drink wine. I told her I hated the French. But then she reminded me they have a huge Punk scene, mostly influenced by downtown NYC. And that was all it took.

We decided to leave immediately, abandoning our cleaning for more mischief, as we discussed how to catch a train into Paris. Kat instructed me to grab my backpack, passport, and any money I had. We were to meet back in the women's locker room to review the plans in 30 minutes.

I ran up to my dorm. Unsure of what to pack, I opted for my Black Flag T-shirt, bondage pants, my leather studded motorcycle jacket, and a few pairs of underpants. I threw those items, some socks, my passport, and my Discman in my patchwork backpack made up of stitched band emblems and safety pins. I laced up my DM's, checked my mohawk in the mirror, grabbed my wallet and chained it to my belt buckle.

Once downstairs, I ran back into the empty locker room and threw my backpack onto the corner of the floor. Kat was not there yet, as I was certainly a bit early. I waited quietly, gazing at my new dew in the mirror, flexed and then looked again at the mess we made. After a short time, Kat arrived carrying a small suitcase and dressed in her best gothic, ripped black tights and plaid mini skirt. She was still very excited and wasted no time as she embraced me and led us into an open stall.

"Let's get this over with," Kat said and pulled down her tights and black panties. I couldn't believe my luck and I fumbled with my jeans as she pushed me onto the toilet seat. Instead of sitting on me face-to-face, she opted for the "reverse cowgirl" position. I stared at the back of her shaved head noticing that she was also shaved everywhere. I was in ecstasy as she grinded and engulfed my manhood with professional ease. She told me to tell her "When I was going to cum."

I cupped her small breasts and told her almost immediately.

It was that fast.

She laughed at me.

Kat lifted up her tights and left me in the stall.

I tried to cover my goo and embarrassment with some quick toilet paper action.

Kat entered the stall next to mine and stood on top of the toilet. She was tall enough to clearly see me over the stall wall, fumbling with my sticky mess of tissues.

"Hey, Rick, she said, "you smell fire?"

"Fire, are you shitting me?" I asked confused.

"No, you're so hot, I think you're on fire," she said.

I looked dumbfounded at myself as she jumped off the toilet.

Kat then appeared back in my stall with an outstretched hand. In it was a red fire extinguisher. She pulled the pin and began to extinguish the stall I was in.

I screamed as the white powder blinded me, I stood pulling up my pants and then I quickly tackled her. I fought the extinguisher free, stood and began to spray extinguishing fluid all over the bathroom. Kat added to the madness by kicking over the mop and throwing the cleaning supplies all about the bathroom. We broke the mirrors, kicked in the doors, and moshed with newfound, unabashed passion.

We were truly crazed and living in the moment, with wild unabashed punk passion.

Unfortunately, we never made it to France.

Instead, we were immediately expelled.

Our parents had the responsibility of paying for our mess (again). They and the school paid special attention to make sure that Kat and I were separated at all costs. We promptly departed at different times, boarded separate flights, and never had a chance to say goodbye. I was angry at having our plans derailed and, of course, having to come home for the rest of that summer. I flew home in despair, listening to a loop of The Misfits, Minor Threat, and a lot of Henry Rollins. I was inconsolable. But I was sporting a fine mohawk and an *itch* that could not be ignored.

This itch was coming from my groin.

And the more I scratched, the better it felt.

I was in the airplane bathroom when I first saw them move through my pubic hair.

I was weak in the knees as I realized what these were.

In a panic, I disrobed in the small airplane stall and tried to furiously wash my groin in the sink. I made a mess. Water and soap were everywhere as I frantically tried to eradicate the infestation.

By the time I arrived at JFK, I was red and raw in the area that once gave me tremendous pleasure. My parents almost fainted at my black mohawk. They were not enthusiastic about paying for my delinquency. And, well, now we needed to go to the doctor.

I never saw Kat again.

And I never forgot her departing gift.

How low can a punk get?

34

Show You No Mercy, *Dongguan City, China—circa 1998*

A week before my thirtieth, Shu Shu threw a party for me.

He invited all his key factory workers to help us celebrate at the local KTV, and we certainly didn't need any other excuse for a celebration! For some strange reason, it seemed I was always in China around my birthday. Tonight, would be yet another ceremonial birthday bash, as Shu Shu rented the largest of the party rooms for me, overlooking the stage; we were in the prime location. Shu Shu also invited all the Filipino workers, his upper management staff, and (of course) Dr. Dave to party the night away in glorious Chinese fashion.

I was still in the *honeymoon* phase of China, where I felt precarious of every situation. Of course, Shu Shu was a great host, always helping to make me feel safe and secure in this strange country. This KTV was an enormous nightclub, elaborately decorated with private rooms where friends could sing, drink, screw, and party. There was a center stage where live performances of singing and dancing would go on all evening. And the place was full of hundreds of young Chinese women. They were employed to entertain, to drink with, and to comply with whatever you felt like doing. And they did it with a smile, hailing from all the Chinese provinces, making the trek down south to where the business was. The air was electrifying, as if someone slipped ecstasy in everyone's drinks. Hell, it felt like Disneyland (for adults) to me.

Thank God for the alcohol, as it drowned out the terrible sappy love songs and general loudness of the Chinese. They absolutely had the worst voices, horrendous musical tastes and yet were so proud to sing. And when they were not singing, they were smoking or enjoying competitive drinking games. Birthday parties also included the ceremonial cake where it was customary to throw it at the party's recipient and everyone else in the room.

There were many drinking competitions involving dice that we all learned to play. These games were not for the timid and increased the alcohol debauchery to an almost frenetic pace. The night ended when everyone got too drunk, or had passed out, unable to continue. It was then decided that those wanting to go to bed (alone or together) would leave, while the others chose to eat in one of China's many all-night noodle restaurants.

I recall that birthday night telling Shu Shu that I was going to walk some of the girls out front so they could catch a cab, and that I would meet him at the car. I walked whatever girls were left standing out of the cavernous building to hail a cab. I'd like to make a point here that I constantly tried to play the gentleman card. I felt sorry for some of the girls and didn't want to mess anything up for the business since I was warned many times by Mei Mei, to "play nice and keep a low profile." Hey, maybe I was also going to teach China something about chivalry... (what a joke!)

The cab was waiting out front, and I made a big show of rounding up the young girls like drunken cattle. I concentrated on keeping the door open for them and did not see the sucker punch when it landed to the right side of my face. I remember spinning around and facing a young Chinese man I had never seen before. I was confused, drunk and taken totally by surprise. Before I realized what was happening, the man was grabbing at the girl's handbags and violently ripping them off their shoulders. The girls were screaming, so I yelled back at him to "stop!"

Instead, he surprised me by grabbing at my Jewish Star charm from my open shirt and threw me to the ground. When I fell, the necklace ripped free in his hands, as the man started to run off. I lied there for a few seconds, embarrassed, and tried to process what just happened and why this guy would want a Jewish Star? I fought through my drunken cloud, piecing together what had just transpired and when my head cleared, I realized that I was just robbed. I jumped to my feet, determined to catch the thief and give him a taste of my vigilante vengeance.

I saw the man up ahead running with an armful of purses, I gave chase and was closing in quickly when Shu Shu's car appeared from around the corner. I quickly changed direction, ran towards his car, and jumped in the back seat.

"Follow that guy!" I screamed. "He just robbed me and the girls!"

Dr. Dave was behind the wheel and did not need to be told twice as he hit the gas on Shu Shu's car.

"That fucken guy blindsided me, took the girls purses and my necklace," I proclaimed with drunken intensity as I tried to get a look at my bruised face in the rear view mirror.

Dr. Dave was quickly on the man's tail as he tried to run out of the parking lot. We were approaching fast and Dr. Dave turned his wheel and sideswiped the man. The burglar flew up and over the car and fell hard to the asphalt. The purses continued their trajectory through space.

"Holy shit!" I screamed in excitement, forgetting about the pain in my face.

Dr. Dave screeched the car to a halt and the man spilled onto the concrete. We watched for a second and saw the man try to stand up. He kept falling and then trying again to stand. He was bleeding and obviously very hurt.

Dr. Dave opened his door and walked slowly out of the car towards the man. He approached silently like a snake, appeared to help the man stand and then suddenly slapped him hard simultaneously with a quick left and then a right. The man immediately lost his balance and fell back to the ground in pain. He moaned something in Chinese and then held up my necklace in a state of defeat to give it back. Dr. Dave took it from him and walked over near the man's feet. They were twisted into an odd position. Dr. Dave proceeded to stomp on both of his ankles until we heard them snap. The man began to scream, and I started to feel sick. That is when Dr. Dave picked the man up over his shoulder, walked over to the back of the car, opened the trunk, and threw the crying man inside. He closed the trunk, went back to gather all the purses, threw them in the back seat, gave me back my Jewish star and returned to the driver's seat.

"What the fuck?" I exclaimed with a shit eating grin escaping from my injured face.

"Shut up!" he said in perfect English as he sped away from the crime scene.

I looked at Shu Shu awaiting some sort of explanation but didn't receive anything from him.

Shu Shu and Dr. Dave did not discuss much as we drove back to the factory, where we were greeted at the gates by the night guards. There were obvious pounding sounds coming from the man inside the trunk. The security guards took notice, but Dr. Dave talked to them quickly. They squelched into their walkie talkies and within a few moments the security boss fully dressed in helmet and boots met us. He proceeded to salute Shu Shu, Dr. Dave and then me. Only I saluted back as he quickly made his way to the back of the car and opened the trunk. He lifted the now screaming Chinese man by his cheap collared shirt and punched him directly in the face. Then the rest of the guards came over, grabbed the man, removing him from the trunk, and manhandled him into the factory. Dr. Dave took out his cigarettes and offered one to Shu Shu and me. We both accepted his offer and lit up. We took our time concentrating on exhaling rings while we heard faint screaming from the inside of the factory.

When we finished our smoke break, we made our way inside the heavy doors to the metal works department and saw that the culprit was being held down in a broken office chair. In front of him was a large wood table where our quality control engineers would inspect goods before final assembly. There were many crude looking tools, equipment and hardware on that table. The man was secured to the wooden chair with thick plastic packing tape. He looked pretty beat up and was spitting out bloody teeth by the time we reached him. The guards were laughing at the man as they took turns punching him in the face. Dr. Dave screamed something in Chinese, and they stopped. The man was weeping, I saw Dr. Dave pull him up by his hair and scream something at him. The man sobbed harder as Dr. Dave walked away. The guards grabbed his arms and straightened them over the workbench in front of him. Dr. Dave returned with a large metal hammer, took a few tall nails from the plastic bins on the table and began violently whacking them into both the man's hands. The man screamed as the nails pierced bone, flesh and nerve. I tasted vile puke as it entered my mouth and swallowed it quickly, afraid to show any weakness.

That is when Dr. Dave looked me sternly in the face and placed the hammer in my hands. I looked at the weapon and then back at him. He shook his head as he read my thoughts. I looked to Shu Shu, and he also nodded. The man began to shriek loudly as spittle flew from whatever yellow stained teeth remained in his mouth. Dr. Dave slapped him hard in the face as I made my way over to the table and swapped out the hammer for a heavier wooden mallet. The mallet was chunky, well-worn with years of good use and felt heavier than I would have thought.

I examined the weapon, increased my grip, looked at the mans impaled hands and raised the mallet high above my head. I released it with all the fury of a berserker in battle. The wooden hammer with its large flat head came crashing down, splitting the man's hand, and shattering his fragile bones. He shrieks were piercing as I continued to pound the man's fingers into mincemeat.

Shu Shu grabbed me forcefully by the arms, snapping me back to reality. I gave my best war cry, looked at the mangled hands, and dropped the mallet on to the dirty factory floor. I was full of adrenaline, punched the man in the face and wanted more. Dr. Dave had enough sense not to kill the guy and grabbed me from behind in a "bear hug" rendering me useless. Both of them, talked me down as Shu Shu forcefully led me back outside the factory doors.

I stumbled outside, breathed in the noxious air, and grabbed another smoke off the guards. I was shaking and laughing maniacally now, trying to contain my nerves. The guards joined me in smoking, gave Shu Shu a butt and then they all talked quietly amongst themselves.

Soon afterwards, Dr. Dave emerged from inside with the bleeding man over his shoulder. The man had a dirty cloth stuffed in his mouth and his eyes appeared to be swollen shut. Dr. Dave did not pay us any attention and walked directly to the open trunk of Shu Shu's car. He threw the bloody man in and slammed it shut. He walked around to the driver's seat, said something to the guards and then to Shu Shu. He then shut the car door, opened the window, wished me a happy birthday, and quickly sped away. We heard the sound of the engine trailing off in the distance.

Shu Shu seemed jubilant as he led me back inside the factory towards his office. He didn't seem concerned that any further consequences would come from this. Tonight, might have been my party but really it was an evening of education about power and how much of it Shu Shu and his entourage had. I also learned more about the culture of our China factory and the power it wielded. It became evident that this factory was not only responsible for my income but was also its own kingdom, and whatever happened in its walls, stayed within its walls. I was also beginning to understand why Mei Mei had such interest in what Shu Shu was up to. He seemed to be able to get away with almost anything and I'm sure that made some people very uncomfortable.

Perhaps tonight I also understood what power really was. *Raw power* was more than another Iggy Pop song. Raw power was something to respect and only those who possessed it, could wield it as they chose. It was as dangerous as the violence it projected and yet somehow it seemed to ensure safety in this cruel world. I now believed that dominance like that was to be admired by few and feared by most. I always wished I had that kind of raw power, since I had been fighting both real and imaginary demons my entire life.

35

My War, *Ann Arbor, Michigan—circa 1987*

My first real attempt at college was to go away to the biggest party school I could find in the Midwest.

Not only was this Big Ten school infamous for its nightlife, but it was also ground zero for the emerging Midwest punk music scene. It was on this sprawling campus of elite students that I witnessed firsthand the debauchery of frat parties and the pure lunacy that went along with it. Even though I was personally against joining any fraternity, or any club that would have me as a member, I could not ignore how much I enjoyed their brotherhood despite the ensuing chaos.

Being a heavily muscled punk rocker from NY *(who was not afraid to fight)* brought me instant respect from the older college students. I loved to drink and didn't mind starting a violent scene whenever necessary. Since this was the usual modus operandi at a frat party, I thought I fit right in. However, I had several problems, and one of them was the morning blackouts. Instead of being in a warm bed or at a diner having coffee with my peers, I would often awake alone at a bus station, bloody, confused with no idea where I was or what I had done.

As you can imagine, things declined rapidly for me during my *fabulous* freshman year. Fraternities never wanted me to officially join them often using the excuse about my violent tendencies and the liability of their fraternal organizations. Instead of ruining their prestigious lineage, they opted just to have me around as muscle or entertainment. I was fine with that, as well, and made their notorious scenes of punishing their pledges far worse than they could themselves! I would often wander around at night to find a frat house in which to drink, fight, and screw. When that house got tired of all the negative attention I was bringing, I was asked to leave. I became *"that guy"* and, like a homeless vampire, would float from party to party, looking to be invited in. When the scene was raucous (as it always was when I was around), something violent would happen to get me thrown out. I made myself an easy target to blame and was often thrown under the bus every time things got out of hand. The more this happened, the fewer places I could go and the lonelier I became. All this self-pity made me sick with depression, and that sickness easily turned into alcohol-fueled rage.

I must confess that I did not only take my aggression out on males. I also had issues with women and made some bad choices when it came to sorority girls. With these girls, I showed the same non-caring disrespect that I had for their masculine brethren. I was like a wild animal in heat, screwing anyone I could. I didn't care about remembering their names or even if they had boyfriends. After all, if they had boyfriends, I wasn't afraid to fight them.

I made enemies of both sexes in what seemed like every fraternity and sorority on campus. I was a hated, felt like a marked man and was convinced that everyone was out to get me. The paranoia became over-whelming, and I imagined that people were going to kill me for beating up their boyfriends or for all the damage I had done to their girlfriends. The alcohol rage blurred the lines between reality and insanity, and I spun out of control.

It got so bad that I would lock myself in my room for days on end, drinking quarts of *Southern Comfort (So Co)* and ordering in Chinese food. The paranoia was so debilitating that it took a lot of doing just to get the front door open a crack to allow my food in. I would also not open any of my dorm windows for fear of being attacked and I was on the eleventh floor! I kept my doors locked and then used the metal mattress platform as a barricade to my bedroom. I knew my suitemates were concerned about me, as well as my folks. However, I didn't really care as I was wrapped up in my alcohol induced paranoia and went a long time without talking to anyone.

But I did listen to the messages left on my answering machine and knew enough that I needed to respond, or I'd be on a one-way trip back home. The future was bleak at school, but I was determined not to go home! There was a particular message left from Dr. Hurtz, letting me know that he had planned for me to go to the school's counseling center. He told me that, "they had my background and all I needed to do was check in with them ASAP."

To get everyone off my back, I made a promise to him and to my folks that I would leave my cave and seek help with the school's shrink department. My Grandpa left me a message as well, "to let me know he thought this was a good idea." I wasn't so sure but was out of options, so I made an appointment and they agreed to see me the following day.

Leaving the safety of my fortress was one of the hardest things I had ever done. It was like stepping in quicksand with cement shoes just to get across the threshold and out of my dorm room. It took sheer courage, a few Xanax and another pint of *So Co* to make this happen. Once outside the safety of my room, I looked frantically around for the inevitable attack to come, and when it didn't, I quickly made my way to the elevator to push the down button.

When the doors opened, there were four boys already in the elevator. Just my fucking luck! I debated turning around, but then corrected myself, counted backwards from five, took a deep breath and cautiously stepped in. I did a quick assessment, eyeing everything and everyone in rapid succession. I must have looked (and smelled) like a hobo train wreck. The boys took notice of my appearance and began to whisper to each other with nervous smiles. I instantly processed this as a threat and was quickly convinced they were laughing at me. I was sure they would be attacking me in no time, and I was positive that I did something to deserve their fury.

Determined to never become a victim, what came next was another instance of my crazy-quick paranoid reaction. Without any thought to consequences, I switched to autopilot, and I turned my back on them, reached down and unbuckled the sharp studded leather straps off my combat boots. I proceeded to wind them tight around my knuckles and flexed my fists. I immediately spun to face the youths and began to attack them with a fast barrage of violent, well-placed punches to the face. There was no order to the attack and certainly no warning. The poor kids did not have a chance to react as I knocked them to the floor with a flurry of violent strikes to their body and face. They were trapped in a small space with a fist wielding maniac, and they dropped hard, transforming their smiling faces to looks of horror, confusion, and pain.

When the elevator opened on the ground floor, I immediately exited, leaving the boys wailing in shock as they grabbed their battered faces in disbelief. I ran as fast as I could across campus, away from the counseling center, to find solace in the only place that always accepted me... *The Black Hole Bar*. It was here that I would often come to seek out the loud jukebox and cheap beer on tap. It was your typical dive bar in the frozen Midwest, dimly lit with tacky Coors neon signs, a small triangle stage in the corner, a large wooden bar with red vinyl stools that were ripped and spun around with your body weight. Everyone knew this was *my place* and within the hour, both the campus and state police found me drunk and swaying to Iggy Pop's, "*Lust for Life*."

I can still recall the scene quite visibly as the cops entered the bar with their nightsticks unleashed and ready for action. The campus security quickly identified me, and that was all it took for the state police to begin shouting commands at me. They unzipped a large body bag that looked more like a strait jacket, placed it on the floor, and shouted at me to drop my beer and to get in it. They planned to remove me like the insane animal I'd become, zipped and tied inside that bag. They yelled that either I do it myself "nice and easy" or they would force me in "against my will."

The choice was apparently mine, and since I was in no mood to compromise, I did the only stupid thing I knew how. It was that damn fight-or-flight instinct—and I never run. Instead, I picked up the closest beer bottle and smashed it against the bar. That was all it took for the closest officer to swing his nightstick to the side of my head. My knees instantly buckled as I crashed to the floor. Then there was the sheer crushing weight of several officers as they pinned me down, handcuffed me and tried to shove me in the bag. I fought to move some more and was immediately hit again. This time my eyes rolled into the back of my head, and I blacked out.

36

Somebody Put Something in my Drink *Shenzhen, China -
Circa 1998*

Shenzhen roared out of the sea like some sort of prehistoric Phoenix.
Its wings blacking out the skyline, while it peered menacing at its democratic brother, the great city of Hong Kong.

The city had been brought to life by sheer willingness to compete and
ultimately destroy its southern neighbor. Shenzhen enjoyed its proximity to freedom and the spoils that came with being the infamous Chinese
city that shared a border with independence. All business channels into
China back in those days, had no choice but to flow through the city
of steel and consummate consumerism. Cultures clashed as the Phoenix was determined to side with freedom and conceal any negative side
effects of its new dawning. The city appeared to breathe on fast money,
drugs and corruption. It was here in the belly of the beast that I was *roof-
ied* for the first time. Like everything else in China, this was no accident.

I knew it as soon as I attempted to stand up. Feeling completely
off balance, I held the table in a death grip, almost turning it over and
dumping all the drinks on the floor.

"Whoa Rick, you, OK?" asked Shu Shu loudly over the deafening house music.

I tried to focus on the scene in front of me, taking notice of Shu Shu's big smile. The club was packed with people much younger than the both of us. They were dancing and smoking homemade cigarettes laced with opium and marijuana. I know this because I remember smoking them with all the patrons partying around our table. They looked like kids to me, but I learned early on that looks can be deceiving, especially in China where no one seemed to age. I white knuckled the table hoping to fight off the dizziness threatening to turn my legs into *Jello*. Shu Shu must have saw me suffering and made a gesture to the two girls sitting next to me. They both stood up and grabbed me by the arms.

"Rick!" Shu Shu screamed, "I think you should take a walk with these two and maybe find a bathroom, you look like you're going to be sick."

The big kid next to Shu Shu stood up as well and talked forcefully to the girls. He had tattoo sleeves which were uncommon in those days unless you were in the *Yakuza*. I had my eye on him ever since we entered the club. He was the son of one of Shu Shu's connections and he organized the table, the girls and the drinks. He appeared to be a tough guy and didn't like that I was casually taking pictures of everyone earlier in the night. I remembered lucidly that he forcefully knocked my phone to the ground and got in my face with his cigarette breath. I didn't fight back because I knew Mei Mei would want those photos and I was just doing my job.

I tried to focus on his glare and snarl back with my best fuck you face.

He shot me the bird and laughed loudly just as the girls were grappling with me to move away from the table. My feet felt like I was floating, while my head felt completely disconnected from my body. It was the strangest feeling that I had in a while and knew that I was a lot more than intoxicated.

I let the girls manhandle me across the busy dance floor and to the WC. (Wash Closet or bathroom). I could barely operate my legs and felt the familiar heat rise to my ears. I was going to be sick. The girls must have sensed this as well, so they quickened their pace and talked loudly to one of the bouncers outside the bathroom doors.

The man quickly grabbed me from the girls, appearing to lift me off my feet and kick open the doors of the closest stool. Thankfully it was more than a hole in the ground. To my surprise there was a porcelain toilet bowl that appeared to call my name. I quickly dropped to my knees holding onto the ceramic bowl for dear life.

The heat in my ears became fire and that flame turned my stomach upside down as I wretched inside the throne of asses. I prayed to the porcelain Gods to save me from myself as I projected my liquid mess all over the stall. I concentrated on breathing in between bouts of sickness. I am not sure how long the misery lasted, but it felt like an eternity before the doors flew open revealing Shu Shu and small army of security guards.

"Jesus Rick!" exclaimed Shu Shu as he raced to put his arms around me and lift me to my feet.

The security guards were flanked around the both of us and screaming something in Chinese. I saw Shu Shu peel off a role of Chinese RMB and give it to everyone around us.

They must have appreciated that, as more arms held me up and started to walk me out of the club. Everything appeared to be in slow motion as I struggled to keep my feet straight and my head up. We passed by the table we were sitting at, and I tried unsuccessfully to glare at the man with the tattoos. Shu Shu said something to him that didn't sound like pleasantries.

Unfortunately, Dr, Dave was not with us that night and I was no shape to help Shu Shu. Both men appeared to argue quickly and the two girls from before quickly came to my side. I saw Shu Shu throw more money and an envelope on the table. The man appeared to quickly snatch up the cash and gave the envelope to another person sitting next to him. I tried to focus on the scene and swore that he appeared to be smiling at me. I did what came naturally and gave him the double bird. He started laughing loudly as the gang walked me outside the club and over to the hotel elevators.

When the elevators opened Shu Shu pushed me inside with the two girls in tow. My legs gave out immediately sending me crashing to the floor. Shu Shu got right in my face.

"Rick, you with me?" he asked slapping the side of my face with intent. I tried to focus on him but felt the strength diminishing from my body.

"C'mon pal," he said and motioned to the girls to help me to my feet.

I felt hands around me tugging me to my feet. Thankfully there was a *safety bar* around the elevator for me to rest my limp body against. I held on to it with all my will and when the doors opened to the lobby on the 6th floor, I practically fell out, landing hard on the hotel floor. I started laughing immediately as I fought to stop my head from spinning off my neck. I heard Shu Shu yelling and a lot of commotion followed.

Hands reached for me again as I was lifted onto the bottom of the concierge's luggage cart. Through blurry eyes, I saw the girls, Shu Shu and other uniformed hotel staff as they wheeled me across the lobby floor and over to the hotel elevators. My eyes felt like they were going backwards into my skull, and I lost my will to sit and lied down on my side, hoping to somehow *ride this out*. My eyes were mere slits as the elevator doors shut and we all rode to the top floor.

I felt the ground move again as the cart was being pushed forcefully across the carpet. I must have been dead weight because the cart seemed to constantly crash into the walls and other doors on the floor. We must have made a lot of noise and hotel security now joined this parade. Shu Shu was talking again to the others as the cart seemed to suddenly stop with a loud bang against the door.

I tried to sit up now and with the girl's help was able to will myself into a cross-legged position. I saw the security guys open the door to my room. They positioned the luggage cart once again and pushed me forcefully into the room. I saw Shu Shu break out more cash as he talked quickly to the security guys and then to the girls. The security guards left promptly and the girls disappeared into the bathroom. I heard the toilet flush and then the sound of water being filled into a tub.

Shu Shu got down to my level once again and started to slap my face.

"Rick, hello, anyone home," he said.

I opened my eyes wide this time and tried to stare back at him.

"Fuck off" is what I tried to say.

Shu Shu stopped hitting me and grabbed me under my arms. He forcefully lifted me off of the luggage cart and let me drop to the ground. I stayed silent for a few beats and tried to focus on my body and sitting up again.

The girls came back and helped me to a seated position. Shu Shu had another talk with them, and I felt hands grabbing at my clothes attempting to disrobe me. I did not fight back as I had no humility left and certainly not the strength. When they wrestled me down to my underpants, Shu Shu took over and man-handled me over to the bath. He quickly checked the water temperature and turned everything off.

I started laughing for some reason and told him, "That I was a very dirty girl."

Shu Shu paid me no attention and wrestled me into the shallow tub. The water felt shockingly cold to my body, but I quickly settled as the water mellowed with my body temperature.

"Rick, I'm going to leave you here with one of the girls." Shu Shu continued. "I will just be next door and she can reach me if you need me."

"But Shu Shu, I got my underpants on," I slurred while trying to wrestle them down my legs and off.

With that, Shu Shu and one of the girls left the bathroom and out of my room. I wrestled with my underpants some more getting them caught around my feet. The girl remaining in the bathroom with me saw me struggling and came over to help. She grabbed at my underpants to free them from captivity and placed them promptly in the sink.

I squirmed in my nakedness and tried to sit up. The girl came back to try and get me to lay back down. I quickly grabbed her and used my weight to pull her into the tub with me. She screamed with the sudden freight of being pulled into a body of water with a naked man. A heavily tattooed *Gweillo* tripping his balls off and smelling rank with puke. The girl fought her way out of the tub and grimaced at herself in the mirror, all wet and obviously scared. She turned to yell something at me, but I paid no attention.

She came back over, pulled the drain and handed me a small bath towel. I starred at the water as it drained down the pipes not built for human waste. When the water was gone, the girl turned on the hand shower head and sprayed warm water over my nakedness. I watched her as she tried to clean me as best as she could. Of course, it didn't help that I was way too tall for this bath and my body was lying uncomfortably half out of the tub.

When she finished, she put the hand nozzle back, grabbed the tiny towel and tried her best to dry me off. I think I managed to croak out a "thank you."

"You out – Zou!" she said repeating this to me several times. I didn't need to be told twice. However, my brain was not cooperating with my body.

I held onto the side of the tub and pushed my nakedness over the side. She grabbed at my wet body and together lifted me over the side where I fell quickly onto the cold marble floor.

"Ouch" I managed to say and smiled at her like I was in love.

She ignored me and went over to the shower and turned it on.

"No, I managed to say. "No more water for me."

"Out" she said forcefully and pointed to the bedroom.

She quickly undressed, put on a shower cap from the hotel toiletries kit and entered the shower before I had a chance to comment. I tried to grip onto the sides of the sink to lift myself up into a standing position. I stood slowly holding on for dear life. I tried to make out my reflection, but the steam hid what I knew to be a mirror of deception.

Despite my efforts, I could not find my legs long enough underneath me and quickly dropped back down onto my hands and knees. Like some sort of pathetic baby, I attempted to crawl out of the bathroom, losing my hand towel in the process.

I made my way past the luggage cart and over to the edge of the bed. The bed was higher off the ground that I wished it to be. The mattress was sunk into a Formica base, and I used the edge to try and stabilize myself enough to stand. I was on my knees for a few beats when I decided to give standing up a try and channeled my inner *homo erectus*. Like a baby, I pulled myself up, unsteadily into a standing position.

Once *erect*, I made a move to the bed and instantly face planted violently onto the side of the platform frame. What came next can only be described as pure horror as I felt excrement flying out of my asshole. The fall must have tricked my mind into thinking that this was the end and in so, activated the *'scared the shit out of me response!'*

Thankfully, there was enough mattress to cushion the fall just enough not to do permanent damage to my face. My eyes quickly closed as the stench started to erupt into my nostrils. I heard the girl come back into the room and started to scream, "No, no, no!" over in a loop.

I could not move my head and felt paralyzed from the neck down. Only my eyes seemed to work as I tried to make out the frantic girl. She came back from the bathroom talking loudly into her phone. I felt another tiny towel in between my legs as she tried to desperately clean up my mess while still shouting on the phone.

The stench only grew as the shit smeared over my naked body. I tried to turn my head away from the stench, but my body was not cooperating with my wishes, and I started to vomit again. I closed my eyes as I began to choke on my own puke.

Here comes sickness…

37

Loose Nut, *Boston, MA—circa 1987*

Grandpa Butch with the help of Dr. Hurtz, bailed me out of the insurmountable trouble I had caused at the University.

They had arranged transportation from Michigan to a treatment facility back East that claimed to have success treating adolescents and young adults. Specifically, those who also had addiction issues. My restraints were replaced with medication to control my violent outbursts. The medication was called *Thorazine*, and it rendered me fat, lazy and useless. Its side effects would cause me to shuffle my feet and drool hopelessly all the time. I was the furthest away from my true horrible self than I had ever been, and I was scared to death of my current situation. I had finally lost my mind. Instead of complacency, I was determined to get off this crippling drug. I needed my Rick Price *mojo* back and was determined to regain my strength and fury. I needed to change my condition and get back to my life no matter how fucked up I or it was.

After a week of being on my best behavior and placating the resident shrinks, they replaced my tranquilizing medicine with a new wonder drug. They called this drug *Paxil* and was in the same class of SSRIs as *Prozac* only this was the new and improved version. Also, it had a sedative side effect that was supposed to keep me drowsy and calm. Sure, I was skeptical, it's *my nature*. I was not happy being anyone's guinea pig, but I must admit that this drug packed a wallop of a Serotonin boost. I don't know if being sober also helped, but the combination hit me hard, and I had to admit that I liked this new feeling of control!

I used this newfound energy to quickly try and get back into shape. At night, instead of sleeping, I snuck in endless rounds of push-ups and sit-ups. During the day, I meditated on retracing every move of my Krav Maga training. After another successful week of good behavior my restrictions were lifted, and I was finally able to take walks outside by myself. The hospital was in rural Massachusetts, and it was easy for me to find a thick tree where I could hide and practice endless hours of forearm blasting and *Iron Fist* training.

Unobserved, I chipped away at the hardest trees and quickly regrew back the bone density on my knuckles, forearms, and shins. I punched and kicked the wood until I could not feel pain. When this wasn't enough, I found the side of a brick building to practice on. I just needed to be careful not to let any physical bruises show or I would lose these privileges. I was still unsure what I was training for, but it felt good, nonetheless. And the pain, well, let's just say that it snapped my brain back into clarity. Welcome home my old friend!

By my second month, it was arranged for me to have my first in-hospital parent meeting. I was a bit anxious, but I knew if it went well, it would be another step closer to me getting out of this madhouse. My parents were on their best behavior and arrived on time, gave me a hug and then took their places around my shrink's office. It was a corner office, with great views of the arbor, and adorned with travel photos from all over the world. My shrink was a balding man who sat in a high back leather chair behind a serious looking desk with a leather blotter, yellow legal pad and a coffee cup with the hospital name on it. My folks sat on a two seater leather couch, and I sat across from them on a plush armchair.

My shrink spoke so softly that sometimes it was impossible to make out what he was saying. He had a slight frame, but today there was a certain spring in his step and a surprising loudness to his voice. It was as if he was showing off to my folks. I noticed the confidence (or cockiness) in his voice as he began to tell my parents all about the positive work we'd been doing and my recent complacency to changes in my behavior.

He began to brag about the institution and how all of his patients eventually came around to making serious changes in their decision-making process, leading them to more productive lives. This got my immediate attention, and I sensed there was more behind his cavalier bravado. I'd never felt complacent about anything, especially my time here, and I began to resent him. I smelled a rat, and this induced my anger and paranoia.

My parents nodded in disbelief as my shrink told them about all the wonderful changes I had acquiesced to. He droned on about his confidence in his ability to change all the patient's thought patterns and impact their ability to make correct choices in their actions. In fact, he took all the credit for my newfound clarity and now my bullshit meter was on high alert. I wasn't sure where he was going with all this, but I knew that reptile smile on his face was not going to be good for me.

The good doctor pressed an intercom button and said to his secretary to, "let them in." In a matter of minutes, six sizeable security officers entered the room. They must have been planted right outside the door. The largest one was carrying a restraining body bag under his arm and quickly unfolded it onto the floor. I knew this drill well, they appeared to be *recreating the scene at the university*. I immediately jumped up, looking for the nearest escape as the men surrounded me. I automatically took a defensive posture, spreading my legs wide and raising my hands into balled fists.

"Rick," my shrink said softly now. "You finally have the chance to show your parents how much you have grown up in the past few months."

"Fuck off," I growled in disgust.

"Now, Rick, life is about making the right choices and understanding the consequences. Right now, you need to make the right choice and get into that bag." He pointed towards the straight jacket on the floor.

The men approached slowly. I immediately recognized this as yet another fight-or-flight situation and, as you know, I do not back down from confrontation. All the Paxil in the world would not help get me back into that bag. My shrink had to know this about me and used it against me to prove his power to my parents. This wasn't a test, but a *power trip* designed to humiliate and emasculate me. It was just a bullshit show to make them believe I had turned a corner. Or maybe it was some sort of karmic payback. That bag again and all it symbolized. My weakness or submissiveness—either way, I was not having any of it!

Instinctively, I picked up my plush chair and threw it in their direction. It was heavier than I imagined and didn't go very far to achieving my target. My mom started to scream as the men held their positions. My shrink stood up and quickly walked to the front of his desk to bravely confront me. Easy to do with six security bouncers...

"Rick, I am disappointed by your decision, I thought you wanted to get out of here and go home," he said. "The only way home is to do as you're told and make the right decision for yourself. So please, I am asking you to lie down in that bag. Show your parents some self-control," he said in his best psychobabble shrink voice.

That was enough bullshit for me.

"Okay," I said and lowered my hands. "Everyone just relax as I make the *right* decision here. Just give me a moment to do the *right* thing." I looked down at the bag and then at my parents.

"Look, this is difficult for me," I said, "but I understand what you are trying to do." I said placating them.

I looked around the room, addressing the situation and making some very fast decisions. I did my best to smile warmly and appear to be non-confrontational.

I started to slowly walk to the bag, but quickly spun around and sent a front kick up between the legs of my shrink. It landed with such force that his feet lifted off the ground. I caught him with an elbow to the neck and then spun him around in a headlock to face the security guards.

I was much too fast for them and screamed for everyone to, "back off!" My father started to scream my name. The men were not easily intimidated and they quickly jumped over the furniture to try and tackle me. I went down with the shrink still in my arms. There were hands all over me, trying to pin me down. Instinctively, I released the doctor and crouched into a defensive position, guarding myself between my elbows.

There were just too many of them on top of me, and their crushing weight was beginning to drain all my strength and whatever breath I had left in my lungs. In a matter of minutes, I was dragged to the open bag. They held me down as someone began quickly zipping up the bag. I tried my best to thrash my legs but had no more room to kick. After they got my arms inside, I was rendered helpless and resorted to screaming incomprehensible insults at my parents as they zipped me up. My folks appeared to be in shock as they huddled in the corner horrified, screaming, and holding onto each other.

A male nurse came in with a large needle. He released my arm from the bag while the rest of them held me down. I tried to fight but they had me good and tight. The needle was plunged forcefully into my shoulder. I felt the drug immediately as it burned through my veins. Before I blacked out, I remember looking at my parents who were now crying loudly and hugging each other. The sight of them sobbing made me ill.

38

Sick Boy, *Dongguan City, China—circa 2002*

Getting sick in China was unavoidable.

These were the days before SARS and bird flu became household names. China was an incubator, a hotbed of disease. It didn't matter what precautions were taken; how much soap you could find, or how careful you ate, at some point you were going to get seriously ill. What you didn't know was when, how bad it would get, and how long would it take for you to recover.

We all tried our best, but the odds were stacked against us. Our spoiled Western bodies were just not prepared for the ugly sickness and bacteria that the common Chinese lived with. Even with a bag filled with *Imodium, Kaopectate, Pepto Bismol, Tums, Advil, Vicks Day/NyQuil, Vitamin C, Zinc, Lysol, Toilet Paper, a Z pack (Zithromax antibiotics)—or amoxicillin*! It still didn't matter; you were a walking target for diseases.

In China back then, the bathrooms never had hand soap, toilet paper, or even toilet seats. Those common-sense necessities were high-ticket items. If found, they were stolen immediately. Since these were the early days before hand sanitizer, it was impossible to keep yourself clean. China was also very slow to understand the importance of the great toilet throne. They were used to shitting in holes, and that was good enough for them.

To us Gweilos, it was impossible to understand how to do this shitting act in a hole. What's the technique? Do you face the wall or the stall door? How far do you need to squat to clear your clothes? What do you hold onto, since there were no handicapped rails, especially if you are a bit backed up? And what do you do with your jeans to make sure they stay off the contaminated floor and remain clean from the shit?

There were never directions, and we all experimented in horror. Fair to say, when toilet bowls started to become the norm, there were graphic illustrations teaching the Chinese how to properly use them. Even still, they would jump on top of the toilet seat and squat over it. I know this because of the clear footprints I saw on the toilet rims. Even though the signs clearly showed proper procedure, the Chinese still felt more comfortable squatting than sitting! Need I say more?

For this reason, we ate in terror, knowing it would ultimately end in our demise. The Chinese tried to help us feel more comfortable by washing our eating utensils in hot tea. This was a tradition at the beginning of each meal. As the tea steeped, the first glass was used to wash our chopsticks and bowls. We poured the hot tea on our eating paraphernalia in a vain attempt to be more sterile and knew that without soap, this was just a ceremony. But the Chinese were adamant about showing us face, and if cleanliness was in question, they were openly brazen to display the freshness of their food. Often restaurants resembled zoos where the animals including rodents, snakes, birds, exotic fish, and what we would consider domestic animals were on full display. It was a source of national pride to carefully pick out what you were going to eat. To save face, we all swallowed our discomfort and blindly followed along.

It didn't take me long to become a vegetarian in China. There was a bounty of vegetables always on hand and a bowl of bai fan (white rice) was just what I needed to keep everything safe inside my body. Actually, it was the soup (or hot pot) that was usually the most disgusting event of the meal. Take it from a pro, never drink the soup, and especially not the hot pot. Let's start with the contaminated water and then add whatever entrails, leftovers, and disgustingness was simmering inside of it. Never stir the broth or be ready to see things you cannot unsee. I reiterate: Never drink the soup! Never entertain the hot pot!

Sickness remained rampant and the norm in those early days consisting of full-on stomach viruses and unheard-of parasites. Even catching nasty colds that made you cough, and your chest hurt for months was commonplace. I am sure it was a mixture of unsanitary conditions and animals that were not meant to be eaten. Hell, there was even a factory in a remote mountain village that would feed me some sort of endangered snake-like animal. They said, "it was good for my *little brother*!" Little brother was the Chinese way of saying it was good for my cock. Nice of them to worry about that!

"I am a vegetarian," I would proudly proclaim as I forced myself to enjoy tofu, rice and some sort of Chinese vegetable reminding me of grass. Despite it all, the sickest I remember was an incident in mid-winter as Southern China had a strange way of becoming unbearably cold in the winter. I believe it had to do with working all day in a cement box of a factory resembling a cold storage freezer. There was no insulation, absolutely no heat, with windows busted open to expel out poisonous air while warehouse doors stood ajar. You quickly got cold, like a wet freezing blanket was set into your bones, making it difficult to concentrate. There was no respite to this bone chill, and most of the hotels back then also did not have heat! And if they did, it was piped through for only a few hours during the morning and turned off during the evening.

This one day was particularly brutal, with an uncommonly strong wind making matters worse. Shu Shu was also uncomfortable and mentioned that we should get a foot massage and put our feet inside a bath of scalding water. Sounded like heaven to me.

We ended up at some dirty shit box of a massage parlor, but they had heat and hot water. We defrosted our bodies, and I felt an uncontrollable cough coming on. I went into my backpack and loaded up on meds, vitamins, and cough drops. The massage felt more painful than relaxing. The pressure hurt me inside where my muscles felt tight and uncomfortable. But it was warm in that little room, and I soon began to sweat profusely.

When it was over, Shu Shu laughed that I looked like a ghost. I did not feel well and mentioned that I needed to "go back to the hotel, hope for a hot shower, and get some sleep." He obliged, paid for the massages, and then dropped me off at the hotel.

I walked to the front desk and asked in my best *Chinglish* for another blanket in the room. Of course, this was not understood, and I heard mention of payment for this request. I called Shu Shu, put him on with the front desk, and all was taken care of.

That night, I slept like the dead, and when I woke up, I felt exactly like I had died. I was freezing and sweating through the blankets with a high fever. I took a drink of water from the plastic bottle next to my bed but immediately threw it up the second it hit my stomach. I retched all over myself. I struggled to get out of bed and to the bathroom. I had trouble finding my legs and felt heat rush over my ears. I vomited some more, projecting my spew uncontrollably all over the tiled floor. I had no idea what to do next as I didn't have the strength to stand. I fell into the tub and proceeded to shit and puke on myself at the same time. I was freezing cold and could not stop shivering and being sick. I managed to strip off my soiled clothes, throw them over the side and turned on the tub, waiting for the hot water to arrive. It was cold for a long while and I believe that kept me from passing out.

When the water began to steam, it was the smell of my own sickness that kept me gagging into the warm water. I didn't care that I was bathing in my own feces. The only thing I needed was the heat. I needed to warm my bones, my insides and just like that, I started to sweat as I began to make myself sick again. There was no stopping the disgust I felt. I knew this was bad and that I needed immediate help. I also knew I needed to get out of the bath before I passed out and drowned myself in my own filth.

I pulled the drain and turned the handheld shower head on cold. It immediately woke me up as I flopped out of the tub and onto the cold floor like a whale at SeaWorld. I reached for a towel and then a robe. Both were ridiculously small, but they did the job. I crawled through the damage that I just made until I reached my cell phone on the side of the bed. The smell wafting around almost made me gag again. I hit my speed dial and waited for Shu Shu to answer.

After some time laying on my side, I heard several knocks on the door. I was in no condition to answer. I heard Shu Shu calling my name and then the door electronically clicked open. My eyes wandered into the back of my head as I noticed Shu Shu enter with Dr. Dave and a few hotel housekeepers. I felt Dr. Dave lift me up as Shu Shu roughly put clothes on me. Before I knew it, I was outside in the cold and gently dumped into the backseat of his car.

"Where we going?" I managed to croak.

"Hospital," is all I heard.

Normally, this would have made me feel more comfortable, but from what I heard about Chinese hospitals, all I wanted was to be home.

We pulled up in front of the hospital, and Dr. Dave carried me out of the car. He threw me over his shoulder like a dead man. He ran inside, screaming in Chinese. I took a drowsy look around in the dim light. There appeared to be people littered everywhere. They were lying on top of soiled newspapers on the floor trying to get comfortable. They all looked infected, and the place reeked of sickness. Two shabbily dressed guards tried to protest Dr. Dave's intrusion. They were quickly put in their place as Dr. Dave impatiently made his move to the front of the line. There were several more protests, and then I noticed Shu Shu's arrival. He quickly made his way over to the front of the line and gave the head nurse a large handful of Chinese money. He whispered something in her ear. She nodded in approval and Dr. Dave made his way over to Shu Shu. We were quickly escorted to a small bed in an overcrowded room. I heard moaning but couldn't tell if it was my own or others.

A nurse came by, spoke with Shu Shu, and returned with a bag of IV fluids. She gave it to Dr. Dave to hold while she forcefully shoved the large needle into the top of my hand. She was not gentle, and I was not given the chance to protest. I closed my eyes and hoped for the best. My mind started to drift away.

I was awakened by the same nurse as she switched the fluid bags. Again, Dr. Dave was left with the chore of holding the fluids. He had a heated exchange with the nurse, and Shu Shu was there to try and calm everyone down. Some more money was exchanged, and shortly afterwards, what appeared to be a doctor, in a white smock with a clipboard entered the room making his way over to us. Some pleasantries were exchanged and then I was lost as they began to discuss the state of my illness. The doctor shook his head a lot and left the room.

Before I had a chance to ask what was happening, he returned with a silver tray. On the tray were two very large silver needles attached to what looked like a silver plunger out of some Nazi concentration camp film. The doctor said something, and Dr. Dave quickly flipped me over onto my stomach. He pulled my pants down and I instantly knew where these shots were headed. I closed my eyes as the first needle pierced my left butt cheek with incredible pain. It did not stop as I felt the liquid plunge deep into my tissue. This was repeated on my other ass cheek. Forget saving face, I groaned loudly this time.

Dr. Dave laughed at this and flipped me back over. The doctor gave Shu Shu two boxes of pills and then said goodbye. He left the room without ever looking at me or checking any vitals. Shu Shu told me we could leave when the IV bag was empty. He also told me to take two pills from each box every four hours until they were done. I didn't bother to ask him what they were, my only thought was that there was no way any of the needles were clean, let alone sterilized.

This thought haunted me for the rest of my road to recovery. It was a slow path of high fever, nausea, and gut-wrenching pain. I could not keep anything down for days and lived off hot tea mixed with ginger root and Coca-Cola. I needed to get well enough to make it over the border into Hong Kong but knew it was useless until my fever subsided. They had guards at the border checking temperatures and quarantining anyone with a fever. I was not going to be one of those escorted off the line, never to be heard from again.

When I was finally well enough to cross that border and take a flight home, I checked in immediately with my U.S. doctor. He asked me lots of questions, took vials of blood, and then had me escorted to the hospital. There they immediately transferred me to the Infectious Disease wing. I was instantly stripped of my clothing, possessions, and my family. They held me in quarantine for several days where I was administered more tests and still more questions. They continued to ask about my whereabouts, what I ate, and what was given to me in China.

Most of these I could not answer nor remember, and it was near impossible to explain Southern China to my Western doctors. We were all nervously waiting for the results of my tests and I was convinced something irreversible had happened to my health. My mind was on overload again about what I did for a living, and was it all worth it? Why continue to put myself in harm's way? Was I just some sort of adrenaline junkie? Or was it (as I feared) just a byproduct of my dance with insanity. Either way, I could not help but feel scared for the first time that I was bringing home a piece of me I wanted to keep hidden from my family. They were innocent and unfortunately, only guilty by association. I swore to never bring home anything that could threaten the wholesome sanctity of my family. I did a good job of keeping myself in check as I tried to protect them from myself. Regrettably, life became much bigger than me and was often out of my control. My family was bound to suffer along with me. I was either a danger to them or a threat to myself.

39

Institutionalized, *Boston, MA—circa 1987*

The hospital considered me a menace to the general population, committing me to undergo deeper psychiatric testing and analysis.

Knowing that I was easily agitated, the staff did their best to keep me contained and separated from the others. At the very least, they kept me doped up on *antipsychotics* and took away all my privileges. With no more free time to displace my aggression with positive exercise, that anger simmered under the surface, looking for an escape.

After a few weeks of good behavior, it was decided that I would attend mandatory group therapy sessions aiming to try and socialize me into the general population again. I complied with all their requests regarding this *second chance* and did my best to appease the staff. I was escorted to these sessions, where the other patients would take turns spouting their mind-numbing bullshit in hopes of being heard. I had zero ability to empathize with others and found these sessions to be a complete bore fest. If anything, *group therapy* did nothing but agitate me further, alienating me from the rest of my group. I hated whining people, with their self-obsessed problems, talking about their feelings. *"Fuck that and fuck them!"* They were not my peers but a bunch of crybabies, still seeking their mommy's and daddy's attention. It was so cliché! You know, the usual spiel about neglect, emotional abuse, addiction, anxiety, depression— *"boo fucking hoo"!*

Just like their parents had done to them, I paid the group no mind and began to occupy my thoughts with blinding agitation. I couldn't stand to hear their sob stories, so I didn't speak or engage with any of them. When I was spoken to, I remained silent and resilient. I built an impenetrable wall of defiance in the form of noncompliance. Like The Who's, *Tommy* character, I became 'deaf, dumb, and blind'... whatever it took for everyone to leave me alone!

The group had rules of engagement and they were not satisfied with my lack of participation. I was convinced that they all just wanted to torture me with their problems, and there was one girl in particular, *Maddie*, who seemed adamant to piss me off. I guess there was always one in the bunch who needed to be heard more than the others. I learned that many years ago at the punk rock shows. Even though it was a collective group of anarchy seekers, there was always one individual who thought they were special. You know the type, the one who got drunk and started fights with anyone not paying attention to them.

This girl Maddie was a real piece of work. She was short and stocky with a bull dyke haircut, who needed to command the room every time she spoke. She absolutely couldn't stand my silence and indifference to her plight. We seemed to have had a genuine hatred for each other and I couldn't stand her stories of emotional abuse or her wild fantasies about killing her parents. Needless to say, she was not a *Rick Price* fan, and I couldn't really blame her for that.

One day, Maddie made the cardinal sin of singling me out and confronting me in front of the others. She stood in my face, invading my personal space, and challenged my decision to remain unresponsive in front of the group. I could see the counselors getting uncomfortable as she yelled at me for having a "holier than thou" attitude. She spat her wrath directly at me and her spittle landed on my stubbled face. I don't do well with physical confrontations and well, enough was enough. I quickly became impassioned with my old friend anger and decided that she needed to be stopped immediately. She crossed the line, and I was going to put her in her place.

Without warning, I quickly jumped out of my aluminum folding seat and grabbed Maddie by the throat with both hands, quickly pinning her against the wall. Her eyes bugged out in fear as I quickly tightened my grip on her neck. I did not hear the others screaming or see or feel anything except how easy it would be to kill her. She was clawing at my arms and then tried for my face in a desperate attempt to free herself from my solid grip. I had my considerable size and rage to keep me safe from her lame attacks. I felt unusually high on endorphins and she grew weak under my control. I could feel her delicate neck bones under my constricted grip.

Time seemed to stop as it often did when I raged. I did not notice the screaming counselors, security officers and other panicked patients. I kept my eyes locked on hers. She tried to claw one last time at my face, but my arms were much longer than hers. I was so much stronger, I had her pinned against the paneled wall and felt invincible. So much so, that I did not feel the shot of Thorazine as it plunged deep into my neck. I did not remember going out.

I awoke in complete misery, restrained to a bed with the worst *hangover* headache I ever had. I lost the ability to move except for slight motions of my head, or maybe it was just my eyes? For what seemed like a week, I was left alone to shit and piss myself like a captive animal. Only once a day I was force-fed with a spoon or other additives that they injected directly into my IV. At night, they gave me more jabs and made me swallow small paper cups of pills. No one communicated directly with me. No one paid me any attention except to change my pajamas, sponge clean my shit and give me the stink eye of disgust. Strangely, I was alright and comfortable with that look.

What bothered me more was feeling completely uselessness, since I had no ability to fight back. I tried to think of an escape but was stuck with incessant brain fog. I drooled continuously out of the corners of my mouth. At night when the meds kicked in, I was plagued with lucid nightmares. I remember distinctively dreaming about Maddie and her fantasies about killing her abusive family. Even though I might have wished to kill her, ironically, she was very much alive and stuck in my head. Throughout the haze of medication, she still managed to haunt me, even in my sleep. She was like a demon I could not shake out of my head. I had nightmares consumed with her presence. I swear she possessed my dreams, and I awoke breathless in a deep sweat.

This is what I remembered about the dream...

House of Suffering

It was the smell of those blueberry pancakes. That meant only one thing: Today was a special day, like a birthday or some other occasion. It was only on those rare weekend mornings that I can recall mom getting up early to cook for us. Dad, of course, could not be bothered to wake up and join the celebration. Instead, he chose to sequester in bed alone, nursing his usual hangover. He stayed there all day by himself, pretending to read the latest weekend edition of The New York Times. *There were so many newspapers scattered throughout that bedroom that it often reminded me of a graveyard where old news was left to die.*

I could not find my mother at this point. I frantically ran through the house looking for her. The smell of blueberries was now overshadowed by the smell of stale smoke. I called for my brother, but he did not respond. I ran to his room and found Maddie sitting on his bed. She was there, in her short haircut talking in a hushed voice to a few firemen. They were dressed in their full fire-retardant uniforms.

I asked Maddie, "What the fuck is going on and why are you sitting on my brother's bed?"

She turned slowly towards me and said, "Mom is dead."

"What?" I shook her in disbelief.

Then one of the firemen handed me a black lacquered box containing her ashes. Maddie turned back into my brother and started to cry.

"It's true, Rick. Mom died in a car fire," he said tearfully.

"What!" I exclaimed. That's impossible. I mean, it's Dad who's supposed to die in a car accident!"

It was then that my father appeared in the bedroom. He had a fresh martini in hand, and exclaimed to us all that, "She deserved this, she never listened to me, and she never took care of her car."

Then he got up close in my personal space, and I smelled the vodka on his breath, and it suffocated me like a wet blanket.

"Fluids," he said. "She never knew how to check the fluids."

Then my brother turned back into Maddie.

"And poof," Maddie said with exaggerated motion of her hands.

The firemen nodded at the box in my hands and left.

"Are you saying it was Mom's fault for not regularly checking the oil? She deserved to die for that?" I screamed in disbelief.

My father smiled a toothy grin, downed his glass, and left after the firemen.

Maddie then suggested that we needed to hide Mom's ashes so my father couldn't find them. I'm not sure why this was, but I followed her out of my brother's room and down the stairs to the living room. Maddie took the shiny box of ashes from me and placed them in a small carved wooden chest that held all of Mom's special candles and essential oils.

My dad reappeared in the room, holding the hand of his hairdresser, Jenna.

There was no mistaking Jenna, the blond hair extensions, her height and the slim, toned body of a young woman. She was the type who "sashayed" when she walked and always seemed to get her way, especially with males. She must have also liked older men and she had Dad under her spell. In a sense, it was not a shock, even for a dream, when my father proclaimed, they were "getting married." They both had martinis and toasted to their recent love affair. Dad gave me and my brother that pinky point, a wink and a smile. I remembered that Mom never liked Jenna and often complained that her "balding husband spent too much time in the hair salon."

Maddie suddenly appeared in my face again and asked me, "How did you let this happen? And why are you not doing anything about this?" She started to scream at me as I instinctively grabbed her neck forcefully between my hands. I held her tight, wanting to crush her windpipe and finally shut the bitch up.

Except it was not Maddie anymore but my brother Josh again. He was turning purple as his tongue projected out of his mouth. I turned my head to clear this vision, only to see Dad kissing Jenna passionately. Again, he gave me that reptile smile. I quickly released my brother from the death grip. I turned, ran outside the room, then out of the house, and headed into the garage.

Once inside, I scoured the garage for a hose, found it, and grabbed one of the large coolers out of the corner. It was the kind on wheels and easily transported drinks whenever Dad decided to take the party with him. I approached the gray BMW coupe first and recognized it as Mom's. It was not burned up but in perfect condition.

I inserted one end of the hose into the gas tank and, attempting to syphon the gas, breathed in deeply. After a few exhausting breaths, I tasted the foul fluid and felt the pressure of the gas rise in the hose. After a mouthful of noxious poison, I released the hose into the hefty cooler and spit the remnants on the floor. After a brief eruption, the gas just stopped. I stuck the hose directly in my mouth again and began to suck with a violent force.

It was a futile attempt, as the tank was already empty. Instantly, my father appeared in my head. He was laughing and said, "See, son, I told you that your mother could not care for the car. Hell, she couldn't even pump her own gas, let alone make sure there was any left!"

This time I agreed with him, although I would never admit to that. I knew that fucker would have a full tank in his Porsche Targa. I quickly shuffled the hose with the cooler to his side of the garage and repeated the same steps as before. Without much effort this time, the gas began to flow at a constant rate and filled the cooler to almost full.

When I was content with the amount, I turned the hose out of the cooler and pointed it at his Porsche. I doused his car with whatever remained in the hose. I started the spray at the top and worked the liquid around to underneath the carriage. Satisfied, I released the hose from the gas tank and laboriously dragged the now heavy cooler out of the garage. My heart and muscles burned with anticipation.

The pungent, acrid smell is what I remembered most. Then there was Dad and all his infinite wisdom, letting me know that if I was ever "too drunk to drive," I should "stop at a gas station." Not to stop and rest or call a taxi, but to "refill the gas and make sure I spilled some on myself." His logic being that if I was pulled over after that, the smell of the gas would overpower any smell of alcohol on my breath.

He was some genius…

I gasped for fresh air and pulled the heavy cooler out back by the pool. Once kept sparking blue and in pristine condition by Mom's vigilance for cleanliness, it was now green with algae and full of dead leaves.

On my left stood the shed where we kept the pool toys when we used to swim in that hole. Before that, it was where we fruitlessly attempted to grow strawberries as a kid. It was just another attempt at lying to us. It brought back more feelings of intense anger.

I pried open the door cautiously, afraid to unleash some feral animal that had made its home in our unused storage shanty.

Instead of finding anything alive, I found it cluttered with death. Dried up spiders, half-decayed rodent carcasses, old cobwebs, and stale air. Covering my mouth, I quickly found the two large water guns I was looking for. They were called Super Soakers due to their capacity to hold large volumes of water. Without shutting the shed, I took the once harmless toy guns and sprinted around the pool towards the cooler.

I opened the cooler and promptly filled one cannon to capacity with gas by pulling back the reserve lever and sucking up the flammable liquid. I needed to test its ability to still shoot, so I opened the garage door, taking aim again at Dad's Porsche. As soon as I released the pressure, a steady stream of gas erupted from its large nozzle, covering the sports car with effortless simplicity. I couldn't help but to laugh at how easy this was.

Without further hesitation, I filled both large toy soakers with an abundance of fuel from the cooler. They were heavy in my arms, and I struggled a bit to bring them inside the house. Once in the kitchen, I dropped them on the large hand-carved wooden table Dad and Mom brought home from a trip to Indonesia. Some of the gas spilled onto the rustic table, and the fuel quickly collected into the recessed designs hand-cut into the wood. I didn't bother to clean it up. It was time to look for my brother, prepare breakfast, and get this party started.

My brother and I had rooms that shared a Jack and Jill bathroom, so it was easy for him to sneak into my room whenever the night terrors plagued him. My brother was afraid of everything, especially being alone with Dad. This fear often resulted in debilitating anxiety, which induced his asthma attacks. I tried my best to soothe his panic attacks, but his weakness only made me angry. I was aggravated by his frailty and found myself at times wishing he would disappear.

I saw my brother huddled under his blankets and jumped on his bed to wake him up. When he turned to face me, it was not him but Maddie again.

I almost screamed in horror.

Maddie stared at me and asked why I "smelled like a gas station." I ignored her question and told her that today I was "going to make breakfast." She smiled at me and said, she would "love blueberry pancakes." I nodded in agreement, grabbed her hands, and pulled her out of bed as we both ran downstairs to the kitchen.

Maddie pulled over a wooden dining chair, eyeballing the water cannons on the table and joined me by the stove. I was super conscious not to get my clothes near the hot red coils, rolling my sleeves up as high as I could.

"What's with the water guns?" she asked.

I ignored her.

"Are we having a water gun fight?" she asked.

"Something like that," I answered as a big smile spread across my face.

Maddie watched me work the premixed batter into small circles on the oiled pan.

I tried to monitor an even number of blueberries that went into the center of the circles, and watched as the pancakes took form. They started to bubble under the heat. I flipped the pancakes to make sure both sides were cooked equally. Occasionally, some of the blueberries would bleed out from the hotness as their juices escaped out of their fragile skins.

I told Maddie that today "Dad and Jenna would be eating on paper plates" and instructed her to set up the bedside bamboo tray accordingly. We separated the good pancakes and kept them aside for us to enjoy later. The burnt ones that we didn't want were placed on paper plates, next to paper napkins and empty paper cups. Maddie filled the cups with water. I quickly took them from her and emptied the water back into the sink.

"No water today!" I exclaimed, and Maddie smiled wickedly.

I went to the wood cabinet that held Mom's ashes, glanced at them for a moment, and then pulled out two large candles. These were Mom's special three-wick candles that we kept in case we lost electricity. In case of an emergency...

I placed the candles at the center of the wooden breakfast tray.

"Are you sure those candles will do the job?" asked Maddie.

"I am absolutely sure," I answered, then told her of my plan.

I explained that I would "quietly bring up the breakfast tray and place it on the side of the bed." Then I would "slip back down" and the both of us would "grab the water cannons, sneak upstairs, and wake up Dad and Jenna with a good old-fashioned water gun fight"—like we used to have when the pool worked.

Maddie looked at me with apprehension and exclaimed how "angry" this was going to make my dad. I stared at her very hard and told her not to worry. The blueberry pancakes would "make everything better. And a little water never hurt anyone..."

She tried to protest as I quickly wrapped my fingers around her throat and told her to keep quiet. She nodded in compliance and started to wheeze under my tight grip. I released her, turned to grab the tray and made my way silently up the stairs. I felt hyperaware and couldn't help but notice all the pictures displayed along the walls of the staircase. I don't think I ever noticed them before. They were only of Dad and Jenna's vacations. I did not see any of my brother or me, and certainly none of Mom.

When I finally reached the top of the stairs, I turned right and silently made my way to Dad's room. The door was shut, so I quickly placed my ear close to the wood to hear any sounds. There was nothing but Dad's snoring, so I gently opened the door.

Immediately, I was assaulted by a wave of stale smoke, moldy papers, sweat, and alcohol. The adults were curled up, fast asleep on opposite sides of the bed. Various debris and clothes littered the room. I could tell they were naked under the sheets, and this thought revolted me.

I slid the breakfast tray onto the table next to Jenna and poked around Dad's side table for his lighter. I found it in the ashtray, under the old butts, took it out and lit the candles on the tray. After a few tries, all l the wicks were fully aflame. I stared at the fire for a moment, thinking of my mother, and repositioned the tray to give me a better angle. I took a few seconds to stare at the flames, did a dry run in my head and then left the room.

My brother now appeared and was impatiently waiting for me downstairs. He was examining the water cannons, smelling them, and I could tell he was nervous about my plan. I pulled him close to me in a big hug, held him for a few moments, and whispered the instructions in his ear.

"You are going to sneak in the room first and aim the gun at Dad. When I count to three, you let him have it with everything you've got. Get him completely wet, and then I will do the same to Jenna."

"Are you sure this is such a good idea?" he asked nervously.

I ignored his question and told him that dad would "really love it if we brought him the Sunday paper in bed." I hugged him again, this time very tightly, and told him, "Not to worry," that I would "handle everything." I let him go and watched as he made his way to the front door to fetch the large stack of newspapers.

This time it was Maddie that came back with the papers, barely able to carry the enormous bulk with her short arms. I quickly took the stack of papers from her and put them under my arm. I grabbed the smaller of the water cannons and gave it to her. She struggled a bit with the weight and complained again about the smell. I grabbed the larger gun with ease.

I motioned for her to quietly follow. We made it up the stairs without incident and approached the open door of the bedroom. We both stood there for a moment looking at the crumpled adults, the prepared breakfast, and the beautiful soft light the candles brought to the room.

I motioned for Maddie to be still while I put my cannon on the floor and gently approached the bed. Once there, I took the newspaper quietly from under my arm and spread it into even piles on the center of the bed, right between where they each slept. I gave the papers one last reposition to make sure they bled over onto the human shapes under the covers. I made my way back to Maddie and picked up my weapon.

I turned to Maddie one last time and mouthed the final countdown.

On three, Maddie nodded, summoned up all her courage, and marched into the room. She stopped just short of Dad and, without hesitation, let out a gigantic stream of gasoline. I followed her lead and positioned myself in front of the lit candles. In an instant my father awoke in shock, covered in combustible fuel. Maddie continued to douse him as I began to carefully spray the other side where Jenna was. Systematically, I raised the stream until it covered her now awakened face.

Jenna began to scream as the horror became evident, and Maddie froze. My father got up and grabbed Maddie by the arm, forcefully lifting her onto the bed. I turned to all three of them, feeling my blood boil between my ears, and sent my cannon stream directly into the candles, fueling a torrent of deadly fire directly at them.

In an instant, the bed and bodies were aflame. Violent screaming was mixed in a pool of burning flesh and heat. I felt like I was dancing around the center of the sun. I quickly dropped the pool toy and backtracked, needing to escape the inferno.

The fire was everywhere and threatened to engulf me. I choked through the smoke and turned quickly to face the carnage one last time, only to notice that Maddie was no longer herself. Instead, she turned back into my little brother, and I swear he was reaching out for me. I felt a twinge of guilt, but there was no time to save him. I quickly turned and ran for the stairs.

Once downstairs, I looked up at the fire now blazing out of my parent's room. It was making its way down the staircase, popping those pictures off the wall. It was only a matter of time before it would come for me, as well.

But today was a celebration of Mom, her blueberry pancakes, and I suddenly felt very hungry. I looked down, cleared the black smoke from my eyes and saw those special pancakes we'd set aside to eat later. I put the plate of pancakes in the microwave and placed it on high for fifty seconds. The blueberries were bursting and blistering from the heat once again. I removed the tray and sat down at the carved wooden table. I notice the spilled gasoline in the open crevices of the wooden table. They reminded me of tide pools.

I felt the heat moving like a dragon, spilling flame from its mouth as it made its way down the stairs, and to the kitchen, overcoming my body. I was suddenly very hungry and began to eat as the rings of fire circled my last meal.

I woke up, trying hard to catch my breath. I was still strapped motionless to the bed. Even more alarming was that I was erect and sticky with cum on my midsection and between my legs. I was confused and uncertain as I have not had a *wet dream* since I was a much younger teenager. My eyes shifted left to find the nurse standing in the corner of my room. She was by the sink, rolling down her sleeves and looked a bit winded.

"Help," I managed to croak. It sounded more like a dry cough. So, I tried again and rattled my restraints for effect.

The nurse finished buttoning her sleeves, looked up, and smiled at me.

"Good morning, Rick," she said. "I bet you would love some ice-cold water?"

I tried to nod my head as she went to the small table next to my bed and poured ice water out of the pitcher into a small plastic cup. The cup had a straw in it. The nurse leaned over to place the straw in my mouth. She was a large lady with a heavenly bosom. I could not take my eyes off her mounds as she bent over. She saw me staring and appeared to swing them closer to my face.

"Here drink some of this cold water," she said placing the straw further into my mouth. "You seem to have had some kind of hot dream."

She said as I heard her giggle to herself and then looked down at my soiled crotch. Without warning, she removed the straw mid-drink, put the water down, and turned to leave.

"I'll let the doctor know that you are awake and see if someone is available to... you know... clean you up." She said and made a cleaning motion aimed at my crotch, let out another small laugh, and left.

I swear, she was swinging her hips *like Jenna*.

I felt odd, vulnerable, and confused. I didn't think it was possible to be so sexually aroused, especially with the amount of Thorazine pumped in my prone body! My mind went into survival mode as I tried to gather my senses. I didn't like hospitals, and I abhorred the notion that I was stuck like a dangerous animal in a cage. I took stock of my situation and swore to do whatever it took to get the fuck out of this madhouse... before I really went insane!

40

Bastard in Love, *Long Island, NY—circa 1988*

When I was *sane enough*, Grandpa Butch had me discharged.

I made a deal with him and my folks to decide and give college another try. My parents weren't convinced this was a good idea, but Grandpa had some connections to a private university on *The Island* and it was close to home. The terms to attend the college were agreed upon by myself, my family, and my private psychiatrist Dr. Hurtz. We had all committed to attending one of those intervention-style meetings, where we all sat around to come to a general consensus on how this would happen. The conditions were that:

- I had to live at home
- Hold a full-time job
- Take my meds
- Stay off the booze
- No violence
- See Dr. Hurtz regularly
- Maintain a B average

Grandpa also insisted that I begin to spar with Boaz again and help instruct his classes. Should I fail any one of these, college was off the table for good! I accepted the conditions and was admitted to the school without even filling out an application. *Thank God for you... Grandpa!*

Going to school on *"Strong Island"* with its proximity to New York City meant commuters like me (and a lot of students) went to college mostly at night, after their workday was done. I spent my days working at a local gym, training overweight women, MILFs, and depressed husbands. The pay sucked, but the benefits of making my own schedule along with the free membership was worth it. For me, those days were largely spent getting back into serious shape by making myself a modern-day Hercules. I did rekindle with Boaz joining some of his classes, and really enjoyed getting back into Krav Maga and helping teach his students.

My physical obsession mixed well with my inner rage and then exploded into something new as I experimented mixing *anabolic steroids* with high dosages of caffeine. Since I had a muscular frame to begin with, to grow bigger I had to work hard by punishing my body with excessive weight training, more drugs and endless repetitions. I worked myself to exhaustion every day in a quest to redefine my body and, more importantly, to tame the beast within. The gym became my salvation and my therapy—as well as my addiction. I never told Dr. Hurtz about the steroids, but he knew of my OCD and my weakness for drugs. He didn't question me, even though we kept up with weekly blood tests, he never brought this up. Neither did Boaz, who must have noticed my sudden strength and muscular appearance. My only thought was that somehow, they both knew that *working out* was better for me than *acting out*, and that I was on so many drugs for my emotions that some physical exhaustion would outweigh the alternative.

The fall of my freshman year started out with a minor uprising by the school's faculty that turned into a full-on teacher's strike. Suddenly, there were no classes and students took this as an opportunity to support the teachers by turning the strike into a drug and alcohol induced vacation. Campus was transformed from an institution of higher learning to a sunbathing park of *higher* students, celebrating the Indian summer and tanning off their hangovers!

Right in the middle of these sunbathing beauties was Heather. She was lying on her belly with her bright pink bikini top undone, tanning that gorgeous ass and showing off her Brazilian thong. She was in top physical condition, completely ripped with D-cups jutting out from the sides of her sculpted chest. All the guy's stares were glued to her, hoping she would grant us a further look at her flawless semi-naked body. I would watch her incessantly as she squirmed, smiled and repositioned herself to get the best suntan. It felt like I was in love at first sight... at least it was for me. I knew I wanted this girl forever and I was going to make her mine at all costs!

Heather was also the captain of the cheerleaders and the admiration of the entire football team. She was tan, gorgeous, *normal* and way out of my league, but I was determined in a *Jack LaLanne* fitness sort of way. I might have had the ripped body, but my crew cut, black combat boots, tattoos, and multiple piercings still gave me the appearance of being a British foreign exchange punk rock student. I wore that costume as proudly as Heather wore that string bikini!

As it stood, I didn't like to settle for second best and bet my new college friends that I was going to make Heather fall in love with me. Then I upped the ante by letting them know that I was going to marry her! The odds were definitely stacked against me, but they always had been. I had learned over the years to never take *no* for an answer. Heather was going to be my girl and there was not much she or anyone else could do about that.

Needless to say, it was a hot day as I removed my Circle Jerks T-shirt, tied it around my waist band, and approached the wall of jocks that appeared to be protecting Heather. The sun was bright and felt good on my taught body as it spread over me like a warm hug. I got closer to Heather making my way through the crowd, as the varsity football team stopped throwing their Frisbee to stare at me in disbelief. I paid no attention to them, focusing instead on a bottle of tanning oil and a bottle of beer lying in the grass next to Heather. I also noticed a large guy with *Bon Jovi* like hair in tight athletic shorts lying right next to her.

I could feel all eyes burning into me hotter than the summer's heat as I approached my bathing beauty with determination. Without hesitation, I picked up the oil and squirted it on Heather's shoulders. Before she could react, I swiftly straddled her backside and began to smoothly rub the oil all over her naked back. She quickly looked over her shoulder, saw me, and gave a little shriek.

The boy with the big hair immediately sprung to his feet and made an aggressive attempt to throw me off Heather. Years of martial arts training had taught me to anticipate my opponent's next move and I was quickly on my feet. I sidestepped out of the way, tripped up his legs, and reached down for the beer bottle. Before he had the chance to look back up, I chugged whatever was left in the bottle, threw it at his head and landed a crescent kick to his solar plexus. He went down hard, as Heather began to scream for "help!" The rest of her posse came running to her rescue.

I instinctively closed the gap between me and the remainder of *Bon Jovi's* gang. One of the boys was quick and sent a fist in my direction. I swiftly parried out of the way, and then landed a hard stomp kick to the outside of his knee. He went down with a loud moan as I grabbed his head in a reverse lock, picked him up, and held him close to my shoulder. I deftly spun him around, landing knees into the kid's ribs and taunted the rest of the pack to come get some! I was finally feeling comfortable and was back in my happy place.

The jocks held their position and looked confused as Heather continued to scream at them to help the boy with the big hair. He was bleeding from small gash in his head and moaning loudly. I stared at her as she strapped up her bikini top and made her way to comfort the big-haired boy. She held him close to her chest as his blood streaked across her perfect breasts. I was mesmerized by the juxtaposition and Heather began to scream at me.

I snapped out of my *love buzz* and turned my gaze back to the rest of the jock pack while they cautiously closed in on me. I still held one of their friends in my tight grip, enticing them once again to come and get some! By now, all the students seemed to be standing and staring at me. I glanced around and saw that campus security was also closing in fast. The jocks saw this too and used it as an opportunity to strike.

One of them made a move in my direction, so I did what came naturally. I released my death grip from the boy's head, stepped firmly on his right foot, held it in place, and pushed him away from me. When he landed, I was sure I heard his ankle break. He screamed in pain and the oncoming jocks got distracted, forgot about me and ran over to help their fallen comrade.

I raised my fists tight to my face looking to see if anyone was brave enough to challenge me. I was loose, muscle ripped, and my eyes burned with ferocity. I was an animal literally 'in heat" and hurried over to Heather, lifting her away from the bloodied boy with the hair. He was dazed, holding his shirt to his bloody head and without her grasp, crumpled into a ball on the grass. His teammates instantly came to his aid, helping him and the other boy that I attacked. Heather's face turned pale with fear as I bent close to her, smiled and then proceeded to ask her to go out Friday night. Horrified, she blinked a few times in shock.

Hence, I asked her again to "go out with me." This time she registered with a slight nod. Even if that was fear talking, it was enough for me. I smiled back at her, winked, made the universal sign to *call me*, and saw the campus police rounding the corner. The boys continued to scream and point the police in my direction. I took off toward the opposite path, running as fast as my legs would go, my heart beating out of my chest.

For the first time in my life, I felt convinced that this girl was my destiny. I also knew this was probably the end of my college career but fuck it... I was a *bastard in love*.

41

Low Self Opinion, *Dongguan City, China—circa 2003*

We exited the Emerald Sauna with the dead girl and took the back stairs down, so I could return unnoticed to my hotel room three floors down.

Once inside, I was happy to find my suitcase in the corner unopened and ready to move. I checked my backpack to make sure all was still there including my passport and cash. Dr. Dave and Shu Shu were right behind me, Dr. Dave was carrying the dead girl over his shoulder in what looked like a heap of wrapped blankets. We made our way back to the rear staircase and quickly labored down the 11 flights of stairs and out the back door of the hotel. Thankfully, it was still late in the evening, and we were protected under the cover of darkness. Dr. Dave ran with the body directly to the trunk of the car, opened it, and threw the dead girls' body inside. We were all out of breath as I made a snide comment that, "bodies in Shu Shu's trunk have become a pastime for me in China."

I threw my stuff in the backseat of the car and got in. Shu Shu reached into the glove compartment and retrieved a FedEx envelope filled with a pile of $100 RMB notes. He then asked me for my passport, which caught me by surprise, but under the present circumstances, I gave it to him without delay. He took the passport, the cash, and left us as he made his way back into the hotel. Dr. Dave got into the driver's side of the car, caught his breath and chain-smoked a couple of cigarettes, then his cell phone began to ring. He picked it up instantly and began screaming at the person on the other end. I didn't know who he was talking to, but he was pissed, and when Dr. Dave got loud, my head immediately began to pound. I opened my window and tried to inhale what I already knew to be noxious air.

After a few moments, Shu Shu jogged back to the car with an empty FedEx envelope in one hand and my passport in the other. He entered the car and handed me back the passport without glancing at me. I noticed some other papers sticking out, so I opened the passport and carefully examined what was folded inside. It was the photocopy of my passport photo that was taken upon check in, along with my paid room receipt and any other incidental records of my stay there.

"Rick, there is nothing you need to know now, except that you were never here, and you will never return!" Shu Shu exclaimed.

"Thank you," I said meekly.

Dr. Dave had a quick conversation with Shu Shu, then started the car and made his way towards the factory.

It was during my early years of doing business in China that I realized how ironic the disproportionate life of the factory worker was compared to its owners. These factories were like self-contained towns, where the workers were housed, fed, and medically cared for. The paradox was that this very same factory took advantage of its workers poverty and need to work, by rewarding them with very little pay and *sometimes* very dangerous work conditions. Although their wages were practically pennies on the dollar compared to what we in America were used to, the factory did take care of their basic needs. There was no need to spend any of their hard-earned money, and the workers had an opportunity to support their families. They endured unbelievable conditions far away from home, just to be able to send money back to their poor village relatives.

At first glance, it appeared that the factory was the perfect sanctuary for the uneducated, low wage worker. It took care of its workers in the same corrupt way the Communist government took care of its people.

The factory painted a glorified picture, but it was really set up to keep workers ignorant by teaching them to obey strict rules and to do the same repetitive job day in and day out. And when families were allowed to have multiple children, the best opportunity for the family was to have those children scatter hundreds of miles away to work in factories to support their parents and grandparents. In fact, there was no greater honor in China than being able to support your elders!

Of course, in today's modern China, the myth of the great factory worker is beginning to crumble. With China's self-imposed *one child rule*, most families will now do whatever it takes *not* to have their child work in a factory sweatshop. With the Internet and the rise of middle management, modern China is suffering an unimaginable shortage of workers, and many factories are closing their doors.

Let's not forget that if you're a woman in China, chances are that you will make six times the amount of money working at a KTV than in a dirty factory. Selling sex can make a young girl the wealthiest person in her family. She might even make enough money to get a visa to travel to Thailand *to make more money*, and even find a rich boyfriend or, in some rare cases, even a husband.

Nonetheless, many private things still happened within those factory walls. The factory became its own self-imposed feudal system where almost anything went. With all its heavy machinery, dangerous equipment, and security, the factory would not fail. Its main objective was to protect its building, its products, its business practices, and its owners.

Shu Shu's factory played by his rules, and inside those walls he could do whatever he wanted. He was the king of a thousand people and made goods that tens of thousands of Americans would buy. He was smart, rich, and fearless. He was also on Mei Mei's *watch list* and that meant he was under surveillance by *me* of all people! All I had to do was sneak some production photos of anything that looked *out of sorts* along with pictures of anyone who appeared to be helping Shu Shu in this *out of sorts* way and send them to Mei Mei. It was my responsibility to keep Mei Mei informed of anything that seemed like trouble. A dead girl was certainly "mafan" (big trouble), and I knew another call with Mei Mei was inevitable. I was conflicted by my role because I was genuinely fond of Shu Shu and Dr. Dave. They both protected me, and I enjoyed feeling safe in this dangerous country. Shu Shu was also, at one time, the lifeline of my family's business and with that came a tremendous amount of respect for him. For a *Gweilo* like myself who was based in China, I never had this type of protection either from an enemy or from myself.

42

Wild in the Streets, *Long Island, NY—circa 1986*

Everyone loves fire.

July Fourth for me, has always been less a celebration of Independence and more a holiday for pyromaniacs nationwide to rejoice. There's something about an evening of blowing shit up that brings out the primal instincts in us. It is part of our collective unconscious, how our nation was born, standing for freedom, power, and danger. As Americans, it is our God-given right to get crazy in the name of independence. "Fuck you, England!" Time to get out the explosives and celebrate our liberation with open-flame barbecues and copious amounts of alcohol. Its the one day of the year *(outside of Halloween)* that we are permitted, *almost expected*, to rage out of control. Like our ancestors before us, we let our inhibitions take a back seat as we celebrate by blowing shit up with reckless abandon.

Even though it is illegal to purchase fireworks in the state of New York, where there is a will, there is always a way! For us, it was the United States Post Office, and that fireworks could be ordered out of Florida (where it is legal) and shipped to your front door! Back then, there were no restrictions on what could be sent in the mail and no known laws on shipping fireworks over state lines. So, all my friends and I saved up our allowances until we had enough to buy the largest bundle of Rockets, Mortars, and other explosives. We would pour over the fireworks catalog that came in the very same mail and study it like the latest *Penthouse*. It would be dog-eared, fingered, fondled, and abused by the time all of us got to ordering our *freedom* works.

Like clockwork, we would receive the massive package a few weeks shy of Independence Day and open it together like some sort of ritual. There was screaming, crying, oohing, and aahing as we fought to get our hands on the brightly packaged explosives. Talk about packaging and marketing to the *Youth of Today*—we were hooked with the graphics, amped about the warning labels and, like a drug, needed more! Fortunately, the companies that sold these rockets, whistlers, mortars, cherry bombs, M-80s, and of course, our favorite Roman Candles, were kind enough to add "freebies" to our order! Imagine our surprise—we order enough and in return receive free explosives! Especially, if those free explosives included more roman candles, that were ignorantly called *"nigger chasers"* in those days.

Roman candles shot five to ten balls of colored fire out of a cardboard tube and were a crucial part of our celebratory evening. We used these Roman candles as actual weapons to shoot at each other in a mock war-type scenario. The rules of engagement were simple. We broke into two teams, each with four Roman candles per person. We drew a line in the center of the street where either team could not cross. When the war commenced, we would run back and forth on our respective sides, trying to shoot each with balls of fire. It was like a demented game of dodgeball where the objective was not to throw (or catch) someone out, but to set your opponent on fire. The more we drank, the more people gained liquid courage and enthusiastically joined our *war games*. I explained the rules to anyone who might care to understand them, belched loudly, and prepared for the self-induced chaos.

We did have a bit of conscience about playing with fire and tried our best to prevent injury by dressing in pathetic plastic ponchos, long sleeves, and ski goggles. When the battle cry commenced, we lit our fire, and dozens of fireballs filled the air on projected paths towards each other's heads. Even though head hunting was completely discouraged, we all aimed high as the balls generally lost steam, bounced off our bodies, and continued to burn recklessly on the ground. But on occasion, our plastic ponchos would catch fire, and someone would scream for the *"fire marshal."* There was always an appointed *fire marshal* chosen to sit off to the side, armed with a small kitchen fire extinguisher. It was usually someone's younger brother who was itching to play. Either that or one of our friends who was just too drunk to play. The person responsible for extinguishing our fiery death was either a minor or a drunk. Come to think of it now, that was all of us!

However, we did have one golden yet simple rule: If you were hit with a burning ball, you were out of the game. This was hard to judge during the blazing chaos, unless you actually caught on fire. So, we operated on some level of a demented honor system while the fire marshal acted as a pseudo referee. The status of the designated fire marshal also meant it was forbidden to purposely shoot this unarmed official. Of course, the winner of the battle was the last man standing and *hopefully not in flames.*

Ok, let me set the scene again for the adults in the room. A large group of underage teenagers (all drinking) have gathered around a small street to watch two teams of about twelve players each shoot four rounds of five to ten balls of fire at each other. In a matter of minutes, upwards of 100 balls of fire would be shot in very close quarters. It would get very exciting as balls of colored fire projected and bounced everywhere. Skill came in dodging, weaving, re-lighting, taking aim, and praying you would not be extinguished.

Over the past few years, our Independence Day War expanded its heated competition and began between rival neighborhoods. We lived in Long Island's south shore where canals separated the neighborhoods, and that separation meant growing up and going to different elementary and middle schools. However, high school broke the water born school lines, putting us together for the first time. It was amazing how a small peninsula of land kept us from knowing each other well before this, but as fate had it, we became fast friends in High School. Perhaps it was a similarity in upbringing, we were all white, privileged, went to the same stores, restaurants and Synagogues. It was like having distant family you never met but felt a kinship toward. Like seeing cousins for the first time, we quickly noticed how much we had in common and how in sync we were.

Most of our parents went away for the summer, taking a much-needed break from their well-off but delinquent children. This allowed us to prepare for an all-day Independence celebratory barbecue. Of course, when both neighborhoods came together for an event, it was usually a momentous occasion. One town was good for bringing the food while we the other took care of the alcohol. Together, we always planned a great Fourth of July, and this year was no exception. Unfortunately, my town had lost consecutively the last two years of fiery war games, and I would not stand to see this happen again. I was determined to win back the crown this year no matter what it took. No holds barred!

The main event started right after the last keg was tapped and the sun refused to shine. The streets cleared as we broke into teams and took our best strategic spots. Onlookers found areas just outside of our fiery range. We lit punks (incense sticks) to keep the fire alive as we needed speed when lighting the fuses. The appointed fire marshal was my friend Harley's younger brother, he stumbled down to the middle of the melee into what was ground zero. He had the ceremonial extinguisher and wore our high school jersey with our *Cougar* mascot proudly displayed. We were revered to be *Cougars*, and we took that as a badge of honor for our hot MILF parents.

We did not have an official *"go"* buzzer or bullhorn; rather, the games began when the fire marshal raised the extinguisher pulled the pin and sprayed a small shot of compressed liquid into the air. I made every attempt to shoot first, trying to defend our honor. What followed was ten minutes of pandemonium as the sky filled with brilliant fire. The crowd cried in unison as the chaos unfolded in the street. Bodies were twisted and thrown in every direction as we tried to escape the glowing balls of fire. Spectators screamed and some hid for cover behind cars or trees or each other. The fire marshal was busy extinguishing my friends and, as quickly as it began, the dangerous game seemed to be winding down.

In the end, on our side it was just me left standing with two Roman candles. On the other end of the street was my friend Harley. I immediately ducked into a low crouch, lit the candle of fire, ran to the dividing line, and took a high shot at his head. He must have seen this coming, and he quickly threw himself to the floor. He responded by lighting both his remaining Roman candles at the same time. In an amazing feat of trickery, he must have tied both the wicks together and sent an onslaught of fireballs soaring to the bottom of my legs. I felt the heat before it registered to my brain that I had been hit, and we had lost once again. Dejected, I fanned the flames off my legs and sneakers and watched the large crowd gather around Harley. Losing is not one of my strong suits and even though this event was over, I was not done.

I remember feeling an out of body experience, where I saw myself lighting that last Roman candle and pointing it at Harley's head. What I did not see, or want to see, was his younger brother, our fire marshal, reaching around to hug Harley with admiration. Instead, I turned my attention away from them and watched the wick burn down my last remaining Roman candle. Then I screamed one more war cry as I sent the burning ball of fire in their direction. Harley's reflexes were always quick, even in this moment, and he threw himself to the ground and out of harm's way.

Unfortunately, I cannot say the same for his brother. He did not move as the fireball blasted towards his face and body. In shock, he grabbed at the fireball attempting to bat it away from his body. Instead, he accidentally got it trapped between his sleeves. Harley's little brother screamed and froze in shock as the flames caught the rest of his shirt on fire. The small blaze quickly engulfed his hands and arms. I stood in shock as he went up in flames and watched as Harley went into action, screaming for the fire extinguisher. He grabbed the handles, squeezed them down with his right hand as his left aimed the hose at his burning brother. There was a lot of screaming at this point, and as I watched the chaos set in (once again), I was only thinking about our ruined celebration.

I dropped the spent Roman candles and ran towards the keg on the edge of the lawn.

My adrenaline was kicking in hard as I lifted the keg and remaining cups into my hands and ran over to the scene. There was a lot of smoke and the putrid smell of burnt flesh in the air. I could see both Harley and his brother screaming as I pumped beer into plastic cups in a feeble attempt to help extinguish the flame. I was spilling beer on the boy, who at this time was practically dowsed completely by the fire extinguisher.

My beer attempt was pathetic at best but was the only thing I could think to physically do at the moment. I knew I'd done something *wrong* but felt numb about it. I was somehow more upset about losing the war, since it shamed me to the core to be seen as a loser. I was angry at myself, pumped a cold beer from the keg, and walked away as the sound of sirens grew louder.

43

Murphy's Law, *Dongguan City, China—circa 2003*

We drove up to the factory gates as silent as the dead girl in our trunk.

Once we approached, Dr. Dave honked the horn twice. The night guards lazily stepped outside, saluted us, and opened the gates. The gates were always slow to open and made an eerie mechanical screech as if being forced ajar against their will. When enough room opened, Dr. Dave gunned it through and continued to drive to the back of the factory where the heavy machinery was maintained. It was also where we kept the fiery kilns on and did our most dangerous work. It was here that we sand casted heavy metal molds with poured molten lava. It was sweltering hot with colorful flames and always felt very *rock-n-roll* to me. I personally loved it back there, probably because it reminded me of the hell, I often found myself in.

Dr. Dave stopped the car, got out, and lit another cigarette. He said something to Shu Shu, then went inside the building. I tried to engage Shu Shu in conversation, but he was not having any of my small talk. He told me to, "get out of the car and get the body from the trunk." I did as I was told, opened the trunk, and gazed at the wrapped body, wishing the blankets would suddenly move and the girl would spring back to life. As I contemplated this impossible reincarnation, Dr. Dave exited the building with the last of the night shift workers. I saw him give them some cash and point to the exit. They quickly fled the scene without glancing in my direction. Dr. Dave walked over, looked in the trunk, and said "Zobah!" (GO!)

I placed my hands under the blankets, steadied myself, and lifted the girl over my shoulder. She was much heavier than I expected. Even at dead weight (and wrapped tight), she could not have weighed more than ninety pounds. Still, I was exhausted, and it felt like I was carrying a load of bricks. I struggled to stand upright as I slowly followed Shu Shu and Dr. Dave into the building. I slung the girl over my aching shoulders and carefully balanced her through the maze of heavy machinery. I don't know why I was so cautious; she was not coming back to life. No real reason to be so considerate but I was still in disbelief.

I'd been in this section of the factory many times. I liked to watch the large vats of molten material as they were poured into the sand-casting pits that were buried underground. Because of the dangerous and poor conditions, casting was done here in the back of the factory where it could be kept out of sight. When the molten liquid filled the pits and craters of the molds, it gave off tremendous heat and light. The fluorescent blaze reminded me of what I imagined the sun's surface to be like.

Dr. Dave and Shu Shu were standing around a large open pit and directly above them was the hot cauldron of molten fire. I saw it all to clearly in my head and my legs grew weak anticipating the inevitable about to take place. It immediately became clear that I was going put the girl in the hole and watch the molten liquid burn her body until there was nothing left. I suddenly felt sick with guilt and overwhelmed with shame. I tried to placate myself with the fact that this was communist China, a girl with me had suddenly died, and her body was in my possession. I rationalized this as necessary to having a business and family to protect. For once, I did not rebel and instead, I put my faith in Shu Shu and Dr. Dave. I made my way slowly to the men, feeling defeated, confused and a bit nervous.

Shu Shu saw me coming, quickly waved me over and told me to, "drop the girl inside." I carefully walked over and gently lowered the blanketed shrink-wrapped corpse into the pit below. No matter how slowly I dropped her, gravity took over and the body toppled to the bottom of the hole. It landed in an awkward position, and I stared at it like some sort of contortionist art installation. I felt a combination of despair and disgust. I promptly turned my attention back to Shu Shu and Dr. Dave hoping they would take over from here. I knew I was about to witness something that I would never be able to forget. It would most definitely plague my already poisoned thoughts. I looked toward the dead girl's body at the bottom of the pit one last time and then thought about my children, their births, and the fact that this was someone's daughter. Dr. Dave, sensing my moment of weakness, walked over and handed me a cigarette. I lit it and inhaled deeply.

I tried to put my emotions into check and talk myself off the ledge. I put the rational pieces together as best as I could. I told myself "*I am in China. Maybe this girl did not have a family. She could have been an orphan. She was obviously sick or maybe it was poison meant for me? Something was horribly wrong for her to die so quickly, so violently.*" I began to convince myself that her death was unavoidable and not my fault. The lit cigarette and the nicotine helped to calm my nerves. Dr. Dave lit his cigarette, looked down at the girl and then back at me. He walked over to chains that held the cauldron of fire and without warning pushed the red button on the side of the wall.

"Zaijian" (Goodbye), I said under my breath.

The cauldron immediately came to life, tipped to one side and released its fiery liquid into the pit. The girl's body was quickly engulfed in flames. I stared in shock as the flames leaped out of the impromptu crematorium and lit up the entire room. Quickly, there was nothing to see but bright blue and yellow flames. Shu Shu and Dr. Dave cupped their eyes to protect them against the light and heat.

Immediately, I recognized the sickly smell of burning flesh as it permeated the air, making it hard to breathe. Shu Shu and Dr. Dave gave one more look, then turned and left the smoky room, talking to each other in low murmurs.

I remained glued to the scene and to the stench. After a few minutes of shock while staring at the incineration of the innocent girl's body, I snapped out of it and left the oppressive heat. I quickly made my way to join Shu Shu and Dr. Dave outside of the factory.

Two immediate sensations hit me at the same time:

<u>One</u>: How good the cold air felt against my face (*no matter how polluted it was*).

<u>Two</u>: Flashing police lights seemed to fill the parking lot outside the factory gates.

I didn't expect to see the police and began to take a mental note of the situation. Outside of that *infamous monthly dinner*, I never really saw any patrol presence in this part of Southern China, and certainly not at the factory! However, I found it stranger still to see Shu Shu and Dr. Dave talking with the officers through the locked gates. I felt a wave of panic as this was absolutely the wrong time for the cops to be here. I was frightened, and I couldn't imagine any other reason that they were here but to arrest me! That thought terrified me as I remember hearing all the stories about, "corrupt China jails" and their "human rights abuses." The way I saw it, I was flat out fucked and, if convicted, I was certain to die miserably.

But before that happened, many secrets would come to surface about me, Shu Shu, Dr. Dave, and hell maybe even Mei Mei. It would be too much for my business and my family to endure. My knees grew weak and I tried to wish myself to be anywhere but here. My better judgement was telling me that Shu Shu would take care of this as he always did. Still, I would not be taken to a Chinese jail, and quickly scanned my brain for options. This would be another fight-or-flight situation, as I was desperate for an exit strategy!

That is when I saw Shu Shu walk in my direction. He approached casually and didn't seem to be concerned. This relaxed me a bit. Then he bent over to speak softly in my ear.

"Rick, someone notified the police about the girl."

"What... who?" I exclaimed in disbelief.

"I don't know," he continued, "but they claim to have photos of the dead girl in your room."

"Bullshit!" I screamed. "That's impossible."

Shu Shu grabbed me by the collar and held my face close to his. He'd never laid a hand on me before. I fought my instincts to bat him away and free myself.

"Rick, you have to go with these men." He said close up in my personal space.

"No fucking way!" I screamed. This time I used my hands instinctively pulling his grasp off from my body and began to take on an offensive position. That's when Dr. Dave grabbed me tightly in a bear hug from behind. I froze in his embrace as he whispered in my ear. His breath smelled like stale cigarettes.

"No worry, Rick; we *know* these men."

Shu Shu interrupted sternly.

"They need to do their job, and you have *no choice* now but to leave *quietly* with them."

"Shu Shu, what the fuck?" was all I could muster.

I decided then to stomp on Dr. Dave's foot repeatedly while I elbowed him in the ribs with short deliberate blows. Instinctively, he let me go as I found the space needed and quickly turned to face them both in a hyper violent manner.

"There is no way in hell that I will leave with these guys!" I screamed.

I cold cocked my fists, planted my feet and got ready to defend my life.

"Remember," said Shu Shu, "you are in my factory now, and we cannot be involved with the police. Not in this way, so please, I am not going to ask you again."

"What about Mei Mei? We need to call her immediately. She'll work this out—"

"She has been fucking told!" Shu Shu exclaimed loudly.

I wasn't prepared for his outburst or the right side kick that Dr. Dave landed directly into my ribs. Before I could recover my breath, Dr. Dave was smothering me again in one of his signature bear hugs.

I looked up drowsily at the cop who was approaching the gates. I quickly recognized him as the same piece of shit police chief from that night at the karaoke club. The one I hit in the jaw. He saw me look at him and smiled a black toothy grin, spit on the ground, and made a remark to the other officer. I moaned as I recognized the other cop. He was also involved in my previous beating at the KTV. I felt my ears turn red with anger. I was not scared anymore; instead, I wanted the chance to beat these men senseless. Dr. Dave must have detected my tension because his grip tightened and turned into a suffocating hug. I thought to stomp on his feet again and follow with a reverse head butt. But something inside me told me that would only make things worse for myself.

Thus, I acquiesced with my better judgement, stood still as Shu Shu opened the gates and let the police officers in. The lead police officer approached, spit again on the ground for effect, and handed me a cell phone. I recognized it immediately as Dr. Dave's phone.

"What the fuck is this doing here!" I exclaimed feeling betrayed.

Shu Shu did not look at me but gestured for me to check the pictures. Instinctively, Dr. Dave's grip loosened enough for me to take the phone. I took it and looked back at both of them and then tapped the familiar *picture* icon. Immediately, I began to scroll through pictures of the dead girl taken in my hotel room. I knew this was Dr. Dave's doing as I remembered him taking the pictures. I spun quickly to turn and face him, confused as to why he was setting me up. I balled my hands into fists and raised them unconsciously to my face in an offensive manner. My only thought was that I needed to take them all out while I had the chance...

Dr. Dave suddenly planted a forceful, short palm blow strike to the center of my nose. My reflexes were slow as I didn't expect that quick of an attack. I was never hit with such force before and my knees buckled, sending me instantly to the ground. I lied on my back, unable to move, and swallowed blood as it drained into the back of my throat. I could not catch my breath, choking on blood; I saw stars shooting inside my head.

Shu Shu started talking loudly to Dr. Dave. Then it sounded as if they were all engaged in a yelling match. Before I could make sense of how serious all my injuries were, both officers quickly grabbed me under my arms and lifted me up to face Dr. Dave and Shu Shu. I tried my best to keep my feet underneath me as I looked angrily at Shu Shu. I was not sure what was happening and why. I felt myself choking on my own blood and coughed defiantly. Shu Shu did not offer any support and turned his head not to meet my gaze.

Instead, Dr. Dave answered my bewildered look by engaging me in a constricting headlock with his left arm while grabbing my right wrist and twisting it until I heard the bones break. I screamed in agony; the pain was too intense for my body to comprehend. Blood flew out of my mouth. I could not catch my breath, and I felt myself drowning in my own visceral fluids as Dr. Dave released his death grip.

With my right arm broken, lying listless and in pain, I tried to focus on getting Shu Shu's attention again, but he had completely turned his back and walked away from me. Enraged, I faced Dr. Dave and spit a big glob of blood in the direction of his face. He moved like a snake, dodging it, recoiled, and suddenly hit me with one of his huge, clenched fists sending my entire world black.

44

Gotta Go, *Kowloon, HK—circa 2003*

I knew I was in Hong Kong as soon as I opened my eyes.

Consciousness was quickly flooding back to my mind like water to a capsized boat. I tried clearing my head by focusing on the English lettering in my hospital room. It was sterile, modern with lots of machinery, and out the window stood the unmistakable gravitas of Hong Kong Harbor.

Also, I saw Shu Shu sitting in the chair next to me, reading the *South China Morning Post*. The TV was silent but was playing *CNN World News*. "*Creature comforts,*" I thought happy to be here and not rotting in some Chinese jail. I tried to turn to Shu Shu, but my body hurt too much. I noticed in horror that my right arm was suspended in a heavy cast. It was difficult to breathe, as I ran my left hand over the bandages splinting my nose.

"Hey, man, what day is it?" I managed to croak.

Behind the paper, I heard him say, "Saturday. You've been knocked out for three days. Glad to see you're alive!"

He put the paper down and gave me a smile. I tried to smile back but my face hurt too much. My hand instinctively found my nose again. I traced the swollen tissue and could feel the packaging and bandages. I tried to sit up, but my head felt dizzy, and I thought I was going to lose consciousness.

"Don't push yourself," Shu Shu said. He turned his chair to face me. "You're in Hong Kong. You're safe here, but you've suffered multiple traumatic injuries."

"No shit," I managed to say. "But how am I—"

"Here, and not in China?" he cut me off.

I nodded slightly as Shu Shu then ran down a list of my injuries.

"Rick, you have a fractured nose, broken wrist, and some bruised ribs. You probably also have a severe case of whiplash. Oh, and did I mention that you are also on a concussion watch." He continued

"What?" I asked weakly. "How? I don't remember a thing."

Shu Shu got up to shut the door, then pulled his chair even closer to me. He leaned over to my right ear to make sure I heard everything he was about to say.

"Correct, you might not remember what happened for quite some time. In fact, you might never remember all the details. I am positive Dr. Dave made sure of that. However, there are a few important matters that you must agree to... no matter how you feel about them." He said in earnest.

"Shu Shu, I don't understand," I said weakly.

"Rick, you killed a girl in China."

I let that sink in and remembered the smell of burning flesh.

"I didn't kill anyone!" I protested, "She died on her own, or maybe it was poison—"

"Rick, it does not matter. A dead girl is a dead girl." He said between clenched teeth.

"But I'm innocent!" I tried to exclaim.

His voice rose as he fought for composure.

"In China, there is no justice. No one is innocent! We are all guilty!"

"C'mon Shu Shu, you know me," I pleaded to his sentimental side.

"I do and very well," he continued with a smirk. "And because of you and our relationship, we made that girl *disappear.*"

"But it wasn't my fault," I tried again to defend myself.

"Rick, for your safety you must now *disappear* as well!" he exclaimed.

"What? How?" I asked confused as my heart began to beat faster.

"Rick, listen very carefully. We have no choice now, we all have too much to lose."

I let this sink in for a moment and he was correct, this was bad.

"There has to be something we can do?"

"There is something we will do!" Shu Shu continued, "I had to pull a lot of strings to make this go away. Everything that happened to you, including your safe journey back to this hospital in Hong Kong, are all part of *the plan*."

"The plan?" I asked.

"Yes! The plan!" he exclaimed. "The plan is to make sure this never gets discussed again!"

"C'mon, Shu Shu, I will never say anything," I pleaded. "You can trust me!"

"Rick, this isn't all about you. There are a lot of moving parts, and a lot of people are now involved."

"Like I said, you can trust me."

"There is no trust anymore. There is only survival. And with that comes the responsibility to make difficult choices!"

"I can do that—"

"Rick," Shu Shu cut me off, "we've always discussed that we needed a *contingency plan* for such *emergencies*. Well now it's time to put into action the difficult choices that we both previous agreed to."

"I know Shu Shu, but this time it's *different*." I pleaded some more.

"The only *difference* is that this is real and now. I'm offering you a way out."

"A way out of what?" I asked feeling sudden precipitated anxiety.

Shu Shu ignored my question.

"There are certain *conditions* that you must absolutely agree upon" he added with sudden discontent.

"Conditions?" I asked. "What conditions?"

Shu Shu took a moment as a stern, but sad look came across his face.

"Rick, you can never return to China again."

"What are you saying!" I almost jumped out of the bed but was frozen in pain.

"Our business together is now over!" he said in a much louder voice.

"What the fuck are you saying!" I exclaimed in disbelief.

"Rick, listen to me very carefully," he said in a very calm but serious manner. "If you are ever found near me or the factory, make no mistake, I will have you arrested on sight."

"What? Are you shitting me?" I asked as the agony and sadness sunk in.

He paused for a moment looked at floor and then raised his eyes to glare venom at me.

"You cannot come back to Mainland China anymore!" he added insult to injury.

I let that sit for a moment as I suddenly felt ill. I tried to plea my case one more time.

"C'mon, Shu Shu, this is all a big misunderstanding... *an accident.* That's all it was."

Instantly, his right hand reached out and squeezed my shattered nose. I felt immense pain as tears flowed freely down my cheeks. He let go as I whimpered for him, *"to stop."* He had my full attention now as his glare pierced daggers into my already swollen eyes.

"Rick, pay attention! This is no *accident,* and I am *dead* serious! No more China!"

I tried to let the idea of *no more China* sink in. All I could think of was my family, my business, and my *needed* expertise in that country. There had to be another way, something I could do or say to make things right again. I was searching through the cobwebs in my mind to come up with something when Shu Shu hit me with another curve ball.

"Rick as far as our relationship is concerned, both in business and pleasure, we are also through!"

"What!?" I began to protest as I felt the world begin to crumble beneath me.

"Rick, we are done. There is no other way!" he said sternly.

I closed my eyes and groaned in disbelief.

"You are no longer welcome to do business with me or any of our associates," he continued.

I persisted my non-verbal protest in the form of guttural sounds and shook the hospital gurney with the fury I was feeling.

"I have already put into motion our *separation agreement*," Shu Shu continued. "Rick, let me leave you with some *friendly* advice: I strongly suggest that you settle down and get a job closer to your loving family."

"What about Mei Mei?" I asked,

"She knows about all of this, and she is not happy," he continued, "I am sure she will be calling you pretty soon and who knows, maybe she already has another job for you?"

"But all this is a *misunderstanding*," I tried to defend myself again.

"Rick, you always say that." He said quickly.

I let that sink in because maybe he was right. I went through my entire life feeling cursed and misunderstood. I always blamed my misfortunes on others, and never took full responsibility for my actions. So now it was all coming back around as what? Some kind of cruel, fucked-up Karma payback? But still, I couldn't help but feel victimized yet again. As a result, I tried to tug at his heart stings once more and manipulate my way out of this.

"Shu Shu, what am I going to do now? What about my family? This business is all I know." I said glumly.

Shu Shu shook his head and looked at the floor.

"About your family, I called Heather." He admitted.

"You did what!?" I exclaimed in anguish, wishing I could jump up and strangle him.

"Relax, I told her you were attacked while trying to protect me against some Chinese Mafia types."

"This is fucking bullshit!"

"This is not bullshit but your *new normal*. This is your truth now!" he said in a raised voice.

"The Chinese Mafia?" I asked incredulously.

"Yes, I told her they were trying to shake me down and you defended my honor. And, well, it almost cost you your life."

I let this sink in as he continued.

"I also told her it would be in your best interest to stay out of China, in case these Mafia types were looking for you."

"You called Heather with this... bullshit?" I stammered in disbelief.

"Yes, and I've also arranged for her to come to Hong Kong to take you home."

"Oh, no," I moaned.

"Rick, I told her you are a *hero*, and I expect she will always treat you like one!"

I listened in disbelief to the story he crafted, and recognized he was *saving my face.*

"Shu Shu, I don't know what to say..." I said with sadness.

"Rick, there is nothing left to say—except goodbye."

"So that's it, then? We're over?" I asked again in disbelief.

"*It's over,*" he continued. "Heather should be here in the morning, there are return tickets already arranged in business class. Also, the *settlement agreement* should hit your Hong Kong account by the time you are discharged."

"What settlement agreement?"

"There will be enough money in your Hang Seng Bank account to give yourself a second chance—to start all over again." He said with a reassuring smile.

"But what if I don't want to stop?" I asked, "What if I can't?"

"Rick, you need to— stop, he continued, "Please, for me, take the money as an opportunity to make your life better. Talk to Mei Mei and tell her you had enough. Maybe she'll let you go or assign you to something closer to home."

"But this is... all I know," I stammered.

"You know enough to stop putting yourself in danger and for once be present for your family." He added.

I took a deep breath and let this sink in.

"Rick, we have been through so much together and you have always been there for me." He got closer and I could see he was somber.

With that, he took the jade Buddha charm off his neck. It was the one he bought me after that night defending him in Cebu. He placed the charm and the chain in the palm of my left hand.

"You've *saved* my life once, and now I am *saving* yours." he said sternly.

With that he walked out the door without looking back.

I stared at the charm, then carefully tried to place it around my neck. It took me a few tries to line up the lobster claw clasp into the female loop, as I only had one functioning hand. I concentrated on keeping my shaky left hand still while I made the connection, locking the symbolic jade charm in place. I grabbed my cell phone and waited for the dreaded call from Mei Mei. I thought long and hard about what had become of my life, my family and my questionable decisions.

Exhausted, I let these emotions flood out of me, as I looked out the window in time to see night falling over the harbor. In between the lights of the skyscrapers, I saw streaks of lightning and noticed the storm clouds quickly approaching. I felt a wave of panic wash over my broken body and willed myself to try and relax as my mind slipped into darkness once again.

45

Return to Heaven, *Angeles City, Philippines—circa 2017*

My right eye fluttered like the wings of a dying insect.

I was tired.

Dead tired.

My left eye tried to focus on the aftermath, the broken glass littering the carpeted floor, the marble that fell off the ceiling, the clutter of empty beer bottles mixed with fallen objects and a halfway packed suitcase with clothes strewn all over my room. There were bloody footprints that led to the bathroom.

The damage in my room looked more like a metaphor of my own life.

A knock on the door snapped both of my eyes open.

"Coming," I barely eked out.

I pushed myself out of the chair and felt my lower back spasm in protest. I took a deep breath, felt pain shoot down my left arm and a strange numbness in my neck. I ignored the discomfort, chalked it up to collateral damage, and shuffled my mangled feet to the door. I was in my usual executive suite on the 14th floor. I always asked for the highest floor.

Lucky me... being a *Platinum Elite* had its benefits, but not today.

I made my way gingerly around the shattered debris that fell from the walls. The bloodied toilet paper that wrapped my feet did little to hide my agony. I checked my watch and noticed it was 2 a.m. Right on time. I opened the door to see a small Filipino hotel worker, whom I immediately recognized as Alyssa from the Executive Lounge.

"Hi, Sir Rick, here is your ice bucket" she said.

Buried in the ice were two San Miguel Light Beers. I thanked Alyssa and asked if she was "okay?"

"I am fine, sir, just a little shaken up. And how are you?" she asked, looking at my bloody feet.

"Better now." I pointed to the beer. "Thank you for doing this."

"My pleasure, sir. Are you sure there isn't anything else you need?"

"Perhaps some new slippers, and maybe something to eat." I winked at her, knowing the hotel kitchen was badly damaged.

"I am sorry, sir; we have no food to offer." She said defeated.

"I know, I know. We should all be *full on life*, lucky to be alive."

I saw Alyssa ponder that for a moment as fear flushed across her face.

"You were in the lounge on the atrium when it hit?" I asked her.

"Yes, sir," she said softly as her eyes began to water.

I took the ice bucket from her, set it down on the desk, and gave her a hug. She seemed to relax a bit in my arms. I released her before it got uncomfortable. She gathered herself.

"Thank you, Sir Rick for your understanding. Would you like me to continue bringing you two beers every hour?"

"Yeah, sure," I said already a little drunk. "I will be up anyway, I am trying to get a ride out of here first thing in the morning."

"Of course, Sir Rick. I hope the roads will be safe for you to travel."

"Me as well, I'm giving myself six hours to get to Manila to catch a flight home."

"Okay, Sir, I will leave you now, as we need to check on all the remaining guests."

"Thank you, Alyssa," I said, and gave her $500 pesos from my front pocket.

"See you in an hour," she continued. "I will look for some more slippers and perhaps a first aid kit."

I thanked her again and shut the door. I cautiously made my way back to the desk chair, removed the beers from the ice bucket, and put my mangled feet inside the cold water. I ignored the pain, cracked open a

SML (San Miguel Light) and thought hard about what happened. I retraced the incident over again and tried to comprehend what I just went through. Usually, I was the one responsible for the damage, but not this time. I was looking for a message and felt truly afraid for the first time in a long time.

It was my first earthquake, and it was a big one.

I was just coming home from our factory and had made a beeline to the elevators. I was adamant about getting the sweat-drenched clothing off me and into a shower. I rode the elevator to the top and entered my suite. I threw my backpack on the bed, stripped off my soiled clothes, chucked them in the corner, and entered the marble bathroom.

The hotel was new and a nice change for this part of the Philippines. We were far away from Manila and the accommodations out here were usually very seedy and full of roaches. We would joke about how long this hotel would remain on the "newer" side, given our experience in the Philippines where everything quickly turned to shit.

Little did I know that tonight would be the first major blow to the hotel's façade of newness. We were in a dangerous part of the Philippines, and I don't mean because of the nefarious people. Rather we were victims of mother nature in what meteorologists called, "The Pacific Ring of Fire." This consisted of a 25K mile long *fault line* responsible for 90% of the world's earthquakes and 75% of its volcanoes.

I never thought about this, or the twenty active volcanoes close to where I now worked. If I had, I would have chalked this up as a metaphor to the danger that followed me my entire life. I had certainly experienced my fair share of violence but wasn't expecting the earth to rebel underneath me as I took my shower.

That's when the world started to violently shake. I heard an unforgettable rumble from the belly of the hotel. I took a careful step outside the shower as the building began to suddenly sway with ferocity. I quickly lost my balance and was thrown to the floor like a sailor without his sea legs. I fell abruptly with all my weight landing on my left side, banging my head on the marble floor. It took a moment to gather my thoughts, and I did a mental check on my injuries. My endorphins kicked in as I tried to stand in a stable position. The trembling continued and the shower door flung open, shattering glass all around me. Tiles from the wall and ceiling started falling like daggers.

My first though was, *Holy shit, we're being bombed,* and waited a few beats for the unmistakable explosion that would engulf and finally be the end of me. But there was no blast, just swaying and shaking... *fuck me,* I thought, *is this an earthquake?*

Ignoring the shooting pain coming from my neck and back, I tried not to panic as I crawled quickly but carefully to the bedroom. I was moving warily, trying to evade the broken glass and tile that had fallen like shrapnel on a battlefield. I reached my bed, threw on a pair of nylon running shorts, a white T-shirt and grabbed my cell phone.

I auto dialed Mei Mei.

She picked up immediately, "Hey, Rick—what's up?"

I was terrified and full of adrenaline.

"Mei Mei, I am in a bad earthquake," I stammered. "I thought you should know in case anything happens to me."

Just then a loud audible alarm startled me as it pierced the room. I immediately knew I had to get the fuck out of there and make it out of the building before it came crashing down.

"I've got to go evacuate; this shit is bad!" I exclaimed.

"Ok, get to safety and I will call you back."

I hung up the phone and thought of those horrible images of the twin towers as they collapsed on themselves, crushing everyone inside.

I used the bed to help me stand up and quickly hobbled out of the room, dodging the sharp projectiles that now littered the carpet. I made my way out the door and toward the emergency staircase at the end of the hallway. I was woozy and had no idea if I was going to make it out in time. My mind was going a million miles an hour, I no idea how bad this really was. *For fuck's sake,* I thought, *this is Philippines construction, and I'm sure it's not built to withstand earthquakes!* The alarms continued to blare and were now coming from my cellphone, warning me of the earthquake, like I needed another warning! I was nervous and knew I had to call my wife while I still could.

I hit speed dial as I entered the crumbling stairwell. The first thing I noticed was the cracks in the foundation. They looked like fault lines running their way around the walls and floor. I saw and heard

the people below me fighting their way down. They were screaming and crying. I kept my phone to my ear as I carefully descended
into hell.

It was 5:30 a.m. New York time when Heather answered.

"Hon, it's me. We just had a major earthquake. I am okay and making
my way down the staircase to safety." I said quickly.

"What—?" she exclaimed in a tired voice.

I cut her off.

"Earthquake!," I screamed like someone would scream, *"Shark!"*

"What!" she screamed back now fully awake.

"Listen to me, I am going to do all the talking now—."

"Rick are you OK?" she said ignoring my last sentence.

I screamed over the noise and chaos, "I'm OK!"

"What is going on—?"

I cut her off again.

"Heather, I'm not sure how bad this is... trying to find safety. Stay on
the phone with me."

In the meantime, I was passing people huddled in the stairway. I
pushed my way through the elderly, the young, and the frightened. I felt
bad about that, but I needed to survive. It was pure instinct.

"Rick!" she sobbed.

"Hon, its bad, you need to let everyone know I'm okay. I'm passing
people now, making my way down, just a few more floors and then
I'm out."

The phone went dead, and I didn't have time to check service or hit
redial. I was in survival mode, and I was close to the ground floor and
finally, out the exit.

When I got outside, there was panic in the parking lot in front of
the hotel.

Sharing the parking lot adjacent to our hotel, was a much older casino.
Black smoke was coming out of the top windows of the building as fire
leaped out in a strange dance of death. People were confused, crying, and
searching for loved ones. Some were clearly injured, holding bloody rags
to their faces. Hotel employees gathered themselves in groups as they
tried to usher everyone away from the buildings. Fire engines screamed
in the night, only adding to the chaos.

I checked my phone and had a *cellular bar*, so I made another call to my wife. I put the phone to my right ear and my finger in the left to drown out the noise.

She answered immediately.

"Rick—!"

"Hon, I'm outside, and I'm safe," I said reassuringly. "They're moving everyone out of the parking lot and into the street," I screamed. "Do me a favor and see if this is on the news or go and check the Internet. Please. Let me know what's happening and how bad this is. I'm going back inside to help with the evacuation. There are a lot of elderly in there, people are hurt, and they can use my assistance."

I hung up before she had the chance to protest.

I went back inside the stairwell and helped evacuate the people I had passed that were still left inside. Despite the sharp pain shooting down my neck, I helped carry out the infirmed and aided with triage to stop the bleeding and comfort the shocked. The scene turned to chaos as the ground trembled again with aftershocks. People screamed, children wailed, and the elderly clung to one another. I was caught up in the moment and felt no pain or fear. In fact, the chaos and the threat of death was somewhat comforting to me now. I'm not sure why but for the first time in a long time, I was not the cause *or the blame*. Simply a victim of mother nature, something out of my control. Yet I was calmly in control. I felt my first aid training kick in, like riding a bike after a long time without being on that bicycle seat... I was on autopilot.

I helped the hotel staff evacuate everyone and then stood out in the street waiting for direction while the hotel did their best to comfort us. They were giving out robes, slippers, and carts full of hotel-branded water. I grabbed a pair of slippers and a water. For once, they were for free. I looked around and felt truly alone, far away from the safety of my home.

Everyone was collecting themselves as we all tried to get phone service to connect with our loved ones. I had spoken to Heather several times by now. She had forwarded me breaking news from CNN, MSNBC, BBC, and several Asian news channels reporting the quake. Its epicenter was forty miles north of Manila, just outside of where we were in Pampanga.

Buildings had collapsed, roads buckled, the local airport was destroyed, and the death toll was rising.

Funny, I didn't feel lucky or relieved or anything at all but shock. Instead of concern, I looked at my phone, waited for more news to arrive, and swatted at the army of ants that lined up and down my bare legs. I knew those little fuckers were going to eat me alive, and I obsessed more about that than surviving the fucking earthquake.

I continued to kill the *fire ants* with fervor and then changed locations to sit on the empty curb. It was then that I felt the familiar twinge in my lower back. *Motherfucker,* I thought, and instantly went into my *back pain mantra.* It went something like this:

This is my back; it is the strongest part of my body. It is an evolutionary miracle that I can walk upright and fight through gravity. The back was meant to sustain great pressure and elude injury. When my back hurts, it is usually attributed to something emotional going on in my life. It is the adage of mind over matter, or the mental/physical connection. I know by now that most back injuries result from severe trauma, both physical and emotional.

My back began to scream as I let the events sink in, realizing that I had taken a bad fall and was suffering from the emotional trauma of having just survived a massive earthquake. I repeatedly told myself "I am alone, and I need to figure out how to get home." The tension was now building, and I felt severe pain in my neck. I began to feel nervous that I would not make it out of there any time soon.

I continued on and off the phone with Heather, letting her know, "I was Ok and was working on getting home!"

A few hours later that evening, word came from Manila that we were pronounced, *"all clear"* of aftershocks. Someone on a rickety bullhorn announced that the hotel had been "declared safe" and because we were "inland," we did not need to "worry about any impending tsunamis."

Just then my phone rang. It was Mei Mei.

"Rick, we have a car coming to get you at *oh six hundred* tomorrow," the drivers name is Manny. You might remember him from a few years back?"

"Manny from Cebu?" I questioned with an insidious smile.

"The one and only," she said.

I thought how good it would be to see Manny again, well despite the circumstances.

"Roger that," I said while eyeing the hotel staff as they began ushering people through the shattered front doors.

"Are you hurt" she asked

I took a moment to take stock of my injuries. My neck and back were stiff from pain, my left arm felt numb and dissociated. But I did not complain to Mei Mei.

"I fell hard," I admitted with a bit of shame. "Also, I'm getting bit up by these fucken fire ants" I said.

"We'll have medevac ready for you," she said and then hung up.

I saw the hotel guests lining up and joined the cue to enter the main floor of the hotel. We ended up waiting for what seemed like another hour while they made additional safety rounds with the hotel staff. Finally, they permitted us to enter, and I noticed that they didn't march us through the metal detectors, as is mandatory before entering any major Philippine hotel. I guess they were no longer afraid of being bombed.

We sat around the hotel lobby while they offered us more free water. There was a lot of busy work going on, as hotel workers tried frantically to sweep up all the glass and debris. I was starting to feel the pain again spreading through my neck and an uncanny numbness down my left arm. I knew I needed medical attention but for now, relief was in the form of a cold beer. I went up to the lobby bar, pulled out $1,000 pesos from my wallet, and asked one of the hotel staff, "to get me a cold beer."

She stared at the money and then me in disbelief.

"Sir Rick, I cannot offer you a beer now, as we just do not have enough—"

I cut her off.

"Listen, I know you have a subzero freezer full of beer. Now, be a doll and bring them *all* to me."

"Sir Rick, we have some fresh fruit juice," she said pointing at the silver platter with some sort of fruit consommé inside small plastic cups.

I became impatient and raised my voice over the low murmur of confused and tired patrons.

"Listen, lady, please drop the *Sir Rick* shit and bring me a mother fucking beer!" I said a little too loudly.

Just then the hotel manager sauntered over. He was overweight and sweating profusely. He held a walkie-talkie in his chubby left hand. I'd seen him before and remembered him having a German accent. I never liked him because of that.

"Mr. Price," said the Nazi in a calm voice, "please follow me to the stairwell. We are going to let the guests start to go up to their rooms. Why don't you be the first one up? And when we are done, I will personally make sure you have enough beer to make the remainder of your stay comfortable." He said reassuringly.

I looked at him suspiciously as he attempted to wipe sweat out of his eyes with an already-soaked handkerchief. I was about to say something clever, but the pain shooting through my body overruled my smart-ass mouth. I followed the heavy German man through the wake of people. The majority were Filipino and respectively made some room for us as we reached the stairwell.

He spoke into the walkie, "Room 1411 coming up."

He opened the door and handed me my room key.

I entered a bit cautiously as I peered at the cracked fault line. It ran the entire perimeter of the stairwell, appearing to show me the way to my room. I followed it up and around knowing I needed to go up 14 floors. I was walking slowly and gingerly as each step became racked with discomfort.

"Good evening, Sir Rick," said one of the hotel workers on the first floor stairwell.

I sneered as I slowly passed him. They had stationed workers on every floor of the staircase. They had flashlights and walkie-talkies. *Good idea,* I thought as I made the arduous climb up fourteen flights. My back and neck were revolting on their own as I concentrated on the steps. I thought sarcastically how lucky I was to be on the top floor! I worked my whole life for that *executive suite!*

A bit winded, I finally limped through the emergency door that led to my floor.

"Good evening, Sir Rick," said another hotel attendant stationed on the Executive Floor.

I gave him a quick salute and followed the cracks in the wall until I was outside my room. I slid the key, opened the door and looked inside.

The room was trashed worse than I imagined. Everything previously attached to the foundation and the ceiling was now broken and littered the floor. I noticed now that the mirrored walls were cracked. *So much for seven years of bad luck*, I thought.

"Hey," I yelled to the hotel attendant. "This room is trashed; there's broken glass everywhere!"

"Yes, Sir Rick," he replied, "they all are. Please be careful."

I ignored him and shut the door. I stared intently at the broken glass littered on the floor. The shards looked sinister, they were sharp and jabbed like a menacing mouth full of broken teeth. It was the same terror that I recognized in my nightmares.

I removed my dirty slippers and cast them aside witnessing the red lumps on my legs that the *fire ants* left behind. I gave them a vicious scratch that only added to the inflammation. To add insult to injury, I slowly moved my neck in a deliberate circle to relieve the tightness. Instead of loosening itself, I felt a dull *'click'* inside my cervical vertebrae that immediately shot fire down into my left arm, hand and down my back. I closed my eyes in pain and then opened them again staring towards the mini bar at the other end of the room.

There was a minefield of glass separating me from salvation.

I took a deep breath,

walked barefoot towards the fridge,

ignoring the pain,

the bloody footprints,

I reached in,

and grabbed a cold beer.

THE END

ACKNOWLDGMENTS

Thank God for the Sinners	Ty Segall, *Twins*, 2012
Here Comes Sickness	Mudhoney, *Mudhoney*, 1989
Victim in Pain	Agnostic Front, *Victim in Pain*, 1984
Seeing Red	Minor Threat, *Minor Threat*, 1981
Shut The Door	Fugazi, *Repeater*, 1990
Think Again	Minor Threat, *Out of Step*, 1983
In My Head	Black Flag, *In My Head*, 1985
I Hate Children	Adolescents, *The Blue Album*, 1981
Family Tree	H2O, *H2O*, 1986
Unsung	Helmet, *Meantime*, 1992
Last Caress	Misfits, *Beware*, 1980
Suburban Home	The Descendants, *Milo Goes to College*, 1982
Furniture	Fugazi, *Furniture EP*, 2001
Born To Lose	Johnny Thunders, *L.A.M.F.*, 1977
Lust For Life	Iggy Pop, *Lust For Life*, 1977
High Hopes	Gorilla Biscuits, *Gorilla Biscuits*, 1988
Betray	Minor Threat, *Out of Step EP*, 1983
Human Fly	The Cramps, *Off the Bone*, 1983
Bloodstains	Agent Orange, *Living in Darkness*, 1981
Sailin' On	Bad Brains, *Bad Brains*, 1981
I Don't Wanna Hear It	Minor Threat, *Minor Threat*, 1984
Cause for Alarm	Agnostic Front, *Cause for Alarm*, 1986
The Eliminator	Agnostic Front, *Cause for Alarm*, 1986

Teen Age Riot	Sonic Youth, *Daydream Nation, 1988*
Give Me the Cure	Fugazi, *13 Songs, 1989*
Back Against the Wall	Circle Jerks, *Group Sex, 1980*
Hard Times	Cro-Mags, *The Age of Quarrel, 1986*
Minor Threat	Minor Threat, *Minor Threat, 1981*
I Love Livin' in the City	Fear, *The Record, 1978*
World Peace	Cro-Mags, *The Age of Quarrel, 1986*
Orgasm Addict	Buzzcocks, *Orgasm Addict,* 1977
Pay to Cum	Bad Brains, *Bad Brains, 1980*
Am I Demon	Danzig, *Danzig, 1988*
Anarchy in the UK	Sex Pistols, *Never Mind the Bollocks, 1976*
Show You No Mercy	Cro-Mags, *The Age of Quarrel, 1986*
My War	Black Flag, *My War, 1984*
Somebody Put Something_	
In My Drink	Ramones, *Animal Boy,* 1986
Loose Nut	Black Flag, *Loose Nut, 1985*
Sick Boy	GBH, *City Baby Attacked by Rats, 1982*
Institutionalized	Suicidal Tendencies, *Suicidal Tendencies, 1983*
Bastard in Love	Black Flag, *Loose Nut, 1985*
Low Self Opinion	Rollins Band, *End of Silence,* 1995
Wild in the Streets	Circle Jerks, *Wild in the Streets, 1982*
Murphy's Law	Murphy's Law, *Murphy's Law, 1986*
Gotta Go	Agnostic Front, *Somethings Gotta Give, 1998*
Return to Heaven	Bad Brains, *Spirit Electrify, 1988*

EXCERPT FROM
THANK GOD FOR THE DRUGS

Gun in Mouth Blues, *Ho Chi Minh, Vietnam - circa 2017*

Today seemed like a fine day to die.

The sun was shining bright, and a gentle warm breeze blew through the bamboo leaves singing with indifference. I was having a Mai Tai at the bar in the Villa River Hotel, while watching trash and debris float lazily down the Saigon River. I was sitting at my usual table, under the shade of palm fronds with a partial view of downtown Saigon. I was amazed by the amount of scaffolding that was as high as the eye could see, as it quickly transformed this great historic city into a modern day metropolis. The bar was cozy, ordained in colonial style and accented with bamboo floors, white plantation shutters and large ceiling fans directing the tropical winds into the highly arched ceilings. This hotel was something of a landmark, being stuck in time and was my favorite in all of Vietnam. It was more of a boutique hotel, featuring prewar architecture and luxuriously decorated with art reminiscent of French occupied Saigon. It was 4PM on a Sunday, and I was in D2 (or Tao Dien), where all the expats lived. Today, I could not muster through the dark thoughts that occupied my "lizard brain." I was caught in familiar tapes, playing ear to ear, stuck in a loop of incomprehensible depression from my past indiscretions and the anxiety that I had about the destructive future that I feared lied ahead. Either way, this historic hotel provided an idyllic landscape, a perfect canvas for my last portrait and ultimate demise.

Mental illness plagued me since birth, having been ripped into this world ass first, suffering multiple physical ailments, numerous operations and psychological abuse. I was a forlorn child to say the least and the black cloud, (the bane of my existence), followed me everywhere, pouring down a maelstrom storm of grief, melancholy and regret. No matter how much I tried to run away from the malevolence, I never could escape its seductive embrace. This dance with the devil, has affected every single moment of my tortuous life and has ultimately been responsible for my decision to finally expire.

My life has been crazy and so has my professional career. My roles have enabled me to travel around the world many times, doing crazy jobs for insane people who would go to any length to achieve the almighty dollar. My bosses amassed fortunes off the precarious situations I found myself in, often quashing them with the sweat off my back. My career pegged me as a "global sourcing and product development specialist," for several American companies in the home furnishing industry. My role was to find the cheapest suppliers to make our "high quality" goods at ridiculously low costs, contributing to our positive margins and demoralizing our overseas partners, whom we would trade allegiance for the penny if we so desired. There was no valor in the amount of time that I spent away to satisfy the pockets of my various bosses and shareholders. I never felt success only the shame of losing face, my relationships, my reputation, and my mental health. But I was a hard worker, fearless at times and was strategically placed into this career at first to appease my family, but eventually to guard me from the pain of living everyday with crippling angst, where I could be shielded from the rest of the world.

Despite the darkness, I was good at my game and a lot of attention was placed on my ability to work long hours away from the people I loved. In return, I received global entry access, an APEC diplomat card, and esteemed club privileges from the world's biggest airlines. To add insult to injury, my talents were also recognized by Mei Mei, my CIA handler who often orchestrated my next professional moves. Mei Mei was one of the most beautiful Asian women that I ever met, standing almost six feet tall of thin, wiry muscle that reminded me of a praying mantis about to devour her mate. She had a hard, chiseled face reminding me of alabaster with large cartoon-like eyes. Her straight black hair, that when not tied up in a fashionable bun, fell down the length of her sinewy back. She was keen, dressed to the nines, dangerous in her stare, but seductive in her English accent. Damn it if the Agency nailed my type!

Mei Mei was first introduced to me my grandfather, Butch. My grandfather was the towns, "kosher butcher," a notorious alcoholic, business Mogel and questionable deep state spy. Butch had protected me from myself (and others) countless times in my life and always involved me in his dubious schemes. When it came time to spread my wings working in China, he arranged for Mei Mei to take care of all my needs and look after my penchant for trouble. Mei Mei was a work of physical beauty and prowess. She got my attention immediately and then quickly let me know in no uncertain terms, that she and her team only had interest in my "profession" and my "ability to get close to China's newly opened doors for international business." My connections, work ethic and ability to speak Mandarin made me an "easy mark."

At first, I thought this was a bit of a joke since I certainly didn't trust myself, let alone trust working for the US government. But Mei Mei (and my grandfather) convinced me (rather quickly) that they would take care of my needs and that my family would never have to worry. That was all I needed to hear, so I dove into my work rather seriously. Although the furniture industry wasn't a direct call to danger, I was definitely a loose cannon and certainly required direction.

My first job with Mei Mei was to befriend Buddy, an American expat living in China, who was stealing antique furniture from the mainland, duplicating them and then selling the fakes as originals to auction houses and the socially elite worldwide. Buddy amassed quite a fortune in his illicit business dealings, and this eventually got him killed by the people from whom he stole. China had an eye-for-an-eye code of justice, and I quickly became aware of its deep corruption.

My last job with Mei Mei in Mainland China was with a Hong Kong tycoon who went by the name of Shu Shu (uncle). Shu Shu became one of my closest confidants as we built a strong business together, creating home furnishings for the mass market retailers in America. Shu Shu had his own empire in Southern China and Mei Mei (and her friends) were convinced that Shu Shu was making illegal weapons with his huge reserves of brass and heavy machinery. Shu Shu was no saint, he was definitely getting away with murder, but we "took care" of each other until it was me, who he could no longer take care of. My outlandish behavior (and black clouds) caused our separation and ended my work with the CCP. Mei Mei never got over this one, often chastising me about my penchant for trouble and my need to keep a low profile.

Mei Mei now had me tied up with some U.S. manufacturer who was circumventing the U.S. anti-dumping laws to avoid the "25% Trump Tariffs" out of China. They were having finished goods from China sent over the border to Haiphong in North Vietnam where they essentially slapped a "Made in Vietnam" label on their items. Not a major crime, except for a company with a billion dollars in sales and a $400 million dollar buying budget, they were evading around $100 million in annual tax dollars from the U.S. Treasury. So, Mei Mei arranged for me to work with this dubious company, spending most of my time in Vietnam where I reported my findings back to her. As it turns out, this was common practice, and I was now a key witness in this anti-dumping scheme.

I liked Vietnam and often wished that I had started my career here instead of China. At least in Vietnam you could get a decent meal with a genuine smile and the pampering of luxurious hotels with western sensibilities. There was also the fact that this unsuspecting city, like others in Southeast Asia, was built for men's pleasure. And Vietnam although oddly communist, still allowed it's "sex-pats" to live out their most devious obsessions and I was certainly no saint.

But tonight, the only thing on my mind in this backdrop of tropical Asian curiosities was bleak depression. I harbored a lifetime of guilt and shame that threatened any joy I had in living. I was consumed with anguish and convinced there was nothing else for me to do but end my miserable life once and for all. The storm clouds that followed me since I was born, threatened to rain on my depressive existence every chance it had. I could not escape its total embrace, and the drugs and alcohol I used to extinguish my emotions, only fueled my flames. Even more, I had just passed my 50th birthday and convinced myself that I had lived enough of a life and that it was time to go. Yes, my family would miss me but maybe they would be better off without Rick's Trip constantly fucking up their lives. The job was definitely killing me, but today, I could take my life back and finally end it myself.

I can't put all the blame of my shitty existence on poor choices, I did make a few good ones. My wife Heather was my college sweetheart, and we have two beautiful children whom I adore. There is still some humanity left in these rotten bones. Enough that I decided it was best to relax in one of Vietnam's sketchy massage parlors. If it was my last night of existence, I was going out with a full belly and a "happy ending!"

I finished my Mai Tai, called the soft spoken Vietnamese server for my tab and took another look around the pristine tropical gardens blooming with fragrant plumeria trees that surrounded the small hotel. Interesting fact is that plumeria's were often planted in Mexico around graveyards to mask the "smell of death!" That's my kind of tree and today it felt apropos for the circumstances. Glumly, I signed for the check as my cellphone vibrated. I could see by the caller ID that it was indeed Mei Mei.

"Evening Mei Mei," I said trying to remain chipper and hide my melancholy.

"Hi Rick, we have a change in plans for tomorrow," she said getting straight to the point.

I came to realize by now that there was no small talk with Mei Mei.

"Oh really?" I questioned with a bit of sarcasm.

"Forget the flight to Hanoi," she continued.

"Oh damn," I feigned. "I was just starting to enjoy myself in Northern Vietnam."

"I'm sure you were," she said and cut to the chase. "You're going back to The Philippines," she added.

"What, are you shitting me?"

"No Rick, when have you ever known me to shit you?"

"I mean, I thought that I was not allowed back in Philippines since that time with Shu Shu?"

"Rick, it has been years since that incident, and I checked with Senior Gabriel, you are clear to travel."

Senior Gabriel was our asset in Manilla and a secret ally to Mei Mei. He initially facilitated a trip for me and Shu Shu to visit The Philippines in order to illegally bring back rare stones to use in our furniture in return for intelligence on where the stones were being used and by whom. Unfortunately, as luck would have it, we never got our hands on the stones and ended up barely losing our lives in a drive by kidnapping attempt. Of course, in effort to protect Shu Shu, I crippled two men with my rage (and Krav Maga expertise) and almost shot the third. Lucky for me, the shotgun was not loaded, however, I promised to never return to The Philippines both out of fear for my safety and my word to Mei Mei.

"But Mei Mei, I'm not sure how I feel about returning?"

"Rick, since when do you care about your feelings?"

"Well, that's true but where the hell am I going?"

"I've booked you on a Cathay Flight from Ho Chi Minh to Clark Air Force base in Pampanga."

"And what's in Pampanga?"

"There is another American company looking to diversify their supply chain from China and Philippines into Vietnam. Word has it that their facility in Angeles City is just a front to store their China made goods, declare them Philippine made and evade the Tariffs. Now they have their sights on duplicating this in Ho Chi Minh."

"So, let me guess, you want me to get close to this company and send you intel on their operations?"

"The price is right again" she said with a snarky tone.

"And what about my trip to Hanoi and what we are currently working on?"

"That will have to take a back seat for now."

"So, what's the story on this company?"

"They are the largest furniture supplier for the U.S. Department of Education (USDE) and have contracts to furnish schools across America."

"So, they are paid by the U.S. government and are also involved in evading the tariffs from the very same government that is placing their purchase orders?" I said with sarcasm.

"Yes, and this company has Billions of sales with the USDE ever year."

"That sounds like a lot of tariff money going uncollected," I continued unamused.

"Exactly why I want you out of here first thing in the AM."

"Sure, and I imagine that my MO is the same as before?"

"Yes, you are simply a logistics and sourcing consultant, hired to help this company expand its supply chain." She added, "I will text you the contact person and a bio on the firm after we hang up. Have a good evening, Rick and for god's sake make it an early one."

With that she hung up.

A few seconds later, I heard the familiar chime of the incoming text. I looked at my phone but did not read the message. I thought about my new assignment and that made me want to plot killing myself all over again. I needed to get off this hamster wheel and stop this lifestyle of incessant travel and deceit. It didn't matter that I was consider an "expert" in both of my fields, the truth was that I was burned out, tired beyond belief and found no joy in my bane existence. I thought about Mei's Mei's reaction when she heard I didn't make it on that plane and was sure they would find another monkey to do the work.

I almost considered staying at the hotel and having a bottle of tequila delivered to my room but opted to a last supper and the massage. I was about to leave when I noticed five small kittens playing under one of the tables. They were roughhousing each other with careless glee. At first it made me smile but that quickly turned to sadness considering the innocence of it all. These cats were feral in a country that would eat them, before going through the trouble of finding them homes.

I took off from the hotel and walked slowly on Thao Dien Road. The sidewalk was beat up with ragged tree limbs busting through the concrete. In some places it was impossible to cross without having to wade through the pockets of trash and stagnant water. I kept my eyes peeled while I thought about those kittens again and then decided to eat my last meat at the Racha Room for some good Asian Fusion tapas and the best tequila in Saigon. I've been coming here for the last few visits as I found the waitresses very cute and the bar well stocked. In addition to the "good vibes" they also had a resident orange tabby cat that I named Nacho. Nacho does a nice job of welcoming the foreigners with some head butts and usually just hangs out under the tables looking for free scraps and some head scratches. I needed a little Nacho tonight.

I entered the red restaurant and let me eyes adjust to the darkness while I looked for the orange cat. I didn't find the feline but was immediately greeted by a tall Vietnamese woman dressed scantily in a sheer red laced ao dai with matching silk pants. The ao dai is Vietnam's national dress and a striking symbol of beauty to anyone wearing it. This waitress was no exception as she sat me at a high-top next to the bar. I gave her my drink order and asked about Nacho.

She of course, did not know my name for the cat but did manage to tell me that, "the pussy cat has not been seen in a few weeks now." This bummed me out even more then I already was. I took the menu from her and glanced around at the patrons. Many were expats like me and the restaurant was quite full for a Sunday night. The main room was adorned with antiques, wooden Buddha heads, palm fronds and bold pictures of half-naked Asian women. The music was some sort of Euro-trash mix with a heavy bass beat. The waitress returned with my double Casa Amigos on the rocks with some fresh limes. I told her my dinner order and watched her intently and she bent over, picked up my menu and turned to leave me alone with a sly smile and a seductive saunter.

I sipped the cold goodness and let the burn find its way home, warming up my belly with seditious splendor. I looked around for the cat again and was dismayed not to see him balled up next to my feet. I decided to go up to the cavernous bar and ask one of the bartenders what they knew of Nacho. I took my drink and flagged down the closest barkeep.

"Excuse me buddy, you happen to see the orange cat around?"

The bow-tied barkeeper did not register my question at first, so I repeated myself a little louder.

"Sorry mate," he said with a slight English affect.

"The cat, Nacho, he's orange, always here, kind of fat"-

"Oh no sir," he continued, "we have not seen the cat for some time."

"Really," I said disappointed.

"Yeah, we think he might have unfortunately been hit by a car or stolen."

"So, the cat is gone and not coming back?" I said somewhat confused and downed my drink.

"No sir, I am afraid not."

I extended my hand.

"My name is Rick Price, and I'll take another Patron Silver on the rocks!" I exclaimed too loudly, shook his soft hand and left the empty glass on the bar.

I returned to my table and sat forlorn, people watching and eaves dropping on conversations. My food and alcohol came but my appetite was nowhere to be found. I took a few bites of spring rolls, ate some satay and had a few scoops of rice before I asked for the check. I looked at my phone again, read the text from Mei Mei and felt more disassociated than ever before. That fucken cat seemed to predetermine my own fate while death consumed my thoughts. The waitress came over with the check and I snapped back to reality. I quickly paid in cash and left the restaurant on a mission to find a "happier ending" to this depressing evening.

I made a right out of the building and walked through the thin streets of Thao Dien. Most blocks had food and bars catering to tourists. There were a lot of Beer and BBQ stands where patrons sat shoeless on plastic chairs drinking and eating with their friends and families. I passed a few "natural" markets and made a left down a smaller street that had a white sign hanging from a tree that said, "Sawasdee Thai Salon."

I followed the dimly lit road through a small residential section, and at the crossroads with another street stood the Sawasdee. It was a small establishment that looked more like a large grass hut then a building. Outside stood an older Mama-San who seemed to be waving at me. I approached and gave her my best western pearly smile. She handed me a menu and pointed at the body massage photo with 500,000 Dong price tag. This was only about $20 U.S. dollars, so I of course complied by saying, "yes."

The old woman told me in broken English to, "tip the girl."

I knew this was coming, opened my wallet, peeled out the Dong's and followed her into the main hut. She went behind the counter, gave me a small towel and a bottle of water. She motioned for me to follow her as we went down a small dirt trail and opened the wooden door to another small hut. She turned on the light and showed me inside.

The floor had discarded palm leaves scattered on it to add to the ambiance. In the middle of the room was a small bed with just a sheet. Next to it was a small sink, soap and tissues. I took this as a good sign. She smiled back at me, led me to the back of the room, opened another small door, turned on another light and showed me the showerhead attached to the wall that was outside the hut. She pointed at my towel, shook her head in agreement and left me in the room by myself. I turned the spigot on the shower and felt a light trickle of cold water as it came out of the shower head. I turned the spigot all the way to the right in hopes of hot water. The pressure remained the same but after a minute, the water began to warm. I put the water bottle down on a small stool, took off all my clothes and hung them on a bamboo hook next to the sink. I grabbed the hand soap and made my way outside and took a tepid shower in the great outdoors. I looked around to make sure I was alone and then quickly washed myself from head to toe, rinsed off the soap and turned off the water.

The short towel barely fit around my waste, I took the soap and entered the hut. I placed the soap by the sink and sat down on the small makeshift bed. I examined the white sheet and hoped to God it was clean as my naked cock and balls were now resting on top of it. I sat for a few minutes thinking of what pills to take to get the job done tonight, when a small knock on the door interrupted my thoughts.

"Yeah, come in," I said in a raised voice.

The door opened and a short Vietnamese woman walked in. She had on a skin-tight white miniskirt, high heels (for added height) and a white tube top that proudly displayed her young full breasts. I took notice of her manicured eyebrows and the pink polish on her long fingernails and felt comforted that she at least "took care of her grooming."

"Hello," she said, gave me a small smile and quickly made her way to the sink.

"Hey, I said back and watched as she took oil out of her bag, hung it on a hook next to my clothes and began to wash her hands. Another good sign I thought and immediately my sour mood started to sweeten as I felt a familiar stir in my groin. I thought I might have had a problem in that department given my mood. Thankfully the primordial impulses trapped inside my "lizard brain" added light to the dark clouds circling

310

around me. After a lifetime battling my depressive episodes, at least I can always count on my erection to cheer up my shitty day. The girl sensing my arousal, wiped off her hands on another small towel, took the oil and made her way over to where I was sitting.

"Wow, nice tattoo's" she said, admiring my full body suit of black and grey Japanese inspired ink.

"You like?" I asked as I flexed my pectorals to do a little left-right dance for her.

She laughed and answered, "very much."

With that she gently traced the tattoos on my chest and my arms and then walked around to examine my back.

"Wow, that is some dragon on your back!" she exclaimed in perfectly practiced English.

"They call me Dalong or big dragon back in China," I said with bravado.

She continued to lightly touch me as she made her way over to my front. I glanced at her tits again and saw her nipples fighting to break free. So, I quickly traced my fingers around her protruding breasts and gave her nipples a light squeeze between my fingers.

"You a bad boy, Mr. Dragon," she said through a smile.

"Please call me Rick," I said still stroking her and feeling more relaxed as I became aroused.

"You like my body?" she asked.

"I like your tits."

"Do you want to see them Mr. Rick?" she said smiling confidently.

"I want to see everything." I said quickly.

"You like oil?" she asked and showed me the bottle.

"Yes, I do!" I quickly answered.

"Tip first," she said.

"Ok, how much?" I answered.

"800 for happy ending," she said with a devilish grin.

I considered this for a moment and decided not to negotiate since it was only $30 U.S. dollars, and this was to be my "last night."

"What's your name?" I asked stalling for a bit of time.

"My name is Minh," she said.

"Like the city" I added. She looked at me confused so I continued to explain, "Like Ho Chi Minh."

She smiled at that and nodded her head in agreement. Then she looked down between my legs and saw my exposed privates laying on the questionable white sheet.

"I like you, Mr. Rick," she continued, "and it seems you like me too."

With that she grabbed the back of my head and gently pushed me into her breasts. She did a little shake, gave me some soft provocative moans and released me.

"How about my tip?" she smiled as if she just won a prize.

"Ok, Minh," I said and then hoped off the bed, let my towel fall to the floor and made my way to my hanging pants. I reached in for my wallet and peeled out the money for her. She counted it and put it into her handbag. Then she told me to lie back on the bed. I planted myself face first, hoping to prolong the experience with a back massage first. I glanced back at Minh as she removed her tank top, slid off her mini skirt, discarded her heels and approach me with just a small pink thong on her narrow hips.

She sauntered over to me with the oil in her right hand and applied it to my back, my buttocks and legs. Once lubed, she climbed on my back, gently rubbing me with her breasts. She began moaning as she kissed my ears and traced my body with her bulbous mounds. The massage was all body contact and little to no hands involved as she maneuvered herself in a swirling motion up and down my back, butt, legs and feet. I felt completely relaxed, forgot about dying for the moment and re-focused my attention on the sexual tension stirring in my loins.

Minh must have felt me growing in anticipation as she quickened her body massage, her tongue flickering my ears like a small snake and then told me to "flip over."

I quickly turned over and grabbed her on top of me. She let out a little shriek and continued her body massage on my front side. Her well-oiled tits, with their erect pencil eraser nipples, seductively caressed my stomach, my groin and then she used her breasts to rub them up and down my now erect shaft. She continued to make sexual noises of excitement and flicked my ears a few more time with her serpent tongue.

At last Minh jumped off and grabbed my cock in her long, delicate fingers. She quickly applied oil to my cock and balls, smiled at me, then closed her eyes and began to stroke with rhythmic precision. She was a pro with her manipulation skills as she pulled, caressed and reversed her grip on my shaft. With her other hand she rubbed the inside of my thighs and tickled my balls.

It didn't take long for that old familiar feeling of sensation to build up in the lower part of my stomach, travel up through my groin and find its home on the tip of my cock. I told Minh that I was "about to cum," and she quickened her strokes. Like Mt. Vesuvius, I erupted with such force that I swear I could have shot my goo all over the Ancient city of Pompeii. Minh let it rip all over her bountiful chest, made a long exhale and gave me another vixen smile. She hopped off to fetch my towel from the floor. She attempted to clean me up, paying particular attention to the tip of my cock, squeezing and allowing for all the jizz to empty from my chamber. I closed my eyes, buckling with sensitivity from her grasp and let myself feel relief for the first time in a while. I was thankful to cum quickly and thought with a grin that at least my dick was still alive.

Minh cleaned me up and made her way over to the small towel by the sink. She turned on the water and pumped some soap onto the towel. I watched as she gave herself a quick towel bath, making sure to wipe all the oil from her bare breasts, her arms and then washed her hands. She returned with the soapy towel and cleaned my deflated manhood with the determination of a saint. When finished, we both get dressed in silence. I took the water bottle from the stool opened it, poured the warm fluid down my parched gullet and followed Minh out of the hut.

"Minh, you want water?" I asked and handed her the bottle.

She opened the cap took a big swig and then spit the water on the floor next to me. I smiled back at Minh, loving her brazen technique. She stood on her toes, gave me a quick kiss on my cheek, took the water bottle and left me on the path to the front door. I watched her disappear into another hut and then made my way onto the path, in my walk of shame, through the palm trees and out the front door.

The Mama-San was waiting for me with a pleasant smile on her chubby face.

"Girl good?" she asked.

"Rất tốt (very good)," I said in my best Vietnamese.

She smiled wider as I turned and left down the dark road. I had the familiar feelings of guilt, as I'm not as callous as you think. Nevertheless, I chalked this experience up to the need for some comfort and a bit of human contact to bring me back to reality. I had planned this night over and over in my head. I rationalized that instead of feeling misery, I would opt for pleasure.

Once I reached Thao Dien Road, I made my way to one of the open markets and went inside. The small market was brightly lit in harsh fluorescents. It was a Vietnamese bodega that had everything like a 7-11 would. I made my way over to the refrigerated section and grabbed two cold Tiger beers out of the cooler. On the way to the register, I went to where the cat food was and grabbed a small can off the shelf and paid for it with my beer. The man behind the counter gave me another polite Vietnamese smile, placed my goods in a cheap plastic bag and waved goodbye. I waved back, grabbed a cold beer out of the bag, turned and left.

Once back on the road, I opened the cold beer and chugged it down with the reverence of a man stranded on a deserted island. I placed the empty back in the bag and hoofed past the incessant mobs of mopeds to my sanctuary at the Villa River Hotel. I stepped over more trash and puddles and made my way to the entrance, opened the grand wooden doors and followed the well-manicured path past the concierge and out the back where the restaurant was.

I took a moment to smell the bright flowers and noticed the bamboo again as it gently swayed in the breeze like a drunken sailor. I continued to walk, slowly now, noticing that I felt alive again as the black clouds quickly dissipated from the torrential storms in my mind. I made my way over to the empty tables, looking underneath for the kittens that I saw earlier. I clicked my tongue as I sauntered around each table. At last, in the corner under one of the smaller tables, there was a tablecloth hanging down to floor and underneath was a scene out of The Nature Channel.

I lifted the tablecloth to find the momma cat, a beautiful grey tabby, laying on her side as her five babies voraciously sucked milk from her mammary glands. The cat gave me small hiss as I bent down to take the food from my bag. She laid still, too tired to make a defensive move and I sympathized with that feeling. I noticed that two of the cats were orange

314

tabby's and I immediately thought of Nacho and hoped that maybe he was the father. Even if he was in fact dead, now his legacy would remain. I also knew that feeling well, as I routinely contemplated my own complicated existence. I watched for a few more minutes, opened the can of wet food and gently slid it under the table. I heard the cat hiss some more at the intrusion, so I dropped the tablecloth and turned to leave. I followed the wooden path and bamboo trees, towards the front door.

Once inside, I climbed the three flights of steep wooden stairs until I reached my room. The room key was an old fashioned brass plated skeleton key, which I stashed behind the fire extinguisher in the corner of the landing. I grabbed the key from its hiding spot, opened the large door with an audible "click" and entered.

The room was like stepping back in time. There was a 4 poster large king size bed, ornately carved and decorated with colorful throw pillows on top of a green silk duvet with bright pink and white lotuses embroidered into it. There was a small balcony toward the rear that overlooked the river, with a large high-backed rattan chair and matching footrest. All the windows had plantation shutters, and several ceiling fans cooled the large room with big "palm frond" blades.

The bathroom had a separate garden like shower with a rainforest shower head, an oversized white claw bathtub and a sink ordained in white marble with brass accents. In the ceiling were two odd-shaped sky lights that were oval in size and reminded me of a pair of eyes. They were visible no matter where I sat in the room and appeared to watch me from above. I felt like I was being constantly watched by the "big man in the sky!"

This thought comforted me as I began to run-through the machinations in my head of what I intended to do. I put the plastic bag on the wooden bedside table, fished out the other beer, opened it, and took a swig before placing it back down. I reached into the drawer of the wicker table and took out my many pill bottles. I had run this scenario through my head a million and was convinced that the combination of Ambien, Xanax and Oxycodone would hopefully do the trick.

I opened the bottles quickly and poured the pills onto my bed to roughly count them. Thankfully, there were enough narcotics to last me for the entire trip and certainly plenty to end my time with the living.

Without hesitation I took a handful to get the party started and stripped off my clothes, throwing them to the corner of the room. I walked back into the bathroom, looked at my monstrous reflection in the tall mirror and made my way to the bathtub. I filled the tub with hot water and poured in some fancy European liquid bath soap. I watched the frothy soap mix with the water while my thoughts ran back to my wife and children. They would be devastated by my demise. I was sure this would fuck them up for the rest of their lives, yet I was trapped in the feeling that I would have to continue to live a double life of agony to keep protecting them. I didn't want to run from my emotions anymore and only wanted peace and quiet in my head. I needed the pain to stop for good, I needed it to go away!

A tear of loneliness and grief escaped from my eye as I checked the water temperature. I added some cold into the mix and went back to my bed where I laid down next to the pills. I looked up at the ceiling, into those sinister eyes appearing as windows to the heavens. I asked God to tell me what to do next since I was out of clues and options. Of course, there were no answers, so I did what I knew would help. I turned over, reached for the beer, grabbed another Oxy and chased them both down with determination. I asked for forgiveness, sobbed a little more and got off the bed.

I reached the bath just as I started to feel a little relief and got in. It was hotter than I would have liked, but I cupped my balls and let my body sink into the cauldron. The water and the drugs enveloped me like a warm hug as I felt my eyes grow heavier. I knew the drugs would knock me out and I would slide into the water drowning out my misery. I relaxed my body, focused my intentions, calmed my breath and closed my eyes.

End of Chapter 1 Preview
Thank God For The Drugs

For sales, editorial information, subsidiary rights information
or a catalog, please write or phone or e-mail
iBooks
Manhanset House
Shelter Island Hts., New York 11965, U.S.
Tel: 212-427-7139
www.ibooksinc.com
bricktower@aol.com
www.IngramContent.com

www.ingramcontent.com/pod-product-compliance
Lightning Source LLC
Chambersburg PA
CBHW050124030726
47505CB00007B/2019